She would force them to see her, to accept her, and she'd reclaim the power that should have been hers, even if it took her years.

But for now she'd have to play the game, smiling and simpering—until they had no choice but to bow before her.

And this was just her opening move.

MISTRESS OF LIES

The Age of Blood: Book One

K. M. Enright

orbit

orbitbooks.net

Cover design by Ella Garrett
Cover illustration by Felix Abel Klaer
Author photograph by K. M. Enright

Orbit
Hachette Book Group
1290 Avenue of the Americas
New York, NY 10104
orbitbooks.net

First Edition: August 2024
Simultaneously published in Great Britain by Orbit

Orbit is an imprint of Hachette Book Group.
The Orbit name and logo are registered trademarks of Little, Brown Book Group Limited.

The publisher is not responsible for websites (or their content) that are not owned by the publisher.

The Hachette Speakers Bureau provides a wide range of authors for speaking events. To find out more, go to hachettespeakersbureau.com or email HachetteSpeakers@hbgusa.com.

Orbit books may be purchased in bulk for business, educational, or promotional use. For information, please contact your local bookseller or the Hachette Book Group Special Markets Department at special.markets@hbgusa.com.

Library of Congress Control Number: 2024936046

ISBNs: 9780316565356 (trade paperback), 9780316565363 (ebook)

Printed in the United States of America

LSC-C

Printing 1, 2024

Content Note

Mistress of Lies contains sensitive material, including but not limited to: explicit sexual content, murder, patricide, gore, blood magic and bloodletting for purposes of magic, discussion of racism and classism, mentions of rape.

There is a scene of explicit sexual content with a trans masculine character. Please note that trans people use a variety of different words to describe our bodies, for reasons as varied as there are trans people. The words used to describe Isaac's body are the ones that he finds comfortable and validating, even though they may not be the words that every trans masculine person would choose.

There is no transphobia, misgendering, or deadnaming.

To Eric, for believing even when I couldn't

Chapter One

Shan

It should have been more difficult to assassinate her father.

Not in the actual execution of it: that Shan had prepared for. Her father was a powerful Blood Worker and had once been considered the brightest of his generation. That had been many years ago, though, and Lord Antonin LeClaire had fallen quite far indeed. But still, he had guards, magical wards and a lifetime of training at his disposal. And she had accounted for all these things.

No, there should have been something—anything—in her heart that railed against this. Despite everything he had done over the two decades of her life, patricide was still the most despicable of all crimes; it ought to twist her stomach and fill her with guilt. She shouldn't relish this kill, shouldn't feel this boundless relief.

But she did.

She was a shattered, broken thing, and this only proved it.

Her father lifted the glass to his mouth, the amber whisky sloshing in the finely cut glass, and took another deep drink as he shifted through the papers in front of him. Shan watched as he licked his lips, taking in more of the poison that would give her power over him.

It was a potent poison, frightfully expensive, but she had learned long ago that secrets were worth far more than coin. It had taken her years to find, and a couple bits of hard-won information to pay for it. Yet watching her father drink it—in a glass handed over to him by his own daughter—Shan knew that she would have paid any price for this moment.

So she sipped idly at her wine as she waited, fiddling through the books that had been laid out across her father's grand wooden desk. Books of their financial records, filled with tables of transactions written in the cramped hand of her father's secretary. They detailed how much had been spent by their estate over the past years—or what remained of the LeClaire estate. Drained and destitute from generations of mismanagement, made worse by her father.

But by morning the books would be hers and that was what mattered.

Her father coughed suddenly, a deep, racking thing that shook his whole body.

Shan cocked her head to the side, eyes wide in the perfect mimicry of a doting daughter. "Are you all right, Father?"

Lord LeClaire looked up, his grey eyes narrowed in that paranoid way of his. He opened his mouth to speak, but was interrupted by another round of coughs, blood splattering on the desk before him.

Shan stood quickly, knocking the books aside. Her glass crashed to the floor, shattering, the wine pooling at her feet. Deep. Dark, like drying blood.

She smiled at the fear in her father's eyes.

Another cough. Another spurt of blood. Shan leaned forward, dipping her fingers in the warm liquid. She swirled them around and brought them to her lips, unminding of the poison. The antidote already flowed through her veins.

"Well," Lord LeClaire managed. "About time."

Shan sucked her fingers into her mouth and felt the power explode through her. The blood acted as a catalyst, a source of power that connected them, forming a bridge that she could use to reach out and—ah!

She bent the very blood in his veins to her will, flinging him against the wall and slamming him into the hard mantle, the sounds of his bones snapping the sweetest music to her ears. Circling around the desk to where her father had fallen, she felt his blood calling to her. Fighting her control with every last bit of his strength. He was strong-willed. He was stubborn.

But she was indomitable.

With a flick of her fingers she had him sprawled out on the floor, his arms pinned to his sides by the force of her magic. He struggled to move, thrashing against the bonds of her will, but for now his blood was hers to command.

Shan produced a dagger from the sheath up her sleeve, feeling its comforting weight in her hands. Her father eyed it, recognition shining in his gaze. Out of all the weapons she could have chosen—the knives he had gifted her for her most recent birthday, the steel-tipped claws she earned from the Academy—she chose this.

Her mother's dagger in her bare hands.

Shan sank to her knees, not caring that her fine, silken dress was stained in the process. "Goodbye, Father." Placing the knife against his throat, she only hesitated when she saw him smile.

"You were always my favorite," he rasped out. "Do me proud."

Grimacing, Shan dragged her knife through his skin, feeling it split under the strength of her hand. She cut deep, down to the bone, embedding the steel in his flesh. The blood welled and spilled, but she dared not remove it, not until it was done.

She couldn't have him healing himself. She doubted the punishment would be as light as it was last time. Then she had been but a child of eight, lashing out in a fit of anger and despair. When he had driven her mother from their home in one of his fits of paranoid violence, and she had taken up her dagger and turned it against him.

She had failed then. She wouldn't fail now.

This was carefully planned vengeance, and she watched until the light faded from his eyes, his blood seeping into her dress and staining her hands. Still she remained, waiting for the body to grow cold, for the skin to pale, for all signs of life to vanish.

The door creaked open, and Bart whispered, "Is it done?"

When her father's guards didn't rush in after him, she knew that he had played his part as well. Shan dragged her fingers through her father's blood one last time. This blood lacked vibrancy, cloying and congealing. There was power still there, but it was dulled.

It was the blood of a dead man.

"Yes," Shan said, relieved, empty and tired all at once.

Bart dropped the tray in his hands, the poison-laced cups clattering to the floor as he rushed across the room. For a moment he just rested his hand on her shoulder, but Shan continued to tremble. He pulled her close, letting her tuck her head against his shoulder. In a brief moment of weakness, Shan buried her face against her friend. "You're free," he whispered. "You're both free."

"We're *all* free," Shan said, clutching her skirt. "But we're not done yet."

"I know," Bart said. "But it's okay to feel."

Shan pulled away, slipping out of the embrace with ease. Bart didn't chase her—he knew better than that. Taking a deep breath, she forced herself to her feet, to put some steel in her spine. "There will be time for feeling later. Now we have bodies to dispose of."

Bart inclined his head. "As you say."

Shan ripped her knife from her father's neck, ignoring the loud, squelching noise that accompanied it. Drawing a handkerchief from her sleeve, she carefully wiped all traces of blood away, scrubbing until the metal shone. She dropped the soiled handkerchief into a small linen bag—the proof of death collected—then slipped it into her corset, tucked safely away.

"The incinerator?"

"Already lit," Bart replied. He was pulling long sheets of linen, sheets with which to wrap the dead, from where he had hidden them in the closet. Shan took one end in her hands, draping it over her father. With ruthless efficiency, she tucked the ends in around him, rolling him into the cloth. It was a clunky, undignified end for a Blood Worker, but Shan didn't care.

He had lost the mercy of a clean, dignified death long ago.

Together they cleaned up every bit of blood, soaking it into the excess cloth they had brought for this precise reason. She was especially meticulous in this regard—aside from what they needed to prove his death to the Council, they couldn't let one drop of blood get away. Lord Antonin LeClaire might be dead, but there was still a lot a Blood Worker could do with his blood.

So, like her father, into the incinerator it would go.

With Bart grabbing the shoulders and Shan scooping up the legs, they made their way past the corpses of her father's personal guards and down into the bowels of the LeClaire townhouse. It was a tricky journey, moving the body round tight corners and down narrow staircases, but it had to be done.

Shan was sweating by the time they made it to the incinerator room, and her arms ached from the awkward burden they were carrying. Bart was breathing heavily, less accustomed to such physical work, and unable to draw on Blood Working to supplement his strength. But he carried on without complaint, and Shan was grateful for that. For all that he was willing to do for her sake—for her brother's sake.

It was more than she had ever expected, even from him.

But the incinerator was there, and they tossed the body in with hardly a care for how it landed. This wasn't a formal cremation. Shan didn't dress her father in his finest, didn't cross his arms over his chest, or make sure his features were peaceful.

What did it matter? Soon he'd be nothing but ashes.

"The others," Shan said, and Bart groaned. She understood his pain, but they needed to get rid of them, too. Leaving her father's corpse where it lay, they returned upstairs to grab his first guard, and then, tired and aching, repeated the trek for the second.

"There," Bart wheezed. "We're done."

"Our clothes," Shan corrected, and Bart sighed. He stepped up behind her, quickly unlacing her dress. Shan let it fall to the ground, landing on dust and soot. Bart stripped her petticoats as well, leaving her in naught but her underthings. "Any blood get through?"

Bart leaned back, studying her. "No, there's none."

Shan nodded. "Now you." Bart wrinkled his nose, but peeled off his shirt, revealing his dark skin. "Don't worry, I'll get you a whole wardrobe of fine outfits to replace this," Shan promised. "Though if Anton had his way you'd never need to wear them."

Bart laughed, the serious expression dropping away, reminding her of his youth. Their youth. They were both so young. "The things I do for love." With a few quick movements, his clothes joined hers on the floor.

Shan didn't pause. She scooped them up, uncaring of the streaks of soot that stained her arms, and threw them into the incinerator with the bodies. "There."

Bart stepped around her to slide the door shut, locking away all the evidence. "It's done."

Shaking her head, Shan grabbed her friend by the hand, leading him away from the incinerator. Together, they left the room, shutting the heavy metal door behind them. Grabbing the lever, Shan pulled down hard and released the fire.

"*Now* it's done," she said, as the flames roared.

Bart grabbed the cloaks that he had stowed away. Stepping around Shan, he placed one across her shoulders, soft and gentle, tucking her away from prying eyes.

It almost made her laugh. She had just murdered her own father and his guards, burned their bodies and stripped down in front of her brother's lover. And still Bart was concerned with propriety, though it was far too late for that. She was a murderess and a monster. But she didn't fight it—the gesture was well meant, and she didn't want any of her father's servants catching her at anything less than her best.

No.

Her servants now.

"Time for the next step, then?" Bart asked.

Shan nodded. "Yes, let's make it official. Before Anton gets home." She saw the look of worry in Bart's eyes, the fear that perhaps they had gone too far. But she forced herself to ignore it. She could handle her twin, and he'd understand soon enough.

All of this was for him.

—+—

It was already past midnight when Shan arrived at the Parliament House, solemn in its grandeur, a high ceiling raised over the marble floors as the sounds of Shan's heels echoed in the vast, empty space. Perhaps it was designed to make her feel small, but as she strode through the atrium, she only felt the calm sense of belonging.

She had made it, at last.

Despite the hour, she was freshly bathed and dressed in one of her finest gowns, one that she had picked for its modestly designed square neckline and pure black color. A perfectly proper choice for a young woman mourning the sudden death of her father. With false tears in her eyes, she told the poor aide who worked the night shift that her father had passed, and he had shuffled her off to a waiting room while the Royal Council was called, left alone with her conscience and an ever-cooling pot of tea.

By the time the Council had been roused and had arrived, the night had slipped away into the early morning, and Shan was summoned to their hearing chamber. It was smaller than she had expected it to be, just large enough for a curved table that they sat around, an impressive piece of dark mahogany with five large, upholstered chairs, nearly grand enough to be thrones, each covered in deep green velvet. There were no windows, perhaps for privacy, and the walls were filled with paintings, a history of Dameral painted from portrait to portrait as it grew from the small seaport of antiquity to the grand capital it had become.

The air was heavy with history and solemnity, and Shan couldn't help but wonder what mark she would leave.

She stood with her back as straight as a rod as the Royal Council entered, her hands folded in front of her, the silver of her claws glittering under the soft, red shine of the witch light.

Lady Belrose, the Councillor of Foreign Affairs, entered first and took the middle chair, the four other Councillors flanking her. The Council—officially all equal with each other—rotated leadership with every year. This year fell to Lady Belrose, and thus she took the seat of honor at the head of the table.

It was part of the way they worked—never did one of the Council rise above another, as they all served as equals, placed above the House of Lords. They each held domain of their own branch of the government, and they were the absolute masters of it, bending only to the wisdom of the Eternal King himself.

Not that the Eternal King had bothered to intervene much in recent centuries, only coming down to pick his new Councillors and allowing them to run his country in his stead. Oh, he performed his duties with care and diligence, but everyone knew that his true home was in his palace, with his studies, far away from the cares of those he supposedly ruled.

So for the moment Shan contented herself with studying the faces of the most powerful people in Aeravin without breaking before them.

Even now, summoned in the middle of the night, Lady Belrose looked incredibly fine. She was a woman of middle years, and she had held this position for over a decade. Like Shan, she had given much care to her appearance, from her neatly pressed dress to the way her hair hung in carefully styled ringlets down her back, making Shan wonder if she had even had the chance to be to bed yet.

"Miss LeClaire," Lady Belrose began, the formal words slipping from her tongue with the ease of a thousand uses, "you have summoned the Council."

"Thank you for coming, especially given the hour," Shan said, taking care to put an extra tremble in her voice. Not too much; overdoing it was just as false as underdoing it, and she had to walk an incredibly fine line. "Earlier this evening, my father passed away quite suddenly of a heart attack."

Lord Dunn, Councillor of Law, leaned forward in his seat, his dark eyes beady and suspicious. He was a thin man of sharp angles and harsh edges, pale and sallow. "Strange to hear in a man of your father's age."

"I'm sorry to say that my father had not been well of late." Shan cast her eyes down, ignoring the twist in her stomach as the lies fell from her lips. "He had been deteriorating for many years, ever since my mother left."

She hated to use her mother in this fashion, but after seeing the collective flinch around the table, she knew that she had made the right choice. It had been such a scandal, and as much as they had reveled in the gossip all those years ago, their foolish propriety wouldn't let them discuss it openly with her.

"Well," Belrose said, pulling the Council back on topic, "do you have the proof?"

Stepping forward, Shan pulled the linen bag from her side and placed it on the table. She had treated it with the antidote and tested it herself—it would show nothing but the death of her father. But she still held her breath as Belrose opened it carefully, letting the bloodstained handkerchief spill out, and the whole Council leaned in as one. Picking it up with the tip of her claws, Belrose spread it out in front of her before lifting the entire thing to her lips. Her tongue flashed out—quick and pale—and pressed against the cloth.

For a moment the whole Council watched her, eyes closed as she did her work, until she breathed out, "Lord Antonin LeClaire is dead." Clenching her fist around the handkerchief, she lowered her gaze upon Shan. "Long live Lady LeClaire."

Muttering broke out amongst the Council, but Shan ignored it, focusing on the weight that lifted from her shoulders. It truly was done.

Stepping forward, Shan held out her hand and Belrose reluctantly dropped the handkerchief onto it. "Take care, Lady LeClaire." Shan tilted her head to the side, and Belrose sighed. "You are young to take your father's place."

"I am three and twenty," Shan replied, with more bite than she intended, but Belrose only smiled.

"As I said." She stood. "Though there are records to update now, you are officially recognized as the new head of the LeClaire line, with all the privileges and responsibilities that come with it."

"I trust we will see you at the opening of this year's session of the House of Lords," Dunn added. "How fortuitous for you that this happened while we were in recess."

"Hush," Lady Holland, the Councillor of Industry, reproached. She had been the quietest of all this night. She was the youngest of the Council, hardly into her third decade, with mousy brown hair and plain features. Shan only knew her by reputation—that she was more interested in numbers and policy that in playing politics, unusual for a Councillor. Typically, such a position required a fair amount of political acumen, but in the case of Lady Holland one could easily believe she had risen on merit alone.

"It *is* auspicious timing for the new Lady," Dunn continued, only for Lady Morse, the Councillor of the Military, to take him by the arm. She was a stern woman of advanced years, but she did not let age soften her. Lady Morse was all lean muscle, her grey hair cropped short in military style.

"Many people's Ascensions seem fortuitous, Kevan," Morse said, "including yours."

"She has you there," added Lord Rayne, the Councillor of the Treasury. He was the eldest of the Council by far, a stooped old man with white hair and prominent veins in his hands. "Let the girl be, she's had a long day."

"And she'll have many long days ahead of her," Belrose added. "You should go rest, my lady. Tomorrow, it begins."

"As you say, Lady Belrose." Shan curtsied to them all, taking care to remain demure and polite, even though she railed at the way they talked about her—as if she wasn't even there. As if she meant nothing. Perhaps she didn't. The LeClaire line had fallen from grace, and her father had ensured that nothing was left but dust and ashes.

But she would force them to see her, to accept her, and she'd reclaim the power that should have been hers, even if it took her years. But for now she'd have to play the game, smiling and simpering—until they had no choice but to bow before her.

And this was just her opening move.

Chapter Two

Samuel

Samuel held his breath as the crowd surged forward, pushing him even closer to the stage that had been erected in the heart of Dameral's main square. It was a large wooden monstrosity, dragged out of storage once a year for this garish display and fitted together over the cobblestone streets. From his position, he could see the dark stains of old blood on the boards—countless years of death marked into the wooden grain.

He didn't even want to be here, but the throng had him trapped. Lowly, he cursed himself for not taking the longer route, the one that avoided this main thoroughfare that lay smack between the warehouse where he worked and the glorified closet he called home. For forgetting that it was the first day of spring and what that meant.

But there was nothing to be done now—there was no way he could fight against the flow of people as the square continued to fill. Well, there was *one* option, tempting and dark. But he ignored the impulse, swallowing down the anxiety that rose through him as he gripped the short iron fence that barricaded the area around the stage. As much as he ached for it, he couldn't dare act out now, not while staring out over the trench before the stage that was patrolled by Blood Workers. Guards in their robes of deepest black.

They kept the crowds back, flexing their metal claws towards anyone foolish enough to press too far. Samuel studied the hands of the one closest to him—the steel claws fitted over their fingertips, held in place by silver chains that crossed over the backs of their hands in a grotesque mockery of jewelry. Those claws were sharp enough to slash skin, to rend flesh so that blood welled to the surface.

Blood they could use to break and control you.

Samuel fought back a shiver, tearing his gaze away from the Blood Worker and focusing on the mostly empty stage. On the spot where the Eternal King would soon stand.

The sacrifice was already there—a beaten, bruised shell of a man bound in chains. Samuel couldn't see his face, even though he was so close that he could hear the man's ragged sobs. His head hung low, the dirty strands of his dark hair falling across his face as the crowd jeered at him.

Samuel ignored them, the merchants and artisans in their fine clothes, the non-noble Blood Workers with their daggers and their claws. The noble Lords and Ladies watched from above, from the balconies of clubs and restaurants that ringed the square. But there were so few like him—poor and tired, trapped amongst the throng—so he closed his eyes and counted his heartbeats, searching for the fleeting calm against the panic that caught his breath like a fist around his throat.

The crowd keep pressing against him, hot and ever moving, the smell of sweat and bodies filling his nose, the sound of chattering nonsense growing louder and more incomprehensible until suddenly, all at once, silence descended.

The Eternal King was here.

Samuel looked up, finding their King stepping through the curtains at the back of the stage. The King was dressed impeccably— such fashions might have been far beyond Samuel's means, but he was still astute enough to pick up on what was *in*. A tailored jacket and breeches, a silken waistcoat with fine, delicate embroidery. A perfectly tied cravat. The only thing that shocked him were the claws. Samuel had expected them to be gold-plated or inlaid with jewels.

But they were simple steel things, more for function than for fashion.

But it wasn't the clothes that made the man. Samuel never had the privilege of seeing his King before, having taken great care to avoid the attention of Blood Workers as much as possible, regardless of political power. But now he saw that the King was not just some dangerous mage hiding in a palace. He was more than that: he was alive and vital and strangely untouchable.

He didn't look more than thirty years old, a man still in his prime. He wore his hair short and carefully cut, a bed of golden curls that cushioned his crown. His features were harsh but striking—a strong jaw, clear eyes, and a tall, lean frame.

It was almost possible to understand how a rebellion had formed around him all those centuries ago, how a nation had followed him when he stole a throne and stayed under his sway for lifetimes, for centuries, for an entire millennium. He still seemed so young, so powerful, fueled by the blood of countless victims.

But he also seemed bored, the expression on his face one of polite disdain, as if he wanted to be anywhere but here. Yet duty called, so he arrived, ready to pander to the will of his people in this extravagant farce.

Samuel bristled with rage, his entire body trembling with the force of will that it took to contain himself. It was a pointless, directionless anger—Samuel wasn't naive enough to think otherwise. He was just a peasant in the crowd, in his patched shirt and dirty trousers, his long hair pulled into a loose and messy bun at the nape of his neck. He didn't belong here—the pointed huffs of the properly dressed woman at his elbow only confirmed that—and he could do nothing but seethe.

On the stage, the King continued to stare idly over the crowd, and a young man dressed in robes of deep, blood red stepped forward. Samuel's eyes darted to him in surprise, taking in the man's youth—hells, he couldn't have been older than Samuel's twenty-five years—and his rich, burnt gold skin tone, one not usually seen amongst the Blood Workers of Aeravin. At least not the ones who would be at the King's right hand. For this was the Royal Blood Worker, the King's official secretary, the man through whom all official business was run.

The King pushed right past him, circling in front of the sacrifice and drawing the eye of everyone there. A collective hush spread across the square as the King pulled the man to his feet, where he stood, shackled and cowed, as he was examined. Coldly and clinically—like he was nothing more than a specimen to be studied in a laboratory.

The Royal Blood Worker cleared his throat, awkwardly drawing the people's attention away from their monarch. "My friends," he said, with a casual smile. Tittering and laughter broke out amongst the crowd, but he kept on smiling gamely, like this was a private gathering between friends, not a state-sanctioned murder to extend the life of their endless King, done year after year, for only he had the right to Eternal.

In that moment, Samuel hated all of them, the Blood Workers and the magic, his country that was drenched in the blood of those like him, born without these so-called gifts.

"We are honored by your presence here today," the Royal Blood Worker continued, his voice deep and clear and gaining in confidence. "For your continued support. It has been a strong year for Aeravin, and we have all of you to thank for that." Placated by his words, the crowd cheered. "Through his sacrifices, King Tristan Aberforth has kept our country strong for centuries past, allowing us to flourish where others see Blood Working banned, has kept our borders strong against those who would see us eradicated for the gifts in our veins. He has done this for a millennium, as he will continue for centuries to come. But in order to do so, Blood Working demands a price."

Samuel clenched the fence in front of him so hard that his knuckles turned white, biting the inside of his cheek as the Royal Blood Worker continued to speak, to justify this horrific act. This murder done in the name of their nation.

"This man is not just any criminal," the Royal Blood Worker continued, pointing a single clawed finger at him. "But a thief and a traitor. He was caught trying to smuggle state secrets out of Aeravin, secrets that would have undermined our position in the world. Our security. Fitting, then, that he will serve his King far more in death than he could in life."

The crowd cheered, accepting the crown's judgement, their hate and anger flowing over him. Samuel himself was almost caught up in the moment, in the sheer power of it as they called for death and blood.

The King tangled his hand in the sacrifice's hair, pulling it so that he was forced to bare his throat, and spoke at last. His voice was gentle but clear, carrying over the crowd as silence fell. "Know that your sacrifice is for the good of your nation."

The man hissed, finding his courage in the final moment. "Fuck you."

The King didn't even frown, didn't even react. He just reached out with his other hand, dragging his clawed thumb against the man's throat. Flesh split easily under the metal tip, blood welling bright and red. The sacrifice gasped in sudden pain, but the King already had his mouth at his throat, his teeth digging into the skin as he sucked the man's blood.

Samuel couldn't look away, even though the scene was a violation of everything good and right. The sacrifice was gripping the King's shoulders, as if he were trying to shove him away, but the King held him in a fierce, almost intimate embrace.

Time seemed to slow as the sacrifice's grip grew looser, his skin turning ashy and grey. It was like watching the body wither before him, all the moisture and vitality being drained from the man as the King seemed to grow brighter, more vibrant, until he practically shone with life.

The sacrifice—the once-man—croaked out his final breath, then slumped forward.

The King looked up, his lips and teeth stained red as he

smiled—feral and alien—then he shoved the corpse aside. It fell to the floor with an ungraceful thump, the body curling up on itself.

Samuel felt bile burn the back of his throat, and he had to look away, sucking in steadying breaths to keep from hurling his lunch onto his neighbor's boots.

"You will be remembered," the King said, though there was a bite to his words. It was ceremonial, Samuel knew enough to realize that, but surely it wasn't normally this sarcastic. This cruel. Then again, they hadn't even bothered to name this man, hadn't bothered to treat him like a person with a life before him. In the end, he had just been another source of blood. A source of life, drained and stolen.

This couldn't be over soon enough.

The crowd was cheering, though, for their King. For the one who had allowed so many of them to practice their Blood Working freely and openly, when every other country in the world banned the practice. For the one who had given them an entire nation without caring about the backs that broke under it.

"Thank you for being here this evening," the King said, blood still dripping down his chin. "Remember, all that I do is for the good of Aeravin, and for you." He bowed then, to his people, then turned to disappear back through the curtain.

Samuel rolled his eyes, focusing on the discarded corpse as the Royal Blood Worker stepped forward once again, rambling about plans for the country—new legislation that was coming as the House of Lords opened for the year, the plans to redo Dameral's central square by midsummer, changes to the policies for requisitioning blood, given the all-time high enrolment at the Academies this year.

It was bullshit. None of it was for him, or those like him. The poor. The Unblooded, born without the ability to use blood magic. Those who kept the country functioning while struggling to simply survive.

At last it was over, the Royal Blood Worker inclining his head before stepping over the freshly made corpse and disappearing after his King. The Blood Workers were moving through the crowd, muttering about the news for the year, eager to be back to their lives now that the entertainment was over.

Samuel didn't rush. He let them fight their way out, following in the relative quiet behind them. It wasn't like he relished rubbing elbows with them anyway, or that he had anywhere to go. Just another night of stale bread and mealy apples for dinner, a book until it was time for sleep, then another day of the same.

Day in and day out, an endless cycle that would repeat itself until he starved or broke, whichever came first.

He shuffled on home as the sun set against the ocean, shivering at the cool breeze that came in off the sea. Spring had just begun but the shadows still rose early, chasing him through the narrow streets to his doorstep, fought back only by lampposts filled with witch light—oil and blood, lit by Blood Working, fire that burned cleaner, cheaper and longer.

He barely noticed the woman slumped in the narrow alley around the corner from his flat, huddled in the shadows between the lamps. He wouldn't have noticed her at all if he wasn't so tired that he couldn't lift his eyes from the ground in front of him. He almost passed her by anyway—it wasn't his problem—but he had just seen a man drained of life, killed by a Blood Worker and a King.

He couldn't in good conscience do nothing. If he ignored her, he knew what would happen—the woman would simply disappear into the night, vanished like so many others. Never to be seen again. Dameral was a dangerous city for those like him, and he couldn't let another be claimed by it.

Sighing, he stepped closer to the woman. "Come on, then," he said, quietly. Carefully—always so careful never to let it slip. "You can't sleep here, it's not safe." He reached out, planning to shake her awake, but jumped back when he realized the woman wasn't sleeping.

She was dead.

Cut open and drained, desiccated and ruined, sliced open along the veins and bled out in a disgusting, vile death. Dried blood lingered at the edges of her wounds, and her mouth hung open, caught in the rictus of her death scream. She had passed slowly and painfully, suffering all the while, and the pain she had felt had been written into her very flesh.

This wasn't some random mugging. She had been murdered by a Blood Worker, then dumped here like just another bit of trash. For a moment he just stared, going cold as he realized what it meant.

Blood Workers, for all their power, still had to follow rules—only a handful—but this was one of them. This was a violation of the very thing that kept Aeravin stable, a promise of safety to the Unblooded. They were not to be taken and tortured this way, used in experiments and cast aside. They bought this protection with their loyalty and their Blood Taxes, and to see it so flagrantly broken?

Gooseflesh broke out across Samuel's skin. Whatever was happening, it was too dangerous for him to be here. If he was found ...

He turned to flee, but there was already movement at the edge of the alley. Black robes. The soft red glow of witch light moving closer.

He was caught.

"Is there a problem here?" the Blood Worker asked, holding up the lantern so that it nearly blinded him. But he squinted through it, taking in her features—she was young, younger than him. He didn't put her at much over twenty. Her features were sharp and harsh, her fair hair shorn close to the scalp. There was something about her that looked dangerous, something calculating and empty as she catalogued him, as academic as if he was a butterfly pinned to a board, and it chilled him to the bone.

Samuel considered lying, considered running. Considered unleashing the dark power that stirred in his chest. But none of these options was viable, so instead he simply said, "I think there's been a murder."

The Blood Worker moved forward, almost too fast for the eye to see. It was the preternatural strength that Samuel knew existed but had so rarely seen. In a heartbeat the Blood Worker was kneeling next to the dead woman, her hand hovering over the corpse's face, as if she were too afraid to touch it.

"Blood and steel," she cursed.

Samuel took a step back. "It wasn't me. I'm not . . . I'm Unblooded. I just found her. I swear."

The Blood Worker didn't even look up at him, staring at the corpse's ruined face.

Her unidentifiable face.

The Blood Worker turned to him, taking in the poor quality of his clothes, the lack of claws or knives on his person, and immediately dismissed him as a threat. "What's your name? We're going to need a statement."

"I said I didn't—"

"I know that," she snapped. "Hells, anyone who looks at you would know that. But you still found her. Now, I don't want to waste my time arguing with the likes of you, so let's just get this over with."

Samuel bit back the surge of power that stole his breath, but he nodded. The Blood Worker was right, after all. There was no way he could have committed the crime, but he was part of it now. "Hutchinson. My name is Samuel Hutchinson."

The Blood Worker finally looked up at him. "Good. I'm Guard Alessi, and I'll come and collect you for your statement later." Grimly, she turned back to the corpse. "But for now, I have a body to take care of."

Samuel didn't fight it. He was, completely and thoroughly, fucked.

Chapter Three

Shan

The day dawned clear and warm, far too beautiful for a Funeral Ball. It was ridiculous, truly, but Shan almost felt like the weather itself was celebrating with her.

It was finally over. Shan was the new matriarch of the LeClaire line, and everything was hers. The estate, the title, the seat in the House of Lords—everything she had spent a lifetime scheming to achieve. She should have been relieved, happy even, but she buzzed with energy, ready to get on with the next thing.

There was so much work to do.

The official memorial would happen that evening, when the LeClaires opened their home to the masses of Dameral. All Blood Workers of rank were invited to mourn their late sibling and welcome the new heir into their midst. For many it was a time of celebration as well as pain. It brought the whole family together as they honored the new head of the House. But the LeClaires had always been a vicious, cruel line, and Antonin had been the exemplar against which all others were measured.

Her father had been the fourth child, far beyond the heir and the spare, but he had been the most ambitious of his generation. He had plotted and killed his way through his siblings till he was the last one standing, had ensured that none of his nieces or nephews lived to take the line back from him, children dead before they even had a chance to live. His exploits had attracted even the Eternal King's attention, and for all his efforts he had been rewarded. He had been drawn into the inner circle of power, into the role that was never named but always known.

That of Aeravin's own spymaster.

The King had elevated him, had given him power and privilege in exchange for turning his cunning and viciousness against Aeravin's enemies. The pressure, though, had broken him. He started seeing enemies everywhere, his cruelty turning paranoid to the point of madness. Within a handful of years, the King had cast him aside, and all of society shunned him for his weakness. With no other outlets, he turned his cruelty on his wife, and, when she fled, upon his children—his legacy. Now it was just Shan and her brother—all that was left of a diseased, despised, nearly destitute House.

Sometimes, Shan thought that if they were wise they would let it end with them.

She was finishing the final touches on the evening's menu when Anton burst into the dining room, his eyes wild and his hair disheveled. His cravat was hanging loose around his neck, and he had not bothered with his waistcoat or jacket, showing up in simple shirtsleeves. It looked as if he had fallen asleep in the clothes he had worn the night before then rolled out of bed to join her. Which, in all fairness, was probably the truth.

Though she had beaten him into the world by only a matter of minutes, they were the same. For all their lives, they had been the perfect image of twins, reflecting each other. They had both inherited the look of their foreign mother—the same rich, golden skin, the thick, dark hair, the wide cheekbones and the narrow eyes. They were both beautiful, but in Aeravin, so terribly *other*.

Shan wore it with a graceful elegance, the kind that moved people to shamed deference. Anton wore it like a challenge, daring them to speak the truth that lurked behind their polite smiles and carefully chosen words.

It was a deliberate, calculated choice. Where she was the perfect daughter, he had adopted the role of the dissolute fop, living only to spend what was left of his father's money as he flitted from scandal to scandal. And though he played his part well, it was far from the truth. Anyone who looked closely enough could see the cunning in his eyes.

They were two sides to the same coin, right down to the cold, calculating mind that he learned at his father's knee and hid behind his scoundrel's persona.

"Good morning, Anton," she said, pouring them both tea. "Rough night?"

Anton slinked over to the table, taking his cup as soon as she finished dressing it the way he liked. A bit of milk, a pinch of sugar. He downed it in one scorching gulp, then poured himself another. "Is it true, then? About Father?"

Shan couldn't help herself. Her smile was soft and cruel. "The Funeral Ball is tonight."

Anton winced. "Shan . . ."

Shan leaned back in her chair as a pair of serving girls entered, carrying their breakfast in on trays. There would be no more wasteful spreads of food—just what she and her brother could reasonably eat—and no more bland breakfasts of toast and kippers.

The girls set the bowls down in front of them—steaming rice, freshly fried eggs, spiced sausages in the way their mother had made them—and quickly departed. Food that their father had loudly banned years ago, that they had to sneak just to have a taste of, now proudly displayed on their dining-room table.

She leaned forward, nudging the bowl closer to him. "Eat up, Anton. We have a long day ahead of us."

Anton immediately snatched his fork, digging in with an aggression that had Shan rolling her eyes. If there was one constant about her brother, it was that he would never turn down food, even if he was angry.

"Oh, don't be like that," Shan said, not bothering to hide her displeasure.

"He's our father," Anton muttered, and, damn it all, there was still a bit of pain there. Despite everything, every cruel word he spat to her brother's face, the way he tried make them hate each other, turning each of Shan's successes into a weapon against Anton, her brother still cared for the man, and it broke what was left of Shan's heart. Their father had deserved what had come to him, and if it took her the rest of her life she'd prove it to Anton.

"Was it you?"

Shan looked up from her tea, staring into Anton's eyes—dark, like hers, but fearful in a way that she had never seen before. Jutting her chin forward, she met his gaze without shame. "Of course," she said, giving him the truth so he would not ask for more.

It was her plan, her scheming, her will. But still, her brother could never know of Bart's involvement. There were some things that even she was not cruel enough for.

Anton let out a low hiss of pain. "How *could* you?"

"How dare you ask me that," Shan whispered, the venom all the more potent for it.

Anton ran his hand through his hair, over the shorn sides and tangling it in the dark strands like he was trying to wrench the words straight from his head. "Please say it wasn't because of me."

"It was for us," Shan replied, even though the truth hurt him. She had grown up in a web of lies, and the only guiding light she had left was that she wouldn't lie to him. Not when asked directly. "But, yes, I murdered our father to protect you."

Anton stood abruptly, not caring that he knocked his chair to the floor. Shan didn't flinch as he stared down at her, as he snarled, "Don't do this. Don't become a monster like him."

Shan laughed. She was already the monster. Their father had seen to that with years of training. Why not use it to protect the one thing that mattered?

But she would never be like her father—he tried to make her a weapon against the one person she loved without reservation, and for that she had cut him down.

"Come on, Anton," she said, turning back to her breakfast. "Don't let your food get cold."

Anton slammed his hands down on the table, causing the plates and glasses to rattle with the force of it. "Look at me, Shan!"

Slowly, cautiously, she turned her head to him, her eyes narrowing as she took in his ragged breathing, the wild look in his eyes, the raw, heartbreaking pain that twisted his expression into something she could barely recognize.

"I am *not* a child," he said. "I do not need you to keep meddling like this."

Shan placed her fork down, squaring her shoulders and folding her hands in her lap, creating the perfect image of serenity. Then—and only then—did she speak. "I will not apologize for what I've done, Antonin." She threw their shared name in his face, a reminder of what their father had wanted of him. Anton had never been more than a means to a legacy, and when he had been born Unblooded, when he revealed that he was disinclined to continue the family line and their name, her father decided that he had no son at all.

She considered going further, flinging every little cruelty they had lived through back at his face, if only to make him understand. For years their father had kept Anton locked away, a shame too great to speak of, a child left to grow in the shadows.

Neglected. Abused. Abandoned.

Sometimes, Shan thought it was worse than what had been done to her—she had been the favorite, special and perfect, struggling with all the weight of cruel expectations. She could never know, but at least it was over.

Her brother was at last free of that burden, and though he might never forgive her for it, that was a weight she was willing to bear. For him, she would do anything.

"Our father was cruel to you, so I removed him as a threat," Shan said, with all the simplicity of truth. "If you cannot recognize that, then perhaps you simply need more time to process."

"Blood and steel," Anton whispered. "You are becoming him after all." Pushing away from the table, he stormed towards the door.

"What about breakfast?"

He paused, not even bothering to look back. "I find, dear sister, that I have no appetite."

With that he disappeared into the hallway, and Shan released the tension she had been holding like a thread unspooling. Of all the reactions she had anticipated, of all the plans she had laid, this was the one outcome she had not expected. She wanted to chase after him, to beg and plead until he saw reason, but she knew that it wouldn't work.

So she remained in her seat, and calmly, mechanically, ate her breakfast. She needed the fuel for the day—there was still much to be done: food and drink to be prepared, a ballroom to be turned out and outfits to be chosen. Eventually, Anton would come crawling back to her.

He always did.

✦

"It's time," Bart said, peering out of the second-story window. Guests had been arriving for the past half-hour, milling about in their drawing room and ballroom—rather quickly redone into more of a parlor, thanks to Bart's ingenuity—and Anton had been down there from the start, accepting condolences.

She had been right in the end. Though he had avoided her all day, simmering in his petty rage, he had still turned up at the appointed hour; freshly shaved, neatly dressed, his hair artfully styled and his expression carefully arranged as the guests poured in.

As the new head of the family, it was Shan's place to come down after the guests had started to arrive, not altogether that different from a debutante's ball. Though it had not been long since hers; since she had turned eighteen, graduated from the Academy, and been accepted as a fully-fledged Blood Worker. Most girls didn't have their Ball and their Ascension in the same decade. Perhaps Aeravin would be better off if they did—the old clung to life and power with a tenacity that choked off the future.

Shan shoved the thought aside. Amusing as it was, there were other pressing matters to attend to. A quick stop before the mirror—her makeup impeccable, her hair still in place—and she was ready to face it all.

"I'll be here," Bart said, sitting at the desk, pulling the family ledgers towards him. Shan had to play the socialite, but why should that stop all the work?

Shan almost laughed. Her father must be rolling in his grave. He would have never allowed Bart—even as well-educated as he was—to sit at the LeClaires' desk. He had given his secretary a small, windowless room to work out of, as *befitted his station*. And he hadn't even hated him as much as he hated Bart. Bart had, after all, found his way into his son's heart and bed, sullying his namesake with his lowness.

Shan swore she would treat Bart better, and all her people for that matter. Blood and steel, for his loyalty and his place in her brother's heart, Shan would give Bart the world.

"Take care," she said, leaving her friend to his work as she left the safety of her father's study—no, *her* study—to face the wolves. She could hear them already, talking and whispering and gossiping. Her fingers twitched, her claws pressing against the silk of her dress, but she forced herself to relax her hands, to smooth her expression into the calm and cool mask that she had mastered long ago.

Tonight, she was facing them not as a child—not as an untested heir—but as a matriarch. This was her house. Her domain. She needn't worry about missing any key bit of information, no matter how small. She had spent years training her birds—her servants and informants and spies—fluttering about invisible and unobtrusive. While they served food and drink, while they served in the background, little more than decoration, they would be listening. Tonight, Shan would act as the center of attention and they'd flit about, following her instructions.

And when it was all over they would come and whisper what they learned in her ear, and she'd reward them for their good work.

So when she stood at the top of the stairs and looked at the people below her, Shan allowed herself the smallest of smiles. One day her web of information would be so strong, so complete, that she'd never have to fear anyone again.

The room quieted as the footman announced, "Lady Shan LeClaire." The crowd turned to her as one, their hungry eyes searching for any sign of weakness. She stood tall, letting them look their fill. They stood in clusters around the room, amongst tables laden with food, stretching from the grand fireplace all along the wide windows—each group its own little battalion.

She was the image of serenity, dressed in her finest black gown, and it shimmered in the glow of the witch light. The silken corset hugged her figure, and the skirt flared out from her pinched waist, but it bore a modestly cut square neckline—which would have been unfashionable if she hadn't been in mourning. It was sleeveless, like most dresses. No Blood Worker worth their salt would restrict their arm movements, even at this time. Not when their power relied on their claws and daggers.

There was nothing to criticize her for: Shan had made sure of that when she had selected this dress weeks ago. After a moment, she began her glide down the stairs, giving her footman a small nod as she passed. She made a note to personally thank him later. Her control of her household would be built on goodwill, a more powerful currency than the threats and fear Blood Workers normally traded in. When one expected pain, a little kindness went a long way.

But the simpering fools who crowded her home didn't deserve such allowances. Behind their sympathetic words and kind smiles lived hearts of stone. Success in Aeravin depended on cunning and ruthlessness, and the Blood Workers flocked to each new pawn, eager to see if they could play the game.

She bared her teeth in a fierce smile as she moved through the throng, her heels echoing on the marble floor. Lord Dunn offered carefully worded condolences and suspicious eyes; Lady Belrose extorted her to come to her next salon; and Lord Craddock leaned on her to join him at the theatre. She kept careful note of every promise she made—and did not make—asking them to please send her a note so she could add it to her schedule.

They met her vicious smile with ones of their own, swearing that their invitations would be sent before the week was out, and Shan demurely gave her thanks. They had their roles and played them perfectly, and Shan knew that every interaction was just the opening gambit in each Blood Worker's personal game of chess. As the invitations rolled in, Shan would respond, picking and choosing each social outing with care as she made her countermoves.

And the game would play out.

"My dear Lady LeClaire," a soft voice whispered at her ear, and she froze as she recognized it, her blood turning as cold as ice in her veins. The Eternal King had accepted her invitation after all, the one she had sent with no expectations. It was a formality, done by every new ascendant in this position. In her lifetime she had never heard of him accepting.

She spun around, her skirts flaring prettily round her ankles, and sank into a deep curtsy. "Your Majesty."

As she stood there, her form perfect and without a single tremble, the King reached down, palm up. "Please rise, my lady."

She took his hand, letting him help her, and she stared up at him. He was studying her, curiosity softening the harsh lines of his face. Despite his looming presence in society, Shan had only personally met him a handful of times—brief flashes of formality through her life. Visiting her father when she was very, very young. Attending the official welcome of her class to the Academy of Dameral. Passing through her graduation to grant the highest honors.

Through it all, he was stern. Cold. Untouchable. The force that had broken her father, her family, her entire world while letting his country slip through his fingers. Though she had worked her whole life for this, she was not yet ready for him to be looking at her. She ached to use her claws or her daggers, to carve that bored look from his face.

"You have a lovely home, and your garden is exquisite," he said, gesturing out the open doors. Though his words were perfectly polite, there was something empty in his tone that sent shivers skittering across Shan's skin. "Take a turn with me?"

"I'd be honored," she said, deliberately casting her eyes low. Her posture demure and perfect, everything that was expected of a young woman who had captured her liege's attention. It was an easy act for her to slip into—and it was certainly better than the truth.

Rage and spite could only get one so far.

The King held out his arm—perfunctory, his movements and actions just so—and the unease in Shan grew deeper. But she took it anyway, and he pulled her away, leading her on a tour of her own gardens. It was meticulously landscaped, filled with lush rose bushes in full bloom, petals scattered amongst the paths and benches. "I haven't been here in years. Your father did wonders with it."

Shan held her head high. "My father was never interested in horticulture. He turned the gardens over to me when I was thirteen."

It was only a slight lie. Lord LeClaire hadn't so much given them over to her as she had seized them—along with control of the rest of the household. In his paranoia, he had let their home go to waste, uncaring of Anton in dirt and filth as the last of the money drained away, funneled towards Shan's education and needs.

She simply did what any enterprising young girl would—she fixed it. She hired new housekeepers in his name, new landscapers, made sure that Anton had all that he needed provided for him, then redirected their investments and kept them just on this side of bankruptcy.

It had left her angry, of course, but she couldn't let it show. When she was supposed to be focusing on her studies, she had to save her family from the shadows while her father took all the credit. That had been the beginning of it all.

The King had stopped by the rose bushes along the stone

wall—Aeravinian roses—and carefully plucked a freshly bloomed flower. He twirled it in his fingers, staring at the petals as they spun. Turning to Shan, he asked, "Blood, then?"

It took her a moment to process his question, but she quickly recovered. "Yes, weekly." Like the rest of the household, Shan had been determined to make her gardens the best in the city. Careful planning and study—and the judicious application of blood, bled into the ground and powered by a simple spark of magic—meant that the roses bloomed strong and fragrant all year round.

"Well done," he said, clenching his fist around the stem. The thorns dug into his flesh, and he turned his hand so that the blood dripped down onto the ground, seeping into the dirt, fuel for their everlasting blooms. "A gift, then, for the loveliest garden outside of the palace."

Shan stared at the blood, even though all she wanted was to run. The King's strange attempts at kindness unnerved her—Blood Workers were normally so careful with their own blood, aware of how powerful even a single drop was. But this King? He spilled it for her on a whim, gracing her roses with power most would kill to taste. "Thank you."

He nodded, as if he had given her a great boon, then dropped the rose to the ground, stamping it into the earth under his heel. The cuts were already healed and gone, as if they had never been there at all.

Then he was walking again, and she had to hurry to catch up. "Still, Your Majesty, I must thank you for attending tonight. I didn't expect it."

"But of course," the King replied. "I simply had to see you after such a sudden coup. I've had my eye on you for years, girl, though I was surprised to see you make your move so soon."

She stopped cold, and as he turned to look back at her, she saw the first bit of true emotion on his face. A knowing smirk. "I don't know what you mean."

"Don't play coy, Shan, it doesn't become you." He caught her chin in his hand, tilting her face up so that he could look her in the eyes.

"I know everything that happens in this country. Your father was a tenacious, paranoid bastard who clung to life with a stubbornness that always frustrated me. But it seems the fool should have watched his own house."

Shan considered her options. Denial? Shock? Anger? No. None of that would do. She held her head high and smiled. "My father was an idiot, and he nearly ruined the LeClaires. I swear to do better."

The King inclined his head to her, the closest thing she had ever seen him give to honoring someone else. "I'm sure you will, my dear. I'll be watching." Their turn around the garden finished, he disappeared back inside, slipping through the shocked crowd. He did not linger—his mission complete, he cut through the crowds and headed straight for the door.

"He's like that," a quiet voice murmured, and she turned to find Isaac de la Cruz, the Royal Blood Worker and her once dearest friend, standing in the shadows of the garden. He lifted his cigarette to his lips, its burning tip a small, bright light in the darkness. "He steamrolls you then leaves you to pull yourself back together."

He dropped the cigarette, stamping it out under his heel, and stepped forward. Shan didn't know what to do, so she clamped her hands behind her back and stood tall, her face expressionless.

He wasn't supposed to be here.

He was the same and different all at once. She traced the familiar features with her eyes, the Tagalan heritage they both shared imprinted in her memories, as she catalogued every change. The line of his jaw, now a bit broader and peppered with the beginnings of a beard. His dark, soft hair, now longer and curlier. His dark eyes, just a bit colder, shuttered. His rich, burnt gold skin, looking a little pale and wan, as if he hadn't seen the sun in weeks.

He was so achingly handsome, grown into his skin in a way that she wished she had been there to see. But his smile was the same, quirked up a little on one side in the way that made her heart ache. "I've missed you, my dear Lady LeClaire."

Shan felt a pang, deep in her stomach. As much as she was

still angry at Isaac, even after all these years, she did miss him. Their constant battles, pushing and pulling each other to be better. Their schemes and their games. The way they were the only ones who understood each other when their classmates had shunned them for their foreignness. In all of the great melting pot of Aeravin, it seemed a miracle that she had found someone so like her.

Once she had been closer to him than anyone else in this misbe-gotten world. She had held his hand as he whispered truths in her ear, as he claimed a new name that fit him better than the one his parents gave him, as he began treatments that would shape his form to match the boy he knew himself to be. Through it all, she had been there, a rock for him to lean on.

But then they graduated, and when he was offered the chance to join the King's cadre, a handful of students selected from each graduating class to be part of his personal team of scholars, he had dropped her like she had meant nothing.

Like *they* had meant nothing, despite all the secrets and fears and dreams they had once whispered to each other.

So instead of embracing him, Shan shrugged casually, as if that wound wasn't as raw and aching as it was when he first inflicted it. "What are titles between us, old friend?"

"Old friends indeed," Isaac said, glancing away. Guilty. "It's been a while. Much has changed."

"Perhaps if you had returned any of my letters," she said coolly, "I would know more about it."

He ran a hand through his hair, swearing. "It was complicated, Shan, you must know that."

"Oh, I do." This time, when she smiled, there was no warmth to it. "I understand that you couldn't be seen associating with someone as low as me."

She almost didn't blame him. It had all worked out in the end, for it hadn't been long at all before the King had appointed him Royal Blood Worker to the shock of all of Aeravin. It had been another one of the dreams he had whispered in her ear, back when they both believed it was nothing more than that.

The position of Royal Blood Worker was prestigious. Powerful. It placed one at the King's right hand, with the privilege and curse of handling all his most important affairs. Most importantly, he had thought it would bring him acceptance he craved so much. It would prove to everyone that he belonged here just as much as they did—and to some extent, it had worked, though there were still whispers about that upstart de la Cruz. But it also bound him to the Eternal King, to do his bidding and represent his will across Aeravin. It would have been hell, in her opinion, but it was everything that Isaac had wanted.

And only a small part of her hoped that his victory was a bitter one.

"I know I was wrong," Isaac said. He stepped forward, but she immediately moved back. Not letting him close.

Not knowing what she'd do if he was.

"You were," she said.

"Please, Shan, is there anything I can do to make it up to you?"

She looked away, wanting to accept his words as truth, his pain as genuine. It probably was, but she couldn't discount the fact that he hadn't reached out to her until he knew that her father was dead.

"I don't know, Isaac," she said. It was the first bit of genuine honesty that she had shown that night, and she forced herself to look upon him, to accept that the pain fluttering across his expression was her fault.

He didn't back down. "Well, I hope you can let me try, at least. I want us to be . . . friends, again."

"Oh, Isaac." She shook her head. "We're not children anymore. Blood Workers don't have friends."

"No, they don't." He took her hand in his, grabbing it before she could pull away. She didn't fight him as he raised it to his lips, placing a soft kiss to the back of it, and warmth spread through her from that single, brief point of contact. "But we were never simply friends, were we?"

Shan licked her lips, her throat suddenly dry as she remembered those nights. The taste of his mouth, the feel of his skin under her hands, the weight of his body over hers as they explored the ways they could bring each other pleasure.

Things between them had never been simple, and they never would be. But she couldn't bring herself to cast him aside in the same way that he had her, so she just whispered, "No, we weren't."

"Is there any hope at all?"

The words fell from her lips before she could stop them. "Give me a reason."

It wasn't quite an admission, but he was smart enough to see it for what it was. A chance.

When he smiled at her, it was like they were teenagers again. Like the last few years had never happened. "Come with me to the theatre, Shan. I have a box."

She nodded, unable to find her voice.

"Brilliant! I'll send an invitation." He bowed to her, the perfect gentleman. "I should let you get back to your guests. I look forward to seeing you soon."

"Me too."

Grinning, Isaac turned away from her, reaching for his cigarette case. And Shan returned to her party, a polite smile plastered on her face to cover the riotous beating of her heart.

Anton was watching from the window, a glass of whisky in hand. He arched an eyebrow, and it was clear from the look that he gave her that he had at least seen everything, even if he had been unable to hear it.

She gave him the subtlest shake of her head. *Not now.*

Glaring, Anton downed the rest of his drink in one gulp, then pushed his way through the crowds and out of the ballroom. The guests tittered amongst themselves, but they were used to Anton's antics. He did always lean into his role.

They knew the real power in the room was Shan. The woman who had taken private conversations with both the King and the Royal Blood Worker. They had all seen the shift in power.

Shan held herself proud and tall. There was still work to do.

Chapter Four

Samuel

"Hutchinson, my office. Now."

Samuel stood abruptly, dropping his pen onto the ledgers across his desk, the long list of numbers and items already forgotten, the careful work of tracking the various goods and payments that passed in and out of this warehouse as they shipped all around the world. The rest of his co-workers all looked away, having all faced the boss's wrath before. They knew what it meant.

It was the end of the day. Cobb was in one of his moods. Samuel had been summoned. But there wasn't anything to do about it. He just straightened his shirt, made sure none of his hair had spilled from its bun and moved towards the manager's office.

"Samuel!" A hand caught his, squeezing tightly in solidarity.

He bit back the emotion he dared not name. Of course, it would be him. Markus was a kind soul, who had repeatedly tried to invite him out for dinners or ales. It hadn't taken long for Samuel to figure out where his interest lay, and if he had been someone else—anyone else—he might have accepted. His interest had never been restricted by gender, but after that one disastrous night, Samuel held Markus at arm's length.

Markus, though, had been so kind about it, even after Samuel told him they couldn't see each other again.

"Thanks," he whispered, returning the squeeze. But he couldn't linger—Cobb was waiting for him, and his patience was thin even on the best of days. Squaring his shoulders, Samuel crossed the room as quickly as he could.

The second he crossed the threshold, he heard the whispering start. He was sure they were already placing bets on whether he'd return to work tomorrow. But he couldn't focus on that, so he faced his manager, studying Cobb's lined face, the grey at his temples and the dark bags under his eyes. "Yes, sir?"

"You have a visitor," Cobb said, nodding towards the glass pane that faced the receiving room. Samuel recognized her immediately— the same Blood Worker who had found him with the body last week, who had promised to be back to take his statement as soon as she had a chance. He just hadn't expected her to come by his work. Hells, he was surprised she sought him out at all. Usually, they didn't bother with Unblooded deaths. But this murder had clearly been done by magic, so perhaps they didn't have the choice to ignore it.

Samuel swallowed hard against the fear that suddenly clawed through him. It was irrational—even from their brief interaction he had sensed that Alessi was not as overtly cruel as many other Blood Workers. But still—those dark robes, the glint of the claws on her hands, the forbidding glare.

It was hard to undo a lifetime of conditioning.

Cobb rapped his knuckles on the glass and she entered the room, standing with her hands folded behind her back as she waited for him to depart. Cobb huffed, moving past her with a frown. But still, he left them alone.

"Samuel," Alessi said, when the door closed. "Thank you for meeting with me." He almost laughed at that. As if he could have refused her. She had shown up at his place of employment, demanding to speak to him as if she were entitled to it.

And perhaps she was. What was he, in the grand scheme of things? Just another Unblooded fool caught up in something far beyond himself.

"Of course," Samuel replied, and Alessi nodded primly.

She sat down at Cobb's desk as if she belonged there, pulling a notebook from a satchel he hadn't even noticed she was carrying. It blended so well with her robes it was like it wasn't even there. She flipped to a blank page, holding her pen at the ready. "Let's start with what you were doing that night." She levelled a stern gaze at him, managing to pack a shocking amount of disdain into it. "You *can* sit, you know."

Cautiously, Samuel settled into the chair in front of her, and she offered him what was supposed to be a reassuring smile. Unfortunately, there was no reason to ever find a Blood Worker's smile comforting.

"Tell me what you were doing that night."

"I was coming home from work when I found the body," Samuel began, only to be immediately interrupted.

"Straight from here, then?"

"No." He twisted his fingers in his lap. "I saw . . . the sacrifice. With our King."

Alessi cocked her head to the side. "We don't get many Unblooded like you there."

"I couldn't get through the crowds." He glanced up at her. "Does it matter?"

"Probably not," Alessi admitted. "Continue."

He took a breath to steady himself, then he did. He told her of how he had waited for the crowd to clear, how he had trudged home in the evening light, how he had seen her there on the ground. How he had tried to help her, only to find she was already dead.

There was something like sadness in Alessi's eyes as she listened to him speak, her hand taking down the notes without her even needing to look at the paper. It wasn't quite pity or compassion, and it made Samuel feel like he was being judged for what he was.

"And that's all you remember?" Alessi pressed.

"Yes," Samuel replied, rubbing the heel of his hands against his eyes. "That's all."

Alessi leaned back in the chair. "And does the name Fiona Molloy mean anything to you?"

"You were able to identify her?" Samuel asked, astonished.

"Yes, with her blood," Alessi said. "It took some time to sort it out, but we found her."

Samuel shuddered, his thumb pressing over the vein at the crook of his arm. It was always blood, wasn't it? It was part of the census, taken from every child who had reached the age of five, for too many died without making it that long. A name, a tiny vial of blood. A way of keeping track of the Unblooded. It was, theoretically, for situations like this. For helping to find missing persons, for identifying the dead, for giving families peace and closure.

It scared him to his very core, for he was not foolish enough to assume there weren't secrets in his blood that he didn't want them to find.

Which is why he always toed the line.

"The name means nothing to me."

Alessi studied him. "Even so, given that you're now part of this case—and given the nature of the corpse—there will be a guard around your flat and your work. Just to keep an eye on things."

Samuel actually scoffed at that. It was absurd. "For my protection?" he asked, with just the slightest bit of sarcasm. "I'm honored."

"I almost like you," Alessi said with a sad smile. "Shame about your condition."

His brow furrowed as terror woke, his power roaring to life in his chest. He nearly spoke—nearly brought Alessi to her knees to demand how she knew, before rationality caught up.

Ah, right. His condition. It wasn't the dark power inside that Alessi referred to, but the lack of power. As if he had chosen to be Unblooded. As if he would have chosen to be a Blood Worker at all.

"Well, that is a shame," Samuel spat, with a fury that surprised even himself. He closed his eyes, reining in the anger that wasn't wholly real—that was spurred on by the power coiled inside him, now awoken.

Alessi's eyes narrowed. "Don't be that way. Aeravin wouldn't survive without the help of you and yours. You're what keeps this country moving."

"Like gears in clockwork." Samuel sucked in a deep breath, his nerves frayed and his temper hanging by a thread. That's all they were to Blood Workers—tools to be used. Cogs in a machine. Nothing more.

"More or less," Alessi shrugged, as if to say, what can you do? "If you find anything else, let us know. Can you do that, Hutchinson?"

"Of course." Samuel stopped himself from showing any reaction. As if he wanted a murderer running through Dameral. It wasn't likely that they'd be killing Blood Workers, not with the way that body had been torn apart. Samuel knew enough to recognize that.

Crueler Blood Workers saw them as little more than bags of blood. Walking, talking power sources to be used as they pleased. And even with the quarterly Blood Taxes, even with the King making forced stealing of blood illegal, it still happened.

Samuel had now seen it first-hand.

Alessi took his answer at face value, nodding like a governess who had just gotten her pupil to do as she asked. Samuel wanted to slap the condescending look from her face. "Very good, boy."

"Don't!" Samuel snapped, the command slipping past his lips, insidious and dark. "Don't fucking patronize me." The power surged from him, hanging in the air. Samuel couldn't see it—no, it wasn't like that, but he could feel it as it bore down on Alessi, shame roiling in his gut as fear overtook him, forming the twisted twins of emotion he was so used to feeling.

Horror, at himself, at what he could do.

Terror, at the prospect of being caught out.

The Blood Worker went slack, all the tension easing from her body as she stared straight ahead, eyes unfocused. Her mouth snapped closed, her voice stolen away as the command wormed its way into her. As it bound her to Samuel's will.

"As you say," Alessi said, and she blinked suddenly, released. The power still clung to her, though, and Samuel knew that it would continue to hold her. Would silence her tongue should she try to address him that way again.

The silence stretched out, sweat beading on the back of Samuel's neck as he waited—sometimes they didn't notice, not really. The truth was too absurd to be taken seriously.

"I should be off then," Alessi said, moving to stand. She was still in a bit of a daze as she packed her notebook away, as she moved towards the door. "If you think of anything at all, please let us know immediately. Lives could hang in the balance."

"I understand," Samuel said, though he knew that he had nothing to offer. He wished that he did. He didn't want another innocent person to die, to vanish, even though it happened again and again in this city fueled by blood.

Alessi stared at him for a long moment, her icy eyes boring into him, like he was a puzzle that needed to be solved. But she only nodded goodbye, then showed herself out.

Samuel slumped down in his chair, his heart pounding an unsteady beat as his panic turned to something sicker.

"You all right, Hutchinson?" Cobb asked, entering the room. "Can I get you something?" He gestured towards the drawer where everyone knew he hid his alcohol.

"Thank you, sir," Samuel said. "But I doubt it would help me with my job." He tried to smile, but he failed when he saw the way that Cobb was looking at him.

Pity.

"I don't think that will be a problem, Hutchinson." Cobb pulled the drawer open and grabbed the decanter. "I really think you should."

That creeping terror came crawling back, sinking its claws into him. "No. No. Sir, you can't."

"I don't have a choice," he said. "We can't have Blood Workers sniffing around. It will upset our customers. I have to let you go."

He laughed—a wild, maniacal thing. He couldn't help it. Let you go, Cobb had said. Like it was a simple, easy thing.

Not like it was his life being shattered.

Cobb didn't say anything, didn't even look at him. He just poured a glass of bourbon and placed it at the edge of the desk.

Samuel studied the amber liquid, considered taking it. Downing it. Then turning the power inside of him onto Cobb and forcing him to let him keep his job.

No.

That would never work. Cobb had supervisors. And this establishment was one of the few that catered solely to the Unblooded, owned and managed and staffed entirely by their own kind as they bought and sold goods across the world. It was the reason Samuel had chosen it as one of the only places he could work, as one of the few places in this entire forsaken country where he could avoid them. And now that he had their attention, he'd lose this, too.

He could, however, make Cobb walk him to the bank, certify the withdrawal and give him all the coin inside. It would be enough for him to flee this brutal, horrible country. He'd get on a ship and sail away, never to be seen again.

His hand hovered over the glass, a new life so close, just waiting for him to reach out and take it.

But he couldn't do it. He couldn't give in to his power. Not like this. He snatched his hand back, as if burned, and looked away, taking deep breaths to still the dark urges that called to him.

"Samuel?" Cobb asked, his brows drawn as he watched. "You okay?"

The laugh threatened again. "I am now unemployed with hardly anything to my name. I have rent due at the end of the week, and only enough food in my pantry to get me through the next two days." He glanced up, just a bit of his power slipping past. "So tell me, what the fuck do you think?"

Cobb closed his eyes, as if pained. "Of course, you're not okay. I just ruined your life, didn't I?" He blinked, startled by his own honesty.

"Right." Samuel got to his feet. "I'll get my things, then."

"Wait." Cobb shot to his feet, the lingering traces of Samuel's power still driving him to honesty. "I'm sorry. I really mean it. You're a good kid. If you need a reference?"

Shaking his head, Samuel turned away. What good was a reference? If he was fired for catching the eye of the Blood Workers, well, that wouldn't change. Any reputable company run by Unblooded wouldn't want him, and he couldn't go to any company that was run by Blood Workers.

Couldn't let them find what was in his blood.

Chapter Five

Shan

"I'll make the rounds tonight," Shan declared, pushing away from her desk. There were notes and letters and invitations scattered all over it, the fruits of her success. In the week after the Funeral Ball, the requests had started rolling in, and she knew that this was important. As a young Blood Worker, as a new Matriarch, her social calendar was everything.

But she itched to move. Only a few days in and she was ready to shed her skin like a snake, to sink into the role she was most comfortable in—the one who controlled things from the shadows, not the woman who danced in the limelight.

The Sparrow.

"Do you want me to come along?" Bart offered, kindly. He, too, had been kept house-bound for the past few days, plotting and committing and cleaning up after a murder on her orders. Surely he felt the same restlessness that she did, but Shan was feeling too selfish. She needed this night to herself.

"No," she replied. "Stay in case anything important comes up."

Shoulders slumping, he nodded and turned away. "Be safe."

"I will." She knew that she was hurting him by leaving him behind, and she decided that she would give him the next day. But it was wiser for him to remain—he was her Hawk, her second-in-command, and if she was busy in the shadows someone had to manage the LeClaire estate. He must understand that.

She hurried to her rooms, cursing every moment that it took her to get changed. She loved her gowns and her dresses, she truly did, but such outfits did not help her move through Dameral at any kind of respectable speed. So, she slipped into her leather breeches and corset, strapped an unholy number of knives to her person, and covered it all with a dark cloak, thankful the nights were still cool enough for such an outfit. She left her claws on the dresser. If it came to it, she couldn't hesitate to use her magic. But a Blood Worker's claws were never inconspicuous, and she wouldn't risk it.

While she was the Sparrow, they would remain here.

Ready at last, she slipped from her room and down the servants' staircase, exiting the LeClaire townhouse via the back entrance, as she had done so many times before.

And, just like that, she was free.

All her life she had been terribly, uncomfortably, aware of who and what she was. A Blood Worker and a Lady, of mixed blood and lesser pedigree. Sneered at by her companions for the golden tint to her skin, for the darkness of her hair.

Shan couldn't change her appearance, but she could change what she was. She had seen how her father had broken her mother, after all, and all that he had done to break her brother. All he cared about was creating the perfect Blood Working family, the envy of Aeravin, but their mother had refused to shed the trappings of her homeland. Her brother had followed in her footsteps, but without even the gift of Blood Working to save him. So their father had locked them both away, prisoners in their own home, till their mother had fled, leaving her children behind with the man who would see them either molded in his own image or destroyed.

And so, Shan had learned to play the game. She could be the perfect, dutiful child of Aeravin with blood on her hands and a smirk on her lips. For years, she had done that, forced by her father to shed everything she had inherited from her mother—the foreign words, her favorite foods, the myths and the bedtime stories whispered in the night.

Even the brother she had loved so dearly, held at arm's length, so long as their father was watching.

It was only on nights like this, when she and Anton and Bart had sneaked out—a terrible trio—that she had learned to be comfortable in her skin. In who she was. By playing the hand that the world had dealt her in the light while crafting her own self—her own power—in darkness.

And now, though things had changed, though Anton and Bart had their own, new roles to play, she still found comfort in the ritual.

Moving away from the townhouse where she had grown up—the district her father had called home, where the noble Blood Workers lived and worked and studied—she felt the weight lift from her shoulders. She relaxed more the further away she travelled, down the cliffside that housed the homes and shops of the noble families, far from the roads that wound their slow, circuitous ways up to the Eternal King's shining palace of marble and gold. Soon she was in the merchants' district, the home of respectable but unadorned buildings, where the Unblooded with money and the Blood Workers without pedigree mixed and mingled, carving out lives of comfort if not luxury. With her dark cloak wrapped around her, and her long hair unbound and hiding her face, she wasn't a Lady but simply a woman going about her business.

But this wasn't the Dameral she was used to—there was a tension in the city, a fear in the air that hung like a cloud. Shan hadn't had the opportunity to walk amongst the people in weeks, so focused on the murder of her father and all that came afterwards, but there had been a shift in the air. It appeared the reports Bart had funneled her way were correct. Something was changing in Dameral, and it was more than a simple murder would bring. Even if, from what she had been able to gather, it was a gruesome, vile affair. This was something deeper, and she had precious little information on it. But she could fix that.

Mind made up, she turned from the main thoroughfare, slipping down a surprisingly empty street as she strode towards one of her drop points. She had several throughout the city, each dedicated to different kinds of information. One was for gossip and rumors on nobles, gathered by her birds who worked as maids and servants. Another was focused on the various Academies across Aeravin, where her birds kept an eye on the up-and-coming Blood Workers from different regions of the country. But tonight she would head for the darkest of them all—where her birds dropped notes about disappearances, deaths and other grim happenings. Normally, it was one of her least useful sources—she was a spymaster and intelligencer, not a detective—but perhaps she could find *something*.

Shan LeClaire was many things, but she was not one to waste an opportunity. Though she or Bart or Anton normally did a weekly sweep of the drop points, she made it a policy to adjust as needed.

Slipping past an all too familiar tavern, she counted the bricks in the wall past the kitchen window. Three to the left, two down—and there. To most, it looked like just another brick, but it slid out easily, and Shan snatched the pile of notes behind it.

Treasure acquired, she retraced her steps back into the tavern, nodding at the young man behind the bar. He smiled at her—recognizing his Sparrow—and she slipped to a table in the corner to shift through her notes.

He appeared at her table a moment later, a fresh candle in his hand and mug of the tavern's best ale in the other. Not that it was that good, really, but in her role as the Sparrow Shan couldn't turn it away. As the Sparrow she wasn't a noble lady used to the finest of wines, but simply someone who would trade useful information for coin.

There were many like the Sparrow in Aeravin, small-time information brokers who worked for both Blood Workers and Unblooded alike. But Shan was determined to make herself different, more powerful than any of them could ever be—and she did so with a simple policy. She simply turned none away, even those who didn't bring forth any useful information. She bought their loyalty with a little bit of kindness and a sympathetic ear. They were used to being overlooked, ignored, and forgotten. But for a little respect, she earned their trust. And when something did pan out, a little bit of coin only sweetened the deal.

She smiled at the young man, thanking him by name, and went back to work. Most of it was useless, a list of names of people who had gone missing, vanished into the night and never seen again. Though it tugged at her heart, she wouldn't be able to do anything about a random Unblooded who had vanished, not unless she could pin it on someone powerful. People went missing all the time and no one cared. One day, maybe, things would be different.

But before she could get there, she needed more power.

She sorted the notes into a pile, planning to dispose of them later. But just as she was about to give up hope, she found what she was looking for. It came from one of her informants in the Guard, and the girl promised her Sparrow important information if she could meet her. A familiar name, a rumor that she had long given up hope for.

A plan that she had dismissed as impossible, suddenly winking back to life.

Shooting to her feet, she dropped a coin on the table—far more than the ale was worth, but her bird would appreciate the extra— and she threw the rest of the notes into the fire. If she were to meet Alessi tonight, she had to move fast. Luckily, the Guard kept their headquarters here, in the merchants' district, not far from where she was now.

Shan hurried through the streets, folding into the crowds that started to thicken in the after-dinner rush, when Blood Workers and Unblooded alike travelled to the theatre, to salons, to gambling hells and clubs. She matched her pace to the crowd as best as she could to avoid standing out, and no one bothered her when she slipped into a building with flats for rent two blocks over from the Guard headquarters. She climbed the stairs in silence, up and up to the very top floor, and from there she slipped through an open window, leveraging herself onto the rooftop. Pulling a mask from her pocket, she tied it across her nose and mouth, hiding her features from prying eyes.

But for a moment, just a moment, she stopped to look out over Dameral, staring down the slope of the hill out towards the docks and the ocean. The closer one got to the water, the tighter the buildings grew, pressing up against each other as they fought for every inch of space. The fine trim and fancy designs faded as well, function taking precedence over style as the districts grew poorer.

Past that, Shan could see that the port was full of ships, bringing merchandise to trade for Aeravinian wealth and goods. For all that the rest of the world feared their Blood Working, calling it dark, unnatural and evil, their judgement was dropped in the face of cold, hard coin. And for those born with the gift and exiled from their homes, Aeravin would welcome them with open arms. As long as they were content with their place, filling the lower ranks of Blood Workers and doing the work that the nobles were above.

Shan turned away, biting her lip hard enough to split it. Blood filled her mouth, warm and thick, as she consumed it to tap into the latent power that flowed in all people. Instantly, she was lighter, quicker, stronger—absorbing the power from her blood and using it to push herself to the peak of physical skill. It wasn't a lot, a small hit to last a few moments, but it was enough.

Ready, she circled back around, then ran across the rooftop, springing up from the very edge and sailing over the narrow gap between the buildings. She stuck the landing, making it as soft as possible, and sprang back up, keeping her momentum strong. She flew across the rooftops, silent as a shadow, but feeling so wonderfully, vibrantly, alive.

When she leapt across the last alleyway, she burned away the remnants of blood in her mouth to give herself an extra boost. She rolled to a stop, her heartbeat pounding in her chest, savoring the moment before her bird approached her in the darkness.

The moonlight from above illuminated her face, her pale skin and eyes. Her hair was shorn short as it always had been, even back in their days at the Academy, when they had been classmates and not partners in crime. Back before Shan had recruited her to her cause. It had been a good choice, one of Shan's earliest successes. Delia Alessi was driven and clever, and she could go far. But she was the daughter of an Unblooded woman and a no-name Blood Worker, with little power of her own. Everything that Alessi had, she had fought for.

And Shan respected her for it.

"You came, Sparrow," Alessi said, a lit cigarette dangling from her lip, her excuse for being up here on the roof. Nothing suspicious, just another young woman indulging in a simple, addictive vice.

"Of course, Alessi," Shan replied. "I received your note."

"You don't always check it," Alessi shot back. "Not fast enough."

Shan kept herself from inclining her head. Whatever point Alessi might have, it wouldn't do to show weakness before her. Perhaps there should be a way for Alessi to contact her directly—unlike most of her birds, Alessi already knew her identity anyway. But that was neither here nor there. "What did you find?"

Alessi rolled her eyes, dissatisfied. But she answered anyway. "A rumor come alive. A young man with a gift to bend others to his will through words alone." Alessi slipped her a piece of paper—notes copied in Alessi's hand—and Shan snatched it up.

"I had started to believe he was just a rumor," Shan said as she scanned the words. The explanation—the murder, the man, the strange power he seemed to wield over a Blood Worker. Alessi herself. And best of all, a name and an address. It was more than she had ever gotten before.

"Aren't all rumors born in a kernel of truth?" Alessi asked, parroting the words Shan had drilled into her birds. Nothing was too small for their notice. A single offhand comment could be the key to tying the whole story together.

But stories such as this? They were almost too good to be true.

"I'll investigate it personally," Shan said, and Alessi nodded. "Did you report this?"

"Only to you," Alessi replied. "Well, aside from the parts that were relevant to the investigation. But that power? No." She tossed the butt of the cigarette over the edge of the building and turned away. "Until next time."

Shan nodded, then bit into her lip again and leapt off the edge of the roof into the night.

—•—

Shan sped through the night once she reached the ground. She ripped off her mask, slipping into the crowd and blending into the masses as she moved closer to the docks. She couldn't wait—not on a lead like this. Not when he had slipped through her fingers so many times before.

Her breath came easier as the crowd around her changed, as she became less *other* and more home. This was the Dameral she loved. The Dameral she belonged in. The one she wanted to save. Where people of all cultures and backgrounds mixed and mingled. A blend of languages crashed over her, words that she had no hope of recognizing flowing over her as conversations melded together, some soft, some sibilant, some guttural, all flowing to their own music. The smells from people's windows floated through the air, sharp flavors that made her mouth water—rich and spicy on her tongue.

Despite the vast cultures they came from, there was something familiar about it. Though their skin ranged from the palest white to the darkest black, though they spoke different languages and came from different traditions, they all brought something here from their pasts.

And Shan ached for that level of connection, that level of comfort. The community that her father had stolen from her when he had made it so their mother could not bear to live in the home that never welcomed her.

She knew that she didn't belong here, not truly. That she had been born to privilege and wealth and power that the people could never achieve, not under the current system. And all because of the magic in her veins.

She had to fix it, even if it took her whole life. Even if she damned herself in the process. It was the only way she could live with herself.

But to do that she needed this man. It was the only way she could make this fool plan work—if she tore down the King with nothing to replace him, it wouldn't just be the system that burned. It would be the whole nation.

But with the right puppet? Well, it certainly changed things.

When she found herself standing outside the address that Alessi had given her, she looked up at the dilapidated building with a frown. It was several stories high, and it was clear that no one had cared for it in decades. It was a heartbeat away from being condemned, the lower windows boarded over, the walls washed out and faded, and Shan swore she could hear it creak in the breeze.

And it wasn't even a strong wind.

It was practically squalor, the worst of Dameral's slums. It was hard to imagine the long lost Aberforth, heir to their legacy, living here. Especially with the power he was rumored to have. If he could bend people to his will, if he could have whatever he wanted, why would he choose to live like this?

Her stomach twisted in sudden fear. The sheer breadth of rumors was one thing, but the facts weren't adding up. What if they were wrong? What if this was just some boy with no ties to the King? What if his power wasn't real? Just a simple mistake born of fear and superstition? What if he had nothing to offer her?

Shan swallowed her anxiety—she knew nothing concrete at this point, and there was only one way to find out. If he wasn't who she was looking for, she still knew how to handle him. She'd turn him into one of her birds or she'd make sure there wasn't a problem. She had plenty of knives to spare.

It would be a shame, but she had done it before. She'd do it as many times as she needed to if it kept her plan safe.

She entered the building, preparing to lay a trap. To strip this young man bare and learn the secrets from his very blood. Before this night was through, she'd have her answers—and if she was lucky, a new ally as well.

Chapter Six

❦

Samuel

Samuel walked the streets for hours, the anger festering inside him. Panic thrummed a heavy beat in his chest, his breath coming hard and fast. He knew that he needed to make a plan, that he should be at home, calculating what little money he had left and putting it into an even harsher budget, rationing out what food he had. He should be looking at other jobs, other opportunities, he should take anything he could find. But it was pointless—no sensible Unblooded would employ him with Alessi sniffing around, and he shouldn't turn to any Blood Worker that would hire chaff like him.

Not with the secrets he carried in his veins.

No, he was well and truly fucked. It was still a shock to him—his entire life, everything he had worked so hard for, gone in a moment. He had been born in the gutter, his unwed, single mother scraping to provide for them. In Aeravin, it was difficult enough to provide for yourself, but add in a bastard son? With no family?

Sometimes Samuel thought it was a miracle he had survived to adulthood at all. But he had, thanks to his mother's hard work. She had made sure he was fed and clothed and educated—taught him reading and writing and arithmetic in the dim candlelight in the dark hours after work. She had kept him off the streets, kept him safe. And when he came into his terrible, terrible gifts, she had not shunned him. Just accepted him and helped him tame it. All she had asked was that he would take care of himself and avoid Blood Workers.

Now he had failed her twice over.

By the time his feet finally carried him home, night had already fallen. Tired and hungry, he fumbled for his keys—once, twice, three times before realizing he didn't need them.

The door was unlocked.

He had definitely locked it that morning. He might not have much, but that didn't mean he could afford to replace anything lost. Especially now. Carefully, he placed his hand on the doorknob, easing it open.

"Well, what have we here?" A woman asked, her voice cutting through the silence.

Samuel stood in the open doorway, his heart pounding in his ears as he looked at the stranger perched on his bed. The woman— young, she couldn't have been older than him—rose gracefully, pocketing the lock-picks she had been fiddling with. She made no move towards him, folding her hands demurely in front of her as she waited.

Samuel released the air from his lungs, taking that burst of fear and shoving it aside. If she was a thief, she would have already taken what she wanted and been gone. If she was here to hurt him, she would have done it while he was cowering in the doorway like a fool.

No, she wanted *something*, but Samuel hadn't the faintest idea what.

Closing the door, he stepped forward, searching her face in the moonlight. She wasn't wearing a mask, like some common criminal, and that intrigued him.

Praying that it wouldn't be the last thing he did, Samuel turned away from her, reaching for the candle and matches with surprisingly steady hands. A quick flick of his wrist and the light bloomed, caught and held on the wick, and he took the candle and lit the stubs he left around the small flat. It wasn't as bright or clean as witch light, but it was what he could afford. If it offended the stranger's sensibilities, at least she didn't show it.

"Well," Samuel said, turning to look her in the eyes. "Who are you?"

"A friend," she replied.

Samuel had to laugh. To her credit, she didn't flinch or frown. She kept her expression composed, and Samuel admired it. He studied her face, from her golden skin to the shape of her features, noting the Tagalan ancestry in her. She was exceedingly pretty, and her skin was clear and flawless. She wore her hair long—longer than most girls in the slums did, given the price that hair like that would fetch—and even in the faint candlelight Samuel could see its healthy shine.

Her clothes were fine as well, though he had never seen anything like them. She wore dark leathers, not quite black, but the same shade of nothingness as the shingles that lined the roofs of Dameral. Her cloak was the same color, that empty shade that would make the eye glaze right over it.

So strange, this girl in fine clothes, breaking into a home that she could afford to buy with the price of her hair alone.

"I've got nothing of value," he said.

Her nose wrinkled in the first sign of emotion he had gotten from her. Distaste. "It is rather quaint," she said, and though the words and tone were polite enough, Samuel still heard the veiled insult behind it.

"So, you're clearly not here to rob me," Samuel continued, his curiosity burning. He could force her to tell him why she had broken into his room, who she was and what someone of her means could want from him.

He could make her do it, and he could make her do it on her knees.

Samuel clenched his fists, disgusted with the way his mind had turned naturally to that. It was the lingering echoes of his power flowing through his veins, tempting him to darkness. Or, at least, that's what he told himself, what he had been telling himself for years. He wasn't his power. That ugliness that was in his blood was a curse, but it wasn't *him*.

He still didn't know if he was lying or not.

But knowing that he could throw it at this stranger was a comfort, a layer of protection he couldn't ignore, though it was one he didn't want to look at too closely.

And still, she just watched him.

"I have nothing to offer you," he said, inclining his head slightly. With no other recourse open to him, and not wanting to fall into the darkness, he turned to the only other option—manners. "No tea, no coffee. No snacks or cakes. I know that makes me a poor host, but I'm afraid that I was not expecting company."

The woman smiled, and in one swift movement there was a blade in her hand, glinting. "Those aren't what I came to taste."

Samuel swallowed hard, suddenly reconsidering his reluctance to use his power on her. "Blood Worker," he whispered, and she nodded.

"I don't want to hurt you, Samuel," the woman offered, turning the blade over in her hand. "I'm a friend. An ally. But I need to know something."

Samuel shook his head. "I'm not ignorant. I know what you can do with my blood."

"I can tell you who your father was," the woman replied. "And everything you can gain from claiming his name."

"It won't matter," Samuel said. "I know enough about my father to know that I don't care about the asshole who sired me." He had seen enough in his mother's eyes, in the fear that she had carried through her whole life. "And even if I did, it wouldn't matter. I'm no Blood Worker."

It was the only reason she would be here. That his family would be looking for him in the first place. It was a common enough fantasy that almost every child of the slums dreamed of it. That out there, somewhere, a Blood Worker family had lost their heirs, that they would come to the slums for the bastard child they had cast aside. That there was magic in their blood and nobility in their future.

Anything would be better than this life, this hopelessness. But Samuel never had that dream, because it didn't take him long to realize that he was one of those bastards. Though his mother had never given him a name, he had figured out the truth, that a nobleman had taken a fancy to his mother, had raped her and left her with a child in her belly and no way to care for it.

And worst of all, he wasn't even a Blood Worker. He couldn't master the simple tests that the Academy gave all their applicants, the magic somehow slipping through his fingers like water.

Instead, he was something far worse.

The woman looked concerned at his announcement, but not deterred. "I'm sure you only need a proper teacher," she said. "Your bloodline is strong."

Samuel smiled sadly. "I thought you needed to test that to be sure."

She cast him a grin that was all teeth. "You're right. Will you give me a little blood?"

Samuel considered it. Despite the anger he carried—or maybe because of it—he wanted to know who the man was. Who had destroyed his mother's life, who left her without a job or references or opportunity. Who had left her with a child she had spent her life protecting from the Blood Workers, at great cost to herself.

He had already failed her. Why not break the last promise he had left if it meant answers? If it meant revenge?

Never let them get your blood, she had said.

But he had nothing left to lose. If anything, this was an opportunity. He could come crashing back into his father's life, demanding retribution, money, answers. Find out if he even remembered his mother's name.

Perhaps even find out *what* he was.

It was certainly better than starving, and even if this woman was playing him, even with a drop of his blood, he could still force her back. Make her forget that she had ever seen his face. Make her take her own knife to her throat and slit it to the bone.

Probably.

"All right," he said. "But first I want your name."

She smiled—just a quirk of the lips, really—but she held out her free hand, dropping into a perfect curtsy. "Lady Shan LeClaire, at your service." She cast her gaze low, the perfect image of sweet and demure, marred only by her strange clothes.

Not knowing what else to do, he took her hand and bowed low, his forehead level with her outstretched fingers. In the game of courtly manners, he only knew the barest basics, but even he knew that someone like him ought to bow before someone like her.

And, strange gifts or not, it would be in his favor to not anger the Blood Worker.

"It's a pleasure, Lady LeClaire," Samuel said as he straightened. "I am Samuel Hutchinson."

"Well, Samuel ..." she flashed her blade again, the small silver dagger dancing in her fingers. "I won't need much."

Samuel steeled himself and stepped forward.

Meeting him halfway, she took his hand in hers. It was soft and small, but there were callouses on her fingertips. A lady's hand, but the type who was used to work, to handling daggers and claws and heaven knows what else. She had held him steadily, drawing her blade against the pad of his thumb, and the blood welled, bright and scarlet. Before either of them could think about what they were doing and the shocking intimacy of it, she raised his thumb to her lips and sucked it into her mouth.

The warmth shocked him, as well as the sudden swipe of her tongue against the cut, and he ripped his hand away before he could stop himself.

He watched her face, the shock and the sudden openness in her eyes, and she grabbed him again—hard. Pulling him closer, she pressed her nail below the wound, forcing another drop of blood out. Then her mouth was on him again, her teeth pressing against his flesh as she worked the wound.

Something flashed through him—an emotion he dared not recognize—and he wrenched himself away from her. "Get away from me!" he snapped, his power slipping. It was dark and heavy on his tongue, fueled by confusion and anger, and he could feel it hanging heavy in the room around him as she *scrambled* away.

All dignity, all pretense, all grace was gone as she mindlessly scurried backwards, eyes empty as she pressed against the far wall, putting as much distance between herself and Samuel as possible in the small room. For a moment they just stood in silence, Samuel's chest heaving and Shan staring blankly, then awareness started creeping back into her expression.

"Do you know what you are?" she asked, still breathless and raw, and Samuel couldn't help the smug feeling that washed over him. He had been the one to shatter her carefully constructed airs, and for the first time since she arrived, he felt like he had the upper hand.

Turning away, he took an old handkerchief from his pocket and held it against the cut. Pressed firmly against it until it clotted. "So," he asked, "am I not who you're looking for?"

He heard her swallow hard. "No, you are, Samuel Aberforth. But you are also so much more."

She stepped away from the wall, coming back into his line of sight, and held out the dagger to him, hilt first.

Looking down, he saw the shine of his blood still on it. Her words still ringing in his ears, he took the dagger and started absently cleaning it as well, till not a drop remained.

"I'm sorry, but did you just . . ." he finally said as he returned the dagger. But he stopped himself, shaking his head roughly. "No, the Aberforths are all dead. All but . . ."

"Yes," she said. She no longer seemed shaken; no, she looked at him with a brightness in her eyes, and he might not know this Lady LeClaire, but he knew a schemer when he saw one. She was looking at him like he was the answer to all her questions, and he felt suddenly, desperately, unbalanced. "All but the King. Until now. You are the last living heir of the Aberforth line and the last descendant of our Eternal King."

"No," he whispered, freezing up. It could not be. Out of every single option he had ever considered, every nobleman he had wondered about, he had never dreamed it was the Mad Aberforth. Fate had already been cruel enough to him—it could not do this now.

"Samuel," Shan said, gently, calmly, like she was speaking to a scared child or a skittish animal. "Do you understand what I am saying? Your father was Nathaniel Aberforth."

"No," he said stubbornly, looking down at her, at her pleading dark eyes and her gentle smile.

She took her hands in his, unable to hide her glee. "You are the answer to everything."

There it was—the scheme. "I am not your puppet," he swore, and she just smiled all the wider.

"And *this* is what you prefer?" she asked. Dropping his hands, she turned around, gesturing to the room around them. To its small quarters and its cheap, mismatched furniture. She pushed past him—graceful and elegant once more—and rummaged through his little pantry.

Rice.

Dried beans.

An apple so far gone that she wouldn't even touch it.

"This?" She gestured again. "This paltry life?" Turning, she obviously, slowly, looked him over from top to bottom in a way that made him squirm. "I see you don't have the strength to be a hard laborer, and your hands are too smooth to suggest that you work as a servant."

"I am an accountant," Samuel muttered crossly, clenching his hands at his side, discomforted by the fact that she had noticed him as much as he had noticed her.

"Ah, well, forgive me then." She pressed a hand over her heart. "Surely keeping numbers for someone else's profits is the life you've dreamed of."

"What would you have of me?" he all but snarled. "Go the King? Grovel for a place at his side?"

"Don't be ridiculous. There is a perfectly legitimate system in place for recognizing bastard heirs," she replied calmly. "No groveling involved."

"But to what end? Don't toy with me. I'm sure you're not doing this out of the goodness of your heart."

"No, of course not," she said, clearly pleased. She stalked forward, into his space, and he could feel her breath hitch as she looked up at him. Something sparked between them, and she tilted her head to the side, exposing the long line of her neck. His eyes followed it, as naturally as the pull of gravity, and he forced himself to look away.

This was not just foolish, it was dangerous.

Yet he could feel her next to him, the warmth of her presence, the pull of her charm. Except for the brief break caused by his power, she had been strong, confident, commanding, ever since he found her in his room. And that momentary slip didn't make her any less compelling—if anything, it made him want to take her apart bit by bit, strip away each layer until he found the true woman underneath.

Closing his eyes, he took a deep, steadying breath. "Just speak."

"The King would welcome you," she said, softly, her words a whisper against skin. "After the passing of his entire family, he mourned them for years. But now, I can give his family back to him."

And just like that, the allure faded, all the mystery gone in the blink of an eye. "You want to ride my coattails to power," he realized. "A simple glory hound."

He might as well have smacked her. She rocked back on her heels, her hand clenched at her side. "I found you, Samuel Aberforth, don't you forget that. I am no mere opportunist. I already have power, more than you could ever realize. This? This is just one of my many plans in play."

Samuel smiled, cruelly, and she leaned in. "And I should thank you for that?"

"Yes," she snapped. "A little gratitude would be nice. Understand this, Aberforth. You have nothing left to lose. I could give you the world."

"I don't want the world," he said. "I've seen what you and your kind do with your powers, your riches. I've lived the results of it." He gestured to the same room she mocked just moments before. "You see this? This is the best life I can hope for, the most I can afford, because you and your Blood Workers exploit us so you can have your riches. Hells, my *very existence* is proof of that. The late, great, mad Lord Aberforth saw my mother and wanted her, not caring that she didn't want him back. And so I was born, and my mother? She was ruined."

She studied him then, the artifice dropping as she took in the anger that flowed through him. He stepped away, raking his hands through his hair as he tried to bring himself back in line. He wasn't normally so open—he couldn't allow himself to be so open—but it had just crashed over him, like a wave, the words that he had held back for so long spilling past his lips.

"Samuel," she said, softly, giving him his space. "I've dropped a lot on you. I know you don't know me, and I am everything you hate about this world. But I understand you."

"And I'm supposed to believe that?"

"I know you can't yet," she replied. "But take this—my name is Lady Shan LeClaire. My father brought my mother from her home, a nation of islands where Blood Working was banned, but she was powerful and feared. He brought her here, made her his wife and his possession. And after he got his heir and a spare, he drove her away, keeping her children hostage."

He turned back to her, drawn by her tale, by the simple way she told it. There were no hysterics, no attempts at drama to earn his pity. It was the simple, honest truth, layered with a pain that was old and well-worn, but none the less potent for it.

"My whole life, I've been shamed for my tainted blood, for my brother who inherited my mother's looks but none of her power. I've seen the cruelty of Blood Workers turned against him. I've seen the way they use people like him—the Unblooded—as laborers and servants and disposable things."

She reached out and he let her take his hand. "I've spent my whole life building power on my own terms, by rallying the very people they dismiss. The people who surround their lives but are too unimportant to be anything more. I've gathered secrets and lies, truth and blackmail, and I'll use it to burn this system to the ground and create something new. I had planned to use you to do it," she paused, that small smile coming back, "but I see you're an idealist."

Samuel openly stared at her. "So, this is what you're scheming."

"And clever," she added. "It's hard enough to enact real change as a LeClaire. As tainted blood. But with you on my side, with an *Aberforth* on my side, suddenly things that were impossible are no longer so."

"You're mad."

"I'm not," she said, bitingly. "You have every reason to hate Aeravin as much as I do, and everything to gain. So, Samuel Aberforth, what do you say? Will you help me?"

For a long moment he didn't answer, weighing what she told him. He did not know this woman, he didn't know her plans or her schemes, just that she admitted to having them. But she was here, giving him just enough information that, should he wish it, he could turn her in to the Guard and have her executed for treason.

So perhaps, if she was willing to take a leap of faith on him, he should do the same.

Shrugging, he said, "What do I have to lose anyway?"

Chapter Seven

Shan

S han sipped her tea, wincing as she realized it had gone cold. Still, she drank it down, needing the boost of clarity it gave her. She stood, stretching, then padded across the study she had stolen from her father and rang the bell for the serving girl. She'd need another pot, and, judging by the light starting to stream through the windows, breakfast as well.

Another night without sleep, another restless day.

But she had a lot to plan for. Last night, she had brought Samuel Aberforth into her dangerous plans with a partial vision of the truth. Soon enough she'd return his title to him, but first she'd have to transform him. For now, he'd be seen as nothing more than common trash when she needed people to see a preening young lord.

Shan collapsed in her chair, tucking her feet underneath her as she settled back down. She knew that it was undignified, wearing the same clothes she had worn to sneak through Dameral the night before. Her hair was a knotted mess, curls falling in uneven strands down her back.

She didn't care. Her mind whirled with all that she had to do, but despite it all she could still taste his blood lingering on her tongue—ancient, alien, rich. Could still feel the weight of his eyes on her, hot as a brand, that bright green—Aberforth eyes. Could still feel his hand in hers—large, warm and strong.

He truly was beautiful. He was pale, yes, and soft, far more than this life should have allowed him to be. But his features were fine, almost elegant, and he had the golden hair of the Aberforths, hanging loose past his shoulders in a way that should have been unfashionable. She wondered what it would look like in the sunlight, and if it was as soft as it seemed.

He lingered with her like a dream, and she dug her nails into her skin to shock herself awake.

Returning to the paperwork she needed to finish, requestioning the next month's supply of blood for the workings of the LeClaire estate, she hardly noticed when the door opened and a tray of food was placed in front of her.

"Morning, sister."

That got her attention, and she looked up at her brother—cleanly shaven, shirt freshly pressed and cravat neatly tied. Even his hair was carefully styled back.

"What happened to you?" she asked, though she knew the how but not the why. Clearly Bart had gotten his hands on him and worked his own kind of magic.

"I should be asking you the same," Anton replied, frowning at her. "It's like you're back at the Academy, studying for exams."

She smiled, taking in the books scattered around her, bookmarks sticking out of them at odd angles and scribbled notes littering the desk. "It does look that way, doesn't it?"

Anton only hummed in response, grabbing a chair and spinning it around so he could sit facing her. "Mind telling me what this is about?"

"Planning," Shan said carefully, knowing that he didn't care a whit about the liters of blood that she needed delivered for her own Blood Working. No, this was about something deeper, something far more dangerous than invoices, and, still, Shan did not know how to address it. It used to be so easy, but things between them had been tense since the death of their father.

It seemed that he was finally starting to warm up to her again, their relationship slipping back into the ease that they used to know, back when they were both young enough to trust each other completely, to share everything.

"Clearly." Anton poured them both tea, downing his while it was still scalding. "Would it have anything to do with the rumor that you went searching for last night?"

Shan didn't answer right way, cutting into the fresh, warm pandesal so that she could fill it with eggs and tapa—a quick and dirty breakfast sandwich. "How much has Bart told you?"

"Blood and steel, why do I even bother?" He leaned back, staring up at the ceiling. "I might as well be talking to a wall."

Shan's smile faltered. "What? It helps to know how much you know, so I know how much I need to explain."

"Did you really find the Aberforth?" Anton ground out, then, to punish her, he snatched one of her pandesal and shoved it into his mouth whole.

"Hey!" She hit his arm as he chewed obnoxiously. "Get your own!" Smacking his lips as he finished, Anton grinned at her. "I hate you, brother."

"No, you don't." He winked. "Now tell me how it went."

Shan considered her choices. Her first instinct, even now, even with him, was to lie, to soften the blow. But she knew that she would end up telling him the truth, even if it wasn't always upfront. "It went well. I explained to him why I wanted to burn down Aeravin and asked him if he'd help us."

Anton did not disappoint. He rocked back in his chair, the whole thing groaning under his weight. "Are you insane?"

"No," she replied smoothly. "I'm proactive."

"We know nothing about him!'

Shan couldn't help rolling her eyes at that, but she kept her voice even. Calm, always calm, even when it hurt. Especially when it hurt. "I've been following rumors of this boy for years. My file on him is nearly as thick as you are."

Anton glared, her words doing nothing to douse the fire in his eyes. "That file is rumors and gossip. It isn't real."

She placed her teacup down with exaggerated care and grace, forcing the anger aside so that he could not see how much his words cut. Rising, she held herself tall, her chin high, daring him to contradict her. "My files are very real, dear brother. They are observation and information, and, yes! Rumors and gossip. A lie can be more powerful than the truth, if applied correctly."

"Of course you'd say that," Anton replied, with no small amount of bitterness. "After all, aren't you more lies that truth yourself?"

She slapped him, hard and fast, right across the face. He reeled back, touching the reddened skin in shock. They both stared at each other for the longest moment, as something between them cracked like glass—hairline fractures nearly invisible to the eye, but still so dangerous.

"I shouldn't have hit you," Shan said, in the same breath that Anton said, "I deserved that."

Shan wanted nothing more than to run to him, to wrap her brother in her arms and beg his forgiveness. But she couldn't bring herself to do it, so she said, her voice as cool and implacable as ice, "It was beneath both of us."

Anton nodded, withdrawing further into himself, and Shan let him. "All right. But my point still stands. We don't actually know him."

No, Anton didn't. But she did, just a little. In their brief meeting, she had seen to the heart of Samuel Aberforth—the control he tried so desperately to maintain over the righteous fire that burned within. He was a man a breath away from catching on fire, and Shan wanted nothing more than to watch him blaze.

But she didn't tell her brother any of this. She couldn't. Those moments were *hers*, and she wasn't ready to share them. She said instead, "The only way to know was to act. And besides, I'm a wonderful judge of character. How else could I have built all this?"

Anton wasn't convinced. "Yes, fine. But you promised us—me—time. This whole plan of yours," he said, gesturing widely, as if to encompass the entirety of her life's work, "is crazy. It's one thing when you're just playing information broker, when we're talking a little blackmail, a little influence, changing a few laws. But that's not your game here."

Shan shook her head. "First of all, I'm not playing at anything, Anton. And this is an opportunity we cannot ignore. We can take down the King and replace him with someone new—someone *human*. Besides, it's not like he knows the full of it. Not yet. He just knows that I want to make changes to Aeravin. Make things better. Fairer. All the same things he wants."

Anton settled back in his chair, chewing his lip. "And you're sure he didn't see through that?"

She frowned. "Are you doubting my ability to lie?"

"I see through your lies all the time," Anton offered, and she huffed. "Fine, fine. I'm just saying that this is a lot."

"It's still our plan, Anton," she said, though it was one they had given up on a long time ago. They had deemed it impossible then—but it wasn't now. "Trust me."

"Trust you?" Anton shook his head. "I love you, Shan, but I don't trust you. I'm not foolish enough for that."

Shan kept her face impassive. "You trust that I love you?"

"Yes," Anton said, instantly and without hesitation. "That's the problem. I don't trust you to hold yourself back. You'll do anything for us, and that scares me."

Shan shrugged. She couldn't fault him there—she had just murdered their father, after all. "You can meet Samuel tonight, if it helps."

"Tonight?"

"I'm having him over to meet with Laurens," Shan explained. "He needs a new wardrobe. And then he'll be staying here for a couple of days, until we get things sorted."

Anton nodded. "Well, since I *am* quite fashionable, perhaps I can be of help—and I can keep you out of trouble. All right. But you must do something for me."

Shan narrowed her eyes in suspicion.

"Finish your breakfast," Anton said. "Go take a bath, take a nap if you can. Stop working for a few hours."

Shan's lips curled into a reluctant smile. "Or what?"

"Or you'll start to smell." He took a big, dramatic sniff. "Nope, too late. You've already started."

Shan laughed—a startled, sudden sound. Perhaps things weren't as bad between them as she thought if he could still make her smile. "Little brothers are the worst."

"Guilty as charged," he replied.

She bit back another laugh, grabbing her sandwich from the plate. He was right, after all. If she wanted to actually be helpful to Samuel tonight, she ought to refresh herself.

Besides, she couldn't let a breakfast like this go to waste.

Chapter Eight

Samuel

Even though he knew he had the address correct, Samuel doubled-checked it against the note Shan had left him. He shouldn't have been surprised—she was, after all, a LeClaire. And in the day since she had arrived in his home and completely changed his life, he had tried to find out everything he could about her and her family.

It hadn't been much, but he had been able to verify a few things. The LeClaire family was an old bloodline, powerful, but the last few generations had been bankrupted. The late Lord Antonin LeClaire, very recently deceased, had found a wealthy family from the Tagalan Islands with a Blood Worker child, and, for an impressive dowry, taken her off their hands.

The family had paid to get rid of their daughter, as if she was some piece of trash. And while he didn't have a lot of sympathy for Blood Workers, even Samuel had to admit that was horrific. No one deserved a life like that, especially if the rest of the rumors about the late Lord LeClaire were true.

But that was the past—the woman had fled years ago in a scandal that had ruined what was left of the LeClaires' reputation, and in the wake of it Lord LeClaire had made them one of the most pitied Blood Working families in Aeravin. It was almost enough to make Samuel feel bad for this Lady LeClaire, but as he stood looking up at the grand townhouse she called home, he found that sympathy waning.

It rose high above him, a good three stories tall to a steeply tapered roofline, the entire structure painted a deep burgundy over the brick exterior. His gaze hopped from one bay window to another, the decorative gables and eaves a stylistic extravagance that was far beyond his experience, purely ornamental and ostentatious.

He had dithered on the street long enough—he was already close to being late. He squared his shoulders and climbed the stairs, knocking twice on the fine wooden door. It opened not a moment later, revealing a young footman in clothes finer than anything Samuel owned.

"Uh, hello," Samuel said, politely.

The footman blinked at him, clearly taking in his ratty shirt and faded trousers. "Lord Aberforth," the footman replied, his voice rising in such a way that it turned the greeting into a question.

Samuel winced at the title—though he knew that he had to get used to it—and nodded. "Just Samuel is fine."

The footman's brow furrowed, but he stepped aside and gestured for Samuel to follow him. "Lady LeClaire is expecting you in the parlor," he said. "Right this way."

He led Samuel into the house, moving at a brisk pace that didn't give him a chance to fully ogle the richness of the home. Just fleeting impressions of the solid pinewood floors, the lush curtains over the wide windows, the fine portraits that hung on the wall.

Everything was pristine and elegant, the design surprisingly tasteful and modern with its dark colors and harsh lines, as if the house had been recently redesigned. Probably with the money that the mother had brought in, now that he thought about it.

But still, the home was lovely, and that made him hate it all the more. It wasn't even something he could mock, gaudy and tacky and reeking of wealth.

"Lord Aberforth," the footman announced, and Samuel glanced up to see Shan in the parlor; a room that had been cleared and transformed into a makeshift tailor's studio, and she was talking with a woman maybe twenty years their senior.

Shan turned to him with a smile, and he was struck with how different she looked. The previous night she had dressed to make herself a shadow, to blend in with the crowds, to hide everything that marked her as different.

Today, she was a proper Lady, dressed in a deep blue gown that could have been plucked from the night sky, sprinkled with little sparkles that caught the eye like stars. It was fitted as if it had been made for her—and it probably had—with a tight corset and a skirt that spun out from around her waist. She wore her hair loose, a cascade of dark curls that edged on just the polite side of messy.

He wasn't a fool; he knew it was a carefully calculated choice on her part. She was showing off the riches that she had, that *he* could have, by wearing such a thing so casually. But even though he knew she was manipulating him, he couldn't deny the effect it most definitely had.

His mouth suddenly dry, he inclined his head to her. "My lady. Forgive me, I appear to be underdressed."

Shan smiled. "That's what we're here to fix. May I introduce Madame Laurens? She is the best tailor in Aeravin." She ran her hand down her bodice and towards her skirt, and Samuel was unable to stop himself from following the path of her fingers. "She made this. It's all the rage in the Courts of Lumerie."

Samuel had heard tales of the Courts of Lumerie, a nation to the south whose court was so decadent it rivalled the Blood Workers of Aeravin. They were the height of fashion and culture—what was popular one year swept out across the world the next, like ripples in a pond.

Laurens scoffed as she stepped up to them, an older woman with dark skin and strong features. She wore a suit of deep red, not the color of freshly spilt blood but of richest wine, tailored to fit her trim figure. "There is no need to talk me up, girl. You wore that dress for yourself, and you know it."

Shan made a noise of polite distress, but there was sudden laughter from the doorway. Samuel turned to find a young man leaning against the door, lounging in so deliberately casual a manner that it had to be affected. From the first glance Samuel knew that this had to be the brother Shan mentioned, the twin that his research had confirmed. The Unblooded one.

He had all his sister's elegance honed to a predator's grace. He was tall and thin and incredibly beautiful, and the smirk he wore proved that he was very aware of it. Samuel couldn't help but immediately compare him to Shan. They had the same features— the wide cheekbones, the wide nose, the narrow eyes. They were mirrors of each other, but he was harsh and brash where Shan was elegant and deadly. He was a club, and she was a blade.

His heavy gaze landed briefly on Samuel, then slid right on by to Laurens. "Glad to see someone here has sense."

"Well, if it isn't my favorite subject." Laurens grinned, holding out her arms, and he crossed the room to give her a quick hug and a peck on the cheek. "But I'm not here for you."

"Unfortunately not," Antonin said, tugging at the sleeves of his shirt. "My sister has more important uses for you."

"That I do," Shan said, at last stepping forward. She linked her arm through Samuel's, guiding him forward, and the light touch sent shivers across his skin. "Samuel, this is my brother, Sir Antonin LeClaire, though you can call him Anton. Anton, this is Lord Samuel Aberforth."

"Ah, yes," Antonin—no, Anton—said, glancing down at him.

"Just Samuel is fine," Samuel muttered, and Shan swatted him on the arm.

"You're a Lord," she said, "and he is not. You should go by Aberforth amongst your lessers, at the least, unless they are amongst your most intimate friends."

Samuel frowned. "And we are not friends?"

Anton laughed. "No. Not yet." The coldness of his gaze made Samuel think that they might never be friends, that Anton might not want them to be friends, and he forced himself to look away.

Perhaps it was foolish of him to even ask. He looked to Shan for help, but she just gestured Laurens forward.

"We still have work to do," Laurens said as she pushed past Anton, who broke off from the group. She took Samuel by the chin, turning his face left and right as she studied him. "He's a fine specimen, though a bit on the skinny side. That's all right, though. Long lines and lean silhouettes are in this season."

"You'll dress him, then?" Shan asked.

Laurens smiled, and there was something hungry about it. "If you're going to parade him around Dameral, girl, he might as well have the best."

Samuel quickly glanced between them. "Is this really necessary?"

"Consider this your first lesson, Samuel," Shan said, as Laurens pushed him onto the pedestal. "Appearances matter more than almost anything else."

He stood there, following Laurens' wordless orders to lift his arms. She circled around him, suddenly quiet and serious, as she took his measurements. "I'm sure there is more to it than that."

"Yes and no," Shan admitted. "But if you came before the King in those clothes we'd get nowhere at all. A proper outfit opens many doors, but it's still up to you to walk through them."

"So that's it? We're getting me a suit?"

Laurens scoffed behind his back. "To start with. Then a whole wardrobe from there."

Samuel looked at Shan in shock. A suit from a tailor, even one who wasn't as talented or popular as Laurens, was already an extravagance. An entire wardrobe was too much to bear thinking of. "No, that's too much."

Shaking her head, Shan stepped forward. "You will be needing the clothes, and, believe me, in a matter of weeks you'll be thanking me for the foresight. And don't worry about money, this is an investment on my part."

"And she's getting a discount," Laurens added, popping up at his armpit. "Don't worry that pretty little head of yours."

"A discount?"

Laurens' grin was predatory. "You're going to be the most talked-about person this season, boy. You'll be a walking, talking advertisement. It'll be great for business."

Shan inclined her head. "Just so. You'll be helping a simple, working-class woman. Aren't you proud of that?"

Before he could fight back—clearly Madame Laurens was not hurting for coin—Anton reappeared at their side, holding up a bolt of cloth against his skin.

"Ah," Laurens said, "the black." She took a half-step back, her eyes going unfocused. "Perfect. You know, Anton, if you get tired of being at your sister's beck and call, I could use someone with your skill."

Anton smiled, but there was an emptiness in his gaze that froze Samuel to the bone. "Thanks, my dear, I'll keep that in mind." He turned away, and Laurens just shook her head.

"Damn Blood Workers," she muttered under her breath.

"I thought he was Unblooded," Samuel said, watching as Anton crossed to where Shan stood, sorting through piles of fabric. Together, they whispered and consulted, occasionally pulling a bolt out, no doubt picking the materials for his wardrobe.

Laurens followed his gaze, her eyes awash with something like sadness. "He is, but he was still raised in their world." She cast him a suddenly serious look. "It's not too late for you, you know. You can still get out of this."

Samuel worried his lip, wishing that he could. That he had any other choice. But there was this dark gift inside him, and this Aberforth legacy to claim. Maybe, just maybe, if he found a way to survive in their world, he could do just a bit of good. "I can't," he whispered, and Laurens deflated.

"All right. Now, be still." She waved her handful of pins in front of him, and he went as still as the grave. "Good boy." Their moment gone and forgotten, Laurens refocused, sticking pins through the fabric as the silk slowly took the shape of a proper suit jacket.

"It's wonderful," Shan said, abandoning her work to look him over. "I didn't think the black would work with his complexion, but ..."

"It makes quite the image, doesn't it?" Laurens sketched in the air in front of him. "With a clean white shirt and cravat, the contrast will be lovely. Especially with that hair of his."

Shan hummed in response. "Yes, he'll be quite lovely." Her eyes were dark, sweeping over him in such a way that he felt like she wasn't seeing the clothes that were being made for him, but, rather, beneath the clothes themselves. "Quite lovely indeed."

He could feel the blush rise in him, staining his cheeks, but he didn't turn from her.

Laurens laughed—a deep, rolling belly laugh. "Oh, this is just delicious."

Shan turned, slowly, arching an imperious eyebrow at her. "I am not paying you to gossip, Laurens." And with that, she turned and sauntered towards the liquor cabinet and the carafe of wine that waited.

Samuel wanted to die.

Laurens, still chuckling, quickly got back to work. "Oh, now I see why you're here. Not that I blame you—if I were fifteen years younger ..." Samuel groaned, and she cackled. "Let me help you out with that."

Kneeling before him, Laurens began work on the breeches, and he could already tell they were going to be far more form-fitting that anything he was used to, and he almost asked her to loosen them a bit.

But then he caught himself. Shan was still watching him from across the room, now with a glass of wine in her hand. Her gaze was hot, a brand on his skin, and any protest he had died unspoken on his lips.

He stood still and silent as the tailor finished her work.

"I'll have the first one delivered here tomorrow," Laurens said, stepping away. "And the rest?"

Shan shrugged. "I'll confirm with you after, but I imagine the Aberforth townhouse."

"I still don't think that is necessary," Samuel said, pointedly. "I already have a home."

"No, you had a hovel," Shan said sharply. "You can't believe that we'd still let you stay there. Appearances aren't just about the clothes you wear, it's everything else as well."

Laurens sighed. "I have much work to do. I'll see myself out. Just let me know where to send this all and I'll send you the final bill." She crooked her fingers towards Samuel in a brisk wave. "Nice to meet you, Aberforth. And Anton, if you can help an old woman carry her materials back to her carriage, she'll give you a discount on your next purchase."

"In that case, how can I refuse?" His foul mood has passed like a summer breeze, or perhaps he was only testy with Samuel himself, and he started gathering the fabrics.

Shan watched them go with a slight smile. "Good, that's done."

Samuel waited till they were out of earshot, then, "I thought we were playing this close to the chest?"

"Laurens can be trusted, as can everyone in my employ," Shan said simply, as if it were a given, like the sun rising in the morning and setting again in the evening. "Now for the difficult part. Wine?"

Samuel blinked at her. Was that fitting supposed to be easy? "No thank you. I don't drink."

Shan studied him over the rim of her wine glass, her expression unreadable. "That makes sense. Can I get you something else? Tea? Juice? Water?"

"Tea would be lovely," he said, and she rang a bell, summoning a serving girl for a pot of tea and refreshments. "Thanks."

"Of course," she said, settling into a chair and gesturing for him to do the same. "We have to work out how to handle this, though. There aren't many teetotalers amongst the Blood Workers, as we're not known for our restraint."

"Is that really so—" he trailed off at the glare Shan shot him. "Right. Appearances." He ran his hand over his face. "Are you giving me a new identity, then?"

"Not a new identity precisely. Just refining the one you have." Shan fell silent as the serving girl returned, setting out the teapot, cups and the plate of desserts. It only took a couple of moments, but they both let the silence stretch out.

Only when the girl was gone did Shan speak again. "You have a unique opportunity, Samuel. You didn't grow up with other Blood Workers; you have a clean slate. You can be whoever and whatever you want to be."

"And what if I just want to be me?" he asked, his voice soft.

"Then I'd tell you that's a very poor decision," Shan replied. "No matter how much they like you, they'll still tear you apart. It's how they test you. So only give them the smallest bits of truth and protect everything about you that's real."

Samuel couldn't help it: the question slipped from his lips. "Is that what you do?"

Her smile was sad, but she didn't look away. "Of course. You have to, if you're going to survive here."

Samuel heard the hint of pain there. "And you don't want me to mess things up for you."

"Well, naturally," Shan said, sipping her wine. "But I also don't want my friends to get hurt any more than necessary."

"I thought we weren't friends."

Shan looked chagrined. "My brother can be . . . difficult at times. Perhaps he is right, that it is too early for friendship. But hopefully one day, no? I can see us working very well together."

Samuel wasn't a fool. He knew that everything about her, from the face she showed the world to the pain she whispered in his ear, was a careful choice. But yet, there was something about it that felt real, a hint of true vulnerability slipping through.

He shouldn't trust her—he shouldn't trust any Blood Worker. It would be too easy to give in to her charms, to let her sink her claws into him. But he couldn't help it.

Perhaps he was a fool after all.

"So let's figure out who Samuel Aberforth is," he said.

Chapter Nine

Samuel

Two days later, Samuel had settled into the LeClaire townhouse, shuffled off into one of the guest suites to wait for his audience with the King, which had finally come. Laurens had sent the first of his outfits along and it hung in the wardrobe, waiting for him.

Samuel didn't need to see the receipt to know that this dress suit was the most expensive thing he had ever touched, a silken masterpiece that felt so delicate under his touch. It was a forest green, only a few shades deeper than his eyes. The materials alone cost more than he wanted to think of, and every bit of the outfit had been tailored to him. Laurens had even sent along new underthings, as if she didn't trust what he had to be worthy of this outfit.

And, honestly, she hadn't been wrong.

In the end, he had needed some help. Shan had trimmed his hair for him, just evening out the ends after he refused to let her take off any length. She provided him with a razor sharper than any he had ever had and used Blood Working to heal the nicks his unsteady hands had left behind, licking the blood from his fingers as she commanded the skin to knit and mend, like he had never bled at all.

After he poured himself into the pants that felt too tight, and the shirt and jacket that hung snug across his shoulders, Shan tied his cravat for him, her fingers swift and soft against his throat. She was so close to him that he could breathe deep of the floral scent in her hair, a faint perfume warmed by her skin. His heart beat an unsteady rhythm in his chest, so loud he swore she could hear it, but if she did, Shan didn't show it.

But as she stepped back, a slight smile on her lips, Samuel swore he could feel her linger.

All the while she was a steady, calming presence. Then she loaded him into her carriage and took him to meet the Eternal King. It wasn't a long trip as the bird flew—the walk would have taken them little more than a half an hour—but apparently it was bad form to appear at the palace on foot.

He let Shan have her way, and they took the carriage through the narrow, winding streets, even though it would have been quicker if they hadn't. Still, it allowed Samuel to see Dameral in a way he never had before. Before he hadn't even been to this part of the city, but now he could watch the people as they passed by. Women in their fancy day dresses, men with their decorative walking sticks and velvet jackets, all lush and dark jewel tones, like so much of Aeravinian style—they might embrace styles and fabrics, following in the footsteps of their neighbors, but some aesthetics would never change. They moved in and out of shops that sold finery and frippery, jewels and soaps and the fanciest teas imported from all over the world, and Samuel felt anxious even *looking* at them.

And through it all, that tiny, dark part of him whispered that this was the world he belonged to. The one he should have been born to.

"We really thought you were all gone, you know," Shan said, suddenly.

Samuel didn't pull his gaze from the carriage window. "What are you going on about?"

"The Aberforths," Shan replied smoothly. "It was such a tragedy."

He couldn't help the scoff. "I might be new here, Lady LeClaire," Samuel said quietly. "But even I know that no one thought my father's death was a tragedy."

Shan folded her hands in her lap, looking up at him through her fine eyelashes. "Perhaps not. But the other deaths were—especially the children."

Funny, how she phrased it. As if the deaths were some mere accident and not murder.

All the Aberforths had been gathered at their country estate for the wedding of one the minor cousins—everyone but the Eternal King himself. Lord Nathaniel Aberforth, known for his cruelty that bordered on madness, killed everyone there then turned the blade on himself.

There were no survivors.

Samuel always suspected that his father was a bastard, but he had never suspected it was the Mad Aberforth himself, though it made a twisted kind of sense. The darkness in him couldn't have come out of nowhere. Yet here he was, entering their world and claiming their name. But at least he had Shan—he might not truly trust her, but he was comfortable in the knowledge that she would not see him disgraced. She was not the type to waste an investment.

"Just be careful," Shan said. "It is still a delicate subject, even after all this time. But he should still be happy to see you."

Samuel couldn't blame him. The Aberforths had been descended from him and his mortal wife, whom he had married when he took the throne all those centuries ago. The Aberforths were his children, his descendants. Then they were all gone. An entire family—and legacy—destroyed.

Until him.

"Are you sure this is a good idea?" Samuel asked, doubt starting to creep in.

"Of course," Shan said. "When have I ever led you astray?"

He laughed at the absurdity of that statement—they were still practically strangers after all—but it did relieve some of the tension, and then the carriage lurched to a stop. Shan glanced out the window. "We're here."

The door was opened by her coachman, who had stopped looking at Samuel like he didn't belong.

Perhaps appearances did make a difference after all.

Shan exited first, Samuel following, and they stepped into a grand courtyard. There was far more greenery than he had expected, not a bit of stone or marble to be seen. Instead, there was a garden of the most luscious red roses—Aeravinian roses—blooming strong and fragrant in the early spring light.

It was more beautiful that any gaudy display of material goods could have been, and Samuel felt a grudging sort of respect for the Eternal King. Yes, this must cost an excessive amount of money and magic to maintain, especially out of season. But it was real and beautiful and tangible, and even he couldn't begrudge them the cost.

Shan watched him admire the garden with a soft smile, her sharp edges softened for once. When she caught him staring, she just held out her arm. "Let's go meet your family."

Samuel nodded, linking arms with her and wordlessly following her into the palace. As they passed through the grand doors, he saw his surroundings slowly morph into the kind of opulence he had expected from the start—the kind that he hated. The walls draped in heavy woven tapestries, the paintings of the glorious Blood Working revolution that had birthed Aeravin, the stained-glass windows that cast streams of color across the marble floors. All fine, yes. Quite understandable and even laudable in moderation.

But throughout the city people were struggling. Starving. Children were scrambling and fighting for bits of stale bread, and the Eternal King lived a life of such wealth and luxury that it made Samuel furious.

Even looking at the servants, he could tell they were leagues beyond the life he had known, maids and footmen and secretaries all passing by in clothes finer than anything Samuel was used to. Shan didn't even acknowledge them, moving past as if they weren't even there. She moved with a casual determination, like she belonged there, and none could tell her otherwise.

Samuel wondered if he'd ever feel the same way.

"We're to meet him in his private study, just past the Royal Library," Shan said, filling the awkward silence.

Samuel couldn't help himself, he perked up at the mere mention of a library, and Shan, damn her, noticed. "Is he an avid reader?" Samuel asked quickly.

"Oh yes, he's quite the scholar," Shan said, as if they were different things. Samuel supposed that they were. "Even to this day he takes his role as the founder of our magic seriously and is always working to push it to new heights."

"I thought that was the Academy's role," Samuel said.

"Yes, but he is head of the Academy still." Shan shot him a quick, pitying look. "It's a lot, I know."

Samuel nodded and squirreled that bit of knowledge away with all the other things he still needed to learn. Unlike Shan, he didn't have the benefit of a lifetime.

They came to a stop before a wide, open casing, as if the architect had simply cut a hole in the wall. Through it, Samuel could see the Royal Library, stacks and stacks of books running back in long rows. He itched to explore, to run his fingers along the spines and see how they were organized, what knowledge and stories and power they contained.

He never had a formal education—his mother had taught him his reading, writing and arithmetic in the dim candlelight after dinner. He had skill with mathematics, yes, enough to build a meager career from it. But it was the novels that consumed him, that he had scrimped and saved for and hoarded.

He had, over the course of his life, managed to acquire a full dozen, favorites that he had read over and over until the spines cracked and the pages frayed. Hardly enough to be called a proper library. But this?

This was beyond any of his childish dreamings.

Shan was watching him, studying the way his face had lit. "Interesting," she murmured. "Most people in your position would be lusting after the jewels or the clothes or the lavish trappings. You, though ..." She gestured towards the library. "I'd love to let you explore, but we do have a meeting to keep."

Samuel followed after her, biting back the retort on his tongue. He knew that Shan was only trying to compliment him, and that she couldn't understand the truth. The LeClaires were a poorer Blood Working family, but they had never been truly destitute. She didn't know what it was like to be starving, that you wouldn't be thinking of books or knowledge, but things that would get you cold, hard coin.

In judging him as better, Shan had just shown her own ignorance.

But Samuel wasn't in a position where he could correct her assumptions. Not yet. Maybe as their plans grew to fruition, maybe as this nebulous thing between them solidified into trust and friendship. So he just kept quiet, wondering if he was damning his own soul by playing along.

"Here," Shan said, stopping fast. There at the end of the hallway was a pair of ornately carved doors. Even from where he was standing, Samuel could make out the delicately etched rose, its thorns standing out in stark relief—the King's seal and the symbol of Aeravin. Two stern-looking Guards flanked the doors, arms crossed in front of them and swords at their sides.

Shan looked at him. "Are you ready?"

He wasn't. Talking about introducing him to the King, planning it, playing dress up—all of it paled in comparison to the real thing. But he was already here and they had a plan. Together, they were going to make this country better.

Licking his lips, Samuel muttered, "As I'll ever be."

"If you panic," Shan said kindly, "just follow my lead." She strode forward, head held high. When they reached the Guards, she pulled a small card out of her reticule. "Lady Shan LeClaire and Mister Samuel Hutchinson here to see His Majesty, King Tristan Aberforth. We are expected."

The Guards barely even glanced at them. "Very well." She knocked twice on the door and then threw it open, repeating the same introductions that she had just given to the man inside.

The Eternal King.

He had stood when they were announced, studying them in a cold, calculating way. Samuel had seen him before, of course, both at this year's sacrifice and through official likenesses spread throughout the city. It was different, now. Now he wasn't looking at him simply as a man or a king, but as an ancestor, and it was like looking in a warped mirror. For all the similarities, the King had a hardness about him, in the sharp cut of his jaw, the harsh slope of his cheekbones, the thinness of his lips. He was carved from stone, looking more a warrior than a scholar, yet here he was amongst a pile of books with ink-stained fingers.

He had the same golden blond hair that Samuel did, though his was carefully cut and styled. And when he lifted his head to them, Samuel saw his own eyes in the Eternal King's face, a green so bright and sharp that it hardly looked natural.

"Lady LeClaire," the Eternal King said, slowly, as if weighing every syllable before it passed his lips. "And a friend?"

"A new friend," Shan confirmed, stepping forward. "But perhaps something more to you. May I present Samuel Aberforth?"

Samuel's breath caught in his throat as a hushed silence fell over the room. So that's how it was to be done? With no preamble and no warning? He stood tall, drawing in deep breaths and trying not to panic as the Eternal King examined him. His gaze was incredibly sharp, as if he were cataloguing every detail about Samuel. He bit the inside of his cheek, holding back the burning words on his tongue—how dare the King look at him so? If not for an accident of blood, he'd care nothing at all.

But he'd have to get used to this. Every time he was introduced from now on, every time the name Aberforth would pass from someone's lips, this would happen.

"It cannot be," the King said, coming closer to Samuel. He was so tall that Samuel had to tilt his head back, and he looked ready to leap forward and grab him by the throat for this affront. "They are all dead."

Samuel glanced at Shan out of the corner of his eye, and she gave him a slight nod, encouraging him to speak.

"My mother was a servant in the Aberforth household, Your Majesty," Samuel said, repeating the information that Shan had been able to confirm for him. "She left Lord Nathaniel's service a few weeks before the tragedy."

The Eternal King began to pace, his movements as graceful as a snake and just as unnerving. He had produced a small knife from somewhere, its blade glinting in the sunlight. "And you claim Lord Nathaniel was your father?"

Samuel nodded, holding out his hand. "If you wish proof, you may have it."

The Eternal King smiled, just slightly, and took Samuel's hand in his. His cut was quick and small, and he simply took Samuel's thumb between his lips and sucked the blood out.

Samuel snatched his hand back, not caring that the man in front of him was his King, or that it was terribly rude, and pulled a hand-kerchief from his pocket and wrapped it around his thumb.

The King simply stood there, his eyes narrowed as his throat worked. "It is true," he said softly. "You *are* Nate's son."

Samuel didn't move, waiting for the Eternal King's reaction. To see if he'd be welcomed or cast out. Then, suddenly, the King moved forward and grabbed Samuel by the shoulders, pulling him into a fierce hug. "I thought it was all lost," he whispered, so quietly that Samuel wasn't sure it was real, and then let go.

"I . . . uh . . ." Samuel stuttered. He had imagined something like this many times, especially after his mother's passing, when he had been alone for the first time in his life. He had dreamt of acceptance, of welcome—but there was something off about this. There was a possessiveness in the King's hug that didn't feel like relief, but cal-culation. "Thank you, Your Majesty."

The King waved his hand. "Please, we're family. Just Tristan will do."

"As you say, Tristan," Samuel said, the familiarity feeling wrong in his mouth. But the King was already turning towards Shan and seemingly oblivious to his discomfort.

"I don't know how you did this, my lady," Tristan said. "But we need to talk. Can you and Isaac give us a few moments?"

Samuel had been so focused on the King that he hadn't even noticed that there was someone else in the room, only then realizing that the Royal Blood Worker was with them. He stood off by an open window, a cigarette dangling from his lips. He looked remarkably different in this context—less like a spectacle, and more like a man— human, handsome, and so, so tired.

Shan curtsied. "Of course. I have been meaning to catch up with Sir de la Cruz anyway." Shan held out her hand, and the stranger from the window moved towards her, like an object caught in her magnetic field. "We'll be close by."

Samuel watched as this handsome man linked arms with Shan, his stomach twisting. And just like that they were gone and he was alone with the King.

"I'm sorry, Samuel ... it is Samuel, isn't it?" The King shook his head, as if he was still trying to piece everything together. "I never expected such luck. How did Lady LeClaire find you?"

Samuel shrugged. "I don't really know. You'd have to ask her—she just showed up at my flat several days past."

Frowning, the King turned a harsh glare on Samuel. "And all this time? You're a man grown. You never auditioned at the Academy?"

"I didn't always know," Samuel admitted, his words coming slowly. "I mean, I always suspected that I was *some* Lord's son, given the way my mother ... acted."

The King looked away, and Samuel caught the briefest glimpse of real emotion on his face. Shame.

Good, let him be ashamed.

"I take it," the King began slowly, "that the union was not—"

"My mother was raped," Samuel said, refusing to allow any dissembling. Not in this.

"I feared that." He sighed. "Nate inherited all my power but none of Abigail's grace."

It took Samuel a moment to figure out who the King was talking about, before remembering that the one queen Aeravin ever had was Abigail Aberforth.

"I know that apologies mean nothing, Samuel," the King said. "That it's not even my place to apologize for him at all. But I am sorry that you grew up fearing your family, and for any indignities you suffered because of it."

Samuel bit his lip. He hadn't faced any more indignity that thousands of others face in the King's city, but, of course, he wouldn't care about them.

"I cannot say what Nate would have done," the King was saying, still talking, "if he had known about you. I hope he would have provided for you and your mother, that he would have welcomed you into the family. After all, your blood is still Aberforth. What I can say, though, is that if I had known, I would have."

Samuel felt his power awaken, and he knew that if he wanted he could find out if that absurd statement had any kind of truth behind it. But he clamped it down, stopping it before it ruined everything. "There is something else you should know," Samuel said quietly. "I never auditioned at the Academy because I can't do Blood Working."

"I'm not surprised," the King said. "But you can do something more, can't you?"

Samuel's stomach dropped. "You know?"

"Of course." The King stepped closer. "It's the gift—and the curse—of the Aberforths. Let me guess, you don't have good control of it?"

Samuel nodded, and the King dropped a firm hand on his shoulder. "I suspected as much. Don't worry—we can work on that. You wouldn't be the first Aberforth I've helped master this gift."

"Thank you," Samuel breathed. It was more than he had ever expected, more than he could have hoped for.

Even if it did leave him indebted to this King of Blood.

"Naturally." The King moved back to his desk, shifting through a stack of papers. "I'll begin the process of transferring the Aberforth estates and funds to you immediately. The country estate will take some time—it's been closed for over two decades—but there is still the townhouse here in Dameral. I'll have that opened for you and find a crew of servants to get you settled."

"That won't be—"

The King cut him off. "It is. I won't have the last of my family living beneath his station. Tonight, you can stay here at the palace, but starting tomorrow you'll live the life you were born to lead."

"You don't have to air out a room for me," Samuel said quickly. "Lady LeClaire has already prepared a room for me, seeing as I'm, uh. Evicted."

There was a flash of steel in the King's eyes. "Someone evicted you?"

"No, no, it's fine," Samuel said quickly. "It was entirely fair. I couldn't make my rent after I was fired—"

"Someone fired you?" the King asked, his voice cutting like a knife.

Samuel winced. "Please, don't even think of it. It's a complicated situation. You see, I was the one who found the body last week—that messy murder? After a Guard showed up at my work to take my statement, it worried the management . . ."

"Wait, that was you?" His eyes narrowed, his mind clearly whirring with some new idea, but he shook his head. "Even so—"

"No!" Samuel said firmly. He couldn't believe it. Here he was, arguing with the damned Eternal King, but he couldn't stop himself. "Until three days ago, I didn't even know I was an Aberforth, let alone my employer or my landlord. What happened to me is what would have happened to any other Unblooded. So, don't be angry at them on my behalf, because they didn't do anything wrong."

The King took a step back, looking at Samuel with a fresh appreciation. Samuel didn't back down—he held his head high as he waited for the King's judgement.

He didn't expect him to look so pleased.

"Well, it seems you have the Aberforth backbone after all. Very well." He inclined his head to Samuel. "All transgressions will be forgiven—just this once."

Samuel couldn't do anything but nod. He didn't trust his voice at this moment, not with the rage that burned inside him.

"But do not expect such leniency again," the King warned. "You are an Aberforth now and will be treated as such."

Chapter Ten

Shan

"An Aberforth," Isaac whispered as they slipped out into the hallway, his arm linked with hers. "I figured you were planning something, but I didn't expect this."

Shan didn't respond right away, steering them past the guards and into a windowed alcove that overlooked the ocean. Only then, in the relative safety behind thick, dark curtains, did she turn to him, taking in the bags under his eyes and the exhaustion that clung to him like a heavy cloak. "I didn't expect to see you today."

"I'm sure you didn't," Isaac said, crossing his arms over his chest. "Especially as I didn't receive any notice about this meeting."

Shan focused her gaze on the curtains over his shoulder. "Oh?"

He nodded slowly. "It's very interesting, seeing that I am the one who manages the King's correspondence and schedule as Royal Blood Worker. Which I am *sure* you know."

"I do," Shan said, oh so softly, finally meeting his gaze. When she had called in her favors to get a meeting with the King—without the Royal Blood Worker's interference—she had expected him to be at most a little miffed. She did not expect him to look so hurt.

He pressed the heels of his hands against his eyes, taking a deep steadying breath. "You know, I'm used to it from the others. They don't like me—they don't trust me. I'm not one of *them*, so they undermine me every chance they get. But I expected better of you."

Shan hesitated—there wasn't a good explanation that wouldn't hurt him. And he knew her far too well to fall for any of her lies. "I had to play this one close to the chest. It was a delicate matter."

"And you didn't trust me to help you." It wasn't a question, so Shan didn't respond, and Isaac cursed under his breath. "I am hurt that you think so little of me, even if I'm not surprised."

Shan's heart ached, beating an unsteady rhythm in her chest. "It's not as if you've given me any reason to think otherwise, is it?"

Isaac reached out a hand, then dropped it—an aborted, harsh movement. "I know, Shan. But can I try?"

"Yes," Shan whispered, "but I'm not—I can't—just accept you back with open arms."

"What fools we are," Isaac said. "And I am the biggest fool of all."

"I'm not going to argue that." She smirked at him, and he laughed, a soft helpless thing. "Give it time, Isaac. Give me more time."

"As you wish," he promised.

They stood there in awkward silence, the tension between them palpable. It had broken something inside of her when he had renounced her, and she still hadn't figured out how to put herself back together. The one time she had opened herself to someone, and he had left her behind as if she meant nothing. Afterwards it had been easy to lock him out—to lock them all out. But understanding? Forgiveness? That was harder.

And Shan didn't even know where to begin.

Thankfully she could put that off till another time. The door to the King's study opened and Samuel emerged—whole and only a little bit shaken. He quickly found them standing together in the alcove, a frown on his face.

Shan arched an eyebrow at him, amused by the way he squirmed.

"Lady LeClaire," he said, executing a small, perfunctory bow. "His Majesty would like to speak with you. Privately."

"Of course." She turned and gave Isaac a curtsy. "Sir de la Cruz."

"Shan ..." His expression twisted into a grimace. "Don't go getting all formal on me."

"And don't go getting too personal on me," she cautioned. "I'll be back as soon as I can, Lord Aberforth. In the meantime, Sir de la Cruz would be delighted to entertain you."

Isaac groaned. "Just volunteer me then. You haven't changed a bit, Lady LeClaire."

"He's fond of books," Shan said, helpfully, and Isaac's eyes lit up. "Maybe you can tell him about the Royal Library?"

"That's really not—" Samuel began.

"Oh, are you?" Isaac turned to him. "Maybe I can do you one better ..."

Smirking, Shan whirled away from them and went to face the Eternal King.

"Close the door," the King said the very second she re-entered the study. He wasn't even looking at her—he was standing at the fireplace, staring into the glow of the witch light. It cast his features in harsh shadows, making him look even sterner. Even more dangerous.

Reminding her that the man she faced was an enemy, even if he didn't realize it yet.

The door was already closing—the Guards following their Liege's orders—trapping her in with him.

"You asked to see me, Your Majesty?"

"You're making quite a wave, Lady LeClaire." He moved to a cabinet, opening it to reveal an extensive collection of liquors. Shan's eyebrows shot up as she took in its breadth.

Blood and steel, even her reprobate brother would be impressed.

"Can I offer you a drink?" he asked. "I have ... everything." He gestured at the cabinet befitting a king—of course he would have everything. A king could never be seen as lacking, not in any single thing.

"Whisky, if you please."

The King grabbed a decanter from the middle shelf and snagged a couple of glasses with his fingers. He placed them all on his desk, then poured a healthy amount into each glass. "Here you are."

She took the offered drink with unsteady fingers. He tossed his back, but she took a much smaller, more careful sip.

"It seems that I have some thanks to give," the King said, sinking into his chair and gesturing for her to do the same. "Tell me how you found him."

Shan settled in. "It started years ago. There were rumors about a child, a young boy. He had a terrible gift. He could make people do whatever he wanted. It reminded me of an old rumor about a recently dead line. But I was young myself, and rumors are fleeting things. I never learned anything more.

"I thought that was the end of it," she continued after taking another sip of her drink. It was good—strong and peaty. The burn moved through her, sharpening her. "But the rumors kept circulating. Little things, never enough. Not until recently. Samuel was caught up in that terrible murder. He slipped, used his power on a Blood Worker investigating the case."

The King arched an eyebrow. "Do I want to know how you got access to that information, young lady?"

Shan shrugged. "Most definitely, but a lady never shares her secrets."

The King smiled, a little cruelly and with far too many teeth, and poured himself another glass. "And then what? You went and dragged him here?"

"Of course not." She frowned. "I first had to make sure the rumors were true. I broke into his flat, I tasted his blood and I made him an offer. I cleaned him up and dressed him in the finest of suits and ensured he understood the magnitude of what was happening. Only then did I bring him to you."

"Well, I am very impressed." He raised his glass to her. "I see my faith in you was not misplaced."

"I didn't think you had faith in me at all," Shan said. She hid the wince that threatened to follow—she didn't know if it was the whisky or her pride that had her speaking so boldly, but from the lazy smile the King gave her it seemed that he approved of such expressions.

She carefully stored away that information, already shifting her outward demeanor. If he preferred that, she could be confident and bold. It would be a welcome change from the normal roles she played. Soft. Shy. Demure. It was closer to the real woman who hid behind the mask, and, as much as she feared and hated the Eternal King, this was the closest she had been to being herself in a long time.

"I've been watching you since you were a child," the King said. "I've had a vested interest in your family. Do you know what your father did for me once?"

Her throat tightened, but she managed to get out two words. "I do."

He inclined his head. "I had high hopes for him. He was clever, like you. He was a talented Blood Worker, also like you. But he lacked strength and conviction." He sighed. "I tried to bring him into the fold, to hone his mind and his ability to see patterns into something useful for Aeravin. But it is a delicate business, sorting truth from lies. Using that information to control people. I rarely make mistakes, but in this I was wrong. Your father was ill-suited for the work."

Shan clenched her glass, holding it so hard that it left indents on her skin. It wasn't that he had been merely *ill-suited*. That made it sound as if he had performed poorly—but he hadn't. He had been terribly gifted at his work, until something in him shattered and he saw enemies everywhere. Then he turned on allies, friends, the very hand that fed him.

Even his own home.

She could never know what her life would have been like if her father hadn't been recruited by the King. It could have been the same. Blood and steel, it could have been worse.

But what if it had been better? What if he had been kinder?

She couldn't think about this now—not here. Not in front of him. "He was," she said, because she had to. Because it was a version of the truth.

"Now I'm thinking that I pulled from the family too soon." The King leaned forward, resting his elbows on his knees as he studied her. "I should have waited a generation."

Her mouth went dry. "Are you suggesting—"

He held up his hand, interrupting her. "You have great instincts for this work. And this was a hell of an audition, girl. But one does not simply become a master of spies and information on a lark. It is hard work, it is taxing work, and I do not intend to make the same mistake twice."

Shan held back her smile—of course he didn't suspect the truth. Even in doing all this, no one would assume that she—young, demure, disgraced Shan LeClaire—would be the Sparrow. And having that up on the Eternal King gave her power. "What if I am interested?"

The King smiled again, and she had to fight the chills that ran down her spine. "I thought as much. You're a bright girl, Shan. You don't need me to tell you that. Continue to do what you're doing and we'll see how things go. But for now, I need you to look after Samuel for me. He said you have a room for him."

"Naturally." She drew up her shoulders. "He was evicted; besides, he needs to learn how to live among us."

"Yes, I heard that little fact." His eyes glinted, and Shan suddenly feared for those who had made Samuel's life even the slightest bit difficult. "I need to ask a favor of you. Help him get acclimatized. Learn who to befriend and who not to."

"I can do that," Shan said, then pushed forward. "But what's in it for me?"

He threw his head back and laughed. "There is the boldness your father lacked! Oh, I like you, LeClaire." Spreading his hands, he gestured to encompass the entirety of the room. "Think of it this way. Samuel is of my blood. I will be supporting him and his ascension to Lord. By tying yourself to Samuel—"

"I'll be tying myself to you," Shan interrupted. "I'll have your support as well as his, and it'll be a much-needed boost to the LeClaire reputation." She knocked back the rest of her drink. "And all that is well and good, but I want more."

Intrigued, he leaned back in his chair and gestured for her to continue.

"I've heard the rumors; I've tasted his blood—I know *what* he is. But more than that, I've seen the kindness in his soul and the fragility in his heart. Whatever your plans are with him, I can help. I've already got him in my grasp."

The King's gaze was sharp. "Gladly. It would be a good way to test you, after all."

"I won't let you down," Shan vowed.

"I don't expect you to. You know what happens to those who earn my displeasure." He let the words settle over her, hanging between them with all the weight of the threat—of the promise—that they were. "Now, run along. I have to see to the Aberforth accounts."

Shan stood gracefully, her movements precise and stable despite the sudden injection of fear to her veins. "Good day."

He nodded at her. "Good day, Lady LeClaire."

She showed herself out, the King already returning to his work. She held her head high, savoring the victory she had earned. She had faced the Eternal King, had bartered and bargained with him, and had emerged with his blessing.

And a most terrible threat, but she wouldn't think of that now.

Chapter Eleven

Samuel

Samuel stood next to Shan, staring up at the townhouse with wide eyes. It was even larger than the LeClaire home, even grander, from the slope of the gables to the decorative trim painted in contrasting shades of blue to the rest of the exterior. Stained glass filled the windows, shaped in the familiar scene of Aeravinian roses, and Samuel didn't even want to think how much that had cost when windows of regular glass would have served fine. And this was only the first of the Aberforth properties to be released to him.

It was still more than he had ever anticipated, and more than he could even understand. It was so much, and Samuel didn't know how to begin filling it.

It had been built by Abigail Aberforth's children, the first generation of the royal line, and maintained ever since, filled with a long lineage that Samuel could never live up to, a constant home until the death of Lord Nathaniel Aberforth and his children just over five and twenty years ago, when it had been closed up but not sold. Shuttered but not dismantled. Waiting for a new owner.

Samuel finally found his voice. "This is ... mine?"

Shan's hand found his, giving it a reassuring squeeze. "I'm sure it'll be a bit of an adjustment, but you'll have help."

That was a relief. She had already informed him that this would involve more than just running a home; there were accounts and estates and investments to keep track of, money flowing in and out, constantly growing and changing.

He might have been a bookkeeper, but this was a step beyond that. Especially with everything else that would be vying for his attention.

Squeezing Shan's hand again, he lifted his chin with a confidence he didn't truly feel. "Let's do this." He dashed up the stairs, grabbed a hold of the knocker on the door, and slammed it several times.

The door opened immediately, revealing a stern and stately man who was old enough to be Samuel's grandfather. That was, if his own ancestor wasn't a fresh-faced man in the prime of his life, despite being over a thousand years old.

His head hurt thinking about that, and he focused his attention back on the man. He was pale and wrinkled around the edges, but his clothes were impeccably pressed and his grey eyes kindly. He showed them in, then immediately dropped into a bow, bending low at the waist. "Lord Aberforth. It is my honor and privilege to welcome you to your family home."

Samuel almost didn't realize that the man was talking to him—he still wasn't used to being addressed by that title, by that name. He swallowed the urge to correct him, to beg him to call him by his given name, and stepped into the role that had been assigned to him. "It's good to meet you . . ." he trailed off, uncertain.

"You may call me Jacobs," the man supplied.

No title. Not sir, the polite way that nobles sneered down at new blood. Not even mister, the title given to commoners with no Blood Working potential. Despite the wage they earned and the security their positions afforded them, they were considered somehow even lesser. "I'm glad to meet you, Jacobs," Samuel said, kindly. "What is your position?"

Jacobs smiled, clearly relieved, and Samuel wondered what he had done to make that so. How cruel his former masters must have been that even a drop of kindness made such an impact.

"I am to be your secretary," Jacobs said. "And to help with the staff and household management while you adjust."

"Did you serve …" Samuel couldn't bring himself to say it, to really claim Nathaniel Aberforth as his father.

"Yes," Jacobs replied. "I did."

"Well," Samuel said, jumping off the cliff without even thinking. "I've heard that he was a harsh master. I don't intend to be the same."

It wasn't a plea. It was a promise.

Jacobs smiled. "As you say, my lord."

"Yes," Samuel shoved his hands into the pockets of his coat—a loan from Shan's brother until the rest of his wardrobe arrived. It was a little too tight around the shoulders, and far too flashy for him with its gold-trimmed lines. "I want to take a look around, but afterward I'd like to meet the staff. Do you think we could call them to the parlor in an hour's time?"

He hoped that would be enough space for them. Because of the short notice, there would only be what Shan called a skeleton staff—a couple of maids, a handful of kitchen workers, a housekeeper and Jacobs. Even that seemed like too much.

"Yes, we can." Jacobs hesitated. "Should I give you the tour?"

He glanced back at Shan, suddenly hesitant, but she nodded at him. "Yes, please."

She smiled, then stepped aside. "I'd like to speak to the house-keeper, if I may."

"Of course, my lady," Jacobs replied. If he was put off, he didn't show it. "She's in the kitchen, right down this hallway."

Shan nodded, turning away. Samuel watched her go, then turned to take in the Aberforth townhouse. While they had been talking, it had been easy to let his eyes go unfocused at the edges, to let himself ignore the opulence and the finery. But he had to learn to live with it, even if he could never allow himself to become comfortable with it.

He wanted to scream.

He didn't.

He was so tired already, but he couldn't be ungrateful. None of this was Jacobs' fault—he was just as much a victim of circumstance as Samuel was, if not more so. At least Samuel had the money, the prestige, the power. Jacobs had nothing, could never have anything, and it was all terribly unfair.

He plastered a fake smile on his face and followed Jacobs through the foyer, their footsteps echoing on the marble floor. Directly in front of them was a grand wooden staircase leading to the upper levels of the home, where Jacobs said the bedrooms and family spaces were. But before they explored that, he directed them to a sitting room on the left, a room that was larger than the one Samuel used to live in, outfitted with the kind of delicate, carefully carved furniture that would have cost a fortune to outfit. Chaise lounges with hand-embroidered designs, a low glass table, paintings and fine statues along the walls—hells, a grand piano in the corner.

Samuel buried his hands in the pocket of his jacket, hiding the way he was clenching his fists.

"Perfect for casual entertaining," Jacobs explained, then stepped past and into the first room on the right—a dining room with a table large enough to seat a dozen people, perhaps more. The walls were lined with portraits, and a quick glance at them told Samuel that he was looking at his family. It was a line of golden hair and pale faces, their cold eyes sharp and piercing.

How was he supposed to eat here, day in and day out?

He wanted to run from the room, but he couldn't tear his eyes away from the judgemental faces of his ancestors, knowing that they all looked down upon him and found him unworthy.

Jacobs cleared his throat. "If . . . if it pleases you, my lord, this one here is Lord Nathaniel. Your father."

Samuel hesitantly approached the last one, looking up at the face of his father for the first time. He had been young when he had ascended, not as young as Shan or even Samuel, but still. His face was unlined, his shoulders strong, his eyes clear. But even in this there was a coldness to him. It was in the way his eyes bored into the viewer, in the frown on his lips, in the haughtiness of his bearing.

Lord Nathanial had been a cruel man, and Samuel had to look away.

Jacobs didn't push the matter—he just let Samuel lead them out of the room.

From there the opulence only got worse, and, bit by bit, Samuel grew cold and distant, smothering the rage that threatened deep inside. He couldn't let this touch him, not now, or else he would break.

———

By the time he met the staff and had settled in, the sun had set and evening was upon them. At Shan's request, the cook had sent up a plate of sandwiches and a pot to tea to the study, bypassing a formal dinner. The wine, she insisted, was just for her. It was exactly what he needed after the immensity of the day, and he could have kissed Shan for her thoughtfulness.

If he were being honest, he could almost kiss Shan in general. She was clever and capable and just alluring enough to make him forget she was a Blood Worker. But that was a thought he didn't want to contemplate at the moment.

She was sitting in one of the large, padded chairs, her shoes kicked off and her feet tucked under her skirts. Her hair had begun to fall out of its pins, hanging dark and heavy against her skin, and her cheeks had a rosy flush from the wine. It was the most relaxed he had seen her yet, the mask slipping to reveal the woman beneath.

A half-eaten sandwich was on the plate balanced on the armrest, and she had his ledgers spread across her lap. She was cozy and contented, and she looked like she belonged here—lady of the house, already running his household and keeping things in line.

Another thought he didn't want to contemplate. Could not contemplate. The memories of a mistake long past still haunted him, and he couldn't walk that path again.

Instead, he steered himself towards safer waters. "You know I have a secretary for that," he said, sipping his tea.

Shan scoffed. "As a bookkeeper, I thought you'd understand how important it is to double-check the work."

"I do," Samuel said. "And I was planning on doing that. But it's not your responsibility."

"I don't mind," Shan said, absently. "I like this kind of work. Books are simpler than people, and it's easy to find the truth in numbers. Besides, there is a lot to manage and you haven't been trained for this."

Like she had. He heard the unspoken words, felt them claw into his gut, not because they were sharp or harsh, but because they were simply true. "I'll learn."

"Yes, but I'd hate to see you bankrupt yourself before you have the chance to." She closed the ledgers, looking up with an easy grin. "Unless that's not the reason. Do you fear I'm going to sell the Aberforth secrets?"

It made him smile. "I wasn't before, but now that you bring it up . . ."

She laughed, standing to pour herself a fresh glass of wine. "Samuel, please. I want to earn the King's favor, not lose it. So long as he favors you, you're safe from me."

"Until you've earned your own place," Samuel said, "and then you'll have no need for me."

Shan shrugged, too casually. "Yes, but don't forget I like you. So, you'd better be careful you don't lose my favor."

"Ah, you *do* like me?" he said, weakly. He wasn't used to being liked, to having friends, to flirting. He might not have much experience in this area, but he knew that there was something here between them.

And as much as it pained him, he needed to squash it before it had a chance to grow.

"Unfortunately, yes," she replied, and from the almost wistful way she said it, he knew it was true. "It's a shame, you'd be much easier to manipulate if I hated you."

Her words hit him as hard as a slap across the face, reminding him that she was a Blood Worker. That no matter how much she claimed to be on his side, she still had her own agenda. "You'd rather that, then? A pawn to manipulate instead of an ally to trust?"

Her expression shuttered; the easy playfulness gone. "It's not that simple, Samuel."

Looking away, he rubbed his face. "Right. Forgive me."

Shan sipped her wine. "Did I mislead you at some point? You know that I have—"

"Schemes?" Samuel snapped. "Plans? Yes, I do. Thank you for your help today, but I can take it from here."

"Blood and steel, there is no need to be so dramatic."

"Good day, Shan." He stood, gesturing to the doorway. "You know the way out."

For a long moment she just stared at him, her eyes narrowed and her lips pulled into a frown. "You know what? Fine." She drained her glass, then slammed it back on the table. "If you have need of me, you know how to reach me. Goodnight, Samuel."

She snatched her shoes then walked out of the study, not even stopping to put them on. Her head was held high, her shoes dangling at her side, and she did not look back at him.

He remained standing until he heard her slip down the stairs, then collapsed onto his chair, burying his face in his hands. He hadn't meant to be so cold, and yet . . .

It was probably better this way, after all. Despite her smiles and her little kindnesses, he had to remember that she'd still use him in a heartbeat. And besides, he still had this awful power, and until he mastered it—*if* he could master it—he wouldn't be safe to be around. He could barely control it when he got angry; he didn't want to think about what could happen in a moment of passion.

What did happen in a moment of passion. The words still haunted him, even after all this time.

Kiss me.

Such a simple thing, and all Markus' choices had been taken

away. In that moment, when Markus had turned to him with that glossy look in his eyes, Samuel realized that he was no better than his father—the nameless figure who had raped his mother and ruined her life.

He didn't need violence. He just needed his voice.

It didn't matter what he wanted—how badly he wanted—he was still a monster, and he could not let himself forget it.

And as Shan LeClaire stormed out of his home, he wrapped himself in the shroud of his loneliness. It was, after all, an old friend. The only one he had.

Chapter Twelve

Shan

Shan loathed to be distracted from her work, especially now, in the wake of her grand transformation of Samuel from gutter-rat to near prince, with things so suddenly and awkwardly strained between them. But she couldn't help but feel a bit of excitement. Isaac had indeed come through—an invitation to the theatre had arrived. A private box. Opening night. A promise of fun and scandal and just a hint of romance.

For a brief moment, she wished that she was anyone but her, someone who could simply fret over suitors and dresses, who could dream of a real romance. Not the woman who had to carry the rehabilitation of her entire family's reputation on her shoulders, or the success of an entire web of spies and a secret plan to undermine a king's regime from within.

But she was not that woman, no matter how much she wished. She had chosen this life, or perhaps it had chosen her, and she had to live with the consequences.

It was nearly time, and she was hurrying down the stairs to wait in the parlor when she was stopped by a sudden, baffled, "Really, Shan?"

She glanced up at her brother with a grin, twirling to show off her new gown. The scarlet silk fluttered around her, and she relished the smooth feel of the bodice that hugged her tight. It had been commissioned in the weeks before she murdered her father, a reward set in place for her success. "It is the latest fashion."

"Not even a little decorum? It's barely been two weeks," Anton pressed, gesturing to his own somber colors. A ridiculous gesture on his part. Their father didn't deserve the honor.

"I'm going to the theatre tonight," she said, as if that explained it all.

"Oh, I see." Anton crossed his arms over his chest, a harsh frown marring his normally carefree expression. But then again, he had been growing colder of late, a change that was coming as slow and inevitable as the frost in winter, but Shan had no idea how to reach him. "And that required a new dress? Shan, we're bleeding money."

"It is not so bad as that—"

"I've seen the ledgers," Anton interrupted. "And, yes, your investments are starting to turn out. And, yes," he quickly continued, before she could voice her counterargument, "I know what you're going to say about appearances and power and looking strong, but that wardrobe you bought for the Aberforth put us back."

"He needed it."

Anton nodded. "He did. But it didn't have to come from us." He leaned against the banister, looking suddenly tired. "Just be careful. Don't spend so much time pretending to be like them that you actually become them."

Shan ground her teeth. "Thank you for the warning, brother. Now if you'll excuse me, my guest will be here momentarily."

"Oh? And who is that?"

Though she knew he'd disapprove, she didn't flinch. She threw the name in his face. "Isaac."

Anton tensed immediately. "De la Cruz? I don't understand. After what he did to you?"

"I know," Shan replied, honestly.

His nostrils flared. "He's the worst kind of traitor," Anton snapped. "It's bad enough for people like Father, but de la Cruz should know better. He should *be* better."

It was an old argument that they had many times over the past few years, but Shan grabbed his wrist, not willing to indulge him. "It's complicated," she said, because it was. When their father had shut her brother out of polite society, Anton never had to learn the complicated dance that people like them had to play. Acceptance, as people with such obvious foreigner's blood in their veins, was a tightrope, carefully managed lest they fall, dashed to pieces against the harsh stone of Aeravin's expectations. "All of it. You know my feelings."

"And so you join him for a night at the theatre?" He gestured at the new dress, her carefully done hair, her eyes lined in kohl to make them all the more striking. "And you doll yourself up for him? For them?"

"That's not it," Bart said, suddenly appearing at Anton's side. Shan narrowed her eyes at him—how long had he been there, silent, watching the two of them fight? But he entwined his fingers with Anton's, and laid a comforting hand on his shoulder, bringing Anton's anger down in his own way. "Not everyone has the opportunity to defy expectations, and, besides, de la Cruz's proven to be a powerful player. We could use him."

Anton grimaced, but Shan nodded. It wasn't quite the truth, but it was close enough. "Listen to your man, Anton. He understands the game we're playing."

"This is not a game," Anton hissed, but Bart was already squeezing his hand, rubbing soothing circles against his wrist.

Shan watched the easy way they laced their fingers together, the way they communicated without saying a word. Anton instinctively leaned into Bart's touch, all the tension flowing out of him.

She told herself the reason she watched was so that she could learn to do the same thing. To mirror their actions and use them to lull someone into her confidence.

It was not because she was envious.

"Well," she said, the sound cutting through the easy silence that had taken over. "I must be off. Isaac will be here soon."

"Be careful, Shan," Anton warned, and Bart huffed.

"Our Sparrow can take care of herself," he murmured, tangling his fingers in Anton's jacket and pulling him close. "Now, come on, it's not often we get the house to ourselves."

"Blood and steel!" Shan glanced away. "At least wait until I leave, please."

Anton laughed, waving goodbye as Bart dragged him towards their bedchamber, and she couldn't help but smile. At least one of them deserved some happiness.

She had barely enough time to make it to the parlor before there was a knock on the door. She heard the footman open it, the exchange of pleasantries on the doorstep. Swallowing hard, she tried to calm the thrum of excitement in her veins. Tonight, all eyes would be on her. She wouldn't be slipping through the shadows of Dameral, having whispered conversations with her informants. She wouldn't be finding the broken and the damned and luring them into her web.

That was simple.

But this? This was new. Now it was time to be the Lady she was born to be. The smiling, charming woman who would be a distraction from all the work she did in the dark. And all she had to do was seduce everyone into trusting her, starting with Isaac de la Cruz.

The footman entered, announcing her guest, Isaac following after. He was dressed exquisitely in his suit, the dark grey jacket molded to his frame, the matching pants so tight they could have been sculpted on. His cravat was a complicated but carefully tied knot, hanging over a waistcoat with elegant embroidery. He had even lined his eyes—lightly, ever so lightly—with kohl, so that their dark depths pulled one in, and his hair hung in perfect waves.

Everything about him was calculated to adhere to the latest fashion. It wasn't enough that he was Royal Blood Worker. With his background, he had to be perfect in all ways, and she was just a tad bit mad for him.

He stepped forward, bowing over her hand. His kiss was warm and gentle, and when he looked up at her with his tired eyes, Shan saw just how desperately he wanted forgiveness. But he had hurt her so badly, and she still wasn't sure she could give it.

"It's good to see you," she said, as he rose.

"No, my dear Shan," Isaac said. "The pleasure is mine."

Shan smiled at him, all the while building new walls around her heart.

—+—

The play was awful, another load of drivel extolling the virtues of Aeravin. A beautiful young Blood Worker born to a homeland that would never understand her gifts, struggling to find a place, risking life and limb to travel to a land that would accept her.

It ended there, as such stories always did, achieving the dream and ending just before the harshness of reality set in.

But at least they had a private box, closed off from the rest of the crowd as they sat next to each other in the silence and shadows. Throughout the play, he kept brushing his leg against hers, and she could feel the muscles of his thigh even through her skirts. His hand drifted towards hers, brushing over her fingers, the tip of his claw tracing across the soft inner skin of her palm till it pressed against the fluttering beat of her pulse.

The whole while she breathed carefully, convincing herself that the heat that flushed through her was because of the tight, windowless rooms of the theatre, not the way his hand continued to trail upwards, leaving a searing path of warmth in his wake. Yet he did not move an inch past what was appropriate, though she wished for him to dig the tips of his claws into the soft silk of her dress, shredding it under his touch until he reached the warm flesh beneath.

At last the curtain fell and the applause began. She leapt to her feet with the rest of the crowd, not because she had been moved in any way by the production, but to give herself a moment's respite from the uncomfortable feelings that swam through her.

Isaac stood, clapping just as enthusiastically, but his eyes were on her as the witch light illuminated the theatre.

Apparently neither of them had been focused on the play.

"Enjoy yourself?" Isaac asked, reaching forward to brush a stray lock of hair from her face.

"It was lovely," she said, choosing her words with care. She didn't want to outright insult the production, since he had brought her, but *blood and steel.*

He laughed. "It was a bit trite, wasn't it?"

"Yes, it was," Shan said, with a sigh of relief. Perhaps they would be able to slip right back into the friendship they once had—Isaac had always preferred friends with bite, and it was part of what made them work so well together. No need to pretend to be something she was not. "But at least the company was adequate."

"Only adequate? You wound me."

"Trust me, Isaac," Shan said, "if I wounded you, you would know." She flexed her hands so that her ceremonial claws glittered in the light, the inlaid rubies shining in their representation of blood.

Isaac's smirk—even more handsome than she remembered— turned into a real smile. "Now that is a challenge I'd like to take."

"Oh, darling, I don't think you'd win that challenge."

"Perhaps not," he conceded, "but I desperately want to try." He held out his arm to her, the formality slipping back in. "Ready, my lady?"

Shan slid into her place, a trophy on his arm, and together they strode out to meet the rest of society. They had not arrived early enough to cause a stir before the play, and for that she was grateful. Shan didn't want to be completely uncouth and ruin anyone's night at the theatre—the play was already bad enough.

Now was the time to shine. She knew they made a stunning couple—a daring couple. Despite the Eternal King's open-door policy for Blood Workers from all nations, the vast majority of Aeravin's most powerful mages were still monochromatic. They valued old blood over new talents and had rigidly kept power in the same families for centuries.

Both Shan and Isaac defied that on an individual basis, and together it seemed almost like a challenge. Their blood might have been mixed, but it was just as strong—stronger even—than anyone else's. They were the best of the best, and none of the pointed stares could do a thing about it.

It almost made Shan wish she could trust him again, foolish as it was. But Isaac had spent his whole life assimilating, and he had proved that he would rather protect himself than risk tearing down the system to help others. It was so self-serving and self-protecting that she almost couldn't hate him for it. His place at the Eternal King's right hand meant that he had finally gotten the one thing he had always wanted—acceptance.

Of a sort.

So, she smiled. Brilliant as ever, knowing the statement it made. Isaac reached over, placing his hand over hers where it rested in the crook of his arm.

"They're all looking at us," he whispered, the soft feel of his breath against her skin causing her to shiver.

"Of course they are," she replied, just as quietly. "They're all jealous that you're the one escorting me."

Isaac laughed. "Naturally. You are the loveliest woman here."

She wondered if it was genuine—a compliment from the boy she had once known or a carefully calculated ploy from the Royal Blood Worker. Because that was the kind of lives they led, moving in an endless dance, swapping affection and power like cheap coins.

"It's because of my dress," she said, suddenly, filled with the desperate need to have just a bit of real honesty.

Isaac kept his gaze forward, not looking at her. "It is a . . . bold statement. But they don't know you like I do." He didn't even hesitate in his judgement. "That you even gave him a funeral was miracle enough."

Shan looked up at him, carefully, trying to hide the panic in her heart. Just how much did he know? His expression seemed almost placid, but there was a hard line to his jaw. His eyes flickered down to her, and he quickly steered her through the crowd, pulling her into an alcove that offered them a modicum of privacy.

To anyone who would have seen it, it would have looked like a quick tryst between young lovers, sneaking off for a hidden kiss. It would send rumors spreading, that she—a LeClaire—had caught the interest of Sir de la Cruz. It would be a huge boost for her reputation, and she was almost thankful enough to let it become truth.

Even if they didn't know—and would never know—that she had already been there.

He was pressed intimately close to her, and she could feel the warmth of his body against hers. Her hands had flown to his shoulders immediately, automatically, as if they belonged there, and she could feel the difference that a few years had made. He no longer had the skinny build of a boy but had grown into a man—his shoulders wider, his body stronger. He lowered his face to hers, and she could feel the brush of his beard against her skin, another new development from the softness of youth, and shivered at the way it felt against her.

She turned towards him, ready to take his mouth with hers, to see if he still tasted as she remembered, but he wasn't looking at her with heat or hunger.

But regret.

"You're just as talented as me," he said, softly. "More talented. If it wasn't for your father you could have easily had my place. You could have been Royal Blood Worker; you could have had whatever you wanted."

Shan blinked at him, shoving aside the lust that clouded her mind as she frantically tried to decide which path to take. She settled on anger, just a careful drop of it, and struck. "What is all this, then? Your asinine way of making it up to me? Of doing me a favor?"

Let him think she was angry. It was better than the truth—that this hurt more than anything else she could have imagined.

"No," he said, flustered and fumbling. "No, no, no. My reasons were true, Shan." He took her hands in his, squeezing so tight it hurt. "I don't want you to think that this is pity."

She allowed herself to melt, just a little. "As you say."

"Let me prove it to you," Isaac begged. "Whatever it takes,

however long it takes. I want you back, Shan." He brushed his lips against her cheek—soft, gentle, and chaste.

It shouldn't have moved her so.

"Why, Sir Isaac," Shan said, forcing a bit of levity into her voice, "what kind of woman do you think I am?"

"The kind who should hate me," he said. "The kind I pray will give me a second chance."

"This is a start," she whispered, and he looked so relieved she feared he might faint. "But I think it's time you took me home."

"Of course." He stepped back, and she immediately missed the warmth of his body. Pulling the curtains back, he gestured for her to step out. "After you."

She stepped into the brightness of the theatre, but no one was looking at them now. There was a new rush to the crowd, and it only took her a few seconds to pick up the words that were being thrown about.

Murder.

Blood Working.

A body.

That was the second in a month, and Shan felt weak at the knees. One death was an aberration—perhaps a draining at one of the clinics gone horribly wrong. But two deaths? That was an emerging pattern, and it seemed the rest of Dameral had picked up on that as well.

Isaac looked suddenly, grossly pale. "I think I have to—"

"Go," she said, "I can get myself a hack." He looked down at her with regret, and she pressed her fingers to his cheek. "It's all right. Duty calls."

He nodded at her, then cut quickly through the throng of bodies towards the door. The crowd turned and watched him go, the whispers getting louder with each passing moment.

This was going to be a disaster, and Shan already itched to get back home and reach out to her birds. To see if they had heard anything, seen anything. But she plastered a bored expression on her face and got in line, waiting for a hackney to come and pick her up, and ignored the looks that people kept throwing her way.

This wasn't the attention she had hoped to get, but it was still attention. And she knew better than to squander it.

Chapter Thirteen

Samuel

S amuel did not recognize his life.

He had spent the last week locked away in his new townhouse, receiving letters and information from both the Eternal King and Shan—things that he needed to learn, accounts to familiarize himself with, an entire city's worth of history and rumors spread out on the desk before him. He was to be isolated, kept safe away from the rest of the country until the proper moment of introduction. One could not simply say the King had found another Aberforth; no, it needed to be a spectacle. So for now he was to stay put in his gilded, extravagant cage.

He hated every last moment of it.

From the moment he awoke, in a bed too big and too soft to be comfortable, a serving girl slipping into his rooms to light the candles. His daily outfits were picked from the wardrobe bought by Shan, which had arrived on his doorstep the day after he moved in, the very wrapping paper it had been packaged in worth more than the clothes he was used to wearing. He was served breakfast—a damned feast—in the dining room under the portraits of the Aberforths who came before, then shuffled off to the study where he was supposed to learn. He stayed there till dinner—not able to bear three meals of such extravagance in a single day—then he was supposed to do it all again.

And again.

And again.

He had a task. To prepare. To educate himself for a life he did not want, all for the murky goals Shan had whispered in his ear. The promises she had made felt distant when he was living a life of luxury he did not deserve while so many others still starved.

He pulled the cufflinks from his suit, turning them over in his hands. They were real gold, and though he did not know precisely how much they were worth, he knew they could feed a whole family for months. Inspiration struck him, like a bolt of lightning, and he knew what he had to do.

Clenching his fist around the cufflinks, he made a decision—and damn anyone who tried to stop him. Feeling alive for the first time since he had stepped into this cursed house, he shoved aside the role that had been given to him, seizing a path of his own.

"Jacobs!" he called, throwing open the door to the hallway. Witch light shone down from the sconces above, casting the already uncomfortable home with an eerie glow. "I need your help."

"What is it, my lord?" Jacobs inquired, appearing at his side as if he had simply stepped from the shadows. He kept doing that—appearing seemingly out of nowhere whenever Samuel needed him.

"Hells, man." Samuel took two steps back as he forced his heart to calm. In some way, it made him a perfect servant, there but never seen, but it was starting to make Samuel deeply uncomfortable. No one should move like that. "Can you walk a little louder? Announce yourself? Something?"

"Should I wear a bell, like a cat?" Jacobs asked, deadpan, forcing a reluctant smile from Samuel. "I will try to be more aware of it, my lord. How may I be of assistance?"

"Right." Samuel squeezed the cufflinks in his hands. "I need clothes—proper clothes."

Jacobs looked him up and down, his normally serene expression faltering. "Is there something wrong with your wardrobe, my lord? We can write to the tailor—it would be her duty to replace anything ill-fitting."

"No, no. I mean, like regular clothes." Samuel pulled at his cravat, tugging at it until it came—reluctantly—loose. "Like what an average person wears—not this foppish shit."

"I see." Jacobs seemed to hesitate, the carefully constructed roles of master and servant slowly starting to erode as the foolishness of Samuel's ask started to settle in. Even in this, even though he was the Lord, Jacobs was the one who knew the most—about their roles, about the rules of their society, about the lives they were supposed to lead. But he couldn't—he wouldn't—step out of his place, and it made Samuel want to shake some sense into the old man.

He didn't need a servant. He needed someone who could help him, if only he could make Jacobs understand.

"I need to get out of here," Samuel said, quietly. "Just for an evening. And not like this." He gestured to himself, to the costume he wore—Lord Aberforth. "As myself."

Jacobs sighed, the barriers between them starting to fall. "If I may..."

Samuel nodded. "You don't need to fear speaking your mind to me, Jacobs. I am not my father."

"No, you most certainly are not," Jacobs muttered, casting his eyes to the heavens. "It is my place to do as you ask, Lord Aberforth, but whatever you are planning, I beg you to reconsider."

Samuel shook his head. "I *need* this."

Jacobs stared at him, and Samuel felt the pity in his gaze. But the old man relented—he had to, he had said as much, after all—and turned away. "I'll bring what you requested to your rooms, Lord Aberforth. Just ... for the sake of this old man, please be careful."

"I will," Samuel said, though he wasn't sure if it was a lie or not. After all, the definition of careful was relative.

—+—

It wasn't long before Samuel had shed the trappings of the Lord he was to become, dressing instead like the man he was. He didn't ask where Jacobs had gotten the clothes, but the rough shirt and trousers felt more comfortable on his skin than the fine silks. He pulled his hair back in a loose bun, and though he still felt a little too soft, a little too clean, he was approaching the person he used to be. He filled his pockets with cufflinks and pocket watches and other pieces of finery, and then—at Jacobs' insistence—slipped out through the back door.

It was a different world from what he was used to, this part of Dameral. It was late in the afternoon, before most of the nobility would depart for their parties and their salons, so he was able to slip down the empty streets, just another Unblooded laborer who had been called to work on some menial thing far too below them to notice. He was, with a simple change of clothes, invisible.

Samuel kept his head ducked low as he made his way back home—even now, with the title and the townhouse and the recognition, home was still the slums where he had been raised. Each step closer eased another knot of tension, the fears that had been choking him for days slipping away like water over a stone. Yes, Shan had her plans, and he *would* help her in them, but there was no reason he couldn't start his own schemes. He had seen his ledgers: the Aberforths had wealth like he never could have imagined. It was more than a single person could spend in a lifetime—so why shouldn't he try? He could afford so much—he could give so much.

Starting with the finery they had forced upon him.

There were hungry children, families who struggled to put day-old bread on the table. With the coin that he could now call truly negligible, he could stop that. He could feed entire families. And just maybe this farce he played would be worthwhile.

Stepping into the slums of Dameral, he breathed freely for the first time in days. He already had decided on the first family he'd help—the neighbors he'd left behind. They were a large family, like so many others. More children meant more mouths to feed, but it also meant that, if they lived long enough, they would become more workers. More coin. It was the worst of all kinds of math, but he understood why they made their choices.

There weren't any other options.

By the time he reached his former lodgings, afternoon had started to slip towards evening. It would probably be a little while yet before the parents returned home from their jobs, but that was all right. Samuel was willing to wait. He had nothing but time.

Rounding the corner, he had to forcibly keep himself from running. For the first time since Shan had found him, he felt like he was achieving something, and his whole being felt lighter. Bubbly. Free.

But the excitement vanished like a punch to the gut as he glanced up at the building he had called home for years. It was boarded up. Closed and shuttered. There was a large piece of parchment nailed to the door, and Samuel didn't need to read it to know what it said. He had seen such things before.

The building had been condemned.

He stood straighter as the tension pulled his muscles taut, confusion spreading through him like the slow, thick drip of wax down a candle. It hadn't been any worse or better than any other building with rooms for rent in Dameral. And it wasn't like such regulations were actually followed. Rules and laws in Dameral were a joke, only enforced when there was some sort of political—

"Hells."

Samuel darted up the steps, pulling the notice from the nail where it had been slammed into the wooden door. The language was formal, rote, nothing out of place to confirm the suspicions that he had. But Samuel was no fool—he knew what this meant, who had been behind it.

His own damned family. The Eternal King. The promise of mercy was a lie after all, and as he crumpled the notice in his hand, that old, familiar, helpless laugh caught in his throat.

It was too late now for him to do anything. The tenants would have been evicted swiftly, kicked to the streets with only what they could carry. Not just the family he had come here to help, but every last soul in this building. And it was all his fault, all to spite the land-lord who had evicted him. A slip of the tongue before the Eternal King, a detail he didn't need or mean to share, and the consequences that were not his to bear.

He could try to track them down, but he had never bothered to learn their names. Given his own situation, the danger in his blood, he had thought mutual anonymity would keep them safer. Ironic, in the end. He had doomed them and then left himself with no resources to help. Like so many others, they were simply gone, swallowed whole by the city that gobbled them up and spat them back out—broken, shattered, or dead.

The crumpled parchment fell from his fingers, caught in the slight breeze that always blew through the street, coming off the sea and smelling of brine. It rolled away in the wind, vanishing into the creeping shadows as the sun sank behind him. "I'm sorry," he whispered, as he tried to impress their faces into his memory. But they were already fading, slipping away.

Gone.

Turning on his heel, he left his home behind. If the Eternal King had taken out his anger on his landlord, then it was likely that his old employer was also a target. He didn't know what he could do, if anything, but he had to get there. At least at work he hadn't been able to isolate himself completely. He had names, contacts, years' worth of memories.

He ran.

It was the time of day when work was starting to let out, the streets filling with the tired and the hungry, but Samuel did not care, ducking and dodging and dancing through the crowds. He ignored every curse that was thrown his way, the looks of confusion and surprise, the attention he was undoubtedly bringing to himself.

In all his years of working there, he had never made it there as quickly as he did then.

The warehouse had just changed shifts, and he scanned the people leaving it—people he had worked with for so long, and yet not a single one glanced his way. He clenched his jaw. Surely he wasn't that unrecognizable? He had shed the Aberforth mask, he was just himself, it shouldn't be so easy to forget—

"Hutchinson?"

He spun around, so startled that someone actually remembered him, let alone came up to speak to him, that all he could do was gape for a long moment. It was a familiar set of dark eyes, and the same soft smile, though there were shadows under his eyes that Samuel didn't recall being there. Of course it was him.

"Markus," he managed, eventually, earning a smile from the man in front of him.

"I didn't expect to see you back here," Markus said, shyly, tucking his hands in his pockets. "After . . . what happened, we all thought you were gone."

Gone. Always gone, gone like so many others. It was simply the way of things, and Samuel wondered when it had become normal. Or perhaps it always had been, and he was the one who was changing.

"I . . . am," Samuel said, wincing. "In a way. I just need to know something—Cobb?"

Markus didn't hide his disappointment, and Samuel felt a little bad for using him like this. "A few days after you. Dunno what happened, really, but the bastard they replaced him with is working us like dogs."

"Dammit." Samuel closed his eyes, filled with a sick sense of relief. At least it was only Cobb. The shipping company itself continued on, and Markus and the others still had their jobs. It was wrong of him to feel happy, he knew that.

But it was better than the alternative.

"What happened to him?" He didn't need to clarify.

"He's been drinking himself to death at one of the pubs," Markus said. He dragged the toe of his boot across the cobblestoned street; Samuel noticed because he couldn't dare meet his eyes. "I can show you."

"Please."

"Right." Markus wiped his hand across his face. "This way." He started leading Samuel down the street, the silence between them thick and tense, when suddenly: "Can I ask why?"

Samuel hesitated—then, "Cause it's my fault."

Markus sucked in a harsh breath through his teeth. "Hutchinson, no. Anyone could have gotten caught up with the Guard. It doesn't do to blame yourself like that."

He didn't know whether to laugh or cry. Markus was far too kind, and if he only knew the truth . . .

Instead, he fell into a bitter, angry silence—one that his companion did not deserve, but it was better than anything else. Samuel didn't know what would happen if he spoke, what danger he might put this man in.

"Here we are," Markus said, coming to a stop in front of a pub that Samuel had never seen before. Though, if he was being honest, he wasn't sure one could call it a pub. It was far too shabby for that.

"Thanks," Samuel muttered, already reaching into his pocket. "Here—"

"No," Markus threw his hands up in front of him. "I don't know what happened to you, but I'd have done this for any friend. I don't need your coppers."

Samuel wanted to say that they hadn't been friends, not truly, and that what he had to offer was far more than copper. But there was a resolute pride to Markus, one that Samuel remembered all too well. "I . . . understand. And for what it's worth, I'm sorry."

For a moment it looked like he was going to ask the question that hung between them for years—the *what happened?* that Samuel had never been able to answer. Samuel's slip had been so small, so natural, that to this day he didn't think Markus even noticed it. That he *had* wanted to kiss him.

Yet Samuel would never know if it was true, and he could not risk it.

But Markus just clapped him on the shoulder. "Don't be. Some things don't work out." He jutted his chin towards the door. "Good luck in there. From what I've heard, it hasn't been pretty."

"Great." Samuel steeled himself and approached the door. It groaned as he started to push on it, and he blinked into the small, dimly lit room, illuminated by the candle stubs on every table, rickety wooden things that crowded the floor. A bar—if you could call it that—ran along the back, and a tired, older woman just stared at him.

Ducking his head, he stepped inside. It didn't take him long to find Cobb, slumped against one of the tables along the wall. In front of him was an empty glass, and he was staring blankly at the whorls in the wood.

Samuel didn't give himself a moment to doubt, knowing that his courage was a fragile thing. He crossed the room quickly, grabbing a chair from the next table, and sat down in front of his former boss. Cobb didn't even react, he just kept staring. Up close, Samuel saw that the table was littered with broadsheets. No doubt he was scouring them for help wanted ads. If there even were any to find. Good work was harder and harder to come by with each passing year, and a firing would only make things more difficult.

The barkeep was watching him suspiciously, but she relaxed when he dropped a few coppers on the table, signaling for two more of whatever Cobb had been drinking. Most likely an ale of some sort. He knew better than to ask for tea, and, besides, one glass of it wouldn't hurt—he didn't have to finish it and most places watered it down so much that you had to drink all night to get even the slightest bit drunk.

The barmaid appeared at the table, dropping down the glasses and sweeping the coins away. Cobb at last looked up as Samuel nudged one of the glasses forward, his bleary eyes unfocused and sad. For a long moment he just stared, then he rubbed his hand across his face, a hand that was still stained, the skin having absorbed years of ink. "Hutchinson? What the bleeding hells are you doing here?"

"Can't I check in on you?" Samuel asked, taking a sip of his ale. He nearly spat it back out. It was like rancid water.

"Didn't expect you to. You're not the type," Cobb replied, with a sad honesty that cut at Samuel. "And if you don't like that, don't waste it. Give it here."

Samuel wrapped his hand around the glass, not out of any intention to drink it, but— "How many have you had?"

"Are you my mother now?" He drained half of his glass in one pull. "Enough that one more isn't going to kill me."

Sighing, Samuel slid it across to him, and Cobb eagerly lined it up. "What happened, Cobb?"

"Hells if I know." He sank back in his chair. "All I know is that a few days after . . . you, a notice came down from on high. No reason, no explanation. And now this." He slammed his hand down on the table, the broadsheets fluttering, and Samuel winced.

"I'm sorry."

"What for?" Cobb blinked at him, awareness starting to cut through his drunken haze. "Looks like we're in the same boat now, friend."

"Not the same, no," Samuel said. He reached into his pocket, sorting through the options he had before him. He pulled the cufflinks out and dropped them on the table. "Here. Take these."

Cobb just stared at them, his eyes going wide, before he clapped his hand over them, hiding them away. "Are you mad?" he whispered. "Trying to start a riot?"

Samuel shook his head, slowly. "No, I—"

"Are these real?" Cobb lifted the edge of his hand to peek at the cufflinks. "Where did you—oh. Hells." He shoved them back towards Samuel. "Not enough to get me fired, eh? Gotta try to get me killed?"

Samuel accepted the cufflinks as they rolled back towards him, but he looked up at Cobb in confusion. "What?"

But Cobb wasn't looking at him, he was digging through the stack of paper in front of him, muttering as he went. Samuel's mind was reeling—what had the man figured out to connect the dots?

"Here it is!" Cobb said, shoving one of the broadsheets under Samuel's nose.

He took the paper with unsteady hands, his eyes dropping automatically to a headline in bold type.

A NEW ABERFORTH?

Skimming the article, he felt a cold dread settle into his stomach as he read an account of his own life for the past week. Yes, the details were muddy and vague, but the gist of it was there—the Aberforth home was reopened, a strange young man had moved in. It was clear that the Aberforths had returned, and Dameral's rumor mills were already churning.

"It's you," Cobb said. It wasn't even a question, and Samuel could only nod. "Hells, it's a miracle I wasn't arrested for treason."

"You didn't know," Samuel said quickly. "*I* didn't know. No one knew. I tried to tell him that. I told him to let it go."

Cobb's laugh was a tinge panicked. "You—you tried to command *him*?"

It seemed foolish in hindsight, Samuel had to admit. Who was he to make demands of the Eternal King? But this was the very reason why he had tried. He had become a poison to those he had known—mere association with him had proved to be dangerous.

"Let me help you," Samuel begged. "Clearly I have the means to."

"No," Cobb replied, firmly. "Your heart's in the right place, but I can't be caught with those."

"Do you have any idea how much they're worth?"

Cobb snatched one of the cufflinks off the table, turning it so that the head faced Samuel. "What do you see?" Samuel stared down at it, at the large *A* in elegant script. "If I am caught with this—if it's found that I sold them—I'd be branded a thief. So keep your jewelry. I don't need it."

Samuel deflated. "I just want to help."

"And the best way you can help me—help any of us—is by going back to your new home and staying put." Cobb drained the drinks in front of him. "Thanks for the ale, but I'm afraid that's all I can accept from you."

"Cobb," Samuel said, his voice cracking. "Please."

"I'm sorry, kid," Cobb said, pushing away from the table. "But getting mixed up with your kind is always dangerous."

"But I'm just like you!"

The look Cobb shot him was enough to crush all of Samuel's hopes—his foolish plans just to walk the streets and give out money and finery to those who needed it were just that. Foolish. Who could they sell it to? Every legitimate pawn shop would think the goods stolen, and then Samuel would just be giving them the means and encouragement to enter a life of crime.

And the Blood Workers were not kind to Unblooded criminals.

It had only been a week, but he had already started to lose sight of what it had meant to be Unblooded. Had he been so surrounded by Blood Workers and nobility and money that the very definition of normal had started to shift already?

"I hope I don't see you around here again," Cobb said. It wasn't unkind, but the message was clear. He wasn't welcome anymore.

"You won't." Samuel hung his head.

"Goodbye, kid."

He heard Cobb's footsteps as he left, heavy and steady, but Samuel just sat there, trying to feel normal. The broadsheet with the article on the Aberforths remained in front of him, taunting him, so Samuel grabbed the stack and shoved it into the pile, hiding it away.

As he did, a smaller pamphlet fell to the floor. Reaching down to grab it, Samuel froze as his eyes caught on the headline.

ANOTHER UNBLOODED DEATH, ANOTHER BREACH OF DUTY

This wasn't a broadsheet—this was something different. Something dangerous.

Something that spoke of sedition.

He scanned the article quickly, fear sticking in his throat as the pamphlet called out the Guard and the Blood Workers who ruled them for the brutalized dead whose deaths had still to be avenged.

It wasn't the first time he had seen something like this—calls for the Blood Workers and the nobility to expand the rights of the Unblooded. There were pamphlets for everything, from eliminating the Blood Taxes to outright impossible demands like this, asking for the Unblooded to have their own seats in the government. Before, he had been terrified of being caught with anything even remotely radical. But now?

The piece of paper felt strangely heavy in his hand, but his heart felt light. Maybe throwing money at the problem wasn't a solution after all. But maybe there was something else.

He slipped it into his pocket and left the rest of the mess on the table.

Chapter Fourteen

Shan

Shan waited in the windowed alcove outside the Eternal King's study, smoothing her hands over her skirts, making sure they were free of wrinkles and blemishes. Her claws glittered in the afternoon sunlight, the silver tips shining and trimmed to sharp points. Though she wasn't going to war today, she still needed the boost of confidence that they gave her as she was summoned to face the Eternal King.

"Shan?"

Shan turned to find Samuel standing behind her, dressed in the fine suit that she had designed for him, a strained smile on his face. Laurens must have sent the final shipment along, and she hated how much the outfit suited him. Looking at him now it was almost impossible to believe there was a time he wasn't one of them.

Now he looked like a Lord, and it stirred something deep in her that she didn't want to acknowledge.

It had been such a short time since she had found Samuel, since she had transformed him into a proper young lord. A week had passed since their spat in the Aberforth townhouse, when she had let her guard down but for a moment and he had left her completely rattled. She had thrown herself into her work since, planning for his grand introduction to society, digging fruitlessly for information on these dead bodies that were appearing around Dameral, but nothing worked. He still lingered.

Around him, it was easy to forget who she was and what she was doing—and why. He had a genuine passion for goodness in him, warring with the darkness his gifts offered. But despite it all—the Aberforth Curse, the utter poverty in which he had been raised, the suffering he had endured—he was still earnest and kind. By bringing him into the courts of Dameral she had either doomed him or set him on a path that would leave him utterly and fundamentally changed.

The twisting, churning feeling in her gut wasn't guilt, surely. It was merely indigestion. It would pass. She had ruined people before and would do so again. What did it matter that he was the most innocent person to ever cross paths with her?

She lied to herself as much as she lied to the rest of the world.

Shan held out her hand, formally, as she focused her eyes on the wall behind him, dropping into a low curtsy. "Lord Aberforth."

Pain cut across his features, but he bowed in response. "Lady LeClaire." Shan thought that would be the end of it, but he stepped close so that his voice was a whisper in her ear. "I'm sorry. About what I said."

Shan uncurled her fingers one by one, several days of tension easing from her at once. "It's all right."

"It really isn't." His voice was low and soft, and Shan pretended that the shiver down her spine came from the cool breeze through the windows. "I'm not good at this. At . . . whatever we're doing. Fixing things. Being partners. Working with others. I'm still learning."

"Oh," she whispered, as everything clicked into place. She had been foolish to assume, hadn't she? He had spent his whole life alone, hiding from Blood Workers, from his power, trusting no one, especially not himself. It was terribly sad. Even she had her brother, Bart, her birds. She had never truly been alone.

"So, yeah." Samuel ran his hand through his hair, a nervous habit that left him just a bit disheveled. It shouldn't have been attractive, but it was, and she ached to grab his hand, to teach him stillness. "We shouldn't keep the King waiting."

"Of course. I had been merely waiting for you." She followed him; her hands clasped in front of her like a proper young lady, as they stepped towards the door. The Guards acknowledged them immediately and escorted them into the study, where the King was pouring a steaming cup of tea. His desk had been cleaned off, turned into a proper tea service that had Shan blinking in surprise.

Surely the Eternal King hadn't summoned them for something as simple as tea.

"There you are. Sit, please." The King took his usual seat behind his desk, the contrast between his stern expression and the delicate cup in his hand throwing Shan off balance. "This blend with the rosehips is a favorite, as it comes from my own gardens."

"That sounds lovely," Shan said, settling gracefully into the seat at his right hand. Samuel sat directly across from her, and the King served them both. "It's a wonderful spread."

Samuel nodded in agreement, seemingly too overwhelmed to speak. His eyes were as wide as saucers as he took in the delicate and clearly expensive array of desserts in front of them—more than they could possibly need. But it would have been in poor taste if the Eternal King hadn't offered them the best and largest spread, even if most of it would go to waste.

Anything less would be a snub.

"It should be, for the amount I pay my pâtissier," the Eternal King said. "And, please, drink. The tea really is a favorite."

They both drank at that. It was indeed wonderful, with its soft floral flavor. It helped soothe some of the unease from her, and Samuel sighed from across the table.

"Delicious, isn't it," the King said, with a smirk. It seemed that even such a powerful man, who had lived for centuries and held such enormous power, was still pleased when his own tastes were validated. Perhaps there was just a hint of humanity in there after all. "But, unfortunately, we must get to business."

"How can we help?" Samuel asked, and Shan took the opportunity to grab a scrumptious looking apple tart.

"It's complicated," the King admitted, folding his hands in front of himself. "And I first want to thank you both for coming on such short notice. You are both clever, formidable people—discreet and trustworthy. But most importantly, you both don't have strong ties to the various factions in my court."

Shan cocked her head to the side. "And our independence makes us valuable, Your Majesty?"

"Yes." He inclined his head towards her. "As always, Lady LeClaire, you are quite astute. Let me get to the heart of it. It is about these bodies, these murders. Shan, I believe you know that a second one was found."

She didn't flinch, even though it was clear what he meant. He knew that she was at the theatre with Isaac when he had been summoned to duty. But the King wasn't looking at her, his eyes cold and distant. "He was murdered in the same exact manner as the first victim, the one that Samuel found, and left in the streets to be discovered. Dead by Blood Working, and not just any Blood Working—but used for dark and despicable experiments. The kind of magics that are illegal in Aeravin.

"I've called you here because one body is an aberration, but two is a pattern."

Samuel spoke first. "I don't understand. You want us to . . . what? Become private investigators?"

"It's not just that," Shan said, and the King turned towards her with a sly smile. "If it was just some random murders, he'd leave it to the Guards. It's their job. He thinks there is something more at play here."

"Very good, Lady LeClaire." The King leaned back, steepling his hands in front of him. "There is a bigger problem here than most people realize and I fear that I cannot trust my own court."

"What is it, then?" Shan asked. Trouble in the court? This was precisely the kind of thing she was looking for—an opportunity to prove her skills.

"What I am about to share cannot go beyond this room. There are many secrets about Blood Working—about its limits and its potential—that have been between me and the Royal Blood Worker for centuries. Am I understood?"

Shan met Samuel's eyes, and he looked as curious as she felt. "Yes, Your Majesty," Shan said, at the same time Samuel muttered, "Crystal clear."

For a moment it seemed the Eternal King wouldn't speak at all, but he let out a sigh. "What you know of Blood Working, Lady LeClaire, is only the beginning. It's only a fraction of the potential that is open to us—and I have worked hard to ensure that Blood Working doesn't surpass the bounds that I have set upon it. Our position, as a nation, is fraught enough. But should we realize our full potential, I fear the fragile peace I have kept for centuries will shatter."

Shan realized that she was leaning forward, gripping the armrests of her chair so hard that her claws were leaving indents in the wood. A part of her had always wondered if there was more to their gift, if there was a way to push their magic forward, but to hear it from the Eternal King's own mouth thrilled her in a way that she hadn't felt in years.

Knowledge was power, and this knowledge might be the most dangerous thing she had ever touched.

"What sort of potential?" she asked, and the King turned his eyes on her—green and burning, and she felt as if he was peeling back her soul.

"All kinds of potential," he said, his voice soft and dangerous. "We can do things to the human body, manipulate it in ways that nature never intended. We can create gods and monsters. I've spent centuries exploring this—both in theory and in practice." He looked over at Samuel. "Including when I gave my family their gifts."

Samuel shot to his feet, trembling with anger, but Shan was already moving. She rounded the desk and took Samuel's hand in hers, taking care to thread her fingers around his so that the claws did not pierce his skin, trying to ground him before he lost control.

But it was too late.

"You did this to me? To my family?" Samuel spat, the kindness bleeding from his eyes, replaced by a darkness that took Shan's breath away. When he spoke again, she could feel that power that slipped past his lips, magic that hung in the air like a cloying mist. "How could you?"

The King flinched, breathing in hard through his nose as Samuel's gift hit him. "Curiosity, mostly." He glanced up at the ceiling, as if he was trying to fight the words as they crawled up his throat. "I had already achieved so much with Blood Working and I wanted to see just how far I could push it."

Samuel snarled, and Shan moved, pressing her hands into his shoulders and forcing him to sit. Perhaps it was because he was so focused on the King, perhaps it was because she had spent years training her body as well as her magic, but he crashed into his chair. "Don't do anything you'll regret," she whispered, and she could feel the fire in him, threatening to break loose. "Let him speak."

The King smiled at her. "Thank you, LeClaire, but it's all right. I understand why he is angry." He turned his attention to Samuel, trying to smooth his expression to something like contrition. It would have been almost believable if he wasn't actively sizing up Samuel and his potential. Shan could see it in his eyes—after all, she had turned the same gaze upon so many others.

If anything, the King might regret the anger and hurt Samuel felt in this moment, but he wouldn't regret the power the Aberforths had brought to his rule. For generations there had been whispers about this, and the Aberforths had been feared and respected for it. This gift was power, and no King regretted that.

She just hoped that Samuel saw it, too.

"This wasn't my decision alone," the King said, far more collected now that Samuel's command had run its course. "The Aberforth I experimented on—Perry—he volunteered for this. He wanted it, too. He was a scholar. Blood and steel, he was the Royal Blood Worker of his time. And what he could do was nothing compared to you.

It was mere suggestion, not control, that was easily broken, and it gutted his ability to use Blood Working. We wrote it off as a failure and we didn't know that it would pass to his children. I didn't know that it would grow stronger with each generation until it happened."

Samuel shrugged her off, and Shan took a step back, watching him and the King with a careful eye. After several deep breaths, Samuel finally said, "I shouldn't have done that."

"It's all right, son," the King said, and Samuel's flinch was barely perceptible. "I know that you haven't had training, that you don't have control. We'll fix that, I swear. But right now, I need your help. Both of you."

He looked to them. "I never repeated the experiment with Perry Aberforth, but that doesn't mean I have been able to hold back the flow of knowledge completely. Knowledge and theory are harmless, on their own, but in practice—in execution—there is no telling what might be done. And it seems that one of our own is determined to find out where the limits lie."

"Blood and steel," Shan swore.

"And what *can* be done?" Samuel asked, his voice small. He seemed to be curling in on himself, and Shan had to hold herself back from comforting him.

The King looked down, seemingly unable to meet their gaze— their judgement. It was a well-played move, and Shan couldn't have done it any better herself. Watching him was like a masterclass in manipulation, an example of what she could be with enough time and practice.

Though she would never have just as much time or practice as one who was Eternal.

"Horrible things," the King said at last. "All Blood Workers are born with a certain amount of power—some with more, some with less. But you can change that, take power from one person and transfer it to another. To turn Unblooded into Blood Workers, to turn Blood Workers into Unblooded. It's not that different, in theory, from what I do annually." He turned back to them, and despite the youthfulness of his features there was an unfathomable, ancient weight in his eyes. "And that's not even getting into the kind of experiments that created your gift, Samuel. There are so many more avenues to explore, but I don't know if what we'd create would be human in the end."

Shan looked down at Samuel, his head hung low and his hands twisting in his lap. There was a fear in him, she could taste it, and that gnawing emotion was crawling its way back into her heart.

She didn't look up as she said, "Yes. You have my aid."

There were so many reasons to assist him. This kind of knowledge, this kind of power, was dangerous, too dangerous to let out into the world. It would be an excellent opportunity to prove herself. And, of course, the simple thrill she would get from a job well done.

But as much as she loathed to admit it, the reason she had been so quick to agree was the pain of the man sitting in front of her.

"What do you want of me?" Samuel asked, taking extreme care with his words.

"That thing you just did with me?" the King said. "That is how you can be the most helpful. You have a gift—no, no, don't give me that look. I know you find it uncomfortable, but it is a boon we cannot ignore in a time like this."

"Please," Samuel whispered. "Do not ask that of me."

"But I am," the King said. "Because we do not have any other choice. We're talking the safety of our nation, of our people. I will help you, Samuel, but I need this in return."

Shan almost smiled, impressed by the way he played his hand. Quid pro quo, tit for tat. And all in the name of goodness and honor.

She wasn't surprised when Samuel sighed. "All right."

The King relaxed. "Good. Lady LeClaire, I'll have all the information I have sent to you—everything the Guard has found, everything my spies know. And, Samuel, we have work to do. We need to take this gift of yours in hand. Do either of you have any questions?"

"Can I see the bodies?" Shan asked, wrapping her claws around the back of Samuel's chair. She felt him tense, but the King just looked up at her with an arched eyebrow. "I want to examine them magically."

The King shrugged. "We can arrange that." He leaned back in his chair. "Anything else?"

"What about the Royal Blood Worker? Does he know?" Samuel asked.

"He knows about the murders, of course," the King admitted. "He is aiding in the official investigation, but he does not know about you two."

"Why aren't we helping him?"

"Because Isaac—" The King glanced at her, and Shan caught herself. "Because Sir de la Cruz is just as much of a suspect, more so than anyone else."

"Listen to her, Samuel," the King said. "Lady LeClaire knows what she is talking about. Sir de la Cruz has a thirst for knowledge unlike any I have seen in centuries—it was a large part of why I chose him as my aide. I do trust him, and I want to believe that he is loyal to the crown, but we cannot discount anything. There is a traitor in Aeravin, and you two will find them."

"I see," Samuel said, though it was clear he did not.

Shan rested her hand on his shoulder, pressing the tips of her claws into his flesh as a warning. "Do not worry, I'll be sure to catch you up on everything. The politics, the magic."

The King's smile turned lazy, almost predatory. "Good. And you'd best get started. Tomorrow de la Cruz is having his annual ball to open the Season, and Samuel—you'll be there. The time for hiding is over. Dameral should know that another Aberforth walks in their midst."

"I see," Samuel said, and the King dismissed Shan with a flick of his hand.

"Now go, Lady LeClaire. The next time I see you, I hope you will have something good to report." He turned his gaze upon Samuel. "I have a few things to discuss with Lord Aberforth."

Chapter Fifteen

Samuel

Samuel was instructed to go to the Royal Library immediately following their meeting. Though he was unable to see to such matters personally, the King assured him that his Royal Blood Worker would be able to prepare him adequately for the ball the next day. And besides, it would do him well to get to know the man—he was one of the many suspects in the court, after all.

Samuel wanted to say no—that he was no spy. In the brief moment that he actually met Isaac de la Cruz, he had seemed kind, charming, funny. A little overworked, yes, but not a serial murderer. It was wrong to accept his friendship in such an underhanded manner, to use it against him in this way. But ... perhaps if he befriended the man, he could prove that he was innocent of the charges laid against him.

After all, wasn't that what an investigator was supposed to do?

By the time he arrived in the library, Samuel had managed to turn himself around in knots, doubting the wisdom of his decision. He took a moment to steady himself, closing his eyes and breathing deep of the smell—the comforting scents of paper and ink and old books.

There were more books here than Samuel had seen in his lifetime, filling well-made shelves that rose from floor to ceiling. The library was arranged by subject matter—labelled by small, engraved panels on the ends of each shelf—and Samuel had to restrain himself from diving in headfirst. History, politics, philosophy, magical theory . . .

Even amidst such wealth, such a thing felt like coming home.

"Can I help you?" asked a soft voice at his elbow.

Samuel turned to see a woman staring at him, short of stature but firm of disposition. Her lips were drawn into a harsh frown, as if he had interrupted her sanctuary, and he realized with a jolt that this must be the librarian.

"Ah, yes, ma'am," he said, inclining his head to her. "I'm to meet with Sir de la Cruz. I was told he would be here."

She gave him a quick look-over, and after determining that he passed whatever standard she was measuring him against, nodded. "He's in his usual corner."

Smiling slightly, Samuel glanced away. "I'm not sure where that is."

"Right." Sighing, she turned sharply on her heel. "This way, Lord . . . ?"

"Samuel Hutch—" He caught himself, biting down hard on his lip. The King had given him a clear directive—he wasn't a Hutchinson, not anymore. "Aberforth. Samuel Aberforth."

The librarian stumbled, tripping over the hem of her skirt. Samuel reached out to help her, but she had already caught herself, dropping into a deep curtsy. "My lord, I had no idea. Please forgive my impertinence."

"I . . . uh." He blinked down at her, utterly baffled. "It's fine, really."

The woman remained bowed, her head low. "Your charity is overwhelming, my lord."

He just stared at the back of her head, searching for the right words. What was happening?

"Samuel!" Glancing up, he saw Isaac walking his way, clearly fighting back laughter. "You made it." Coming up beside the still bowing librarian, he helped her up. "Thank you, Charlotte. I'll take it from here."

"As you say, sir." She bowed her head towards Samuel once more, then hurried off into the stacks. But he swore he could still feel the weight of her gaze upon him.

"Thank you for your help," he said quietly, and Isaac grinned. "But what the hells was that?"

"Come on, Samuel." Isaac rolled his eyes. "You're practically royalty. Such a reaction shouldn't surprise you."

Maybe it shouldn't. But it definitely disturbed him. "I'm just the same as she is," he muttered, "except for a small matter of blood."

"We both know that's not true. You are so much more than that."

Samuel shot him a sidelong glance, wondering what precisely he was referring to, but Isaac was already walking away, slipping deeper into the library. Once they were past the opening, it became so silent that Samuel felt his very breath would disturb it. Isaac, too, seemed to have the same reverence, and led him past the tables and stacks in a companionable quiet.

They rounded the last corner, coming upon what looked like a small study built right into the corner of the library. There were tables, oversized chairs with plush cushions, even a damned couch shoved up against the wall. It was out of place and homey at the same time, and Samuel turned to Isaac with a frown.

"It's the King's private corner," Isaac explained, "and the closest thing I have to my own space here." He dragged the toe of his boot across the floor, and Samuel glanced down to see what looked like an inlay of blood sketching a border around it, a thin line of glass built into the floor itself. "If he requires privacy, he can activate this ward here, protecting those inside from eavesdroppers."

"That's impressive," Samuel said, unable to stop himself from being awed by it. Blood Working was both great and terrible in equal measure.

"It is, isn't it?" There was a hungry look in Isaac's eye, and Samuel recognized it. He had seen it in himself, after all—the thirst for knowledge. It was part of why he was drawn to books in the first place, and he supposed that even the most powerful of Blood Workers felt the same.

"Anyway," Isaac said, clapping his hands together. "I know what

His Majesty wants us to discuss, and we'll get to that. But I believe I promised you a tour of the library?"

Samuel flushed a little at the memory. It was sweet of him to offer, but— "That's not necessary."

"I believe it is," Isaac said, grinning. "As you are family of the King, you're welcome to help yourself to anything you find here— just check it out with Charlotte before you leave. Besides, I've heard the Aberforth estate's library is lacking, so hopefully this suits you better."

"It is," Samuel said. "Lacking, that is." It had been the first room he had truly explored, before even his own bedroom, and he had been filled with a crushing disappointment. It seemed that the Aberforths before him hadn't cared much for reading and they had simply purchased books by the foot, not caring about the quality or the value of the words they carried, all decorative spines and impressive titles, but drivel within. It was all style and no substance.

Isaac clapped him on the shoulder. "Well, the last few generations of your family hadn't been scholarly, from what the rumors say."

No, they had been cruel. Vicious. A long, terrible fall from grace. Their passing had been tragic, but he couldn't deny that there had been a sense of relief that had spread over Dameral afterwards.

"You are familiar with the rumors, then?" Samuel asked, and Isaac turned away. Shan had given him some of them, but he knew that she was withholding the worst. He was uncomfortable enough, and she seemed hesitant to push him. He didn't know if it was a kindness or an attempt to manipulate him—it was hard to tell with her.

"I am," Isaac said, at last. "They were not nice people, Samuel, and though I've just met you, I can already tell you are far better than them."

"Flatterer," Samuel chided, but he was smiling as he said it.

"Is it flattery if it is the truth?" Isaac asked, his dark eyes sweeping over him. It was different from the way that Charlotte had studied him—that had been reverence and fear. This was pure interest, with just a hint of heat.

Samuel sucked in a harsh breath as he realized what was happening. Hells. This wasn't some mere stranger. Not someone he could brush off with paltry excuses, like Markus had been. They were to be allies or enemies in the complicated game of cat and mouse that his life had become. This had potential—and that terrified him.

And it was bad enough that there was already attraction growing between him and Shan.

Isaac laughed softly, breaking the spell between them as he ran his hand over the back of his neck. The tension hung thick between them, and it was clear that he felt it, too. "So, books then. What are you interested in?"

"History," Samuel answered. "Politics. Philosophy. And fiction, of course."

"Of course," Isaac said. "What kind of fiction? Do you prefer the dramatic stories? Adventure tales? Sweeping tales of romance?"

Blushing fiercely, Samuel looked away. "Just fiction."

Isaac burst out laughing, and Samuel wanted to sink into the floor. "Oh, Samuel. Don't tell me. You have a soft, bleeding, romantic heart, don't you?"

"There is no need to be cruel," Samuel muttered.

"Cruel?" Isaac stepped around him, and the expression on his face was achingly fond. "I'm not being cruel. I'm delighted. The world needs more idealists, if you ask me."

Taking a deep breath, Samuel tried to force some of his embarrassment to fade. "I see."

"Unfortunately, you won't find many of those books here," Isaac said, sadly. "Or the ones that you do will be unbearably chaste. Something about decorum or whatnot. But I'll be happy to loan you some from my own collection."

Samuel stared at him.

"What? It's well known that my parents were deeply in love," Isaac said, shrugging. "It's part of what made them so unpopular. Growing up with them, well, it tends to give a boy hopes."

"Hopes?" Samuel licked his lips, and Isaac's gaze dropped briefly to them.

"Hopes," he repeated. "Even when they are foolish. Come, Samuel, let me show you where to find things. This library can satisfy your academic needs, but don't worry, I'll be sure you have your fun, too."

Isaac's smile was a wicked, brilliant thing, and when he grabbed Samuel by the hand, Samuel let himself be pulled into the stacks.

—⊢—

After Isaac had shown him around and explained the basic layout, Samuel devoted himself to learning the ins and outs of the library. Isaac had given him a friendly smile and retreated back to the study area, but Samuel? He explored—it was exactly what he needed after the meeting with the King and he would be eternally grateful to Isaac for giving it to him.

In the space of an hour he had brought a dozen books back to the table, books on history and Blood Working and politics, the look on Isaac's face growing more incredulous with each successive trip. By the time he added the thirteenth book to the already precarious pile, Isaac reached out and grabbed him by the wrist.

"I think you have enough for now," he said. "The rest will still be here when you're done with these."

"But what if someone checks them out?" Samuel asked, deadly serious.

"Then you can take out different books!" Isaac shook his head. "And besides, I haven't even given you the fun ones yet." His voice dropped low on the word *fun*, sending chills running down Samuel's spine. Isaac's voice was deeper than it had any right to be, rich and masculine, and Samuel sat so he could hide his rising blush behind the stack of books.

"Fine," Samuel reluctantly agreed. "This is a good start." Isaac did have a point, after all. There were more than enough books to keep him busy, and besides, it wasn't like the palace was far from his home. Or that he wouldn't be back here often enough.

This was where his only living relative was, after all.

"You can see sense!" Isaac quipped. Rising to his feet, Isaac stepped over to the line in the floor he had pointed out earlier. A small dagger—fine and sharp—was in his hand, and he sliced his finger open, letting blood drip slowly onto the floor.

The ward sizzled to life around them, invisible to the naked eye, but Samuel could feel it as it rose. All the hairs on his arms stood up, as if a rush of electricity was washing over him, and he stared as Isaac licked the blood from his own wound.

"There." Isaac slid the knife back into a tiny sheath at his waist. "Now we can talk."

Samuel's smile was forced. "And we weren't talking before?"

"Well, yes," Isaac said, coming to sit next to him, instead of across from him. They were too close for Samuel's comfort—not even a foot separated them. "But there are a few things I am to update you on privately."

"Afraid of spies in the library?"

This time, when Isaac laughed, there was no humor in it. "There's always someone listening, Samuel. You need to learn that. The only question is how they'll use it against you." His hand hung from the edge of the armrest, his fingers just close enough to touch. "I recommend you be careful."

"And you?" Samuel asked. "Are you going to use this against me?"

Isaac's gaze sharpened, and Samuel noticed just how striking his eyes were. Not simply brown, but so dark one could lose themselves in them. "No, I won't."

"And I'm supposed to believe you?"

"You're cleverer than you let on," Isaac said, inclining his head. "I like you, Samuel. You don't belong here, that's clear." He bit his lip. "And without help you'll be eaten alive."

"Charity, then." Samuel clenched his jaw. It was barely a step up from pity, but Isaac wasn't wrong.

He was as helpless as a lamb led to the slaughter.

"Vested self-interest," Isaac countered. "You're the last Aberforth. Having your friendship could be very helpful." The brush of his fingers, clearly intentional, against Samuel's helped to temper some of the unease. "Besides, I meant what I said."

"Thank you."

Isaac grinned. "Anything for a friend. So, first things first, I know about this power you have."

Samuel wrenched his hand away, sending his chair skittering back. "You *what?*" he gasped, his throat tightening as fear gripped him hard. His breath was coming in short, hard bursts, a slightly off-putting wheeze, as he stared at Isaac imploringly.

"Don't be so afraid," Isaac said, soothingly. "I am the Royal Blood Worker—the King himself asked me to help you. He's a very busy man," he paused, his expression hardening, "and then there are the deaths. He doesn't want your training to be put on hold, so I will be stepping in."

Samuel shook his head, gasping turning to trembling as the fear radiated outwards. It was too many people. First the slip-up with the Guard. Then Shan. The Eternal King.

Now Isaac.

A noose was slipping around his neck, and Samuel didn't know what to do.

"Hey, hey," Isaac was moving closer, his hand sinking onto Samuel's back, rubbing soft, soothing circles on it. It was tender, comforting, and Isaac kept repeating the motion until the tension started to ebb away, whispering gentle words of comfort in his ear.

"It's fine, you're fine," Isaac whispered, as the last of the panic melted away.

Samuel looked up to him, Isaac's face close as he leaned in. "And you're not ... afraid?"

"Of what?" Isaac asked, so genuinely earnest that Samuel almost believed him. "Of the Aberforth curse?" He laughed. "Even if the power itself is frightening—and it is—that means I'd have to be afraid of you."

"You're not?"

"Please, Samuel." Isaac smiled at him, flashing a dimple he hadn't realized had been there. "You collect books and pine over romance novels. You get flustered when someone curtsies to you. I think I'm fine."

Samuel tried to force a smirk. "You don't know. I could have a dark side."

Isaac's snort was enough to prove him wrong.

"Fine," Samuel said, though he pulled away. Isaac let him. "You know. Great."

"And we'll get the power of yours under control, I promise." He leaned in his chair. "But there is your reputation to think of as well."

"Oh?"

"Yes," Isaac said. "Did His Majesty tell you about the ball tomorrow?"

Samuel swallowed hard. "Yes, he did. I'm not entirely sure it's necessary—"

"Please, Samuel," Isaac interrupted. "The rumors of you are already spreading fast, and we have to get ahead of them."

"You sound like Shan," Samuel muttered. It always came back to this, didn't it? Image. Reputation. Power.

"Ah, yes," Isaac said, glancing away. "Shan LeClaire. I suppose I should warn you of her as well."

"Shan?"

Isaac nodded. "Yes, Shan." He raked his fingers through his hair. "I'm sure you've noticed that she's very clever, but you need to be careful. She could do amazing things for you—she's going to be a very powerful player. And yet . . ."

He drifted off, and Samuel leaned closer. "And yet?"

"You don't want her as an enemy, Samuel," Isaac said, sadly. "Once you lose her trust, I don't know if you can get it back."

Samuel studied him closely—Isaac wouldn't quite meet his eye. "Speaking from experience?"

"It's complicated." Isaac stood, cutting off the conversation. "Just be careful with her."

"For my sake or hers?"

Isaac hesitated, then, "Both?"

Samuel wanted to push—he knew that he could get the full story out of him, if he wanted. If he just gave into the lure of his power. But Isaac seemed so sure of his goodness that the impulse died as soon as it bloomed. He believed in him, and Samuel might not know much, but he knew that he couldn't just throw that away.

"Okay," Samuel said, and Isaac relaxed.

"Let's get these books checked out for you, and I'll call you a hack." He held up his hand, stopping Samuel straight out. "You are not carrying all this on your own."

Samuel laughed. "Oh, fine."

"Good. You go home and enjoy your ill-gotten gains." His lips curved into a too-tempting smile. "Read a bit. I'll stop by tonight with other books, and I'll give you the rest of the details about the party."

"You really don't have to—"

"I insist," Isaac said. "But I promise that I won't take up too much of your time. Now come on, let's get you over to Charlotte." Taking half the stack, he made his way back towards the entrance, the ward shattering around him as he passed through.

Chapter Sixteen

Shan

Shan stood off to the side, nursing a glass of vintage wine and watching the couples move around the dance floor. She had to give Isaac credit—he sure knew how to throw a party. He had taken the ballroom of the Royal Palace, rarely used despite its regal design, and transformed it into the party of the year. All the best people of Dameral were here. The musicians were exquisite. The food simply divine.

Though she was here as Isaac's particular guest—it seemed he was indeed sincere in his attempts to woo her back to his side—he was off performing his duties as host. He had given her the first dance, the most important dance, then begged off to see about something. Whatever it was, he didn't do it simply because his duty demanded it. She had seen real excitement in him.

And she was nearly certain that the task had something to do with Samuel. The King had demanded that this was to be his introduction to society, and though he didn't attend functions such as this, it only made sense for the introductions to come through Isaac. The Royal Blood Worker. His right-hand man. She was only mad that she couldn't have been the one to do it herself, but he was the King's now, and they were running out of time. Despite their attempts to keep this from getting out, rumors were already spreading about the sudden reopening of the Aberforth home and the stranger who had moved in.

So she waited in the shadows, taking shallow sips of her wine to keep intoxication at bay. Tonight the nobility of Aeravin would be completely upended and she wanted to be sharp enough to take it all in.

The whispers started suddenly, moving from one end of the room to the other, spreading fast and furious as fire. There! Isaac was showing Samuel in, and already the vultures were starting to flock. Even from her hiding spot, she could hear some of the things that were being said, caution thrown aside in the desperation to be the first to know.

Who is that?

Handsome boy.

Bette, look. The hair.

Shan hid her smile behind her glass, letting her eyes wander over Samuel. Everyone else was, so it did her no harm to join in. What an image he made. Mysterious and different, yes. But he looked every bit like he belonged, right down to the clothes he wore.

Laurens had outdone herself indeed.

It was the suit they had designed, stunning in its simplicity. The colors flattered him, the depth of the blacks against the simple starkness of the whites. Instead of washing him out, they made him sharper and more focused in their contrasts. His cravat was a slash of white at his throat, expertly tied, and he wore his long hair tied back at the nape of his neck in a style that would have been fashionable twenty years ago.

Shan was glad he hadn't let her cut it. Seeing it now, like this, she realized not only did he wear it well, but it made him look like his father. The late, lost, last Aberforth, back from the grave.

The older people were already whispering it, before Isaac even had the chance to formally introduce him. But he didn't seem to mind. He looked like the cat who caught the canary, and suddenly Shan didn't begrudge him taking her spot. Because every eye in the room was on them, and Isaac was cutting his way through the crowd towards *her.*

Samuel followed in his wake, looking just a little lost and far too innocent.

Shan handed off her mostly full glass of wine to a passing servant, leaving her hands free as they came to a stop in front of her. Every move of this game was carefully calculated. Not only did Isaac bring this young, Lost Aberforth to the world of Dameral, this Lost Aberforth when the world thought they were all gone, he was introducing him to Shan first.

This was the King's promise fulfilled, Isaac trying to mend the mistakes he had made. She was valued, she was worthy, and the stain on the LeClaire name would start to lift.

This was how the game was played, and everyone watching saw it, too. But Shan saw the confusion in Samuel's eyes, saw him putting it together just a half-step behind everyone else.

Shan flicked her gaze up at Isaac, and he nodded. He saw it, and more surprisingly he didn't seem to judge Samuel for it. In that second, they made a silent pact to protect him, to protect the asset. Even beyond what she had promised the King, she would act as interference, as help, guiding Samuel while he found his footing like a baby deer learning to walk.

And Isaac would provide aid.

"My dear Lady LeClaire," Isaac said, formally, as he bowed. Samuel bowed after him, a beat too late, keeping his head low. "May I have the pleasure of introducing my friend, Lord Samuel Aberforth?"

Shan smiled, holding out her hand. "Aberforth, you say? I'm honored."

Samuel did well to hide his recognition of her, but she could see the gleam of amusement in his eyes. He took her hand in his, and she fell into a deep curtsy. "Lady LeClaire."

"Please," she said magnanimously. "Any friend of Isaac's is a friend of mine. You must call me Shan."

"Then you must call me Samuel," he replied, as he continued to hold her hand, far past what was proper. And despite everything between them, a thrill ran through her, one that she didn't have words to explain.

Before she could politely step away, Isaac asked, "Would you be kind enough to give Lord Aberforth the next dance?"

"I'd be delighted," she said, turning and entwining their arms. Samuel looked a little green, but she just offered him one of her kinder smiles. It wouldn't be so bad.

Side by side, they walked towards the dance floor to wait in line for the next song, leaving Isaac alone to be swarmed by the guests. They couldn't have Samuel yet—no one was crass enough to interrupt a dance—so they would get what they could from the second-best source.

The host.

As the current dance entered its final movement, Samuel dipped his head, his lips mere inches from her ear. She could feel his breath warm against her skin, and she had the sudden, ridiculous wish that she had worn her hair down.

"Uh. Shan?" Samuel whispered. "I can't dance. I never learned."

Shan clenched her hand against his arm, surprised by how lean and hard his muscles felt under his sleeve. "Of course you can't. And Isaac still sent you out here?"

"He didn't exactly tell me his plan."

Blood and steel. Isaac didn't intend to humiliate Samuel, she was sure; this was just an oversight. Dancing was simply a part of growing up for them; there was never a need to imagine it otherwise. Her mind raced as she considered the options—there was only one thing she could do.

Fate must have been on their side, for the song the quartet was starting was a simple one. She could still salvage this.

"Follow my lead," she ordered.

"*What?*"

"I'll lead," she said, twirling around him as she guided them into place. "You follow what I do. It's really simple, Samuel." She took his hand and placed it on her shoulder. "It'll be fine."

Samuel blinked down at her, panic creeping into his eyes. "But it's not proper."

She was grinning before she had even decided on it. "And are you the type to really care about what's proper?" She leaned close enough that their breath mingled. "I know you can do it. Don't disappoint me. And now ... one. Two. Three. Four."

As the rest of the couples began to move, she pulled him into the dance, guiding him with a strong hand as he stumbled through the first few measures. He kept his gaze down at her feet, and she counted the beat to him, drowning out the whispers and the gasps, until the stumbling smoothed into something more graceful.

"There," she said. "You're dancing. Now look up at me."

"I am looking at you," he said, and she could hear the wonder and amusement in his voice. But he slowly moved his eyes up, and she could feel the heat rolling off him as his gaze slipped slowly upwards. Up her skirts to the tight pinch of her waistline. From there to the corset that bound her tight, past her décolletage and at last to her face.

He was *blushing*.

Shan's heart pounded a loud, unsteady beat in her chest. This was ridiculous—she had danced with countless others before, been subject to their leers and their greedy hands. Samuel hadn't moved an inch beyond propriety—blood and steel, he was barely touching her, with her leading—but his cheeks were flushed the most delicate pink, and his lips were parted ever so slightly.

She wondered how he would taste—if his kiss would be soft and sweet, or as fierce and passionate as the fire that burned within him.

Shan closed the extra space between them, stepping closer and turning her head so that she couldn't see his face. There was something far too intimate about this, and she tried to ignore the longing that spread through her, warming her from the inside out.

"Your dress is lovely," he whispered. "So ... lacy."

Shan breathed out a laugh, relaxing against him. "You're so talented with words, my Lord Aberforth."

"What? It is." His voice was low and gentle, and Shan ignored the shiver that rippled across her skin. "It looks good on you. You're my own lace-wrapped hero."

"Casually saving you from disaster."

"I'd hardly call fumbling a dance a disaster," Samuel huffed.

Shan's throat clenched. "That's where you'd be wrong, Samuel. It would be." There was so much that he didn't know, but he had her. He was investment, she told herself, and she would be sure that he was worth the cost. She was already thinking of ways to spin this—there would be rumors throughout Dameral, sparked by this scandalous dance. She could take him under her wing, play into the expectations. It wouldn't be the most ridiculous thing; everyone would be trying to.

She just got to him first, long before anyone would even have guessed.

"Well, then, I'm lucky to have you on my side."

Shan laughed. "Yes, you are. And I promise that next time you won't be so unprepared."

The tempo picked up, and she led him into the next movement, spinning him out from her and then back in again. The eyes of the entire crowd were on them, and Samuel was no master but she was strong enough to guide him where he needed to go. It was rather crude and inelegant, but she didn't mind. It was shockingly fun.

He rolled back into her arms with a surprised "Oh."

"That's just the first one," she warned, and then they spun and twirled their way across the floor, Shan leading them expertly through the pattern.

"How do you know this?" Samuel asked as he pressed close to her again.

She spun him out for the last time, then pulled him close and flush for the final movement. "I never do anything by halves, Samuel." She braced herself for the censure, for the judgement, for quite literally leading him into this madness.

But when she looked up, his smile was soft and genuine. "You continue to surprise me, Shan."

She swallowed hard, then looked away, guiding him through the end of the dance. The last notes of the song rang heavy over the room, low and ominous, and Shan swore she could feel it reverberating in her blood.

And then it was over, and couples were stepping apart from each other all across the dance floor. They clung to each other for a moment longer than necessary, their hearts still beating in time.

"Thank you," Samuel said. "For everything. I hope we can do this again."

She wet her lips. "I hope so, too," she said, her voice strangely rough.

As he walked away from her, Samuel glanced back over his shoulder. His eyes burned with a question Shan didn't recognize, and his lips curved into a smile just for her.

It was foolish, but it felt like a balm against the jagged edges of her soul.

She turned away, biting the inside of her cheek until blood welled and burst across her tongue, ready to face the questioning throngs that were desperate for whatever gossip she could give.

With a demure smile, she allowed herself to be swarmed.

Chapter Seventeen

Samuel

Samuel dragged his eyes away from the black-robed Blood Workers who lingered at the edge of the crowd—extra security pulled from the ranks of the Guard, provided for the protection of all. It was ridiculous. This murderer had not yet attacked a Blood Worker, and if the Eternal King's theory was correct, they would not anyway. Besides, who would be foolish enough to strike in the middle of a ball?

Still, he had seen the same Blood Worker who had come to his old workplace on the day he had been fired, who had been responsible, however indirectly, for all the changes that had happened in his life. Alessi's shorn blond hair made her stand out in a crowd of prim and proper Blood Workers, and she caught him staring at her. For a moment they locked eyes, and she inclined her head with a smile that chilled him. He wasn't sure that he wanted her attention, with her too sharp eyes and her cunning smile.

But there were more important things to keep track of, even if Samuel was completely lost. Hoping that his smile hadn't faltered in the brief distraction, he turned his attention back to the men Isaac had introduced him too, accepting the goblet of wine that Isaac pressed into his hand. Between the wine and the conversations he was drowning in, filled with references to people and places and things that he did not know, Samuel wasn't sure he'd be able to remember any of it come morning.

Except, perhaps, the feel of Shan's hands on him, guiding him in the steps of a dance he had never learned.

"Don't worry," Isaac was saying, and Samuel forced himself to pay attention to Sir Morse, who was looking at the both of them like they were the most fascinating thing in the room. "I'm sure we can arrange something."

Samuel didn't have the foggiest idea of what he was agreeing to, but he inclined his head just the same.

"Now, if you don't mind," Isaac said, clapping a hand on his shoulder, "I need to introduce Aberforth around."

"Quite so," Morse agreed, with a smile. "But I shall see you at the club soon!"

"I am looking forward to it," Samuel added, though he would rather launch himself headfirst out the nearest window, but thankfully Isaac was already steering him away, before twisting and pulling them up some stairs and onto a private balcony, where they could speak alone while looking down on the crowd.

It was a blissful reprieve, but Samuel knew that Isaac had not done it as a kindness, but to impart a lesson. He turned his gaze on Isaac's face, though he felt the urge to look for Shan like the pull from a lodestone.

They were separated by the full length of the ballroom, and a height difference of at least ten feet besides, but he felt her presence as acutely as if she were right beside him. She stood near the windows, chatting with a group of young women.

"I'm sorry?"

Isaac laughed—no, *snorted*. "I was saying, Samuel, that you shouldn't look so worried." He leaned in, a conspirator's smirk turning his handsome features into something cruel. "They'll keep introducing themselves to you for the length of the Season, at least. They'll be vying for your attention, and you can have your pick of the lot."

"Joy," Samuel replied, taking a careful sip of the wine. It was bitter and dry, and Samuel nearly choked on it. Isaac had assured him it was a very fine vintage, though Samuel had no way of knowing. It didn't matter, really. No matter what he was drinking, he couldn't allow himself to have enough of it to affect him.

"Don't be like that. You've got to trust me on this. This is an opportunity."

Samuel clenched his jaw, tired of being talked to about opportunities. "I am aware."

"Then don't waste it," Isaac said, spinning him around so that they both faced the crowd once more. He began again, this time from the top. It was an endless list of names and titles, parsing out those who were truly worthy of his time and those who were simply there to fill the space. It was bad form to throw a ball of this caliber without a certain number of guests, apparently, and Isaac coldly told him that's what the fodder was for.

Samuel kept his mouth shut at Isaac's judgement, even though he would've been one of the fodder—or worse—not so long ago. One of the nameless, anonymous servants who cut through the crowd, invisible and unnoticed.

Instead he focused on committing the names to memory, wishing for parchment and pen to keep track of it all. The woman in red was Miss Lynwood, and she was the mistress of Miss Rayne, granddaughter of Lord Rayne, the Councillor of the Treasury. And there was Sir Morse, who so desperately wanted Samuel to join his favorite smoking club. But he was the second son of Lady Morse, who acted as the military strategist on the Eternal King's council, and so any connection to them would be useful.

Samuel hadn't even been aware that the Council contained a military strategist. The Eternal King had kept Aeravin out of the wars between other nations for centuries, despite the countless rulers who had courted them and their legions of Blood Workers.

It was funny. Every other nation—who called themselves civilized—banned and criminalized Blood Working, calling it an abomination and a perversion. But when they had need of it, they came crawling to Aeravin with their pretty words and petty bribes. For what little good it did. The Eternal King had never given in, keeping their magic free and separate.

Isaac kept going until Samuel's head began pounding, his power pressing against the confines of his chest. He could feel the command burning at the back of his throat, and he wanted to snap. To unleash this gift and make Isaac stop his endless prattle.

It kept on pressing, and when at last he felt like his power was going to burn him from the inside out, Samuel broke.

"Please," he said, just a whisper of magic leaking past his lips. "A moment."

Isaac's eyes glazed over, his expression surprisingly soft. "Yes, of course." It came and went so quickly that Samuel could almost believe that he hadn't noticed, but then Isaac's brows furrowed and his lips curved into a frown. "Blood and steel, did you just—?"

"I'm sorry!" Samuel blurted. "I tried to stop it but sometimes it just—"

Isaac shook his head, like he was trying to clear it of fog. "That was truly bizarre. I almost didn't notice it, but there was this almost imperceptible feeling of wrongness." He grinned at Samuel. "I'm looking forward to our testing—I must know how this works. Is it always so subtle?"

"I don't think so?" Samuel blinked at him, still waiting for the anger and hurt to come. "It's easier if you were already likely to do it in the first place."

"Interesting," Isaac said. "We shouldn't be talking about this here. But soon, I promise. The King and I will help you figure out this thing in your blood, and you will master it."

"Thank you?" Samuel waited for the catch, but there didn't seem to be one. Everyone wanted something from him, but perhaps all that Isaac wanted was a friend. As important as he was in court, he seemed to have shockingly few of them.

"Naturally. And I *am* sorry about all this as well." He gestured to the crowd. "Next time we'll go small. Just a handful of people, and I'll make sure Shan has time to prepare you properly beforehand. She's even better at this than I am."

"That would be nice."

"You understand that it had to be this way, right? It had to be a show."

Samuel didn't understand, but he was too tired to argue. "Why are you doing all this, anyway?"

"For the King," Isaac said, as if that explained it all.

Perhaps it did. The King was the most powerful man in Aeravin, and it was clear that Isaac had worked hard to put himself at his side. Samuel didn't know his story, but he could see the sacrifices writ in Isaac's face—in the bags under his eyes and the exhaustion he tried so hard to hide. In the callous way he studied the people around him, so at odds with the genuine kindness he had shown Samuel.

Isaac would do anything it took to climb in Aeravinian society, and Samuel didn't really blame him for it. They made bastards of them all.

Samuel felt a heavy gaze on him, and he turned to find Shan staring at him. Unlike the others, who kept stealing coy glances, she looked straight at him, daring.

"Is there something I should know about?" Isaac asked.

Samuel didn't look away from her. "What do you mean?"

Isaac tsked, lowly. "Already playing with fire, I see. Despite my warning." He leaned against the banister, turning so that he faced Samuel, his eyes shrewd and cold. "She could have had my place, you know. She had the skill and the mind for it. But between the disgrace that was her father and the shame of her brother everyone knew it wouldn't happen. Better to risk it on an unknown like me than a LeClaire."

"The shame of her brother?" Samuel frowned. Anton might be a bit of a walking scandal, but he wasn't that outrageous.

"Oh, yes." Isaac looked at him, surprised. "Did you not know? She has a twin, just as beautiful as her, but Unblooded."

Samuel blinked. *That* was the shame? "And that is a problem?"

"It doesn't help," Isaac admitted. "It's bad enough being a LeClaire, but, as Shan is proving, that is a stain that can be forgiven. Antonin, though, is a bit of a radical, and Unblooded to boot. Those things do not mix, not in polite society. Shan is the LeClaire you should be seen with, not Antonin."

Samuel scoffed. "I didn't know the court of public opinion was so fickle."

"Blood and steel, Samuel," Isaac cursed. "I know you're not stupid, so stop acting like it. You're new to the game, fine, but there is no need to pretend you don't get it."

Samuel ran his hand through his hair, knocking it from its carefully arranged queue and letting it fall around his face like a curtain. "I don't like it."

"But you do understand it?" Isaac asked sharply.

"Yes," Samuel hissed. "I do. I understand that you all lie and cheat and hide behind fake smiles as you prove—what? That you're cleverer and more powerful? That you can be crueler than the next person? That you'll sacrifice anything and anyone? And what does it gain you?"

Isaac shrugged. "Stability. Safety. Comfort." He reached out, pulling Samuel's hand into his.

Samuel did, taking in the dark circles under Isaac's eyes, the slight wrinkles in the corners of them—strange in one so young. For just a moment, he was not the Royal Blood Worker, second-in-command to the Eternal King. He was just a man, frayed to the point of near breaking.

Samuel squeezed his hand, a useless bit of comfort. Isaac clung to his fingers as if they were a lifeline, and Samuel felt a sudden fluttering in his stomach.

"Don't pity me," Isaac said. "I've got almost everything I've ever wanted."

Samuel bit his lip. He was nearly sure he knew what that "almost" meant. Or, rather, who. Apparently, it was complicated. But he didn't pry, not on that. Not when his own feelings were suspect. "Is it worth it?"

Isaac shrugged. "It's hard to say. But it's better than anything I could have had."

"I don't understand. You were already a Blood Worker. A noble."

"Not a noble," Isaac said, laughing bitterly. "A de la Cruz—an immigrant family. My parents immigrated when they were young, hoping to find a sanctuary that would embrace them for the magic that everyone else fears. And they were clever and talented and good, but still." He raised his hand, pulling Samuel's with him. Their fingers were still entwined, Isaac's burnt gold skin in stark contrast to Samuel's pale white. "They were still different, and the child they bore carried the same stain."

"I didn't realize . . ."

"You wouldn't," Isaac said. "Aeravin pretends it's some great haven for Blood Workers, that anyone with the gift can come here to find training and a home. And, yes, it's true, but there is a catch."

"But now you're Royal Blood Worker."

"Yes, I am. I am the King's right hand, the one he turns to, who executes his will, who stands with him and for him." Isaac's eyes blazed with fire, and Samuel recognized a bit of himself in that drive, the part of him that he had spent so long burying. "Because if they couldn't accept me, I would force them to. I would be the best so they couldn't deny me."

"And have they accepted you?"

"Yes," Isaac whispered. "As long as I don't disappoint them in any way."

If it was this close to destroying him already, Samuel wondered what he would be in ten, twenty, thirty years. Would the person he grew to be have even the barest reflection of the young man he was? Or would he become something worse?

But more importantly, why did he care so much? Isaac wasn't a friend, or an ally. He was supposed to be a suspect in his investigation, and yet, looking at him now—a hair's breadth away from being broken, Samuel couldn't imagine him as anything other than lonely.

And hells, he wanted to do something to ease that pain.

"Isaac," he whispered, "why are you telling me this?"

Isaac flinched, as if he had been slapped, and Samuel knew he had made the wrong move. "Because I didn't want to see you hurt, like my parents were. Like I was."

He pulled back, and Samuel let him draw his hand away, watching it fall to the side. Samuel wrapped his arms around himself, trying to ignore the feelings of warmth that still lingered, and the strange way that Isaac was watching him through his eyelashes, like he was waiting for a rebuke.

"Thank you," Samuel said. "I appreciate it, I really do."

"Then don't let it go to waste, Samuel." Isaac turned away. "We've been hiding long enough. Come on, there are still plenty of people left to meet."

Samuel nodded. "Then introduce me."

Chapter Eighteen

Shan

It should have been illegal to schedule the opening of the House of Lords for the day after the opening ball of the Season. Granted, it wasn't something that Shan ever had to deal with before and so she never gave it much thought, but for some things it only took once.

The House of Lords met in the largest chamber of the Parliament House, in a room of circles that rippled ever deeper. The topmost row was a long bench that ran along the curve of the room, and each consecutive row down ran smaller and smaller, till at last it bottomed out at the platform where the current speaker could hold the attention of the entire assembly.

The first row—the ground row—was reserved for the Royal Council, but outside of that the House of Lords was arranged in play at equality. The seating was determined alphabetically, and Shan had found her seat nearly halfway down, a shiny silver plaque displaying her name.

Lady Shan LeClaire.

She ran her fingers across it immediately, savoring the moment. It had taken her so many years, but now she was here, amongst the most powerful people in Aeravin. Those who presented and debated laws and regulations and changed the very structure of their society. One amongst equals.

There was a part of her that never thought, truly, that she would be here. That for all her father's schemes and betrayals, they would find a way to take this away from the LeClaires as well. But she had done it. She was here.

And everything she had worked for could, at last, begin.

But by the end of the first session she found that she was terribly underwhelmed. Though the chamber had been designed with things like acoustics in mind, it had not been designed for comfort. The only windows were near the ceiling, narrow things that hardly let in any breeze. Her dress stuck to her skin, sweat trailing down her neck, and her back ached from sitting on this bench for over two hours. Logically, she knew it was designed to keep them from getting too comfortable, to remind them that they were here to work in service for Aeravin, but *blood and steel*.

Discomfort could be just as distracting as too much comfort, and, besides, it seemed that most of the nobles had stopped paying attention long ago. Aside from Samuel, of course, who watched the entire thing with a rapt concentration that she envied. Shan had only managed to keep her attention by digging her claws into the soft flesh of her hands, just shy of drawing blood, but the pain kept her alert.

Each of the Royal Councillors had given a speech, laying out their goals and visions for this season's work. But there was a shocking lack of detail—it was all dreams and goals and useless platitudes. Flexing her fingers beneath the grip of her claws, she struggled for patience. She hadn't worked so hard and for so long just so that she could waste her time here.

The rest of her fellows were starting to file out, just as eager as she was to be gone, but she remained in her seat, taking deep breaths as she sought to find her serenity once more. She had just managed to unclench her hands when a soft but authoritative voice spoke above her. "Lady LeClaire?"

"Lord Dunn," she replied, opening her eyes to look at the Royal Councillor. He hovered above her, his willowy form casting a shadow across her. Up close, he seemed to be a creature made entirely of angles, harsh and unforgiving, but the worst were his eyes—narrowed, suspicious, judging. "You gave quite a fine speech," she lied. "I am intrigued by your policy proposals and I'm eager to hear more details."

That part wasn't a lie. Details would be useful—it would allow her to figure out who was best to befriend and who best to spurn, who could potentially be recruited to her side and who would forever be an enemy.

His lips quirked up at the sides, looking less like a smile and more like a threat. "In that case, perhaps you can spare a few minutes to join me in my office? I'd be happy to tell you more."

Her decision was made quickly—he might have a history of being conservative, but he was still a Royal Councillor. One could not simply spurn *him*. "Of course," she said, glancing over his shoulder to meet Samuel's gaze across the room.

It seemed the new Lord Aberforth had waited for her, but alas that was not an opportunity she could seize today. She shook her head, just barely, and Samuel slumped. There was nothing she could do about it, so she turned her attention back to the man in front of her.

He held out his hand to her, and she took it, allowing him to help her up. "I hope your first session was interesting, my lady. As I said before, it really is fortuitous that you were able to join us at the start of a session. Joining in the middle can be rather ... disorienting."

She lifted her shoulder in an elegant shrug. "I've been following politics for years."

Dunn watched her from the corner of his eye as he escorted her from the room, and Shan shivered in relief as the cooler air hit her skin. "Naturally. But I daresay you are more politically inclined than most of our fellows, are you not?" She didn't know what to say to that, and Dunn smirked even wider. "Don't worry," he continued, not bothering to lower his voice, not caring who heard him. "I meant it as a compliment. I hardly recognize Dameral anymore.

Most of your generation care more about parties than their duty as Blood Workers."

She waited till they had turned down a hallway before responding. "I believe you are right, but, then again, most Blood Workers my age have not been elevated to our level of responsibility. Perhaps when the time comes they will impress us."

Dunn laughed. "A true diplomat's answer. Yes, Lady LeClaire, I think you will do well here. I can always use someone with your skills on my team." He came to a stop before a large wooden door. "Right through here."

She stepped into his office, the one set aside for him here in the Parliament House so that he could handle his work as a Royal Councillor at his convenience. It was finely furnished, as was to be expected, and the window overlooked the city. But there was nothing of Dunn here—no knick-knacks or personal touches or even the smallest bit of comfort. Despite the fact that he had held his position for well over a decade it still felt as if he had just moved into the office yesterday—a plain room with no heart, no soul.

He closed the door behind her, and Shan had the sudden, wild feeling of being trapped. This man was not her ally, and she was in his territory now. But she was a LeClaire, she could not afford to show weakness.

"Please, have a seat."

She sank into the chair gracefully, waiting with her hands folded demurely in her lap. Dunn bustled around the office, gathering his papers and thoughts, before he turned to her suddenly. He didn't sit in the chair behind the desk or the one beside her. Rather, he leaned casually against the desk so that he could tower over her.

Well, if he sought to intimidate her, he would be sorely disappointed.

"I'm sure you're wondering why I asked you here, my lady," Dunn said, staring down at her. "And the reason is that though I am quite skilled in my role—His Majesty wouldn't have appointed me otherwise—I do not have the skill to reach the younger Lords amongst us."

"And that's where you think I can come in," Shan supplied, and he grinned.

"You are quite clever indeed," Dunn said, clapping his hands together. "Even with your—" he hesitated for a long moment, then sighed. "Let's be blunt, LeClaire. I am tired of all the politicking. Even with the bad history around your family, and your own ... shortcomings," his lips curled as his eyes raked over her appearance. Even though she had dressed perfectly, there was nothing she could do about her skin or features, and the contempt was still there, even when he was asking for a favor. "You have a lot of talent, and if you help me I can help you."

Shan didn't let her anger get to her—though she ached to lash out. To unleash her Blood Working upon him, forcing him to bend and break before her—as her father had. To show that her magic was as good as his. No, better.

But it would only set her back, so she took it and locked it away, deep inside, where it couldn't touch her.

All of a sudden she understood Isaac a little bit more.

"And how precisely can I help you, Lord Dunn?"

He nodded, pleased by her proper words and her gentle tone. "I have been working on this bill for a while, and I believe we can get it passed." Passing the papers to her, he continued, "Though I doubt it will be a popular bill, I hope that with the aid of someone with your skills, we can make them see that it is necessary."

Curious, Shan looked down at the paper he passed her, reading quickly. Of all the things she had expected, she certainly hadn't thought she'd see something like this, especially from Lord Dunn. She kept the expression on her face mild, but she couldn't stop her mind from whirling with the possibilities.

Tensions between Blood Workers and the Unblooded were fragile at the best of times, but she knew that things were reaching a tipping point. If something wasn't done, and soon, she wasn't sure how long the Unblooded would remain peaceful. And this bill, this bill from one of the most conservative Lords, would give in to some of their demands.

But what did Dunn have to gain from it?

"It's bold," she said, and Dunn preened like it was the greatest compliment in the world.

"It is, isn't it?" He pushed off from his desk, clasping his hands behind his back as he started to pace. "Between you and me, LeClaire, things are not looking good for Aeravin. The Eternal King has been protecting us for a millennium, but while Blood Workers have thrived the Unblooded grow frustrated with their place. Ungrateful, the lot of them. We give them so much, and this has been how they treat us?"

He sneered, and Shan realized that this was not motivated out of any kindness or sense of justice, but out of the sheer political practicality of keeping peace. "But I cannot discount that while they may not be strong, they are many. So, if we give them just a hint of what they want, we can placate them before they truly push for more. Nip this dangerous sentiment in the bud."

Though she disagreed with his morals, she couldn't argue with his logic. "Perhaps you should use that as part of your speech to the House, my lord."

He snapped his fingers. "Yes, I should! Let me write that down."

While he was scribbling she turned her gaze back to the document in her hand, trying to wrap her mind around it. "And you believe the solution is to give them a place in the government?"

"Not precisely." He turned back to her. "Rather, we'd create an office that would be dedicated to hearing their complaints and concerns, an additional branch of the Council." His smile was cold and calculating. "It would give the illusion that we are taking steps, but in the end it will still be up to the House of Lords to pass any new laws."

She bit back the retort on her tongue. He wasn't helping the Unblooded, and he knew it. All he was doing was wasting resources to create an elaborate form of trickery. At best, it would buy them a few years until the Unblooded figured out they were being played.

But still, a few years of peace would give her more time to get ingratiated into her role, to gain more power, and perhaps, just per-haps, she could use this to her advantage. She could be seen as an ally to the Unblooded, and when it was time to move—well, there would be some frameworks already in place.

"You think a lot of my opinions if you believe that I can get all of Aeravin behind this. Especially considering my," the word almost stuck in her throat, "shortcomings."

"I do," Dunn confirmed, "though you shouldn't be so hard on yourself. It's not your fault your father chose poorly. Besides, the fact that you have done so well in spite of it only proves your strength of character, does it not?" He didn't give her a chance to respond to that, luckily for him, continuing on with his planning. "Anyway, it needn't be all of Aeravin. Just enough to get it passed. Besides, the first step is not so controversial. As I said, the truth will be clear."

Again, she took that anger and locked it away inside. She was used to it—a lifetime of tiny cuts had made her numb to the pain, though she feared the day when the smallest of slights would tip her over the edge.

"Yes, it will be," Shan said, focusing on the issue at hand. The truth behind his bill. If she could see it—if all the nobles of Aeravin could—why wouldn't the Unblooded?

"It is the perfect solution," Dunn said again. "Only it is one I cannot present myself. I have a—" he coughed, looking away from Shan. "A certain reputation when it comes to the Unblooded. This plan would be too gentle to be believable as a proposal from Lord Dunn."

"Yes, you have tended towards," Shan hesitated, "conservative policies."

"The Unblooded are coddled, and if I had my way we'd remind them of their place before they start getting out of hand." He grabbed something off his desk, passing it to her. "Such a travesty would not have been allowed when I was young."

It was a pamphlet—the kind that the Unblooded passed among themselves. Usually harmless, but a quick glance confirmed that this was not the normal kind. This was outright seditious—demanding change to the very structure of the government itself.

While the Blood Workers revel, it read, *leeching off our labor, we are not given even the slightest consideration. If they cannot be bothered to legislate for our needs, perhaps they should allow us to do it for them. For, unlike them, we are accustomed to hard work.*

"Disgusting, isn't it?" Dunn sneered. "Keep it, read it. It's good to know what these rats are thinking. But I am not the hot-blooded young fool I once was. If there is a chance to settle this peaceably, then we should. But if they reject it?" There was a hunger in his eyes, barely restrained, that chilled Shan. "That's another matter entirely."

"I understand." Shan folded the papers, slipping them into her reticule.

"Good." He leaned forward, resting his hands on the armrests of her chair. "Of course, I don't expect an answer on this now, but I want you to understand that I have eyes and ears everywhere. Should the details of my bill—or my grander plans—become public, I will know how. Am I understood?"

Shan didn't flinch. "If I am not to discuss the bill, how am I to sway people to your side?"

"Oh, you are. But it's not my *bill*. It will be yours."

"Ah," Shan said. "I see."

She was to be the tool to be used, the pawn he played when he couldn't make the move himself. It was a degrading role, but still . . . there would be advantages.

"Precisely." He stepped back. "I think we understand each other well, LeClaire. We can help each other, if you want it." Shan opened her mouth to respond, but he held up his hand. "Don't. Prove it to me with actions, or not at all. Good day, my lady."

Shan stood and curtsied. "Good day, Lord Dunn." She let herself out without turning back to him, focusing instead on the potential he offered her—not the pain, not the insults—with a clear mind.

Yes, this plan would fail. Eventually. Yes, she would be his tool.

But the favor of a Royal Councillor would be quite the currency to collect, and the prestige of building up power in the House of Lords itself would pay out quite nicely.

All she had to do was hold her nose and close her eyes.

"Lady LeClaire!"

She spun, turning to see a young woman in Royal Livery running her way.

"A message for you," the woman said, holding out an envelope.

Shan took it, hesitating only for a second as she studied the seal— a rose in dark red wax. A message from the King. She hid a smile as she turned away from the messenger, though it faded quickly as she opened the note.

Well, there was an investigation to be done. Another body had been found.

Chapter Nineteen

Shan

S han entered the morgue with her hood still raised, her face hidden and the note clutched in her hand. There had been another body found—left brutalized and bloody in the streets. The Guard had got to it before her birds could find her, thanks to the damned opening of the House of Lords. But Shan did not have to worry. The Eternal King had kept his promise, inviting her to meet with the lead investigator and examine the body at her leisure—though it would be best if she were quick. Blood Working was strong, but the longer they kept the body in suspended animation the more contaminated it would become, the two sources of magic mixing together until it was impossible to tell one from the other.

She had come at the first opportunity, leaving Bart to handle all her official business while she handled this, waiting only till night had fully fallen and most of the Guard had retired. She was, after all, still supposed to be circumspect, and though the King promised in his note that the lead investigator was sworn to secrecy, Shan knew she had nothing to fear.

The lead investigator was Delia Alessi.

"Alessi," Shan said, by way of greeting, lowering her hood as she stepped into the glow of the witch light. Alessi stood from her perch by the window, looking out over the night-darkened sky of Dameral.

She bobbed her head once in greeting—as effusive as Alessi ever was—and gestured towards the metal slab in the middle of the room, and the covered shape that could only have been the body.

"It's strange, Sparrow," Alessi said. "Having you here with the permission of the King instead of sneaking you in during the dead of night."

Shan shrugged, carelessly confident, and stepped closer. "Things are changing, Alessi, and this is only the beginning."

Something hard glinted in Alessi's eyes, a blue so pale they could have been ice. "Indeed, they are. I suppose congratulations are in order for winning the King's favor?"

"I haven't won it yet," Shan said, watching the careful changes in Alessi's expression. "But I will soon." She knew that the girl hated the King as much as she did, perhaps even more so. For all that the Eternal King had done to destroy her family, at least she still had relative wealth and luxury. Even the poorest of the nobles had far more than Alessi's family could ever hope to have.

Shan kept her smile cold and cruel—not a promise, she was not foolish enough to make such things, even to such loyal subordinates. But a hint could be wonderfully reassuring, and she trusted Alessi to know how the game was played. She had tried for years to get one of her birds into the palace, but she had never succeeded. The Eternal King was too smart for that—his servants too well vetted, too loyal. If she was to succeed in her plans, this was the only possible way.

Vengeance was slow, almost painfully so, but Shan wouldn't let that stop her.

"Right." Alessi crossed her arms over her chest, fixing Shan with a surprisingly firm glare. "While you're doing that, I hope you don't neglect your other responsibilities, Sparrow. It's been hard to reach you as of late."

Shan bristled at the tone that Alessi turned on her. How dare she? "I am playing an important role as Lady LeClaire. Besides, you can always turn to Hawk with information." That was what Bart was there for—he was there to handle things in her absence, and now that she was playing Lady LeClaire, he had stepped up to the role admirably.

Alessi shook her head. "Of course. That's how it is."

"How what is, Alessi?"

"Nothing," the girl spat, but Shan reached out and grabbed her arm.

"I am not unreasonable, Delia," she said, her voice low. "I know that you care about this work, it's why I recruited you. If you have concerns, you can talk to me."

Alessi stared at her for a long moment, her blue eyes unreadable. "It's nothing. Just some frustration at how long things are taking."

Shan let her pull away, even though she had a feeling that wasn't the full truth. But she couldn't force Alessi to confide in her, and even if she could, trust was a delicate thing. "I know. As am I. But we cannot change a nation in a night."

Alessi sighed. "Of course, Sparrow. Forgive my outburst."

"There is nothing to forgive." She took a step back. "Now, the body?"

"Right this way." Alessi stepped over to the metal slab, pulling off the sheet that had hidden the corpse from view the whole time.

Shan gripped her own arms, digging the points of her claws into her own skin as she fought back a scream. It was far worse than she had anticipated, even with the notes the Eternal King had sent her way.

She had been but a child when she had first attended one of the Eternal King's annual sacrifices, dragged there by her father to see their ruler in his full glory. To understand the power that lived in her veins, and the place Blood Workers held above all the Unblooded. Her father had held her in front of him, not allowing her to turn her face or hide from the brutality of it.

She had only been nine years old.

After that, she had stopped trying to fight her father, had embraced her magic in all its brutal glory. She had learned all the Blood Working had to offer—all the good and evil, all the potential and the pitfalls.

But nothing had prepared her for this.

Her stomach turned, bile making its way up her throat as she studied the corpse. The remains of the woman—for it was a woman, no more than five and twenty—were all that was left of a once vital life. Her eyes were shut, her hair fanned out underneath her head. Shan ran her fingers across the strands, golden, yes, but brittle to the touch, as if all the life had been sucked out of it. Her skin was little better, papery and thin, over desiccated muscles that been drained down to the bone.

There were deep cuts in her forearms and thighs where the blood had been carefully drained. It wasn't like the King's sacrifice, which was done with brutal, ruthless efficiency. This was slow, methodical—*academic*. The multiple wounds meant the blood was likely being drawn for some arcane purpose, but Shan hadn't the faintest idea what. And with the way the cuts were made, it would have been done while she was still alive, and it would have been excruciatingly painful. But the end results were the same.

It was as if someone had taken all the blood and moisture and squeezed it out of her, leaving behind only this broken, brutalized body.

"Were you able to identify her?" Shan asked.

"Jessica James," Alessi said, softly. "Unblooded. She owned a bookshop in the dock district."

The name sounded vaguely familiar, and a cold pit settled in her stomach as she asked, "What bookshop?"

Alessi stepped aside, flipping through a file that she had left on an adjacent table. "*Pages*."

Shan clenched the edge of the slab—it was the proprietress of the shop her brother liked to frequent, the one who had imported a variety of Tagalan books for him. Histories, novels, books on mythology—all things they had lost when their mother had fled.

He would be heartbroken to hear of her passing.

"How unfortunate," Shan said, with a forced air of calm as she made herself relax, her fingers popping off the table. "Were you able to discover anything else?"

"With Blood Working?" Alessi shook her head. "Nothing more than the obvious—she was drained for power. We did a mundane autopsy just as a well, to cover our bases, but the results were the same." She gestured to the Y-incision on the corpse's chest, where they had cut into her with their scalpels and rooted around in her body, looking for clues.

What a disgusting way to do medicine, Shan thought as she studied the rough stitches that had sewn poor Jessica back together like a broken doll. And people dared to call Blood Working unnatural?

Still, she had to try. Raising her hand, she let one claw hover over the corpse. "May I?"

"You can try," Alessi said, shrugging. "There is very little blood left, though."

Shan took Jessica's hand in hers, sorry for adding to the desecration that had already been done, but there was no other choice. She drew the tip of her claw against the inside of the corpse's wrist, where the pulse would have been on a living body, digging for the slightest bit of moisture. Of blood.

Alessi watched with a sharp eye as she rooted around, pressing through the skin and the ruined flesh to the bone. When Shan removed her metal claw from the dead flesh, there was the slightest stain on it—the color of rust.

It would have to be enough.

She sucked her claw into her mouth, her whole body rebelling against the blood that hit her tongue, bitter and acrid. Her senses screamed out—*dead, dead, dead*—but more than that, it felt corrupted. This was vile, wrong and against the few laws of nature that Blood Workers still adhered to.

Shan turned and spat on the floor, desperate to get the taste out of her mouth, and Alessi rushed to her side, pulling a flask from her jacket.

"Here, Shan," she said with surprising kindness, as she held the open flask to her lips. Shan tipped it back, the burn of pure liquor spilling past her lips and washing away the remains. She coughed and sputtered, turning away from the corpse and shaking. "It is vile, isn't it?"

"It's wrong," Shan agreed, and Alessi stepped back, her face shadowed. "What?"

"This is what happens with the King's sacrifices," Alessi hissed. "They are just the same, and yet we praise him for it."

Shan shook her head quickly, glancing around even though she knew they were alone. "Alessi! Be careful when you speak treason."

"I speak the truth!" she spat back, and Shan shivered at the pure hate there. But the anger passed quickly, replaced with a calm that was far more terrifying. "Just remember your promise to me."

"I will," Shan swore. "We will see justice for these souls."

Alessi shook her head. "I meant the King. He's the real monster we need to fear."

Shan held her breath, not knowing what to say. "You know that I am working towards all of our goals."

Alessi shook her head. "Yeah, I know. Now you'd better get out of here before the shift changes. I'll put things to right."

For a second Shan hesitated, knowing that she should say something, anything, to comfort Alessi. To let her know that she wasn't in this alone. But that wasn't her way, and besides, Alessi was a good bird. She had never failed her before. Shan just flipped her hood up and stepped towards the door. "Let me know if anything else happens and keep an eye out for my instructions."

There was so much she had to tell Alessi—about the investigation she was running, about needing to loop in Samuel as well. But this wasn't the time. Her rules were simple. In and out, no lingering.

"I will, Sparrow," Alessi responded, sounding tired and drained. "And good luck with the investigation."

"You as well."

Alessi's smile was brittle. "Please. What I'm doing is just a formality. Now that the King has called you in, we both know who he's going to be looking to."

Shan didn't know what to say to that—it was, after all, true. So, she simply nodded and turned away.

Chapter Twenty

Samuel

When Samuel had been instructed to meet Isaac at the palace, he hadn't expected this. Instead of the lush, fine furnishings that he was starting to get used to, this was a stark, bare room that reminded him of a laboratory. The hard marble floor caused his steps to echo, and there was a metal table laden with all sorts of devices he had never seen before—contraptions to draw, contain and test blood. Knives of all sorts. Blood Working tools far beyond his imagining that had his stomach twisting.

"It won't be that bad," Isaac assured him, following his gaze. "I doubt we'll use anything too scary today, anyway. We're keeping it simple."

"Simple is good." He forced out a deep breath, grasping for calm. "I'm sorry that you have to do this."

"It's my job," Isaac said, easy as anything. "Come on, have a seat and roll up your sleeve. Non-dominant hand, please."

Samuel settled onto the stool, shucking off his jacket and laying it on the table. "What are you doing?"

"Just taking a little blood for study." He already held a wicked looking device in his hand—a sharp needle attached to a long, thin tube. "If you don't mind."

"I was always warned to be careful," Samuel said as Isaac lined up a series of vials. "Never to let a Blood Worker get my blood."

"Ah." Isaac turned to him. "I understand your concern, and it is good advice. But we are friends and allies here. If you want, I can help you … master your gift without studying your blood. That is His Majesty's general strategy—practice and willpower and control. But …"

Samuel leaned forward, drawn in by the pregnant pause. "But?"

Isaac moved forward as well, meeting him partway. It felt powerfully intimate and private—ridiculous as they were already alone in the room. There was nobody there to overhear them, yet here they were, leaning into each other and whispering. "But I want to know how the magic in your blood works, and if there is any way to strip it away."

His heart stopped in his chest. "Is that really possible?"

"I don't know," Isaac said, open and honest. "We won't know for sure until we try. Blood Healing is a tricky business—there are limitations that many Unblooded don't realize."

Swallowing hard, Samuel asked, "Such as?" It was such a foolish question, he knew so little of how Blood Working actually worked, but if there was even a chance …

Isaac considered him for a long moment, some internal debate warring across his face, before he let out a sigh. "Blood Healing is powerful, but it is at its core restorative. When I heal a cut, it knits the flesh back to where it had been; when we purge a disease, it cleanses the virus. In all things, it restores a body to its peak, but natural, state. Trying to … change that is complicated, and it requires consistent monitoring and treatment."

Isaac glanced away, for the first time too timid to meet Samuel's eyes. "It is what I do, weekly, for my own treatments."

"Your—" Samuel began, only to be cut off.

"Yes," Isaac cut him off, barreling forward to keep Samuel from interrupting. "I wasn't born … I wasn't recognized for the man I am, when I was younger. My parents, society, they thought they had a daughter, until I was old enough to have the words to correct them."

"Oh," Samuel said, as understanding hit. He had known a couple of people like this, people whose gender did not align with the bodies that they had been born with and the expectations that society put upon them. But they had been Unblooded and poor, and what Isaac was describing was something beyond what they could achieve. "Blood Working can help you transition?"

Isaac's shoulders relaxed at the simple question, at the way Samuel hadn't flinched away in confusion or disgust. "Yes, it can. It can manipulate my body, the hormones in my blood, but it cannot create the organs which would synthesize them naturally. So, here I am, working on it constantly."

What a fascinating bit of magic, what a wonderful potential for good—if one had the ability or money to access it. Still, there was the matter of his own problem. "And my gift . . . might be like that? Unalterable?"

"I don't know," Isaac said, simply. "That's what I want to investigate."

It wasn't a promise, it wasn't more than a hope. But still, there was another aspect they needed to consider. "And what of the King?"

"What of him?" Isaac stepped back. "I'm just finding out what's *possible*. What you—what *he*—decides to do with it is beyond me."

Samuel stared down at his hands, suddenly imagining a life where he didn't have to be so careful all the time. Where he could allow himself to let loose, to be free for just a moment. "You can take what you need," he said, rolling his sleeve up past his elbow.

"Thank you. Now hold still." Isaac grabbed a long, thin bolt of cloth from the table and wrapped it around his arm, pulling it tight. Samuel hissed in surprise, and Isaac shot him a comforting look before running his fingers across his veins, tracing the dark lines that stood out in stark relief against his skin. His touch was hot—burning almost—and Samuel wanted to lean into it.

Instead, he forced himself to focus on the procedure. "What's this for?" he asked, fingering the cloth with his free hand.

"Makes the veins easier to access," Isaac replied, grabbing the needle and tube contraption. "Be glad for it, you don't want me stabbing around trying to find the vein." He dropped the open end of the tube into the mouth of the first vial, then carefully pressed the needle against his skin. "This might hurt a bit," he warned, then immediately pierced him.

Samuel grunted, instinctively flinching away, but Isaac was holding him in a firm, tight grasp, his hand large and warm around his arm. It felt strangely comforting to be held so—to be grounded and controlled—and he didn't want Isaac to let him go.

But Isaac wasn't paying attention to him—he was pulling the tourniquet loose, watching the flow of the blood through the tube, filling the vial. "Not so bad, right?"

"No," Samuel managed, past suddenly dry lips. "Not bad at all."

The first vial was nearly full, and Isaac pinched the edge of the tube shut as he moved it to the next one. "Two more should be enough, for now."

Samuel nodded, not quite trusting his voice or control. There was something thrilling about leaving himself entirely in Isaac's power, and he really didn't want to think about that. So, he sat in silence, biting the inside of his cheek, until Isaac was done draining blood from him.

"There we are." He still wasn't looking at him, focused on pulling the needle from the vein. Tossing it onto the table, he pressed his thumb over the tiny pinprick, forcing the blood to well out. At last, he met Samuel's gaze as he wiped away the last of the blood, his eyes dark and fierce. Isaac sucked his own thumb into his mouth.

Samuel couldn't tear his eyes from it, from the soft press of teeth against skin, the flash of a tongue past his lips.

And then the fucker *smiled* at him, and Samuel realized he knew exactly what he was doing.

"And now," Isaac said, grabbing Samuel's arm. He could feel the tickle of something in the back of his head, the faintest connection, as the skin knitted itself back together. "All healed. Just give me a few moments to clean up and then we'll get to the real work."

"Right," Samuel said, shaking himself out of his daze, slowly putting himself to rights as Isaac washed the remains of his blood away. Of course, this room had its own plumbing—the Eternal King really would spare no expense, would he? It was the kind of thing that should make him mad—that *did* make him mad—but he was still feeling so off-balance that he couldn't quite muster the proper response.

Hells, this was embarrassing.

"You okay there, Samuel?" Isaac asked, suddenly appearing at his side. The knowing smile he wore made it abundantly clear that he was aware of what was going on in Samuel's head.

"Fine," Samuel said, scowling up at him. It did little to discourage the Royal Blood Worker. Isaac just laughed.

"All right, all right. Let's talk magic."

"Like that wasn't magic," Samuel said with a huff, and Isaac inclined his head to him.

"It's more like alchemy when you get down to it—ah, never mind." He ran his hand through his hair, blowing out a little huff of frustration. "That doesn't matter now. What matters is what we're going to do. From what I was told, what you need to practice is control."

"Yes," Samuel said, then started. "Wait, *practice*? You can't mean for me to use it!"

"Well, yes." Isaac cocked his head to the side. "How did you think you were going to master this gift?"

"That's the entire point! I don't want to use it!"

"But if you do not practice you never will have control." Isaac grabbed him by the hands. "I know your gift frightens you but if you do not master it, it will master you." Samuel wanted to roll his eyes at that inane bit of advice, but Isaac was rubbing soothing circles on the backs of his hands. "As I said before, I'm not afraid of your power and you shouldn't be either."

"But I am," Samuel whispered. "You don't understand—you can't understand."

"Then try me."

Samuel wanted to run, to hide, but Isaac was still holding him, looking at him without fear or judgement in his eyes. He had never thought it could be like this, that someone could know about the darkness within him and not turn away. Not only that—despite the orders the King gave him, Isaac wasn't using him for his own power or glory. He was helping him, as a friend.

Or, given the way he kept holding his hands, perhaps something more.

So he did something he never thought he'd do—he told the truth.

"It's not simply about what I can do," Samuel began. "The fact that I control people, or the fear that I'll slip up. It's deeper than that. This power is part of me. No—it lives inside me. I can feel it." He pulled one hand free from Isaac's, placing it over his chest. "Here. It breathes and it hungers and it pushes, and every time I give in to it, it gets harder to push it back into its cage."

"You think practicing will only make it stronger," Isaac said.

"Yes." Samuel hung his head. "And as it gets stronger, I'll get weaker."

"That's not true. You'll get stronger with it—it won't be able to fight you anymore."

He could feel his hands trembling. "But what if we're wrong? The King said it's getting stronger with each generation. Even if my father could control it—and from what rumors held he didn't really bother to try—that doesn't mean that I will."

And there it was. The fear that had haunted him his whole life. It was easy to write off one or two mistakes. But it was never just that. He had spent his whole life trying to pull himself away, to limit the damage he could do to others, but it still kept happening.

It would keep happening, until the man was gone and all that was left was a monster.

Isaac looked away. "That's why I took some of your blood, isn't it? If this fails, we'll have another option."

"You said it wasn't a guarantee."

"Nothing is guaranteed," Isaac admitted. "Except if you don't try, you will fail."

He pulled away, and this time Isaac let him go. He wanted to flee—to find some space from the truth that Isaac was speaking. He was right, after all. Ignoring it had never been an effective tactic, and even if it was, the Eternal King wouldn't allow him to let such a talent lie fallow.

"Why are you risking so much for me?"

"You keep asking me that," Isaac replied. "And ... I can't give you an answer."

"Can't?" Samuel whirled to face him. "Or won't?"

"Heh, you're learning." He shrugged. "Both? I'm the Royal Blood Worker, Samuel. I've aided the Eternal King in matters that leave me damned. But if I can do even just a little good in this life, then I will. So, what do you say? Are you ready to begin your practice?"

Samuel looked pointedly around the room. "There is no one here to practice on."

Isaac smiled, slowly and sadly. "Yes, there is."

"Hells."

"Hells indeed," Isaac echoed. "But it's all right. I know what I signed up for. Besides, I know you won't make me do anything too bad. Perhaps pat my head and rub my stomach at the same time? Hop on one foot? Quack like a duck?"

Samuel couldn't help it—he laughed, and Isaac laughed with him. It was just such a ridiculous idea. Sir Isaac de la Cruz, the Royal Blood Worker.

Quacking like a duck.

"I told you it wouldn't be so bad." Isaac shook out his shoulders—loosening himself up as if for a fight. "But, sadly, this isn't a childish game. Let's just keep it simple and straightforward, yes?" When he met Samuel's eyes, there was no hesitation there. "I trust you."

For a moment Samuel considered his options, just having him hop on one foot or some other innocent thing. But, no, he was right. If he was to master this power—if he was to please the Eternal King—he needed to take this seriously. He looked at Isaac and said the first thing that came to mind.

The thing he had been aching for, but was too cowardly to admit. But they had shared something here, something soft and vulnerable, and Samuel ached to know what it would be like if he could just reach out a little bit more.

"*Kneel.*"

Isaac went ramrod-straight, his ease vanishing as his eyes went wide with surprise. For a second, just a second, he resisted, his body trembling as he fought with every ounce of his will. Then Isaac sank in front of him, struggling the whole way, but he still managed to land on his knees with grace. It was only in the tension in his neck as he bowed his head that Samuel could see the fight—the way that Isaac needed to cling to control, to his image, to his pride—and he wondered what this moment must have cost him.

Samuel forced himself to watch, unable to turn away. He told himself it would be dishonorable, but in truth, there was a part of him—deep and shameless—that stirred with a dark kind of thrill. The pleasure curled through him, low in his stomach and intoxicating, knowing that he was the reason Isaac was now on his knees. That he had taken this proud, stubborn, brilliant man and brought him low with a single word.

That no matter who or what he would face, he'd always have this power.

And then it was over. Isaac scrambled back to his feet, his breath coming hard and fast while his cheeks colored. The slip in his control lasted only a moment, then he was grinning up at Samuel like they had just played the most marvelous game. "You cheeky bastard."

"What was it like?" Samuel asked. "Please—I've never known."

Isaac paled slightly, but he faced Samuel unflinchingly. "It was like ... being trapped in my own body. I knew what I was doing, I knew I was supposed to fight it and I tried. But I knelt anyway. I couldn't do anything else until I was done."

Samuel turned away, pressing the back of his hand against his mouth as he tried to keep from retching. Finally, he managed, "And you couldn't resist. I really am a monster."

"No, Samuel," Isaac grabbed him by the shoulder, spinning him around until they were face to face. "It's all right, really." His smile turned sly. "Besides, if you wanted me on my knees, all you had to do was ask."

"You're a damned menace," Samuel said, pushing him away, but he couldn't help it. He was laughing.

"Perhaps," Isaac admitted. "But it works." He was so close that Samuel could feel his breath against his skin.

"It's just . . . a lot," Samuel admitted.

Isaac's laugh was so soft that he felt it more than heard it. "We'll figure it out. Now, if you stop getting lost in that damn head of yours, let's back to work?"

"Okay," Samuel whispered, and Isaac stepped back.

"Have at me, then."

It was easier after that. It seemed that no matter what they did, Isaac didn't hold it against him. It was knowledge, it was science, and he was determined to help Samuel figure it out. It stirred a feeling of fondness in Samuel's chest, something he thought he'd never feel again, not after the death of his mother.

It felt almost like trust.

Chapter Twenty-One

Shan

"You look ridiculous, Shan," Anton said, his arms crossed over his chest as he took in her outfit, her cloak discarded on the carriage floor now that they travelled quickly through the streets. He fiddled with a flask in his hand; even on route to the gambling hell, he needed a drink, unable to wait. But then again, he was probably looking for anything to occupy himself as he was unable to look at her directly.

Her dress was short—scandalously so—and the bodice was little more than a tight corset with decorative lace frills. It was black as midnight, studded with fake diamonds that would catch in the light. And around her neck she wore a simple necklace in the shape of a bird in flight—a sparrow for a Sparrow.

Shan loved it.

"It's the uniform," Shan said, her voice deceptively sweet, but her red-stained lips were pulled back in a grin. Anton squinted at her, as if he was trying to find the real face behind all the makeup she had applied, exaggerating her features so that no one would recognize the prim, proper Lady Shan LeClaire underneath.

"Well, the Fox Den prefers to hire tarts," Anton said, rolling his eyes. "Or at least dresses them as such."

"There's nothing wrong with dressing this way," Shan chided, and Anton winced.

"It's just not you."

"Maybe not," Shan agreed, twirling a strand of her curled and blown-out hair around her finger. "But it's fun for a night."

"I could handle this on my own, you know."

"You can handle the nobles and their friends," Shan said, "and that's important. But it's good for the Sparrow to mingle with her birds. Besides, they're the ones I need right now."

The murderer hadn't killed a single Blood Worker yet—they targeted the Unblooded exclusively. It wasn't the nobles who were worried and talking and planning—it was everyone else. And that wasn't even getting into what Lord Dunn was planning.

Which was exactly why Shan had to don this particular outfit.

Besides, she had Anton with his friends among the noble children tonight, the gamblers and the players who saw him as a riotous good time, despite his Unblooded nature—or perhaps because of it. And with Samuel weaseling his way into Isaac's good graces, intentional or not, his innocent eyes and pleasing features cutting through the Royal Blood Worker's defenses, she was free. Free to be here in one of her many disguises, answering to a name that felt more her own than the one her parents had given her.

Sparrow.

"I still can't believe that you're doing this," Anton said, and Shan knew who and what he was talking about without him needing to say. "That you're working for *him.*"

"I can handle it," Shan said. "And it's not like I can allow a monster to run my streets killing Unblooded. Besides, this will help us in the long run. We've never been able to get a bird in the palace—"

"You're gambling with your very life," Anton interrupted. "Remember Father? And that was only because of his paranoia. If he finds out that you're treasonous—"

"He won't," Shan swore. "Not until it's too late. Listen, we can put all of our plans in place. We can seed dissent for years if we want to. But to make actual change we need this access—we need to know how he works."

Her plan was madness, she wasn't too proud to admit that to herself. It was like a mortal fighting a god. It didn't matter how talented a Blood Worker she was—the King's power had been augmented by centuries of murder and blood, and if they couldn't find a way to tear him back down to their level nothing they did would matter.

Anton glanced up, his dark eyes burning as realization struck him. "That's why you're back with de la Cruz."

She shifted uncomfortably. "I was never with him, precisely."

"Liar," Anton snapped, the hurt etched across his features. "I thought you didn't lie to me."

"I'm not lying!" Shan rubbed her temples. "It was never anything formal, never anything . . . serious."

It had been their last year at the Academy, when their stress was at their highest, tumbling into each other's arms more times that Shan could count. But it had never been anything more than two friends blowing off steam, not until the end.

After finals, when they were waiting for their grades to come in. They had celebrated in the flat Isaac had inherited from his parents with several bottles of wine that Shan had sneaked from her father's cellar.

And, for just a single night, they had believed that they could make a future together.

Then the next day the final rankings were posted, and the King summoned Isaac to his side.

And nothing was the same.

"Besides," she muttered, "it was just a stupid, childish infatuation. It meant nothing and it changes nothing."

"Blood and steel, Shan." Anton sighed. "You're playing with fire. I'm not fool enough to miss that he wants you back—and neither are you."

She wasn't so sure about that. She had, after all, seen the way he had looked at Samuel—so sweet, so innocent, so tempting. "I can handle it."

"Please tell me you're not thinking about it."

Shan shrugged. "It would be a useful alliance; you have to admit that."

If he isn't the serial murderer.

Anton made a noise of disgust, and she couldn't help the bristle of anger that rose, sharp as her own claws. "Just because you found yourself a love match doesn't mean that it's possible—or even feasible—for everyone. I have a duty." She held up her hand to stop him from arguing, always with the arguing. "We're here."

The carriage pulled to a stop around the back of the club, and Anton leaned forward. "Fine. But just hear me out—if de la Cruz hurts you again, I don't care how strong of a Blood Worker he is, I will break him."

Shan laughed. "Nothing like a display of gross masculinity to warm a sister's heart," she said, pressing a kiss to his cheek. "But I am glad that you care. Have fun in there."

He caught her hand, squeezing it once for luck. "You, too."

Throwing him a final grin, Shan slipped from the carriage and into the seedy back alley before the carriage took him round to the front where he'd enter with all the other patrons. But Shan wasn't here to gamble. She was here to work.

Holding her head high, she walked in as if she belonged. With her outfit and her attitude, no one questioned her. The girls who worked here rotated in and out so quickly that there was always a new face, new girls filling in, scraping out a night's wage when it was offered. It was better than the other options, after all. The Fox Den kept their patrons in line—they tolerated no wandering hands or private back rooms. It was frequented by Blood Workers of all types—and the occasional Unblooded with enough money or prestige—but the customers were there for the tables and the alcohol, not for the *company.*

And if a few of the serving girls or table dealers caught snippets of their conversations, what of it? If the Blood Workers never bothered to learn the names of the people who served them, barely treated them as human, what harm could it do to sell those little secrets to the one who treated them with respect and lined their pockets with gold?

It was a good system, and Shan had missed this work in the past weeks. Being Lady LeClaire was its own kind of thrill, stepping into the games of Dameral and earning the respect of those around her.

But this? This was just fun.

Shan grabbed a tray of goblets from the kitchen, lifting them up over her shoulder as she sauntered out onto the floor of the gambling hell. She was immediately assaulted by the noise—the shouts of the patrons over the craps table, the groans from the vingt-et-un, the rattle of the roulette wheel.

And while she slipped between the tables—between the Blood Workers she had grown up with, their brothers and sisters and cousins—not a single one of them recognized her. They just took fresh goblets as she snatched their empty ones, their eyes passing over her as if she were just a piece of furniture.

But the workers? *They* took note of her, they were the ones who recognized her, who bothered to learn her face, her name—well, the false name she used for this—and the Sparrow she wore around her neck. As she dropped off her tray in the kitchen, they leaned in and whispered in her ear. As she brought fresh, cool water to the dealers, they, too, thanked her and whispered in her ear.

There was an undercurrent of panic, though, that Shan hadn't encountered before. For every bit of gossip they brought to her, there was another whisper of fear. Who was this murderer? What did they want? Who was next? How could the Blood Workers not care at all? Why wouldn't they do anything to help?

She didn't have any words of comfort. What was another Unblooded in the streets to them? There were still so many others to drain blood from, anyway.

But Shan turned none away, not even those who didn't bring forth any useful information. She bought their loyalty with a little bit of kindness and a sympathetic ear. They were used to being overlooked, ignored and forgotten. But for a little respect, she earned their trust—and the promise to send word through the normal channels if something did come up.

If there was any real lead. She might not be a member of the Guard, and to most of them she wasn't even a Blood Worker, but all of them knew that information was power. And in this case, safety.

Even if they did know something, most of them would never go to the Blood Workers and Shan didn't blame them for that. The Eternal King wanted this murderer caught, but not for the safety of the Unblooded. It was for the affront to his rules, for the shame of this happening under his watch, for the unrest it was causing.

But she would see these people protected.

After a few hours her head was swimming with information, her heart heavy with their fears. It was still a little too early for her to slip out without raising suspicion, even though all her contacts had come to her. Even though it was unlikely that one of the nobles would notice a worker leaving early. So, she continued to work, keeping one eye on her brother as he charmed his way through the night.

Shan might have been the mastermind of their schemes, but Anton had his own brilliance about him. He could twist a conversation round and round, leading people to the very thing they did not wish to talk about, but in such a way that it seemed natural. And since Sir LeClaire was nothing more than an Unblooded drunkard and gambler, they never suspected him of anything—they bragged and gossiped around him like he was a simpleton, never realizing that they were being used.

It wasn't the path she would have taken, but it was effective, and it brought Anton a wealth of information that Shan could never have earned.

She was turning away from his vingt-et-un table after he had pulled another winning hand—what luck!—when she was grabbed by the wrist, pulled off the floor and shoved against the wall.

Her fingers clenched around the empty tray, an instinctive need for her claws. Tilting her head up, she prepared to chastise the patron for breaking the rules, but the words died on her lips as she stared into a pair of familiar dark eyes.

"Shan?" Isaac breathed, so low and quiet that she wasn't sure she heard it at all.

Her heart thudded in her chest—he wasn't supposed to be here, and, even worse, he wasn't supposed to recognize her. Wrenching her arm away from him, she whispered, "Not here." She glanced pointedly over to the servants' corridors that led back to the washrooms. Isaac's gaze flickered back and forth, and he nodded.

"I'll be right back with your wine, sir," Shan said loudly, and Isaac smiled slightly. Tucking the tray against her chest, she moved through the crowds, but she could still feel his eyes on her. She didn't look back, despite the urge to. Tonight, she was just a plain working-class woman, and he was one of them.

Blood and steel, she hadn't even realized he frequented the Den. He had never shown interest in gambling when they were young. When had that changed? And worse, why hadn't she realized it? Despite everything—maybe *because* of everything—she should have kept better track of him, of what he was doing without her.

He was the Royal Blood Worker, after all.

Ducking into the corridor, she pressed against the wall, taking deep, steadying breaths. Moments later Isaac rounded the corner, as if he were headed to the washroom, but Shan grabbed him and shoved him into the storeroom, closing and locking the door behind them.

For a minute they simply stared at each other in the dim glow of the witch light, Isaac's eyes roaming all over her outfit, but Shan was more focused on the bags under his eyes, on the smell of cigarette smoke and alcohol floating from him. On every bit of him that looked frayed.

Isaac was the first to speak, arching an eyebrow at her. "If you wanted my attention, you have it."

Shan ignored his gibe. "How did you know it was me?"

His brow furrowed. "What? Did you think a bit of makeup and a short dress would do that much? I'd recognize you anywhere, Shan."

She closed her eyes for just a moment, letting his words sink in. It was only natural that he would—they were imprinted on each other, after all. Even after all this time, after everything. He had always *seen* her, and she couldn't hide from him now. "I'm working, Isaac."

"I hadn't realized the LeClaire fortune had fallen quite this far."

Rolling her eyes, Shan dropped the tray and perched on a pile of boxes. "Not like that."

His eyes had fallen to her chest as soon as she removed the tray, and it only took a second for him to make the connection, his mouth popping in a soft *oooh*. "Your power isn't in money or name," he said, reaching out to brush his fingers against her necklace. "But in something even less tangible."

"But far more useful," Shan said, smiling because she couldn't help it. She was proud of everything she had done, all that she had created, and even though Isaac had left her, she needed him to see it. To understand everything she had done and become.

And be proud.

When his eyes lit up, the haze of alcohol fading just a bit, she felt her heart soar.

"You are utterly, amazingly, wonderfully brilliant," he said, locking eyes with her. "You're the Sparrow."

She knew it was foolish—beyond foolish—for him to know, but she could not stop herself. Not with the way he was looking at her. "I see you've heard of me."

"Every information broker in Aeravin has," Isaac said. "But I don't think anyone suspects someone so young." He laughed, catching her by the hand and spinning her around, taking in her costume once more. "And no one recognizes you?"

"People see what they want to see," Shan said with a shrug. "They see the color of my skin, my outfit, my features—and they draw their own conclusions."

Isaac stepped closer, cupping her chin and tilting her head up. He ran his thumb across her cheek, and he was close enough for her to smell the wine on his breath. "They're all fools if they can't see you."

Her heart stopped, and she knew they were standing on the precipice of a mistake. "You're drunk."

"Not that drunk," he said, leaning closer and catching her mouth with his. His hands found her back—large and warm, she could feel the press of them through the thin material of her corset—and he was pulling her close, pressing her against him. Her hands landed on his waist without her even making the decision, old instincts flaring to life, and he dipped his face down.

As he caught her lips with hers.

As she lifted herself up on her tiptoes to meet him halfway.

He kissed her roughly, desperately, one hand rising to tangle in her hair, pulling her back so that he could dominate the kiss, holding her in place as he licked into her mouth like he could wipe away the last few years with the pressure of it.

And though it lit her up like a fire, heat rising low in her core as it forced a whine from her throat, she could still taste the undercurrent of alcohol on his tongue. A bitter reminder that, as hungry as he was for her, this was an indulgence that he might not make sober.

It was always like this with him, stealing her affections in the shadows. He was so cautious about his reputation, his goals, his plans, walking that careful line between taking what he wanted and doing what was expected of him.

She pulled back, though it was the last thing she wanted, though she ached for him to keep touching her, and whispered, "Not like this." Isaac dropped her, looking up at her with such pain in his eyes, old wounds ripped open, and she forced herself to be cruel. "This is your problem, Isaac. You don't know what you want. You never did. And until you do this cannot happen."

He turned away, and she wasn't sure what he was going to do. But he just whispered, "You're right," and slumped forward, curling in on himself. He wasn't angry, she realized. He was shattered.

"Fuck, Isaac." She didn't push him away, and after a second's deliberation, she whispered. "Talk to me."

Isaac just stared blankly ahead, his dark eyes cold and empty. "It's nothing, Shan."

"Clearly."

"It's been a lot," he said, at last. "I've worked so hard, sacrificing so much."

She bit her lip, watching him as he struggled for words. He had given up everything to become the man the King needed him to be, including her. But there was something more going on, even if he wouldn't say it. She knew him well enough to recognize that. "What has he threatened?"

He flinched, spinning away from her. "You know nothing, Shan."

"Then tell me!"

Isaac stood, staring at her, his chest heaving as he warred with himself. She wanted to reach out, to grab him and shake him till he saw sense. It had been years, yes, but there was still something here, and perhaps they could claw their way back to it—together.

If they both learned to trust just a little bit.

But he turned away, his expression cold and grave, and that tiny spark of hope died in her chest.

"I should go," Isaac said. "I am sorry, though." He trailed his fingers down her arm one last time. "About that ... well. Goodnight."

She said nothing in response, waiting till he was gone, then collapsed onto the floor. This day was altogether too much, and she needed a few moments just to breathe. Blood and steel, she was a horrible cliché of a woman, to be reduced so because of a man, and she hated herself for it. So she made a decision—if he couldn't reach for her, she wouldn't reach for him.

She had wasted enough of her life on Isaac de la Cruz.

She didn't let herself linger. She allowed herself three long, deep breaths, and then pushed herself back to her feet.

Chapter Twenty-Two

Samuel

Several days after his meeting with Isaac, Samuel was summoned to meet with Shan. The footman showed Samuel in, directing him to an area of the LeClaire townhouse that he had not yet explored. It was ridiculous, really, how many rooms these houses had—far more than any family would need. But at least Shan had her brother, so it couldn't be as lonely as the sterile place he now called home, just him and the servants who didn't know how to treat him, tiptoeing around him like his kindness was just a mask and his true nature—his Aberforth nature—would soon rear its ugly head.

There were only a handful of people in this new life who treated him like a person, and one of them appeared before him. Shan took him by the hand, throwing a coy smile over her shoulder as she led him on. They could have been lovers heading for a secret tryst, or two friends preparing for a twisted scheme. For the briefest second, Samuel let himself believe that was true. That Shan was interested in him for who he was, not simply the blood in his veins.

It was a sweet lie, but Samuel was too cruel to allow it more than a breath to flourish. He shoved it all aside to focus on the reason he was here—to discuss the task the Eternal King had given them: murder and mystery and bloodshed.

But Shan didn't lead him to a study or a library, as expected, but to her own Blood Working laboratory. He recognized the same instruments the Eternal King had in his, though he didn't know their names, strange and shining along the walls. But there was more than that—everywhere he looked he found signs of Shan. They were in the books and journals scattered around the room, notes jammed in between the pages. There were diagrams of the human body that stripped away the skin to reveal the veins beneath, with annotations scribbled in an ever more familiar hand, and Samuel stepped forward to read Shan's theories of magic.

She didn't stop him, though it didn't matter. He couldn't decipher her secrets anyway.

"Why are we here, Shan?"

She smiled, leaning casually against the door as she slid the lock in. "It is the safest place in my entire home. Every Blood Worker guards their laboratory—and I worked hard to make this one mine."

"It's rather . . ." Samuel searched for a word, one that wasn't *intimidating* or *gruesome*. He couldn't find one that was also true.

"It's a lot," she admitted. "Especially if you haven't studied Blood Working. But there is nothing here that you wouldn't find in any classroom in the Academy. Or, I'm sure, in the Eternal King's own sanctuary."

He heard the unspoken question there, and he turned slowly, taking in all the details before he spoke again. "He has a sink in his."

"Of course he does." Shan shook her head. "I'd love to make that addition, but finances being what they are . . . Anyway, I know you've been having meetings with Sir de la Cruz about your magic. What has he had to say?"

"Keeping yourself informed, I see," he muttered, his hand automatically going to the place where Isaac had drawn his blood just days ago. He swore he could still feel the echoes of his touch, and he wondered if he was going mad.

"It is my job," Shan reminded him. "And I want to help you as well. I'm sure you realize the King has ulterior motives for your training."

"I'm not an idiot." Samuel pulled his hand through his hair, absolutely destroying the proper queue his valet had spent so long on. Oh well. "I know what he wants of me. It's mostly been . . . practice." He still couldn't keep the distaste from his voice—yes, Isaac had been right. Control was getting easier.

But he still didn't like using it.

Shan, though, was always so attentive. "Mostly? What else have they done?"

He turned away from her, not wanting to see the disappointment in her eyes when he told her. It was bad enough when he was breaking the rules left by his dead mother—he suspected that Shan would somehow be worse than her spectre. "Not them. It's just been Isaac."

"Just Isaac," Shan repeated. "And what did *just Isaac* do?"

"He wanted some of my blood," Samuel said. "For study."

Shan exhaled sharply. "You did not."

"I did." He turned around before she could even begin. "Shan, he thinks he might be able to fix it."

Her anger melted away, replaced by something softer and somehow harder to bear. "Oh, Samuel."

"You don't think it's possible?"

She didn't answer right away. "I . . . honestly don't know. But if you like, perhaps we can try."

He could barely breathe. "You'd do that?"

"Naturally. I've always been fascinated by the Aberforth Gift, and—" she hesitated, that pitying look back on her face "—it's clear it makes you terribly unhappy. Besides, such a talent is just as much a liability as it is a boon."

"A liability?" He was surprised. "I doubt the King would agree."

"Trust is valuable in politics, Samuel," Shan explained, "and if the truth about you ever got out that trust would be lost. Forever. So while it certainly has its uses for the life you want, you'd be better off without it." She stepped over to a metal table, gesturing for him to follow. "Now, take off your clothes from the waist up."

Samuel flushed, crossing his arms in front of himself. He must have misheard her. "Wait, what?"

"Your clothes," Shan said again. "Off."

So much for that. He had to clear his throat to get the next word out. "Why?"

"Because I don't want to get blood all over them," Shan said, as if he were a complete simpleton. "Because then we'd have to burn them, like we do with all bloodied materials. And unless you're hiding a second outfit somewhere, you'd have to head home half-naked." She ran a hand down her dress—a simple dark cotton affair with no frills or baubles. "Why do you think I am wearing this?"

His cheeks were burning even more now, but he couldn't stop himself from following the movement of her hand. Even in such a plain outfit, she was still a beautiful woman—and he knew that she knew it, too. The simple dress hugged her curves, drawing his attention to the fullness of her breasts, tapering down to a thin waist he ached to feel under his hands. She was beautiful in the most exquisite of dresses, she would be beautiful in rags, she would be beautiful in nothing at all.

Turning away, he stopped that line of thought cold as he shrugged his jacket off. "Isaac didn't make me do this."

Shan laughed, and he heard her step closer. "And here I thought Isaac was a clever man. What's the matter, Samuel? Are you shy?"

"Don't be ridiculous," Samuel muttered, throwing his cravat over his carefully folded jacket. "I'm fine."

"If it helps, this is all for purely academic purposes," Shan said. "Nothing untoward at all."

Samuel stopped himself from calling bullshit on that. She was clearly drawing some amusement from it. But he would not let his nervousness show any more than it already was. "I'm fine, Shan," he repeated, with far more confidence than he felt, and he quickly pulled his shirt over his head and added it to the pile.

When he turned back around, Shan stood staring at him, her hand at the base of her throat as her eyes roamed. Samuel didn't say a thing as she took him in, the weight of her gaze as heavy as a physical touch, the silence thick and impenetrable between them.

At last she forced her eyes back up to his, her mask in place as if nothing had happened. "Please, have a seat over here." She drummed her fingers on a table that was just a slab of metal, cold and unyielding, and Samuel slid into one of the sterile metal chairs that surrounded it.

"I hope you don't mind sharing a little more blood," she began, and he made a face that had her laughing. "Don't worry. I have a safe." She pointed towards one of the bookshelves. "Hidden back there, behind a series of wards keyed to my bloodline. Only Anton and I can access it. It's not foolproof, but it's pretty damned good. If you don't want to, I'll only take what I need for immediate tests, while you're still here, and burn the remainders. But . . . you gave Isaac your blood, correct?"

He could already tell where her argument was going, and his resolve was crumbling like a wall of sand. "Yeah."

"Then let's make it so I can be truly helpful, don't you think?" Shan looked at him, and he nodded. "Also it's easier this way. Now we don't need to keep coming up with excuses for you to visit me."

"Ah, my company isn't wanted, then?" Samuel pouted, and Shan smiled slightly.

"You know that's not true. But we both have reputations to think of."

Samuel rubbed the back of his neck, annoyance rising. "I'm getting pretty tired of hearing that advice. I can make my own decisions."

"Yes, you can," Shan admitted. "But you still need to be careful. People will start to think we're lovers."

"Won't that help you?" Samuel asked, then felt heat rise through him. He cursed his pale skin—he knew without seeing it the sight it must have painted—but continued digging himself deeper. "Your reputation, I mean. Not that I'm some great—it's just that I'm an Aberforth—" She watched him sputter on with a smile, until he eventually shut up and buried his face in his hands with a groan.

"You're not wrong," she admitted, "but it could hurt other

opportunities—especially yours. As you said, you're an Aberforth. And an Aberforth can do so much better than a LeClaire." She lined up a row of vials in front of him. "Ready when you are."

He didn't know what to say—that despite the fact that he barely knew her, really, he'd still take her over any of those other Blood Workers. When she looked at him, she didn't see only a title, or a power, to be used, but the man behind them. And damn it all if that little thing didn't make all the difference. Besides, he didn't care if he could do *better*, whatever that meant, because she was already better than all the others combined.

He just held out his arm to her. "Take as much as you need, but you're not getting rid of me that easily."

Shan's smile was so brilliant that he felt as dazzled as if he had looked directly into the sun. "I wouldn't dream of it." Reaching up, she pulled the white ribbon from her hair, the dark waves falling down past her shoulders, making her look strangely soft and ethereal.

He kept his focus on her as she went to work instead of the needle and the blood. He concentrated on the soft way she touched him, so different than Isaac, but just as burning. Her touches were feather-light, almost teasing, guiding where Isaac's were grounding, and she worked in a quiet way that soothed him as the blood flowed.

As the second vial filled, she looked up at him. "Not too bad, right?"

"Not really," Samuel admitted. "Just . . . strange."

Shan glanced aside. "Sometimes I forget how different it must be, growing up without Blood Working. How strange and macabre it must seem."

"Seem?" Samuel laughed. "Shan, this is the very definition of macabre. You take blood and use it to control and twist a person to your will."

"Is it any different from what you can do?"

Frowning, Samuel replied, "No, but I wouldn't call my ability comforting, either."

Shan only shrugged. "Not all Blood Working is so dangerous.

We can heal, reunite families, create the strongest protective wards. There is a lot of good in my power."

Samuel hummed in response, remembering the details of what Isaac had shared with him, what Blood Working had allowed him to achieve. And yet, there was still so much harm being done. "But at what cost?" he asked, even if he didn't know the answer himself.

"Is it better to be weak?" Shan countered. "To have no power, no control, nothing to offer?"

"Shan." He moved his free arm, reaching to brush her hair away from her face, and she leaned ever so slightly into his touch. Her skin was so delicate, and he found himself wishing he could explore it further, find all the other places where she was soft and warm. "I refuse to believe you are just your magic. You are brilliant and cunning and even without all this, you have gathered enough power to threaten a kingdom." His smile widened. "And you did find me."

"Perhaps." She straightened her back, moving away as she focused on filling the vials. His hand fell limply to the table—he didn't know what to do with himself if he wasn't touching her. "But I don't know if I could have become that woman if I didn't have Blood Working to guide me."

"Maybe," Samuel said. "Maybe not. It doesn't really matter, though. Whatever you might have been, you are still a remarkable woman."

Shan laughed—a real, sudden laugh that left him breathless. "Blood and steel, Samuel. I see I don't have to worry about you. Soon you'll be charming all of Dameral."

"I'm not trying to be charming," Samuel stammered. "I really mean it."

"I know you do." Shan refused to look at his face, instead focusing on pulling the needle from his arm. She swept away the needle and tube, and while she was distracted he carefully swiped the ribbon she had left on the table. He palmed it and slipped it into his pocket.

"What now?"

"Put stoppers on four of the vials," she instructed. "Leave the last open. We'll need it."

He did as she instructed, carefully sealing away most of the blood she had drawn. The last was left sitting open in front of him, and he stared into the pool of his own blood until Shan returned to his side.

"Drink it," she ordered, and he looked up at her in surprise. "It's how we access the power. In consuming the blood, we can gain access to the very life it holds."

"This is pointless," he said. "I tried the tests as a child. I never could do it."

"Maybe," Shan said with a shrug. "Maybe not. But whatever the case, I need to know if you can access it at all. Blood Working is difficult to explain to someone who doesn't have the power, but if you can get even a sense of it, that will help. Even the barest bit of power from the barest bit of blood. Indulge me."

"All of it?" he asked, his throat suddenly dry.

"Yes." She smiled at him. "Or can you not? It's something that children do in the Academy all the time. You cannot be afraid."

"Disgusted, more like." He snatched the vial and tossed it back, the taste of his own blood heavy on his tongue. It had only been out of his body for a few moments, but it was already viscous, sliding down his throat and making him shudder.

Shan watched him the whole time, her eyes never leaving his lips. "What do you feel?"

"Nauseated?" She smacked his arm, and he bit back a laugh. "All right, all right." He closed his eyes, waiting for something—anything—that felt like magic. He could still taste the blood on his lips, copper and salt, but he felt none of the power that Shan had promised him. Something *was* stirring inside him, though, something like his gift, but it was faint. It was a treacherous, fragile thing that kept slipping through his fingers whenever he tried to grasp it. "It's like—there's almost something? Am I doing it wrong?"

Shan reached out, her thumb tracing its way across his mouth, spreading the blood that still lingered there. "This might seem weird," she said, "but I swear it's for the magic." She gently pulled him towards her and sucked his lower lip between her teeth, her tongue lapping across it and wiping away every last drop.

It was the most exquisite torture.

"Hells, Shan," Samuel said, pulling back from her as his head spun and lust shot through him, an insistent thrum in his veins. "Warn me next time."

But Shan wasn't paying attention to him, her eyes were wide and unfocused. "That *is* odd." Grabbing the same needle she had used on him, she pricked her own finger and held it out to him. "Here."

Samuel's vision narrowed to the small bead of red on her fingertip. "You can't mean—"

"Come on," she said, exasperated. "Let me help you build the bridge. It works better when we both imbibe." She leaned across the table and pressed her thumb to his mouth, pushing past his lips. His teeth caught it, and he could taste her skin and blood on his tongue.

Forcing himself to meet her eyes, he worried the wound and forced even more blood out.

"Good," she whispered, then pulled back.

The whine that followed had nothing to do with magic.

"There," Shan said, settling back in her seat. "Do you feel me?"

"I ... uh," Samuel spluttered, "hells." He dug his nails into his thighs, trying valiantly to ignore the way his cock hardened. But with Shan sitting there, so alluring, the thrum of magic electric in the air, he could barely concentrate on her words. What sort of nonsense question was that? Of course he felt her. She was all he could focus on when they were this close.

Even when he shouldn't—when he should be keeping her at arm's length, not dancing dangerously closer to her in this game of desire.

"The bridge, Samuel."

"Oh, right." He closed his eyes again, ignoring the call of his own body and focusing on the tremulous connection between them. She was right—he *could* feel her. He ran his tongue over his teeth, focusing on the fading taste of her. It was different from his own blood—there was a headiness to it, a burn to it, like the cleanse of a strong liquor. It was rich and overpowering, just like her, threatening to overwhelm his senses and pull him under.

"There you are."

"Good." Her hand found his, clenching tightly. "Reach for me, Samuel."

He did, clawing his way through the power of the blood within to draw her closer. She was reaching back towards him as well, the connection between them growing stronger and more real with each passing second.

He could feel her heart, stepping ever closer in sync with his. The slow, steady beat of it guiding him, pulling him towards a well of power he never realized he had. It was there, hidden below the darkness that had grown within him, untapped and untouched. "This is . . ."

"Blood Working," Shan confirmed, wrapping her hands even tighter around his. "This is what we call the bridge. It connects two— or more—living sources of power. You can feel my magic, right?"

"Yes, you're here with me." He could feel her, a gentle touch across his veins, stirring his blood and his heart and his body in a way he had never known before. He breathed and she was there. His heart skipped a beat, and hers skipped with him. The power in his blood stirred in response to the power in hers, and they were somehow one.

Shan was sliding closer to him, falling off her chair and pulling him down with her. They tangled together on the floor, Shan perched on his lap, skin against skin as they pressed together. She slotted over his hips, fitting against him like she was made to be there, and Samuel had to lean back and press his hands into the floor, forcing himself to remain still when it would have been so easy for her to hold him down and grind against his aching hardness.

Wrapping her hand around his throat, Shan pressed her thumb against his pulse as the bridge between them grew stronger—a blazing path of blood that seemed as real as anything. As real as the pressure of her hand closing around his neck. If he leaned forward just a bit, Shan would cut off his breath, leaving him entirely at her mercy.

He had never wanted anything so badly in his life.

He could feel her *inside* him, running her fingers along the dark well of power that stirred in his chest. It woke under her touch, coming to life with the all-consuming anger and viciousness that he normally tamped down, fighting her invasion tooth and nail.

"Blood and steel," she swore, pulling back from his embrace and his soul. "You live with this?"

"Always."

"And is it usually this . . . hungry?" Her hands roved over his chest, settling over his heart, warm against bare flesh.

Samuel swallowed hard, her very touch inflaming him. His hands settled over her waist, and though she was small, he could still feel the strength in her, and he prayed she wouldn't break, no matter what he did. "Yes, it is. I've been learning to fight it, to keep it in its place, but it's underlying everything, begging to be unleashed."

Shan trembled. "You could break anyone to your will, force them to follow you, to do whatever you asked." She looked up at him but there was no fear in her eyes, just a hunger that had nothing to do with power. "You want to be rid of this, but you could be a god."

"I don't want to be a god," he whispered, though the darkness in him stirred with possibilities. It would be so easy to let go, to unleash it. To force Shan to bend and break. To take her, make her his—utterly and completely and in every imaginable way.

Hells, that was too appealing an image, as it would be so easy to make it true. She probably wouldn't even resist him. She probably wanted it, too, with the way she leaned against him, sharing the same breath, her hands roaming his body, like it was her due.

All he had to do was take.

He shoved her off him, leaping to his feet as he tore at his skin. He wished it was gone, that he could reach inside and grab this monstrosity and tear it out by the roots. But it wasn't that simple.

It was as much a part of him as the very blood in his veins.

Shan caught his hands before he could break skin, stilling him with a touch. "Don't, Samuel."

"Do you see now why I need it gone?" he asked, the question spilling from his lips, and the pitying look she gave him tore him deep. "What it's making me?"

"It's not making you anything," she said. "But I'll keep my promise. I'll share everything I know with Isaac."

"Can it be removed?"

"I don't know," she admitted. "It's part of your Blood Working—it *is* your Blood Working. It's completely taken it over and that's why you can't grasp it."

Samuel huffed out a broken laugh. "So it's hopeless."

She shook her head roughly, her hair falling around her face. "No, don't. Even if we don't have an answer yet, we've only begun. And you've learned a bit about Blood Working."

"And you've learned what kind of monster I am."

Shan frowned. "Stop it." Her fingers twined with his. "This power, it's part of you, but it isn't you. That you've resisted its call for so long is what makes you a good person. But me? I'm not one." Her voice was soft, and she looked so terribly unsure. "I have no illusions about that."

"Neither do I," Samuel said, "but you're wrong."

"I've killed, Samuel." She looked up at him, not with tears in her eyes, but with a fierce, desperate pride. "I've lied and cheated and blackmailed. And if I had to, I'd do it all again."

"So?" Samuel said, brushing a thumb across her cheek. "We all do what we must to survive."

"And you're a damned fool," she snarled, reaching up and pulling him into a kiss.

It wasn't anything like he expected a kiss to be—it was rough and vicious, more teeth and biting than anything else. He tasted blood— his or hers, he couldn't tell—and she moaned against him. But with her mouth on his, any logic—any reason he was holding onto—to keep her away, vanished. There was only this moment.

And it felt right.

He pulled her close, wrapping his arms around her as she tangled her hands in his hair, holding him captive in her embrace. It was a battle and a promise and everything he had never known, and he wanted to kiss her until the world came crashing down around them.

Shan pressed her mouth against his jaw, his neck, biting and nipping her way across his flesh as he lifted her up. She was so light in his arms, and he slammed her down on the table, the bottles rolling and sliding as he crawled over her, sliding himself into the waiting gap between her legs, her skirts rucked up around her hips. He pinned her down with his weight, and she didn't resist him, only rose her hips up to meet his, as her hands wound in his hair, pulling him where she wanted him. Shan bared her neck to him in an open invitation, and Samuel pressed his mouth against her skin.

It was so easy to bite into the soft dip of her throat, flesh catching between his teeth as he sucked hard. Shan gasped, pressing even closer to him, and that familiar darkness rose within, crawling up his throat as a single word tore past his lips—guttural and harsh and not at all him. *"Mine."*

Shan locked up in his arms, her dark eyes wide and afraid, and he saw a second too late what had happened. The power he had tried so hard to deny had crept up when he wasn't looking, when his control had slipped, and Shan slumped against the table, her eyes wide and vacant as she lay there, unresisting, unresponsive, unknowing.

For him to take a warm body with no soul, to find pleasure that was only his.

"No," he gasped out as reality crashed back in, his lust fading against the horror of what he had done. "I didn't mean it!" He grabbed every bit of his power, bending it to his will, and threw it at her. A command to counteract a command, fighting his own magic. "Shan, don't!"

She shuddered again, her body and mind struggling between the contradicting commands, then went slack all at once. Silence filled the room, broken only by the harsh sound of their breathing.

Eventually, she pushed herself up on her elbows, and he couldn't bear to face her.

But she was fine. It was over.

Sliding himself off the table, Samuel turned away as tremors ran through him. He was such a fool, a damned fool for not seeing this coming. He thought it was bad before, he thought he understood the depths to which he could fall.

A stolen kiss seemed childish in comparison to this.

"We can't do this," he whispered, barely audible.

"Oh, Samuel," she began. "It was an accident."

But he just spun around, silencing her with a soft, gentle kiss to the forehead. "I cannot risk, I cannot ... becoming him," he explained, and her mask cracked. He didn't even need to say his father's name, to utter the crime that had led to his own creation.

He would have her when he knew she was entirely willing, entirely of her own choice, or not at all.

"All right." Her hand came up to cup his cheek, and he leaned into the softness of her touch. "If that is what you want, I'll respect it. But we will figure this out, one way or another."

"Thank you."

She nodded, then slipped off the table, putting a deliberate amount of space between them. "I still have much to study."

"That you do."

"You'd better put your shirt back on," Shan said, heading towards a bookshelf and grabbing a thick tome. Her tone was brisk, professional, though her cheeks were still flushed and her hair askew.

Samuel was sure he looked no better, but he grabbed his clothes from the chair where he had left them, determined to act as normal as she was. "And can I help?"

"Naturally." Shan's smile was quick, there and gone, and Samuel breathed out hard.

She was going to be the death of him.

—†—

"Lord Aberforth," Jacobs said, bowing as Samuel entered his town-house. "You have a visitor."

"I . . . do?" Samuel rubbed his temples. He was tired and confused and energy still thrummed relentlessly through his veins, aching for something he could never have. He wanted nothing more than a cold bath to kill the fire in his blood, then his soft bed, but he was a Lord now. And appearances must be kept. "Who is it?"

Jacobs looked uncertain, only the slightest hesitation in his words. "Antonin LeClaire the Second."

"Anton?" Samuel blinked in confusion. Why would he be *here*? Samuel had just been at the LeClaires; wouldn't it have been easier to meet there?

"He's in the parlor, my lord. He would not be dissuaded," Jacobs said, and the thinness of his lips showed how he felt about that. Arriving here without an invitation, without even a title or the power of Blood Working to lean on, and then insisting on waiting. It was the height of impropriety.

Samuel smiled, slightly, at Jacobs' loyalty and devotion to order. It had only been a few weeks since he had begun living there, but already Jacobs had started to feel like a staple in his life, there in the background, always ready to help. They were starting to get a feel for each other, and even a grudging kind of respect.

"It's all right, I'll see him."

"As you say, my lord." Jacobs bowed again. "Should I send for anything?"

Samuel glanced at the clock—it was already well past dinner, and he didn't have a damned clue what the appropriate thing to offer was. "Uh, what do you recommend?"

Jacobs chuckled, a little surprised, but if he was judging him he did a good job hiding it. "At this time? Brandy, whisky, the hard liquors."

"Right. That would be great."

"There are some in the parlor," Jacobs offered, kindly. Then he stepped forward, adjusting Samuel's cravat and smoothing down his jacket. He shot an exasperated look at the state of Samuel's hair, but there was nothing to be done about that. "There, you're ready."

Samuel nodded. "Thank you, Jacobs." Jacobs patted him kindly on the shoulder, and Samuel pressed past him towards the parlor.

Anton was facing away from him when he entered, already searching through the previously untouched cabinet of alcohol that had come with the townhouse. Well, at least that made this easier—he didn't have to pretend he knew which liquor was which.

"Close the door," Anton said, without looking at him. He was very focused on pouring his drink. "I don't want us overheard."

Samuel considered rebelling just for the hell of it. Anton did barge in on him, after all, and he'd had a very long day. But his better judgement won out. If he was here on Shan's orders, privacy would not just be wise, but necessary. He closed the door and locked it for good measure.

"I was just at your townhouse, you know."

"And I said I don't want to be overheard," Anton said, turning around. "All of the servants are in Shan's pocket. It's not safe there."

Samuel couldn't help staring. There was so much of his sister in him. From the fall of his hair to the tone of his skin. Their eyes, their cheekbones, the curve of his smile. Even the way he carried himself. It was a strange reflection of Shan, and Samuel couldn't look away.

"Easy there," Anton said, at last breaking the silence. "I'm spoken for."

He flushed. It wasn't that Anton was unattractive—his attractiveness was an objective fact—but this was Shan's *brother*. "I didn't—it wasn't like that."

"Ah, I see." Anton gestured to his face. "You see her in me, don't you? Funny how that works, being twins and all."

"You do share some similarities," Samuel admitted.

Anton snorted. "Trust me, it's all in the looks. Aside from that, my sister and I are like night and day." There was bitterness in his voice, and he downed his drink in one gulp. Turning back to the liquor cabinet, he said, "You have a great collection."

"I'm glad you enjoy it. But why are you here?"

"Well, I'm hoping you can give me some answers, Aberforth." Anton sipped his drink this time, his dark eyes watching him closely. "About some of the schemes my sister is planning."

Samuel tensed. "Why would I have that kind of information?"

"I might not know all that my sister does," Anton said coolly. "And I might be privy to more of her mind than most, but I know that she still conceals as much as she can from me for my own protection." He clenched his glass so tightly that Samuel feared it was going to shatter in his hand. "But don't you think me a fool, Samuel Aberforth," he whispered, stalking closer, and Samuel felt suddenly like prey.

Perhaps he wasn't as different from his sister as he thought.

"I don't know why you would think I would know any more," Samuel repeated. "I am just one of her many pawns."

"Are you playing with me?" Anton snapped. "Or are you that foolish? I know the two of you are involved."

Samuel could feel the burn of blood in his cheeks, and he knew that his skin was stained red. "We are not!"

Anton studied him closely. "I didn't mean it like that, though clearly you'd like to be. Interesting."

Turning away, Samuel suddenly understood the desire for a drink. He couldn't, obviously, but something about Antonin LeClaire made him wish he could indulge. "We are associates, nothing more."

Anton's laugh was surprisingly sharp. "Oh, Aberforth. You are fucked."

"I'm not looking for romance," Samuel said simply, because it was true. He couldn't risk it, and he learned that lesson well.

"What's that saying?" Anton snapped his fingers. "Right, those who have sworn off romance are bound to find it. But anyway, fascinating as this is, I'm not here to speculate on Shan's love life. Or realistically, lack thereof."

"I was telling you the truth, Sir LeClaire."

"Oh, no," Anton grimaced. "None of that."

"Fine," Samuel snapped. "I'm sorry I couldn't help more, *Anton*."

"I really didn't expect you to," Anton admitted, setting his empty glass down. "I don't know why I even bothered coming."

Samuel couldn't help the way he bristled. He knew, logically, that it wasn't personal. That Shan clearly thrived on secrets, that she had plans within plans, and she used people as needed, confiding in no one. She had admitted as much this very night. And if even her twin didn't know the full extent of her plans, then who would?

It was understandable and disappointing all at once.

This was like the worst game of poker. They both had their cards, but they couldn't compare them without betraying Shan. And Samuel knew that neither of them would. It was an exercise in futility. "Then why did you?"

"Curiosity," Anton replied. "And misplaced hope."

Samuel shrugged. "And how did that work out for you?"

"Not well." But he looked up with a grin. "If you think that means I'm giving up, you're wrong. I don't give up. If we're going to be working together, you'd best learn that."

"We're going to be working together, then?"

Anton's grin turned sharp. "Haven't you learned anything yet? We all work for Shan. She's seen to that." Samuel sucked in a harsh breath, and Anton's facade cracked. "I'm not being cruel, Samuel. My sister is ... challenging. She has her plans, but she doesn't trust easily. Or at all."

Samuel bit his lip. Anton was right about that much. She was like ice, slow to melt, and Samuel feared that the very act of thawing would destroy something fundamental about her. It didn't stop him from wanting to try, though. "So now what?"

"Nothing," Anton said, without hesitation.

Samuel could only blink in confusion. "Nothing?"

"Nothing," Anton confirmed. "I learned what I needed to know."

"And what is that?"

"That it is too late," Anton replied. "You are already thoroughly her creature. She has that effect on people."

"You don't know anything about me," Samuel said, but Anton's words were true. He was her creature and he didn't know precisely when that had happened. But there was only a small part of him that feared what would happen when she realized it, too.

Anton chuckled. "It's funny. I wouldn't have expected the heir to the most dangerous family in Aeravin to be so innocent." His smile was all teeth, and he looked so much like his sister that Samuel's breath caught. "I can read you like a book, Lord Aberforth. I don't know her plans with you, or what she's going to do to you, but I can tell you care about her."

"I'm her ally, Anton."

"For now," Anton said, leaning back against the wall. He pulled off such a pose of elegant disdain that Samuel almost rolled his eyes.

"I'm going to help your sister in her plans," Samuel said, keeping deliberately vague. "To make Aeravin better. But I will not go behind her back. If she needs my help, I'll offer it directly."

Anton studied him for a long moment. "You really don't belong here, Aberforth."

Samuel met his gaze head on. "I really don't."

"Fine, then." Anton pushed away from the wall. He inclined his head—a mocking little bow—and swept out of the room with a dramatic air.

Samuel just stared after him, chilled to the bone. There was something off about this whole LeClaire family, even if he hadn't figured out the particulars yet. And he was entirely too caught up in their schemes.

But, strangely, he felt no desire to get out.

Chapter Twenty-Three

Shan

Shan directed her guests with a gracious smile, her entire expression and posture that of a woman who knew that she was being granted a second chance. It sickened her to have to pretend to do so—that she couldn't be the proud, strong woman that she was. But no one wanted that of the Lady LeClaire. Not yet. The Royal Blood Worker and the Lost Aberforth might favor her, might have earned her a spot back in this world, but she was still what she was.

Stained. Foreign. Inferior.

And she would be reminded of that for years to come. The game was a long one, Shan had known that from the start. But somehow it had been easier to be ignored completely than be welcomed but pitied.

Still, for her first salon this was turning out to be a resounding success. Samuel, of course, was here—thus securing the attention of the other nobles. Even if he never came to another one, the mere chance that the latest curiosity could show up meant that any gathering she threw for the next year would be well attended. Even if all he had done all night was sit awkwardly by the window, cup of tea in hand.

But the other guests were far livelier—Miss Lynwood and Miss Rayne had both accepted her invitation, and they had kept the conversation flowing pleasantly from topic to topic, from the balls they were the most excited about to the stunning new dresses they had commissioned. They chittered on with a larger group than she had expected to show up, all young heirs of Aeravin and their siblings, eager to see how the new Lady LeClaire presented herself.

Honestly, Shan only paid them the most superficial attention, noting instead the sly way they kept looking to Samuel. They would be the ones who spread the news of his attendance, and thus they served their entire purpose at this party.

No, the one she kept her eye on was far quieter. Young Amelia Dunn—daughter of her new secret partner. Shan had no doubt that she was here on her father's orders, but even so, her attendance helped. She was a jewel of Dameral society, despite the fact that she was a Blood Worker of only middling ability and looks, her face far too sharp and angular to be called pretty. But her father was on the Council of Lords and so everyone had sought her favor.

Though she was younger than Shan, having only been out for two Seasons, Shan's network assured her that she had already received and rejected five offers for her hand. For many it would have been a disaster, but for her it had only driven the price higher.

Amelia set her sights high, and though she was no beauty or skilled mage she was ruthless and clever enough to do everything she could to secure a stable future for herself. If Amelia hadn't been the daughter of a man she despised, Shan might have admired her.

But Kevan Dunn was everything wrong with Aeravin, and the plan that he had trapped her in only proved that. But like this salon—like her reputation—she was prepared to play the long game, even if she found it terribly distasteful in the moment. Now, she'd had to pay more attention to young Miss Dunn—and she decided to have Bart dig up what he could on her.

It would be helpful to have something on Amelia.

And Amelia, it seemed, would be kind enough to set things in motion.

"Have you heard about these dratted pamphlets?" she said during a lull in conversation. Everyone turned to her, but Amelia kept her eyes on Shan. This was the test she had been sent for—to see if Shan would keep her end of the bargain. "It's all the usual trash, but the latest ones have gotten rather incendiary."

Miss Morse leaned forward, her eyes wide. "You cannot expect me to believe you've read this nonsense?"

"I have," Amelia said gravely, raising her teacup to her lips. "If the rabble is becoming a problem, we need to know what they are plotting."

"They're not rabble. They're people."

A hushed silence fell at Samuel's words, and Amelia smiled.

"Ah, yes." She turned to him, every bit the predator who had found her prey. "You grew up amongst the Unblooded, didn't you?"

Shan watched as Samuel bristled, the anger flashing in his eyes, and weighed her options. She could jump in before things got ugly—but no. No, she'd let it play out, and then she'd swoop in with the reasonable, moderate option, swaying the crowd onto her side.

An Aberforth—especially one with as unusual a story as Samuel's—could recover from these odd beliefs. She could not.

Hopefully he would understand.

"I did," Samuel said, jutting his chin out in that way of his. So proud, so righteous. "Lived and worked as one of them."

"Fascinating," Amelia said. "So perhaps you should be the one to educate us, then, about their needs and wants. Since you know so much about them."

The crowd tittered, but she had played him expertly. Samuel was ready to fight, and the event could not have been more successful if Shan had planned it. She signaled for the maids to fetch fresh pots of tea while she waited for the perfect moment to enter the fray herself.

"It's simple," Samuel replied, throwing the words in Miss Dunn's face. "We start treating them like people instead of like cattle. Do away with the Blood Taxes, let them organize their labor unions, give them seats in the government."

"Lord Aberforth!" Amelia held her hand over her breast in a play at dramatics. "It appears that you are a radical."

"Maybe I am," Samuel admitted. "If it's considered radical to realize that those without magic aren't that different from the rest of us."

"But they're Unblooded," Miss Lynwood started, only to be cut off by Samuel slamming his hand down on the table.

"And that doesn't matter!" Samuel said, and Shan felt the stirrings of something dark and familiar in his voice. "The majority of these people are living in conditions that you cannot even begin to understand. The food you waste on a daily basis can feed a family for a week, and that is not even getting into all the other things you waste so much coin on. Maybe before you go deciding what's best you should—"

"Lord Aberforth does have a point," Shan said, catching the moment before it slipped past. Before the darkness that she recognized in Samuel slipped into his words into a command he couldn't take back. The memory of the previous day and the single word he had whispered in her ear still lingered with her, no matter what she did. It had been dark and terrifying and just a tiny bit appealing, not that she would dare admit that deviant thought aloud.

And she couldn't risk anyone else discovering that gift.

"Of course," she said, once she had everyone's attention, "it would be foolish to go as far as he's suggesting. But we are the noble families of Aeravin, the best of the Blood Workers, and it is our duty to take care of country and lead it into prosperity. And to do that we must take care of all our citizens, including the Unblooded."

"Don't we already do that?" Miss Morse asked. "We give them a home, protect their livelihoods, their streets, and all we ask is for a few pints of blood a year."

"Naturally," Shan said, "but our efforts are outdated."

Amelia leaned forward. Though her expression was concerned, Shan saw the sparkle in her eye. "Yes, what do you mean by that?"

"I'm curious as well," Samuel said, and the harshness in his tone cut like a knife.

She couldn't show any reaction to that, though. No matter how much it hurt. They might be friendly, but as far as everyone else knew, they weren't allies in this. Still, the pain and confusion in Samuel's eyes was real.

He was too good for their world, and sometimes Shan hated the game.

"It's simple," she began, looking everywhere but at Samuel. "The landscape of our country has changed in the past millennium, and what started out as a haven for Blood Workers has grown into so much more. While the laws and structures that were put in place then made sense at the time, the demographics have flipped. Instead of there being almost one Unblooded to every three Blood Workers, there is something like . . ."

"One Blood Worker to every ten Unblooded, according to the most recent census," Amelia supplied. "Like rats, they are out-breeding us."

There was a harsh sound from Samuel's direction, but Shan cast a warning glare in his direction before he could get a word out.

"Yes, and because of that we need to re-evaluate our position," Shan said smoothly. "While we are very powerful, we cannot discount that the Unblooded have the numbers. It would be the height of foolishness to forget that."

"We can take them still," Sir Morse said, speaking up for the first time as he drew up his shoulders. Oh, he looked so much like his grandmother, the fierce Councillor of the Military, ready to solve any problem that presented itself with force.

Shan didn't even have to argue his point, however. Miss Rayne did that for her, turning to Sir Morse with a frown. "Perhaps, Edward, but wouldn't there be losses on both sides?"

He blanched at the thought of loss—such a brave young fool he was—and conceded the point. "It is a possibility. But they would lose far more than we would."

"There are other options beside force that could be tried first," Shan said, softly.

Miss Lynwood tapped the edge of her teacup as she thought. "So because there are more of them, we should give in to their demands."

"Oh, no," Shan said, with a cruel little smile. "When negotiating, one does not simply give in to the first round of demands. No, we should put something else forward, a compromise. A way of letting them think they have power, that they are getting what they want, without giving them too much."

"It doesn't sound like that's a *compromise* you are proposing."

Shan could feel the burn of Samuel's eyes on her skin, and she forced herself to meet his gaze. "I suggest allowing them to unionize under the guidance of Lady Holland. She is the Councillor of Industry, and she understands their specific needs and requests more than we can."

"I don't think," Samuel said, slowly, "that if the union is under the organization of the government, that is still a union."

"No, but this is brilliant," Amelia said. "This will give them a place to air their grievances, and if they are legitimate, to move on them."

"And it will let them know they are being heard," Miss Rayne added in, "and hopefully will stop things before they turn to bloodshed."

"They are just Unblooded," Morse said, crushing a biscuit in his hand. "They would not be that much trouble."

"I understand your drive, my friend," Shan said, "but society runs smoother when there is peace, does it not? Should the Unblooded prove to be unreasonable, we will need bold souls like you."

That seemed to appease him, and the group, and Amelia leaned forward, capturing her hand as if they were good friends. "You should draft a bill for the House, Shan—this is too good of an idea to simply let it pass."

"Oh, I don't know," Shan demurred, "it's only my first session in the House, after all."

"No, Amelia is right," Miss Lynwood said. "We might be young, frankly, but it is our duty to put forth solutions to problems that we find, and you can do that. And I think we can all agree that the Unblooded are becoming a problem."

"Perhaps you're right." Shan twisted her hands in her lap—just a moment's worth of calculated dithering—then lifted her head. "No, you *are* right. I will get to work on drafting this bill and I'll present it myself. Thank you all for your support."

Amelia smiled. "Excellent. It's always good to have another bright young mind join us, especially one who does sit in the House." She squeezed her hand. "I think we'll be good friends, you and I."

Shan returned her smile, letting the conversation slide away from this dreary bit of politics to the latest opera. Yes, this salon was indeed a success in every conceivable way. Except for the way that she felt Samuel's gaze linger on her—confused, angry, and full of judgement.

Well, there was no such thing as the perfect day.

Samuel was one of the first to leave, ducking out of the salon when it was just barely acceptable to do so. Shan didn't linger on it—didn't *let* herself linger on it—as she focused on the rest of her guests. She smiled at Miss Rayne, curtsied before Sir Morse, clasped hands with Miss Lynwood.

Last of all came Amelia Dunn, who only smiled at her knowingly. "We must meet again soon," she said, and Shan murmured in agreement.

Of course, she had to please her new handler.

But soon enough they were all gone, leaving Shan with an empty home and an even emptier heart. Despite the successes, it had been harder than she had anticipated to play that role, to fold herself into a shape that was socially acceptable as she played the part politics demanded of her.

It was easier to be the Sparrow than the Lady LeClaire, and, somehow, she thought she might get fewer enemies that way.

Turning towards the scattered remains of the party, she wanted nothing more than to tidy up, even though it wasn't her place. Even though it wasn't something any lady of quality would do. Her hands ached to do something—anything—and a restlessness filled her as she clenched them at her side.

Useless.

"Well, well," Anton said, appearing behind her as stealthily as a shadow. "That was an interesting meeting, wasn't it?"

Shan didn't even turn to her brother. "Were you eavesdropping?"

"Naturally." He slipped around her to grab a couple of biscuits off the table, shoving them both into his mouth whole. "Ugh, dry."

"They're popular."

"They're shit," Anton replied. "There is this recipe of Mother's—"

She shook her head, a quick, sharp movement. "You know I can't serve those."

His jaw clenched. "I didn't even say which ones they were."

"It doesn't matter." She crumbled a biscuit in her hand. Her brother was right. They were awful, dry things, hardly sweet at all and with no discernible flavor. "I cannot serve Tagalan food. I'd be laughed out of society."

"Oh, foolish me." He wiped the dry crumbs off his hand. "I should have remembered. We can have adobo and sinagang and pancit when it's just the two of us, but we can't let anyone else know that we dare defy expectations."

Shan just slumped into a chair, too tired to be angry. "Are you just here to fight, Anton? Don't you have better things to do?"

"Probably," Anton admitted. "But there is something I wanted to talk about." She just waved her hand, urging him on. "I didn't know you had planned to be so ... political."

Ah, so that was it. Of course that would have caught his attention. "It wasn't precisely something I planned, you know. Sometimes I have no choice but to react to things as they happen."

"And you just so happened to fall into monarchist sentiments?"

"As opposed to what? This democratic nonsense that's been filling the streets?" Anton didn't respond, and Shan looked at him in shock. "Really, Anton? I expected such things from Samuel, but I thought you knew better."

A dark silence hung over them as Anton chewed on his lip. Blood and steel, but when had they grown so distant? He had always been interested in politics and frustrated that he could not actively participate in them because of his Blood, but she never would have pegged him as a democrat.

"I thought," Anton said, with more calm than she expected of him, "that we are working to change things."

"We are," Shan said, then dropped her voice low. "I haven't changed my plans."

"And what do you expect to happen, then," Anton said, "when your little coup succeeds? You're only trading one King for another."

"I'm trading that hidebound ancient fool for someone who can listen to change."

He laughed, low and dark, and he might as well have slapped her across the face. "Nothing will change, not really. Maybe you'll pass a few laws, maybe things will get better for a few decades, but once that pet Aberforth of yours is gone things will return to the same old ways."

"He's not a pet," she snapped, and Anton just stared at her, unmoved.

"Perhaps not," he said, leaning back in his chair. "After seeing you today he probably has some doubts about the validity of your claims. If you really cared so much about the Unblooded you would want to help them."

"I *am* helping them!" Shan shot to her feet, stomping right up to Anton's face. "I'm trying to keep them from getting killed."

"You're keeping them in their place," Anton countered. "Used and exploited by the nobility who think them nothing more than cattle."

"You are nobility yourself," Shan spat, and Anton recoiled.

"I might have LeClaire blood," he said after a moment of deliberation, "I might have their name and their money, but I am not like you." He grabbed her, entwining his hand with hers so that her claws cut into his flesh, his blood spilling to the floor. "My blood is nothing like yours, and you and your kind will never see me as anything but fuel to be used."

He shoved her back, so suddenly and forcefully that she almost fell. By the time she had caught herself, he was already gone, the echo of his words hanging over her like a weight around her neck, pulling her down and drowning her in a pit of despair.

The ice around her heart cracked just a little bit, but she caught the sob in her throat. She wouldn't cry, she wouldn't show weakness. He was angry, that she could sympathize with, but he was wrong. These Unblooded fools protesting in the streets and making their wild demands wouldn't fix Aeravin. They'd only tear it apart.

Even if he didn't understand now, he would soon enough. This was the only way forward, and she would fix things for him. He was still her brother, and she'd move mountains to keep him safe.

Chapter Twenty-Four

Samuel

"This is a bad idea," Samuel muttered under his breath, low enough so that only Isaac could hear him. They walked side-by-side through a crowded street, both dressed in the cheap, low-quality clothing of the poor. Isaac kept scratching at the fabric, no doubt unused to its roughness, but for Samuel after weeks of silk and finery it felt like coming home.

This whole adventure was like coming home as they made their way down into the slums, where they were not surrounded by nobles or Blood Workers, but by Unblooded laborers and working people. The kind of people Samuel had grown up with, had lived and worked with, the people who were more like him than those his heritage revealed he was born to. And they were here to use them as nothing more than test subjects.

Perhaps he was becoming more like a Blood Worker after all, even if he couldn't use their magics.

"It'll be fine," Isaac replied, just as quietly, and Samuel glanced at him. He hardly looked like himself in the simple shirt and trousers, and he had even gone so far as to smudge his face and hands with dirt and grease. "We can't keep practicing on me."

Samuel forced himself to look away—he had to keep reminding himself to not stare at Isaac. It was a messier, more unkempt version of the man he knew, but Isaac wore it surprisingly well. As if it wasn't the first time he had disguised himself so. "This isn't right," he argued, even though there was truth to Isaac's words.

It was getting hard to master his ability when his only subject was Isaac. He could keep forcing his will on him, seeing how far against Isaac's own instincts he could push the man, but that was not all that the King wanted from them.

His ability was supposed to be subtle, insidious and undetectable, and one could not perfect it on a subject who was constantly on his guard.

Isaac knocked his shoulder against his, a friendly bump to anyone looking, but Samuel took it for what it was. Reassurance. When he was presented this idea, he hadn't done it as Isaac de la Cruz, the surprising friend he had never expected to find, but as the Royal Blood Worker, doing the duty his position required of him. But he was here as a friend, as support, because he knew that Samuel could never do it alone.

And for that Samuel was thankful, even if he didn't have the words for it.

"Here we are," Isaac said, pulling him to a stop. They stood outside one of the larger taverns, where desperate people with hardly any coin came to spend what little they had on some alcohol to dull the pain. Samuel had never been there, not out of snobbery or disgust, but because he could not afford to let loose.

If anything, he was a little jealous of them.

Before he could argue—one last, hopeless attempt—Isaac was already pushing his way through the door, and he had to hurry to not lose the man in the crowd. For it was a crowd—the tavern was packed to the brim with Unblooded from all corners of the slums and despite their conditions, despite the harshness of their lives, there was a vibrancy here that Samuel hadn't felt in ages.

They were alive and vital and spontaneous in a way the nobility weren't, and a knot of tension deep inside him finally relaxed.

Isaac was grinning at him, the mood infectious, catching him by the hand and dragging him over to the bar. Isaac's hand felt right in his, and he followed along automatically. For a moment it was easy to feel like they weren't there on a secret training mission for the Eternal King, but simply as two men looking to get to know each other better. But that wasn't the truth—nothing in Samuel's life was a simple as that.

The bright burst of happiness he felt faded, so he just turned to the barkeep and held up two fingers. A moment later, two glasses of cheap ale were deposited in front of them and Isaac was slipping some coppers into the man's hand.

"Okay," Samuel said, leaning against Isaac. He knew what it would look like, but Isaac had asked him to be subtle, quiet, and no one would take a second glance at the two of them cozying up like this. And besides, Isaac wasn't pushing him away. "Target?" he breathed, his mouth dangerously close to Isaac's skin.

Isaac shuddered, but turned around, leaning back against the bar all casual as he studied the crowd around them. His free hand came around Samuel's shoulder as he played with the hair that was coming loose from the bun at the nape of his neck, fully committed to this charade, and Samuel sucked in a harsh breath.

This was a mistake.

But it was too late to turn back now, so he pressed against him, savoring the warmth from his body that he could feel even through the unnecessary layers of clothing between them. Isaac kept toying with his hair, and Samuel bit the inside of his cheek, using the pain to ground himself.

This was just a ploy: there was no potential here, he had already learned that lesson with Shan. "Isaac," he said again, warningly, but it came out as more like a groan.

And the bastard had the gall to smile.

"Easy, I'm looking," Isaac said, softly. "It would be easier if you agreed to scam the barkeep."

"No," Samuel replied emphatically. Practicing it on the Unblooded was bad enough—taking money from someone who needed it was even worse. Isaac didn't push him, though, just raked his nails across his scalp, back and forth in a soothing motion.

Samuel hated that such a touch was effective, but the immediate bristle of anger that had risen in him faded right away.

"Fine, fine. There." He followed the line of Isaac's gaze to a group of rowdy young people—around their age or younger—who were attracting the attention of a large corner of the bar. "Let's go see what that's about."

"And what am I supposed to do?" Samuel asked, but Isaac only grinned.

"Be adaptable. Maybe stop a fight." He didn't give Samuel a chance to argue as he dragged him across the tavern, pulling him through the crowd as they got closer to the commotion. But the closer they got, the slower Isaac moved, and it only took Samuel a moment to realize why.

This wasn't a bar fight. This was a political rally.

"We have been silent long enough! The Bloodsuckers can't keep us back if we join together!"

The leader of the group—a young boy, hells, he couldn't have even been nineteen—was waving something around in his hand. Another one of those pamphlets. His friends were walking through the crowd, passing them out, and it wasn't long before a young girl had pressed one into Samuel's hand.

The paper was thin and cheap, the typeface smudged and offset. But the title blazed across the front was clear enough.

A DECLARATION ON THE RIGHTS OF THE UNBLOODED

Samuel ran his thumb across the paper, tracing the letters of the author's name—or, rather, the moniker they wrote under. The Friend of the Unblooded. Of course. He swelled with pride as he flipped through the pamphlet—at the demands they were making.

Removal of the Blood Taxes.

Representation in government.

Protections in the workplace.

All things that Samuel knew from experience that the Unblooded needed, and all things that he wanted to fight for. And here they were, without the seat in the House of Lords that he had, without the money that he had been gifted, without the political power that he had stumbled into, fighting for it themselves.

Perhaps he was unnecessary after all.

But Isaac glanced back at him, and the pride he felt popped like a bubble as something more serious replaced it. He wasn't Samuel Hutchinson anymore, able to simply support his fellow Unblooded. He was Lord Aberforth, and he was training for a duty he never wanted, to do what the crown needed.

What the Royal Blood Worker needed.

What Shan would have asked him to do.

What the King would want from him.

This was the very thing he had been training for. To gather information, slyly and subtly, to help the nobles. To give them the ammunition they'd need to stop this movement before it ever had the chance to grow. All he'd need to do was talk. Talk to this young boy, this brash leader, and find out where the pamphlets came from. Stop the movement before it grew into something more. But he knew what the Blood Workers would do to them. Even the sympathetic ones—Shan with her compromises, Isaac as the Royal Blood Worker—would save them by keeping them in their place.

He was a tool to be used, and Isaac was watching him with unreadable eyes.

Samuel dropped the pamphlet and ran from the crowd.

"Wait!"

He heard Isaac call after him, but that didn't stop him. He could feel his power stirring in his chest, ready to be used, but he just clenched his jaw and pushed through the crowd, back past the way they had come and out the door into the cool night air.

It hit his skin like balm—soothing the darkness within—and he turned and stalked away into the shadows. He turned the first corner he found, desperate to get away from everyone.

He didn't want to be seen like this, a hair's breadth from falling apart.

"Samuel, wait." A strong hand grabbed him around the arm, jerking him to a rough stop, and Samuel spun with a sudden desperation, grabbing Isaac by his shirt and shoving him back against the wall.

"Please" was all he could get out, was all he could trust himself to get out, lest the power swirling within him twisted his words into some horrible mockery of everything he intended.

"It's all right," Isaac said, raising both his hands in surrender. When Samuel made no move to fight him, he laid them on his shoulders, squeezing tightly. "I wouldn't have asked you to."

He buried his face in Isaac's shoulder, a choking sob bursting past his lips as Isaac wrapped his arms around him. "I thought—I thought that—"

"Well," Isaac said, one hand slipping down to rub soothing circles on his back while the other tangled in his hair, "given my . . . position, I wouldn't have turned it away if you had. But I know how difficult it must be for you."

It wasn't quite what Samuel had wanted to hear, but it was enough and he relaxed into Isaac's embrace, drawing what solace he could from it. Isaac held him like he was afraid that Samuel would break apart if he let go, and, in all honesty, Samuel didn't know if he would.

But he couldn't deny the effect of Isaac's hands on him, of the press of his body—hard and warm—against his. The brush of Isaac's mouth so close to his—almost a kiss, almost something more—and the way he slotted one leg between his, brushing against him in an indecent manner.

They hung together on a precipice, Isaac hardly even breathing, as he gave Samuel the chance to choose.

Samuel caught Isaac's shirt between his teeth, gagging himself on the cloth as he gathered his wits. Then, gently, he detangled himself and pushed away. "We *can't*."

Isaac huffed out a groan, leaning his head back against the wall with a thunk. "If you insist."

"I want to," Samuel said, though guilt tore at him. He wanted to so much that it nearly tore him apart. Isaac. Shan. Both of them. It made him feel greedy and selfish, because he knew he couldn't have either of them. And yet, he kept reaching, playing them both like some sort of terrible rake.

Isaac, though, was looking at him with such kindness that he nearly turned away. He wasn't worthy of such a look. He ran his hand down Samuel's cheek, drawing his thumb down the line of his throat until he rested his hand across his heart. "I've changed my mind."

"What?"

"I said I'd make you no promises," Isaac whispered. "But I will figure out how to take this gift from you even if it's the last thing I do." He wrapped his hand around the back of Samuel's neck and pulled him in for a quick, rough kiss.

Samuel didn't fight it, he just leaned into it, the hard press of Isaac's mouth against him, the dig of his nails into his skin, and then they broke apart. Isaac didn't push him for more, and as much as Samuel wanted to press against him, to learn all the ways that he wanted to be touched, he knew that he couldn't ask for more.

Didn't dare risk more.

He closed his eyes, pressed his face against Isaac's chest, seeking the safety and comfort of his embrace. "Thank you."

"Of course," Isaac said, before stepping to the side, gently disentangling himself. "Come, then. I have work to do."

Samuel blinked at him for a moment, then— "But what about the training?"

He shrugged, so carelessly handsome that it made Samuel's heart hurt. "We'll figure something else out. Clearly this wasn't the right, ah, venue." Taking Samuel by the hand, he led him out of the alley. "Let's get out of here."

Heart lighter than it had been in a long while, and his lips still tingling from the kiss, Samuel let himself be led through the slums, his eyes only on Isaac.

Until there was something blocking them—a crowd gathered along one of the major intersections, and the whispers carried back through to reach their ears. For a second they just stood there, letting the information process, and Samuel prayed that he was just mishearing it. But no.

"Find a Guard," a women cried, as her companion let out a hysterical sob, burying her face in her friend's shoulder.

"Don't look," a man snapped, grabbing a young child and turning him away from the scene.

Isaac dropped his hand, shoving his way past, Samuel following in his wake to the front of the crowd. There, in the middle of the street, was a body. No, not a body, a mutilation. A corpse torn and ruined, blood spilling from the wounds and seeping into the cobblestones.

Chapter Twenty-Five

Shan

S han had never seen a crowd this large in her entire life—not at any social event, not at any of the annual sacrifices, not at anything at all. The streets below were filled with people—with Unblooded citizens—gathered in protest.

They filled the main square of the capital, crowding around the construction work in the central park, spilling out to fill the gardens, packed between rose bushes and standing on benches. They filled the cobblestoned streets around the square, pressing up against the windows of restaurants and shops, fully blocking access to them, a veritable sea of bodies. But Shan and a host of other Blood Workers watched from the balconies above, safe in their second-story restaurants and clubs as the Guards below struggled to keep the Unblooded in check.

As the chants rose.

No Justice! No Peace!

If we don't get justice, you don't get peace!

So far there was no violence. No threats. But their chants were loud, organized, and steady, and she wondered when they had found the means to prepare so.

And how she, as the Sparrow, had missed it.

But she couldn't ignore it any longer. Not after a fourth body in as many weeks had turned up on the street, bloody and brutalized, and fear moved the people to such lengths. Blood and steel, she had studied her history as diligently as the next student, but she had never read about anything like this. If this had happened in Aeravin before, such tales had been suppressed, wiped away like a blot against the pages of history.

And from the tension rolling off Lord Dunn, she was not sure that something like that wasn't about to happen now. He had invited her to his favorite club when word of the protest had started to spread, along with a handful of others from the House of Lords, and she had readily accepted.

How else would she have gotten such a good view?

"Absolutely unacceptable," Lord Dunn growled, low and dark, then he downed the rest of his wine. Snapping his fingers, he summoned one of the servers, who shuffled forward and refilled his goblet. "How dare they."

Shan just fiddled with her teacup. Many of her brethren had turned to wine, or worse, spirits, but it was only mid-afternoon yet and she did not want to be addled. "I am curious how they gathered so quickly," she said, taking care to be calm, composed. "It's been less than twenty-four hours."

Dunn huffed in response. "Yes, I've been considering that as well. They must have planned this in advance, but simply been looking for an excuse to gather. It's too well put together to have been done last minute."

Shan pursed her lips. "Exactly. That said, they picked a good time. This cause will earn them sympathy, at the least. They are not entirely wrong. People are still dying, and we have no leads."

"No, they're not." Dunn sipped his drink, some of the anger fading as the talk turned to politics. "That's what is the most frustrating about all this. They almost have a leg to stand on."

Lady Belrose slid up beside them, greeting Shan with nothing more than a nod. "Almost? They're dying in the streets, Kevan, and we are doing nothing about it."

"There are investigations happening," Dunn started.

"Investigations mean nothing," Belrose interrupted. "Results do. And all they see is that more bodies are appearing and we continue to go on as if nothing has changed."

"Everything is changing," Dunn muttered under his breath.

"And how is that?" Belrose sighed, and Shan noticed that the normally impeccably put together Councillor looked terrible today. Every year of her life stood out on her face in tired lines and dark circles. "As much as it pains me to say it, we are failing them. Our Guard is failing them."

Dunn cast Shan a look out of the corner of his eye, and she drew up her shoulders, already knowing what he expected of her.

"We are failing them," Shan agreed, and Belrose looked up at her in shock. "It's no surprise that they've taken to such measures, especially given the . . ." She trailed off, deliberately looking troubled.

"The rubbish they've been spouting?" Dunn supplied, perhaps with a bit too much vigor. "Absolute nonsense. Have you seen the latest? They want their own Parliament House."

"Yes, I've seen," Shan said demurely. One of her birds had dropped off that one the other night, and it had been an illuminating read. "But surely we can do something. They are our citizens after all, and for the Blood Taxes they pay they do deserve some protection."

"Exactly," Belrose said, straightening. She studied Shan with a new appreciation. "Perhaps I underestimated you, LeClaire. Do you have any suggestions?"

"Aside from catching this killer?" Shan said with a shrug. "The Unblooded need to feel like they have a place to go when they have issues. A safety network, a way for their needs to be addressed. Not their own Parliament, obviously, but perhaps a council of some sort. Something that is organized and recognized by the government."

Belrose nodded as she listened, turning the thought over in her mind. "Yes, like the unions their little pamphlets and books go on about, but not so . . . drastic."

"Precisely," Shan said. "We give them some protections, a little of what they want, and things like this," she gestured at the protest below, "won't happen again."

"It's all pointless," Dunn said. "A foolish fancy of youth."

"No," Belrose said. "LeClaire is right. Things are changing, Kevan, and sometimes I worry that you and I are too stuck in our ways to see the right solutions." Turning back to Shan, she added, "Do you have anything formal written up?"

Shan swallowed hard. "Yes, but it's only a draft."

"Send it to me," Belrose said. "I'll look it over." When Shan hesitated, she smiled. "Don't worry, I don't plan to steal your idea from you. Dunn has overheard all of this anyway, so even if I tried, he could vouch for you."

"No, it isn't that. It's just—thank you," Shan said, dropping into a curtsy. "I am in your debt."

Belrose waved her hand. "Nonsense. We might be on the Royal Council, but it's still our duty to ensure that the next generation of nobility is ready to take the lead. Now, if you don't mind, it's been a long week and I'm going to see if they have anything stronger than wine."

She took her leave of them, and Dunn leaned close enough to whisper, "You're doing well, LeClaire."

Then he too was gone, leaving Shan alone with the strangely bitter taste of success. Everything was proceeding exactly as it should. So why did she feel so used?

Stepping back out onto the balcony, Shan let the warm afternoon air wash over her. Below, protesters continued their chants, and she tilted her head back and let their voices wash over her—a strangely soothing rhythm.

"Shan."

She opened her eyes to find the Royal Blood Worker standing next to her, having slipped to her side while she was waiting. He, too, looked hopeless and bedraggled, and Shan realized that was the new normal of their lives. For once the nobles faced true tension and fear—and a deep, dark part of her relished it. "Hello, Isaac."

His lips quirked into the briefest of smiles, but it faltered as the chants rose. "I didn't expect you to be here today."

"Honestly, I didn't expect to be here either." She glanced over her shoulder at the rest of the crowd, but it looked like they had all gathered in small groups around tables. It was easier to ignore the truth of the situation if one didn't have to look at it. "But there are a lot of things happening this Season that I didn't expect."

"I'm sure." His hand drifted towards hers, barely a brush, but she felt it anyway. "I've heard rumors about you, my dear."

"Only good things, I hope."

"Only the best. But we need to talk. I never had the chance to thank you for those notes you sent me."

Ah, the notes on Samuel. She wondered when they would come back around to her. But they had both been busy. "All right. Tonight?"

"My, my, Lady LeClaire. Are you inviting me to dinner?" He bared his teeth in a smile that sent chills down her spine.

"If you'll deign to join me."

"I wouldn't miss it for the world."

It took her longer than she wanted to get out of the club. The protest had been broken up peacefully—a miracle, in Shan's opinion, but Lady Belrose took a great risk. She put herself out there in front of the crowd, swearing that she would increase their efforts to find this killer. There would be extra Guard patrols, a drop point for them to share information anonymously and a vague hint of new legislation to come.

It had appeased them for now, but Shan knew the truth—if they didn't find this killer, and soon, nothing the Blood Workers did would keep them in line.

But Lady Belrose had bought them time and Shan knew better than to waste it. Her first task when she finally made it back home was finish up the last of the changes on her draft of Dunn's bill then to send it off to Lady Belrose. After that, she had an important meeting with the Royal Blood Worker.

She considered her options—as hostess, there were many things expected of her. A certain type of menu, a level of decorum. But Anton's words from the other night still grated on her, and if there was anyone who'd understand, it was Isaac.

She still remembered that night, once, when she had sneaked to the flat he shared with his parents at his insistence, had sampled the rich flavors of their food in an atmosphere she had never known before. It was the anniversary of the de la Cruzs' move to Aeravin, and they had made lechon, a whole roasted suckling pig in the Tagalan tradition, to celebrate, complete with a rich wealth of side dishes. It had been the most delicious dinner, and one of the few times she had felt at home somewhere since her mother left.

Perhaps it was time she returned the favor.

She ducked into the kitchen to speak with the Tagalan cook whom Anton had hired after the death of their father; despite his misgivings about her methods, he had quickly taken advantage of the change in status.

That settled, she went to change and wait. Evening came quicker than she expected, and she was shamefully relieved when she realized that her brother wasn't home. He still wasn't pleased by her rekindled association with Isaac, and though she had done everything she could to keep them apart, she wasn't sure what would happen should their paths cross.

It wasn't that she was more forgiving than her brother, it was just that she knew when to let things go for political reasons. And this was one of them.

Her past relationship with Isaac had no bearing on it.

It was harder to believe her own lie when the footman escorted Isaac into the parlor. He, too, had changed, trading his formal robes of office for a simple suit, finely made but without any ostentatious bits. Somewhere along the way he had shed some of the roughness from before. No, that wasn't quite right. Isaac hadn't done away

with the pain and exhaustion that seemed to plague him lately, but
it seemed that he had been soothed in some gentle, unknown way.

"My darling Lady LeClaire." He took her hand in his, bowing
over it as he placed a kiss on the back of it. "Thank you for your
invitation."

She rolled her eyes, just a bit more dramatically than usual.
"Please, Isaac. Such formalities never suited us."

"No, they didn't," he agreed, as he straightened. He didn't let go
of her hand, though. "Yet still I am compelled to give you the honor
you deserve."

The honor that she did not yet get from others. She felt a slight
blush rise to her cheeks, and she let it happen. "You've become quite
charming."

His smile faltered. "It's what's expected of me," he said quietly. "I
must keep them entertained, after all."

She squeezed his hand, sympathetic. They would never be good
enough to be considered simply on their own merits, would they?
They'd always had to be more—more entertaining, more successful, more charming—to simply be considered on the same level as
the others.

"Let's have dinner," Shan said. "I've requested something I hope
you'll like."

"Oh?" His mask slipped away, revealing the boy she remembered.
"And what is that?"

"You'll see."

She led him to the dining room, where there was a minimalistic
dining set up for two around the corner of one end of the table. It
was a lot more casual—and personal—than Shan would dare with
almost anyone else. Even she and her brother sat across from each
other, on those occasions when they dined together, an increasingly
infrequent event.

Isaac, though, seemed pleased by this turn, and settled down at
the table. One of the servants entered, carrying a single large bowl,
which she set down in front of them. Lifting the lid, she revealed a

steaming pile of noodles, vegetables and chicken, all cooked together with spices and broth in one pot.

The girl looked between them, and Shan nodded, and she quickly served them. The wine had already been poured, so she just curtsied and left. It was much simpler than her usual work—one course, one dish.

Nothing like the normal dinners in Dameral.

"Pancit bihon," Isaac said, with just a hint of awe. "This looks—and smells—amazing." He leaned over his plate and taking a deep breath, savoring the aromas.

"I'm glad you think so," Shan said, grabbing her fork and spoon—another deviation from the normal setting.

"Thank you for sharing it with me," Isaac said sincerely, and Shan felt a burst of happiness inside her, though she'd never admit it.

She simply tucked in.

They ate in companionable silence, despite the important topics she knew that they needed to discuss. But it was nice to simply be able to enjoy a meal, to enjoy someone's easy company, without having to worry about playing word games or keeping up with a conversation that was more deception than truth, without the calculations that went into every single thing that she did.

It was relaxing, and she almost wished she didn't have this moment. Now that she knew what it was like, she knew that she would miss it. Such things could not last forever, though, and soon enough the meal was finished, and she had no choice but to usher Isaac into her study, leaving behind the fleeting moment of peace.

There, in her private study, behind the wards she erected as soon as they entered, in the safety of her magic and with a glass of strong whisky in her hand, she turned to Isaac and forced herself to be strong.

"So."

"So indeed." He had placed his drink aside right after she had poured it, resting his hands on his knees. "I . . ."

The words died on his tongue, but Shan didn't press him. She knew him well enough to know his process, that if she wanted to get to the real Isaac she couldn't push him.

Pushing him only led him to putting his mask back up.

She sipped her whisky, savoring the burn on her tongue, until he looked at her with sad eyes—regretful eyes. "I made Samuel a promise."

"Promises can be dangerous things." She settled down next to him on the couch, her skirts fluttering out so that they brushed, barely, against him. "What did you promise?"

"The very thing I told him from the beginning was not a guarantee." He reached for his drink then, downing a large amount of it in one go.

"You foolish man," she whispered, and he flinched.

"I thought you'd understand," he whispered. "You sent me your notes."

"I do," she replied, "believe me, I do. But this is Blood Working beyond the likes of what you and I have ever seen, beyond even what the Eternal King expected. As much as I hope that we can succeed, teasing him with the potential of success only to fail will just hurt him even more."

"I know," Isaac growled. Literally growled, and Shan looked up at him in surprise. "But we have to do something. He's getting better at controlling it, Shan. Soon there will be no reason for the King to wait. Blood and steel, he wants to see Samuel in action."

Shan bit her lip, weighing her options. How much to sympathize, how much to demur. She had not expected to see this side of Isaac—hadn't realized that this side of him still existed—and that the thing to bring it out would be Samuel.

She had spent her whole life planning her schemes, laying out her plans, and there was a part of her that wished she could reach out to him here. But she played a very dangerous game, and in the past few weeks she had started to attract the attention of so many dangerous people. The Eternal King. Lord Dunn. Lady Belrose. And despite the yearning to open up to him—as she had so many years ago—Isaac was still the Royal Blood Worker. This Eternal King's right-hand man.

One of the most dangerous pieces she had in play.

Yet here he was, looking at her as if she could save him—as if she could save them all—and she couldn't simply turn him away.

"What you are saying," she said, carefully, "sounds almost treasonous. Even if we discovered a way to cure Samuel that doesn't mean that the King would allow it to happen."

He didn't look scared at her words; if anything, he looked even more determined. "Perhaps this shouldn't be the King's decision. After all, it's not his life at stake."

"No, it's not," she agreed. "I am only surprised that you seem . . . willing to defy the King. And for Samuel, no less."

"Do you think he's not worthy of protection?" Isaac asked hotly, turning on her with a sudden rage. "Or do you, like the King, find that his gift is too valuable to be wasted—morality be damned?"

Startled by his vehemence, she slid to her knees in front of him, grabbing his hands in hers. Her movement surprised him enough for him to pause in his rage, looking down at her as she seemed to kneel in supplication at his feet. "No, Isaac. You misunderstand. I cannot lie and say that I have not considered the usefulness of his gift, but I would never *force* him to use it."

She meant it honestly—such a tool would never be useful. He'd only grow to resent her and her schemes and eventually turn against her. She wouldn't waste an Aberforth—a king—for such a short-term asset.

Her feelings for Samuel did not play into this at all. She was ever so practical.

Isaac stared down at her, the anger replaced by a pain so sharp Shan almost couldn't bear to look at it. "So, it's me you thought a coward."

"After everything you did," she said, softly but not cruelly, "after everything you didn't do, can you blame me?"

"No, I suppose not." He was still holding her hands, brushing his thumbs against her skin. "But I am not the King's man through and through. I am still my own person. And I will prove it to you."

"And Samuel?"

"Him, too," Isaac said.

"No, I meant—" Shan trailed off, for once words failing her. She didn't know what she meant, how to put it all into a coherent thought.

"Ah." He moved his hand, stroking his thumb down her cheek. She leaned into the touch, and he cupped her face against the palm of his hand—it was large and warm, and even with the years between them it was so easy to give in. "This was also something I wanted to talk about. Last night, I kissed him."

Shan froze completely, her heart not even beating. "Why are you telling me this?"

"Because I've kissed you, too," he said. "And I've a feeling that I wasn't the only Blood Worker to steal a kiss from Samuel."

She pushed herself away from him, too flustered to speak, and he let her go. Returning the favor from earlier when she had given him time to gather his thoughts. Eventually, she found that forced calm she had spent years perfecting, and she turned back to him. Cold, impassive, unhurt. "What is this? Are we to fight over him, like he is some prize to be won?"

"Not at all," Isaac said. "I was serious when I meant that I want to court you. But I also want to court him as well. And I think you want that, too." She sucked in a harsh breath, and he smiled. "Am I wrong?"

He wasn't. She was a lonely creature, and perhaps her heart had been so starved of love that, now that she had the option, she didn't want to give up either. And Isaac—she had suspected there being something between him and Samuel, blood and steel, she had eyes, but she had no idea that it was this strong.

And if Samuel was open as well . . .

Maybe she could have it all.

He was offering her everything she wanted on a silver platter, and yet. "This isn't our decision alone to make."

"I know. And Samuel doesn't feel comfortable entering a relationship as long as his power hangs over him. But it is something to think about, isn't it?"

She remembered the way his command had rung in her ears—a single, simple word. *Mine.* It had cut through her with a shocking, brutal pain, stripping her of all sense of self and identity for a single moment.

It was terrifying. It was thrilling.

But his fear was understandable, and she was relieved that Isaac understood it.

"So that's why you're so determined to cure him," she said instead, twisting the moment into a bit of levity, and Isaac snorted. "I can't say I blame you then."

Isaac threw back his head and laughed, and Shan smiled. "All right, de la Cruz. You say that you are your own man? Then prove it. And maybe, just maybe, I'll take you back."

"And then we can talk with Samuel?" he added, and she nodded. "Well, then, I guess I have to prove myself."

Chapter Twenty-Six

Samuel

"Is this entirely necessary?" Samuel said as he climbed into Isaac's carriage. The door slammed shut behind him, and Isaac knocked once on the ceiling for them to get moving. "This isn't the time for parties."

"Samuel, it's always the time for parties," Isaac replied, taking a drag on his cigarette as his eyes wandered over him.

He couldn't help feeling like he was being undressed. His outfit was perfect and incredibly fashionable—Jacobs had assured him of that while he had carefully tied his cravat—but Samuel still felt terribly uncomfortable in it. Tight breeches, starched shirt, an *embroidered* waistcoat for goodness' sake. The jacket was tight across his shoulders, making him broader and more substantial than he actually was, and Samuel felt dreadfully exposed in it.

Isaac, however, seemed to approve, and he leaned closer, studying the suit. "Blood and steel. Laurens, is it?"

"Uh, yeah." Samuel fiddled with his cufflinks, wishing he could fade back into the seat. He wasn't used to being so seen—Isaac's eyes looked darker, sharper, boring into him with an intensity that made him shiver. He remembered the feel of Isaac's lips against his, quick and firm, and part of him wanted Isaac to look at him that way forever.

Another part of him hesitated, recalling the feel of Shan's body under his, the way she had pressed into him.

Hells, he was making a mess of things, wasn't he?

"Fuck." Isaac shook his head, finally looking away, and Samuel felt a surge of relief. When he wasn't looking at him Samuel could almost pretend that this thing between them wasn't there—that they were simply friends, that they weren't betraying Shan. Not that there was any real future with either of them, anyway, not with this gift of his hanging like an albatross around his neck.

He finally understood why people turned to drink.

"Laurens won't even respond to my requests," Isaac continued, blessedly oblivious to Samuel's internal panic, "let alone dress me. Royal Blood Worker or not. Being an Aberforth has its benefits."

"Actually, it was Shan." He hated the way her name tasted on his lips, even when she wasn't there, hated the way Isaac's gaze sharped for just a second. "She's the one who got me in with Laurens."

"Of course she was. She can do anything, it seems." Isaac flicked ash off the tip of his cigarette, his hand resting against the open window, his long fingers golden in the fading sunlight. "How have you been doing since . . .?" he drifted off, not quite mentioning the body they stumbled upon. "I know it must have been hard, seeing something like that."

Samuel eyed him, wondering what his angle was. Isaac had been walking on eggshells around him, treating him like something fragile about to break. But now? To address it directly? There was a part of him waiting for the trap to spring.

"It . . . goes," he said, since it was not like he could question Isaac about his motives. Well, he could, technically, but it would be poor form after everything Isaac had done. "It's not like it's my first."

"I suppose that's true," Isaac said, softly. "Still, it changes you. I know from experience."

Samuel wanted to lean forward, to ask how he had coped. What tragedies he had seen as the Royal Blood Worker, and how he managed it all. But perhaps Isaac had been right after all. Perhaps Samuel was still a bit too fragile. So he ignored the impulse, turning towards something safer. "Unfortunately, we don't have time. Training must continue. Are you sure this is a good idea?"

The corner of Isaac's mouth curled up. "Don't worry, I doubt there will be anyone here you'll feel bad testing your power against. It's a far better plan than the one we originally had."

"I never said thank you for that."

Isaac waved his hand. "Don't worry about it. It was my mistake." His eyes grew cold, distant. "Besides, just because I am the Royal Blood Worker, and the King has his orders for us, doesn't mean we should turn our practice on the innocent. I should have never asked that of you."

"It's okay." Samuel shrugged. "It's not like we have much freedom, anyway." Isaac looked like he wanted to press further, to dig into that statement, but the carriage rolled to a stop. "We're here."

"It seems we are." Isaac's lips twisted into a frown, and he tossed the remains of his cigarette out the window. "Remember, nothing too drastic. Keep it natural."

Samuel stepped out of the carriage, Isaac immediately on his heels, and he looked up at the large estate before him. Unlike the townhouses at the heart of the capital, Lady Lynwood's home was more like a manor. Three stories tall and three times as wide, the entire structure was lit up from within, music and laughter drifting out into the night air. When Isaac had showed up at his house this afternoon and demanded they attend, he swore an invitation from Lady Lynwood wasn't to be ignored.

Apparently, she knew anybody who was anybody and she threw the best parties in Dameral. From what he had been able to gather from Isaac, she was what Shan hoped to become—the women everyone knew held all the power. A single word from her could make or break a reputation.

And besides, this was a perfect opportunity to make up for their lost session.

Still, the timing of this fête felt all wrong.

"Hells," Samuel hissed. "There's been four murders in three months—and that's not even getting into the protests."

"And it's turning this into one of the most active Seasons in a decade," Isaac said, clasping him on the shoulder. "This is how we deal with stress, Samuel."

"Endless parties?"

"Well, not just parties." Isaac shrugged. "There are also dinners, and salons, and balls, and coffees, and plays."

Samuel thought back to the pile of invitations in his study that grew daily, left unopened and untouched.

"You can go to these events alone, you know," Isaac said, quietly. "I shouldn't have to drag you to them."

"Please, Isaac." Samuel did his best to smile, but it came out more like a grimace. "You think I can take this on without backup?"

"I think," Isaac said, taking his time in choosing his words, "that you're afraid. But you shouldn't be."

Samuel didn't respond. He just stepped forward and left Isaac behind. He wasn't afraid, not really.

He was angry.

Angry at the extravagance of it all—at the fine clothing and the expensive food and the even more expensive wine. At the lies and the gossip and the rumors. At the way everyone looked at him like he was a piece of meat to be inspected and bought for the right price.

But Isaac had never known anything else. Nor had Shan. They were born into a world that would drive most good people mad, and he couldn't fault them for being what Dameral had made them. Like he shouldn't blame himself for what Dameral had made him—*was* making him. But it was easier for him to forgive others than it was for him to forgive himself.

He walked up the stairs with his head held high, Isaac a breath behind him. The footman smiled as they handed over their cards, and they were ushered into the ballroom with the rest of the crowd.

It was a large open space, made of glittering white marble and lit by wide chandeliers from which witch light hung. Against the far wall was a series of glass doors, thrown open against the cool night air, and the musicians formed a perfect quartet in the near corner. Complete with a buffet of light snacks and drinks along the inner wall, it was a perfect image of a noble's ball—fine, lustrous, and just a bit gaudy.

At Isaac's instance they were what he called "fashionably late", and the ball was already in full swing. The dance floor was crowded, filled with all kinds of couples as they spun their way through the song. There were dresses of every color, a rainbow of flowing skirts that swirled round and round, and finely cut suits in greys and blacks and blues. Samuel couldn't tear his eyes from the beauty of it.

"Do you want to go again?" Isaac said, and Samuel didn't need to look to know he was smiling. "I'm not quite as talented as Shan, but I'm sure I could manage to lead you."

"You're not funny."

"I'm not joking."

Samuel glanced over, seeing the same dark look in his eyes that he had found so compelling in the carriage, in the alleyway.

"I thought you were courting Shan," Samuel said, the words he'd been holding in for days bursting out.

Isaac bared his teeth in a grin. "Did she tell you that, or did you learn it yourself?"

"Please, Isaac," Samuel said, clenching his jaw. He might be new to this world, but he wasn't a simpleton. "Rumors fly."

"Maybe I am," Isaac admitted. "Maybe you are, too, from what I've heard. But a single dance won't hurt, will it?"

It could hurt far more than he wanted to admit, but he didn't stop himself from putting his hand in Isaac's, from letting himself be drawn onto the floor in the breath where one song ended and another began.

If it was strange to see them dancing together, the Royal Blood Worker and the Lost Aberforth, no one said anything. There were just the deep reverberations of the strings as the musicians drew their bows across them—the violins, the viola, the bass. The counterpoint of the piano. There was Isaac's voice, deep and low, counting out the beat in his ear.

Then they were moving. It wasn't like the other dance he had shared with Shan, where she had twirled him in and out across the floor. This was more intense, more intimate. Isaac pushed and pulled him across the floor, counting all the while, but Samuel didn't follow the beat.

He followed the movement of Isaac's hips, the brief press of his thigh against his, the brush of his fingers against his skin.

It was maddening and intoxicating, and for a few moments Samuel just let himself *be*. Isaac didn't give him a moment to worry or stress, and he focused only on the music and the beat of his own heart in his ears.

But when the song came to an end, when Isaac pulled him flush against him for the final few measures, Samuel spotted a familiar face in the crowd.

Shan—her face red and her expression utterly unreadable, but her attention was riveted on them. When she caught him watching her, she simply raised her glass, drained it, and turned to walk away, her dark skirts the color of dried blood fluttering out behind her.

"Ah," Isaac said.

"Are you embarrassed for the dance, or at being caught?" Samuel said, disengaging from Isaac and stalking away, following after Shan.

"Wait—" Isaac began, but Samuel shrugged him off.

He needed to find Shan, he needed to talk to her. To say what, he didn't know, but he just had to reach her somehow.

He followed her to the doors at the end of the ballroom, and Samuel saw the flutter of her red dress disappearing through them. He hurried after her, emerging in a garden filled with alcoves and hidden pockets of space. He came to a stop as he realized what it was—unlike Shan's carefully cultivated garden, this was a labyrinth, the hedgerows tall and twisting around each other in a circuitous maze. It was for lovers and allies and enemies, for secret meetings under the guise of a party.

He had the feeling that Shan had fled there not out of business but out of a need to hide.

He ran right into the maze, searching through open spaces and alcoves, turning down twisting paths and doubling back. He passed couples and groups as he went, all in various states of intimacy. Samuel didn't care. He passed by all of them without a second glance, looking only for Shan.

Except she had found him first.

A hand grabbed him around the wrist, dragging him into an empty alcove and shoving him against a hedge. Her other hand clamped over his mouth, muffling his cry of surprise, until they met eyes and she was sure that he wouldn't fight her.

"Shan," he whispered, and she lowered her hand to rest on his chest. "It wasn't what it looked like."

She smiled, and he realized suddenly that she didn't look mad. "You shouldn't lie. I think it was exactly what it looked like."

Samuel blinked at her, confused by her easy manner and her gentle smile. "You're right."

"Of course I am," she replied. "You're a terrible liar." She looked up at him, not demurely through her eyelashes like many of the nobles did at this party. She met him head on, unashamed and unafraid.

"You're not mad?"

"No," she said, simply. The familiar flush rose to her cheeks, and Samuel suddenly recognized the heat for what it was. "I just . . . ah. I needed some air. You two made quite the image."

He couldn't help the smile that split across his face. "Oh, we did?"

"Yes," she replied, primly. She took a step back, and Samuel wanted nothing more than to follow. She was like gravity, and he was already caught in her orbit. "So. Isaac. Tell me what's going on there."

He laughed at her directness. "And here I thought you excelled at secrets and insinuations."

There it was—a hint of relaxation. A promise of something

more. "Perhaps, Samuel, I find it refreshing not to have to constantly play the game."

"Well, in that case . . ." He flexed his hand against his side, wanting to reach for hers—but he could still feel the warmth of Isaac's hand against his skin.

How was he supposed to react when both of them felt different, but still *right*?

"I don't know, Shan."

Though she was still flushed, Shan otherwise showed no reaction. She had mastered that cool and impassive expression—forever in control—but there was a hunger in her eyes that Samuel prayed wasn't faked. "Something I never fully understood, Samuel, is why one does not simply go after what they want."

Samuel licked his suddenly dry lips. "I don't understand."

"Well, when I was young," Shan said, very softly, "I had no power, no respect, just a tainted name and the blood in my veins. But I didn't settle for that. I created my own power, carved out my own respect, and I will bring Aeravin to its knees. Why? Because I want it so."

Samuel stepped in front of her, forcing her to tilt her head back to look in his eyes. "And what of me? Of Isaac?"

"I'll have you both," Shan said. "If you'll allow it."

Samuel gaped at her, the possibilities unravelling through him, leaving him breathless and aching. "Are you—"

"Quite." She stroked his cheek. "Isaac and I have already discussed it, but we know that you will not be comfortable until you have this handled." She laid one hand over his chest, and he knew she meant the power that lurked within him. "But once that is settled, then the three of us will talk. But for now, we'll keep on as we are, if that is all right with you."

"Yes," he gasped. "I mean, it's all right."

She grinned at him. "Now, correct me if I'm wrong, but I assume Isaac brought you here for more than a dance?"

He gaped at her. "How?"

"Please," Shan said. "I'm not a fool. Let me help. The sooner we figure out this," she brushed her hand across his chest again, "the sooner we can figure out this." Pushing herself up on her tiptoes, she brushed her lips against his in a kiss.

It was soft and unbearably chaste, but the promise was there.

"Now come on." She stepped around him, and mute, he followed. Twining her hand in his, she led him expertly through the labyrinth, back to the entrance of the ball.

She must have done this before.

Isaac was there waiting for them, lounging on a bench, cigarette in hand. He didn't look the slightest bit worried, and Samuel felt such the fool for jumping to conclusions.

"Shan," he said, his eyes burning with a passion that Samuel had seen before. "Samuel."

"I found our wayward sheep," Shan replied, pulling him forward. "Now, I believe there is work to be done."

Isaac laughed. "Naturally. Well, don't wait on me." He took another drag on his cigarette. "I'll catch up."

Still a bit stunned, Samuel let Shan lead him back into the party, drawing him towards a cluster of people he vaguely recognized. She cast him a look over her shoulder, one eyebrow elegantly arched, and he reached for the power deep within.

It responded instantly, like a cat waking from its slumber, and when he asked about their thoughts on the recent Unblooded problem he was able to lace the darkness into his words with a shocking ease.

And he pretended that it didn't feel good.

Chapter Twenty-Seven

Shan

"Y̲ou're not listening to me."

"I am," Shan insisted, though she didn't tear her gaze from the streets below. She stood with Bart on the edge of a sloped rooftop, tracing the movements of the people through the district—or more accurately, the lack thereof. It was a heartbreakingly lonely sight—there was hardly anyone out, and those who were moved together in groups, rushing through the night.

There was fear in Dameral, and she could feel it in the air.

"If you were listening," Bart continued, his voice quiet but sharp in her ear, "then you'd be more cautious about this."

She cast him a glare. "I have to investigate them, Hawk," she said, using the code names for their street work. It was safer that way, and Shan didn't want to risk it. Especially when she was investigating something so important.

She had yet to find a connection between the four victims, but she had to keep looking. Their names ran through her head like a mantra.

Fiona Molloy. Charles Hahn. Jessica James. Thomas Menken.

The street was clear, and she dropped from the rooftop to the alley below, softening her landing with a bit of Blood Working. Bart scrambled down after her, his descent less dramatic but no less effective, appearing at her side as she inserted the lockpicks into the keyhole.

"And just … like that," she murmured, as she maneuvered the tumblers into clicking free.

Bart slipped past her, easing the door open and entering the small flat. Shan bit back a smile—even though they were arguing, he still insisted on accompanying her on this mission, going so far as to take the lead when he could.

As if he could do anything against a Blood Worker. She let him have his pride, though. She was familiar enough with the sensation—and besides, if they did run into any trouble, she could protect them both.

When Bart waved her forward, the all-clear sign, she stepped into Thomas Menken's flat. He had been the latest victim, found dead in the middle of the intersection in one of the poorest districts of Dameral. He had been found by the Royal Blood Worker and Samuel Aberforth, and from the reports they had given it had been a gruesome affair. Just like the previous ones.

And now she was here, in his home, digging through his belongings in hopes to find some clue as to why he had been targeted.

"What was his job, again?" Bart asked.

"He was a foreman for one of the larger shipping companies," Shan replied, going through the contents of his pantry. It was well stocked, though starting to go off in the week since Menken had been murdered.

Bart simply hummed to himself, and Shan glanced his way. "What?"

"It's just … he did well for himself."

Shan turned around, taking in the space. The furniture was well made, sturdy and solid. The space itself was fairly large, and there was even a private washroom. It was, admittedly, a nicer home than she had expected, though it was perhaps unfair of her to judge it. Her only real experience was with the flat that Samuel had rented—and, well, he had been practically destitute.

"I suppose so," Shan said, "but he was a foreman."

Bart continued to search through Menken's things.

They worked together, letting the silence grow, as they carefully searched every corner of the flat. They were meticulous to leave everything as they had found it, though Shan wasn't sure it mattered—the Guard had already been through, and they hadn't found anything suspicious.

And neither did they.

"Everything is perfectly normal," Bart said, rubbing his hand across his eyes. "There is nothing here to suggest why him."

"Exactly like the others," Shan said. "It must be random, then." It made a certain kind of sense. Whoever this murderer was just wanted them for their blood. There was nothing else to it.

"Unfortunately, this means we have nothing to go on as to who they'll target next."

"Perhaps it's for the best," Bart muttered.

Shan whirled on him. "What?"

He hesitated, gnawing his lip. "Never mind."

"Oh, I will mind." She stalked forward. "Speak your piece."

For a moment she thought he wouldn't, thought he would turn away from her. But he jutted his chin forward, his eyes alight with a burning fire. "Hasn't it occurred to you that this is a trap?"

"A trap?" she repeated, eyes narrowed.

"Yes!" he glanced away, running a hand through his short curls. "Isn't it odd that the King turned to you for this?"

"He took a chance on me, when I found Samuel."

"And how long before the King realizes who you are?" Bart hissed. "Lady LeClaire is not this well connected. Lady LeClaire is not the type to run about Dameral, breaking into people's homes for information. Lady LeClaire is not the type to find a killer."

Shan didn't hesitate, the words flying from her lips. "That's irrelevant. If we succeed I could have my father's role." How could he not see the value in that? "It's a risk worth taking."

"And when he discovers you're the Sparrow?"

Shan rolled her eyes. "He won't. No one will." Aside from a handful of her birds—and Isaac, now—no one knew who the Sparrow was. No one would dare think that it was Shan LeClaire.

No one would expect her to have that kind of ambition. She played her part well, too well sometimes. It chaffed at her, pretending to be what she was not. But it brought her ever closer to her goals.

Bart was just watching her with a sad look in his eyes. "He will. One doesn't remain King for this long by being a fool. You're playing right into his hands."

"I have everything right where I want it," she spat.

He just shook his head. "Your pride will be the death of us, Sparrow."

"You're wrong."

Bart stepped away, and she let him go. "I hope I am." Pulling his hood up, he turned towards the door. "We're not going to find anything else here, and I have birds to see."

Shan watched him go, not calling him back, not fighting him any longer, though his doubts cut her to the bone. It was bad enough that Anton had been turning away from her—she didn't need this from Bart. Now not.

They were the pillars that had held her up her whole life, and now the very foundation she stood on was cracking just as she was reaching new heights.

Everything was playing out better than she could have anticipated. Lady Belrose was considering *her* bill, the Eternal King had turned to *her* for aid. She had both the Lost Aberforth and the Royal Blood Worker eating out of *her* hand.

It was everything she could have hoped for.

A small part of her rebelled at the thought of counting Samuel and Isaac amongst her accomplishments, but she was not fool enough to discount them. Regardless of her feelings for them, they were assets, and she had to be cognizant of it.

She was building power faster than she had ever thought she would. How could they not see it?

Clenching her fist at her side, she strode out the door. This might have been a dead end, but she was not done for the night. Samuel had picked up a couple of interesting leads at the Lynwood party the other night, and she had time.

She would gather every other secret and lie in Aeravin to her and prove that she was able to do this.

She would not destroy them.

She would bring them to glory.

Chapter Twenty-Eight

Samuel

Samuel's lessons had been proceeding well, according to Isaac, as he twisted the man round and round to obey his commands. Kneeling had only been the beginning—Samuel forced Isaac to crawl on his knees across the floor, to grovel, and once, even, to turn his own blade against his throat, the steel pressing against the soft skin until blood blossomed.

Samuel had no idea how Isaac separated it in his mind. In this room—this grim chamber of the King's—it was as if they were different people. As if what happened here couldn't touch what they were building outside. Where they met over coffee and talked books, where Isaac escorted him to balls and salons when Shan was busy, where they shared heated glances that spoke of promise.

Not the pain that the King's training put them through, honing Samuel's gifts and testing his limits—tempered by the promise that maybe, just maybe, they could take all this away.

But after the failure of the tavern experiment and the success of the Lynwood party, they were running out of options. They needed fresh subjects, new ways to push the limits of his power. He might be able to bring himself to pull some secrets from Blood Workers, but he couldn't dare risk exposure, and so Isaac did the only thing he could.

He filed his report to the Eternal King. And the Eternal King? He was curious, and so Isaac was dismissed.

So tonight, Samuel stood in front of the King and his books of notes, alone. The King had shed his fancy coat, standing there in only breeches and shirtsleeves, the cuffs tucked up almost to his elbows. Witch light highlighted the scars on his arms, the faint white lines crisscrossing their way across his skin.

He was caught staring, and the King's lips curved into a small smile. "Blood Working has come a long way in the past millennium. Our methods didn't use to be so refined."

"Can't you heal them?"

"I could," the King acknowledged, "but I want to remember where I came from, and what I learned. You should be thankful, though, that the Blood Workers of today heal clean. We wouldn't want to ruin Isaac's pretty skin."

Samuel blanched, and the King's smile turned a little bit cruel.

Speaking through a suddenly dry throat, Samuel asked, "What is today's lesson?"

The King turned to him. "You're strong, Samuel, even stronger than your father. I am proud of your successes, but we need to know just how powerful you are. If you can overcome even the strongest wills—and so we will test you."

"I see," Samuel said. "On whom?"

"Oh, I have the perfect specimen."

"Specimen?" Samuel furrowed his brow. "I don't understand."

"Yes. She's resisted all traditional forms of interrogation. Her strength of will is incredible, and if she wasn't so dangerous I'd be impressed." The King snarled. "She's a criminal, Samuel, and you're our last hope of getting the truth out of her."

Samuel took a deep breath, wondering if this was better or worse than experimenting on Isaac. At least this would be a stranger—but then again, did she deserve this? "What was her crime?"

The King cocked his head to the side, like a cat studying his prey. "Does it really matter?"

No, it didn't. It wasn't like the King would find some other person for them to practice on if Samuel wanted to spare her—Samuel had already learned that the King never spared anyone, despite his claims otherwise. "Just curious."

The King sighed, but acquiesced. "You do need to know for the purpose of this interrogation. She was a handmaiden to one of my Councillors, and she stole from her employer. Information, state secrets, anything she could sell to foreign spies."

Samuel clasped his hands behind his back to hide their shaking. Information, then.

The King continued. "We never found who she sold the information *to*. Your task is to get her to tell us."

This was the way they could get them back, a tangible benefit to his training. He had known that this would happen eventually, that the King would use him for justice. But this was different from hunting a murderer—that saved lives. But this?

Well, he didn't rightly know. But he didn't have a choice. "All right."

"Don't look so sad, Samuel," the King said. "It might seem unsavory, but it is an unfortunate necessity. You need to build up your talents, so that when they're needed you can use them instinctively and without fear."

Hanging his head, Samuel said, "I had hoped that I wouldn't need to use them much. That it would be control I was learning."

"With mastery comes control. But I understand." The King clasped his shoulder, squeezing tight. "But for the first time we have an opportunity to take this … power, the one that so many Aberforths used for ill, and use it for good. To protect Aeravin."

Samuel wrenched himself away, anger making him bold and foolish. "Please don't put that on me. My father was—"

"A monster," the King interrupted. "And it's not your job to atone for his sins. But you can change your legacy, restore respect to the Aberforth name."

To the King's name—it wasn't Samuel that he cared about

precisely, but his own legacy. The blood of his blood, the flesh of his flesh. He could have married again, could have had another family. It had been over nine hundred years since the death of his wife, after all, but he had never sought out another.

It was a bit romantic, Samuel had to admit. But it also meant that everything he was, everything he did, was a reflection on the King. And that was a weight he didn't want to carry, even if he did want to be better than the bastard that sired him. But perhaps, in this particular case, it wouldn't be so bad to give in—to use this monstrous power for a bit of good. If he could save even one Unblooded life, it would be worth the stain on his soul.

And it would help him continue to win the King's support, and with it he could help Shan with her plans to change things. It was better than holing up in his home, never speaking to anyone or doing anything for fear of accidentally using his power. He just needed to play the game first.

Feeling resolved for the first time since the King had proposed this plan, he stood tall. "I'm ready."

The King smiled. "Good." Walking over to the door, he opened it and spoke to the guard. "Bring the girl."

Samuel took several deep breaths, closing his eyes as he reached for his gift. The King had been right about one thing, at least. It *was* getting easier with practice. As soon as he reached for it, it stirred to life, filling him with power and confidence—with the knowledge that while he drew on it, he was the one in control.

Most of the time.

It was addicting, this comfort. His whole life had been one of caution and fear, bowing to the whims of others, to the things he couldn't control. His place as Unblooded, mistaken though it was. His poverty. His mother's illness and death.

But now? There was nothing to fear.

The Guard had returned, escorting a young woman. She was a slight thing, pale and with a long, thick braid of dark hair. Samuel could tell that she had been pretty, though now she was wan and thin from her imprisonment, and her eyes shone bright and clever. Her arms were covered in bruises, and she moved gingerly—as if she was wounded.

The effects of the *interrogations* the King had mentioned. Torture, Samuel was sure.

Hopefully, his method would be less painful.

"You can take those off," Samuel said, looking at the manacles that still bound her. The Guard glanced up at the King, who nodded his assent. Only then did he unchain the woman, and she stood there rubbing her wrists. "And you can leave us now."

"As he said," the King added, and the Guard left.

The woman was staring at them both, not ducking her head in deference like most of the servants that Samuel had encountered in the palace. She was no longer cowed, and Samuel had to respect that.

"Thank you for helping us," Samuel said, stepping forward with a smile that wasn't entirely forced. He gestured towards a table set in the corner that the King had brought in for this exact purpose. "You can have a seat if you like, Miss . . .?"

"Kalyn," the woman replied, eyeing the chair distrustfully, as if searching its wooden frame and soft, white cushions for deception. "And what shall I call you, sir?"

She managed to make the honorific sound like an insult, and Samuel felt bad. In another context, in another life, he would have liked her a great deal, but the Eternal King hadn't brought her here so they could make friends. "My name is Samuel Aberforth, but you can just call me Samuel."

Kalyn glanced up, her dark eyes narrowed. "It's you, then."

"It is," Samuel said, biting back a frown as he slid into his seat. News spread far and fast, and he supposed that even prisoners could get their hands on the gossip rags that kept detailing his activities since his introduction to society. "Would you mind answering a few questions?"

"Depends on the questions," she said carefully, settling in the chair across from him. She glanced over at the King, who stood watching them a few feet away. "I can't promise to have the answers."

This was the time: he released just a tiny bit of power, weaving it into his words. "I'll keep it simple," he said, and she relaxed, her eyes going soft. "Why don't you tell me about yourself?"

"Not much to know," she replied. "I worked in Lady Belrose's home for years, making my way up to handmaiden." She clenched her hands in her lap. "Four weeks ago, she caught me stealing from her and she turned me over to the Guard."

Samuel felt a bit green, but he reached down into his power, pulling on it until he was steady and strong again, until he was flooded with its calming presence. "How did she catch you?"

For a second it looked like she was going to resist, but he could feel the power hanging between them, slowly sinking its claws into her and making her malleable. "I was in the wrong place," Kalyn explained, "at the wrong time. Lady Belrose was supposed to be out to lunch with her daughter. She found me in her study, going through her notes, and when she searched my chambers she found the copies I had made. I hadn't had my free day yet to drop them off."

The King shot Samuel a pointed look, but he waved him aside. He wasn't a fool. "What did you do with the notes?"

"I met a man at the docks, every Sunday at noon, and traded the notes for a bag of coin."

Samuel couldn't help himself. She had been better off than most, having a coveted position as a handmaiden, and still she had risked it all for coin. "So you did this for money, then?"

"Of course!" Kalyn frowned at him. "I needed the money for Res's treatment."

Samuel paused. "What?"

"They don't take barter," Kalyn explained, rather unhelpfully. "Just coin. And blood—but I didn't have enough blood to pay for this."

Afraid of the truth, but desperate to hear it, Samuel released just a little more magic. "You were ill?"

"Not me," Kalyn said, staring down at her hands. "My younger brother, Res. I don't know if he's still alive." Perhaps it was the effects of his power, but she didn't seem particularly bothered. Her gaze was soft and unfocused, her voice quiet and empty of emotion.

Samuel looked away from her, his mood thunderous, but the Eternal King was unmoved. He simply rolled his hand at the wrist, signaling for him to get on with it. Samuel had to bite his lip to hold back the rush of anger that almost had him demanding to know if the King knew all along.

But he just turned to face Kalyn. "And your contact?"

"I never knew his real name," Kalyn said. "He went by Storm, but we always met at this tea shop."

"Which shop?" the King asked, finally stepping forward and joining the conversation.

Unable to take any more, Samuel just funneled a raw punch of power into his next command. "Tell him whatever he wants to know. Names. Locations. Everything." Kalyn turned her head to the side as if she had been slapped, and Samuel pushed away from the table. He left them alone, letting the King pull the information he needed from Kalyn's unresisting lips.

He pressed his hands against his face. It wasn't supposed to be like this.

He turned around just in time to see a flash of steel in the King's hand, the other tangled in Kalyn's braid so that he could pull her head back and bare her throat. Before Samuel could even say a word, the King had drawn his knife through the girl's neck, cutting enough to bare the white of the bone.

Kalyn clasped her hands around her throat, as if she could hold her skin together through sheer will alone as the blood poured through her fingers. Her eyes were wide with panic as she struggled to speak, to breathe, but she was only able to make a strangled, gurgling noise—a noise that would haunt Samuel for the rest of his life.

He rushed to her side, catching her as she fell from her chair. There was nothing he could do but watch her die, holding her in his arms as she stared up at him, until she stared at nothing at all.

Samuel held her still warm body close, his shoulders shaking as he struggled to not break. He heard the King walk away, drop his knife in the sink, turn on the water to wash the blood away. Calmly cleaning away the murder he had just committed.

As if he could wipe away his inhumanity with a bit of soap and water.

"You killed her," Samuel gasped.

"I did," he said, his voice so terribly calm.

"But why?" Samuel snarled, turning to look at his King. His ancestor, standing there, a towel in his hand, wiping away the last of the blood that had splattered on his skin. "She gave us what you wanted."

"Only because you forced her," the King said. "Besides, why are you crying over her? She wasn't just an Unblooded thief—she was a traitor to our nation."

Samuel wiped his face, only then realizing that he was even crying. "Her brother was sick." She was only trying to save him, to pay for the medicine that Blood Workers could easily provide but demanded so much coin for. Was what she had done illegal? Yes.

But he couldn't call it wrong—and even if it was, he couldn't stomach this as the price for her crimes.

"That doesn't matter." He threw the towel to the side. "I am a king, Samuel. It is my job to enforce the law for the protection of all, and I cannot allow a traitor to live. But I am not without mercy—I made it quick. Clean. Now, let go of the body."

Samuel did, not caring that he was covered in blood, that he was facing the King with tears in his eyes. "She didn't deserve to die."

"That is not your choice to make," the King said, his eyes cold and hard as he looked Samuel over. "Treason is a capital crime."

Samuel started to tremble, and the King turned away. "We're done for today. Go home, rest up. Justice is hard, but you'll adjust in time. You'll see this is the only way."

Wiping away his tears with the back of his hand, Samuel turned away from his king. He didn't do as he was told, though. He left the palace, but he couldn't simply go home. He couldn't be alone with his thoughts, with the image of Kalyn's dying face burned into the back of his eyelids.

He wanted to forget about it—he wanted a friend who would treat him like a person tonight, when he felt so much like a tool. But he couldn't turn to Isaac—he had no clue where the man lived. So it would have to be Shan.

First, however, he had to return home—just for a moment. Even the Lost Aberforth couldn't wander around Dameral in blood-stained clothes.

Chapter Twenty-Nine

Shan

S han heard the commotion from her study—the raised voices, the crash of something fragile, shattering as if it had been flung against the wall. She was on her feet in an instant, hiking up her skirts and running out of the room and down the stairs. The sight she came upon was something out of her worst nightmares—Isaac and Anton at each other's throats, seconds away from bursting out into a bare-knuckled brawl.

Her footman—no doubt unwillingly drawn into this conflict—huddled in the corner, next to the destroyed remains of a very fine vase. The two men were screaming in each other's faces—vile words of censure, and Anton was advancing on Isaac with an anger that scared Shan.

She had never seen him so enraged before, but then again, he had been walking a knife edge these past few months since she had killed their father, and it looked like he had found an outlet at last.

At the very least she was thankful that Isaac had the decency to restrain from Blood Working, though he held his ground against Anton's advance, cruel words dropping from his lips. "Useless man, hiding behind your sister's skirts."

"Enough!" she shouted, and both of them turned to her in shock, as if surprised to see her standing there at the foot of the stairs. As if they didn't think their row would draw her to them.

"Shan," Isaac breathed, a plea, and she turned her eyes upon him in worry even as her brother began to rant.

"Ah, there you are, sister," Anton spat. "I was just telling our *esteemed guest* that he has to leave, seeing as he is not welcome here—"

Shan held up her hand without even looking at her brother, shushing him as she took in the ragged look around Isaac's edges. She had never seen him like this before—so worn and weary, seconds away from falling apart. "Why are you here, Isaac?"

Isaac didn't respond. He just looked to Anton helplessly, shaking his head.

Shan understood. He wouldn't—couldn't—speak in front of her brother. He was too vulnerable for that. So, silently, she took him by the arm.

"What are you doing?" Anton turned on her, his anger not diminished in the slightest. "Shan, you cannot trust him, not after—"

"I told you before, brother," Shan said softly, so very quietly, "that I know what I am doing. I do not need your protection."

Anton stared at her for a long moment, clenching his fist, then spun away sharply. He snapped his fingers at the footman, who hurriedly grabbed his jacket. The second he had it in his hand, he slung it over his shoulder and stalked to the door. "I'd warn you not to do anything you'd regret, but you're with him."

He slipped out, slamming the door behind him and leaving them standing there in painful silence.

"I shouldn't have come here," Isaac whispered.

"Nonsense," Shan replied. Glancing at the footman, she instructed him to have one of the maids bring up some wine, then waited until she was gone before she spoke again. "Please don't take my brother's words to heart."

"He isn't wrong, though." Isaac wrung his hands. "I have only brought pain and regret. To both of you."

"We're not children anymore, Isaac. Now come on." She tugged him by the arm, leading him to the stairs. "Let's talk."

He followed her in maudlin silence. She carefully smoothed her skirts, rolling her shoulders to release some of the tension that had crept up in the last few minutes. She led him again to her study, seating him by the fire, and when the serving girl arrived with the glasses and the wine, she poured them both a generous amount and placed the goblet in his hand.

He didn't speak right away. He just sipped his wine and stared into the fire. Shan didn't push him. Settling in the chair across from him, she waited. He was scared and hurting, and he would speak when he was ready.

"We're too late," he said at last, looking up at her with haunted eyes, and suddenly everything became clear.

"Samuel," she whispered, and he nodded. "Where is he?"

"With the King," Isaac spat. "Where else? I tried—" his voice broke, a terrible, haunting sound. "I tried to be there for him, but I couldn't. I wasn't even allowed to be in the room, and so—"

"So you came here."

"I tried to stay away," he admitted. "I walked the streets for hours, Shan. Hoping I could just ... I don't know. Disappear. But still, I found my way here." He drained the rest of his glass, and fear rolled off him in a wave so strong that she could taste it.

"What happened tonight?"

"I am the Royal Blood Worker, and it is my duty to do as the King commands," Isaac began, and she stepped forward to refill his wine glass. His hand caught hers as she set it down, keeping her close to him. She didn't resist. "Even if it means delivering Samuel to him like a lamb to the slaughter."

Intrigued and a little bit terrified, Shan sat at his side as she encouraged him in his tale. It didn't take much, just a nod of encouragement here, a simple question there. Isaac spilled it all, as if he couldn't stop himself, as if it was a compulsion.

A confession.

He told her everything, all that he had done in his trainings with Samuel, and the reports that he had sent to the King. How the King had been pleased with the progress but kept pushing for more—for more practical applications, for darker things that Isaac couldn't bring himself to ask of Samuel. Frustrated, the King had taken it into his own hands, had summoned Samuel to the castle for a test.

And though Isaac had begged him not to force Samuel to be alone, the King had not been moved.

She held his hand through it all, all her masks fading and her responses becoming more and more real as he continued to speak. It had been years since they had opened up to each other like this—speaking of pain and fear and vulnerability. And as he proved what he had promised her before—that he was not the King's mindless puppet—it was painfully easy to slip back into this, the time melting away as if it had never passed.

Shan knew that she was standing on the edge of a cliff, and the slightest push would send her falling.

When at last he finished, his eyes closed and his head tilted forward, she couldn't do more than whisper his name. He glanced down at her, his dark eyes empty and framed by his soft eyelashes, and he looked so beautiful and broken that she couldn't breathe.

"I failed him," he whispered. "I promised him that we'd find a cure."

"You haven't failed him." Shan squeezed his hand. "We can still find a cure for it, and Samuel knows that you are fighting for him. He knows the power of the King, and he will not blame you for it."

She hoped so, at least. But Isaac just looked at her, a frown on his face, and said, "I still feel like a failure."

"You're not," Shan said. And she believed in Samuel—he was stronger than Isaac knew, and she had to have faith that he could survive this test. "Trust in him, as he would trust in you."

He bit his lip, and he looked so vulnerable, so shattered. "What if I don't trust in myself?"

"Then let my trust be enough." She leaned forward, capturing his mouth with hers, and Isaac grunted in surprise. For a second she thought she had miscalculated, that this wasn't the kind of comfort he needed, but then he grabbed her, his hands on her waist, pressing in with an almost bruising intensity.

She didn't fight him as he pulled her onto his lap, slotting his lips over hers as he pressed their bodies together. Her knees spread automatically as she settled over his hips, locking them together, her hands clenching his shoulders as she clung to him, tasting the despair and desperation on his lips.

He breathed her name again and again, a benediction, as he peppered her cheeks, her throat, the tops of her breasts with kisses. Shan pressed against him, an offering, knowing what he sought, the friction they both needed, driven by the desperate desire to lose themselves in their own bodies. To drown their fears and emotions in a few moments of pure physicality.

Letting him hold her up, she reached behind her, pulling at the stays of her dress so that they came loose, sliding down and revealing the corset beneath. Isaac let out a shocked breath, suddenly stilling as she allowed the dress to fall. He kept staring as she moved his hand to her corset, and he gently pulled it free, letting it fall after the dress and leaving her in just her shift.

"Shan," he gasped, looking everywhere but strangely afraid to touch. "Are you—"

"I am," she said, sharper than she intended. When he still didn't move, she ripped her shift off, leaving herself wonderfully bare. She pulled from his embrace to slide down his body, enflamed by the feeling of her naked skin against the silk of his suit—him, still perfectly dressed, looking down at her in awe as she knelt between his spread knees.

Trailing her hand down the long length of his torso, Shan felt the flutter of each of his breaths, the barely held restraint that coiled through him. Her fingers lingered where his shirt tucked into his trousers, and she glanced up at him through her eyelashes, coy and sweet. "May I have a taste?"

His hand found hers, fingers twining as he eased the button open. "Yes," he breathed, lifting his hips as she pulled down his trousers and underthings, baring himself before her.

"I've missed this," Shan confessed as she leaned forward, dragging her tongue across his leaking cunt. Isaac bucked up into her mouth so she wrapped her hand around his hip, holding him firmly in place as she refamiliarized herself with him. "Let me suck you."

"Please," Isaac gasped, moving to pull his lower lips apart, letting his small cock jut forward, his bud grown and engorged and perfect for Shan to wrap her lips around. The result of the Blood Working treatments he had spent so long on, and Shan knew how to work it for his pleasure.

So she did, pulling his cock into her mouth as she suckled, working her mouth up and down his length, flicking her tongue against the sensitive head before taking him all the way in. His scant inches still felt heavy against her lower lip, twitching and eager, and she released her grip on him so that he could thrust into her mouth again and again, until he at last shattered against her with a low groan.

She leaned back with a smirk as he struggled to catch his breath, her fingers warm on his thighs. "Feeling better?"

He didn't respond—he just seized her in his arms, rising to his feet and carrying her to her desk. She clung to him as he swept it clear, pressing biting little kisses against his throat until he groaned. He dropped her hard on the desk, the wood shockingly cold against her naked skin. She grinned up at him, daring and defiant, and he swore under his breath. "You are a marvel, Shan."

She pulled him down, clawing at his clothes now, desperate for him to touch her. He laughed, and she felt suddenly lighter, as if she could float away on the very sound of it. He kissed her deeply, unmindful of his own taste on her lips, as he dipped his hand between her legs, driving into her aching warmth with a roughness that had her gasping. He fucked her relentlessly, twisting his hand so that the heel of his palm pressed up against her clit, falling into that old, familiar rhythm of skin and sweat and pleasure as they both chased the release they were looking for.

Chapter Thirty

Samuel

"*Blood and fucking steel.*"

Samuel came to a sudden stop, sliding on the damp cobblestones as he narrowly avoided colliding with Anton, who had barreled around the corner like a man possessed. He carried his jacket slung across his shoulders, frowning and exasperated all at once as he looked at Samuel in disgust. "Not you, too."

He blinked at Anton, his words fading on his lips as Anton rolled his eyes up to the sky, as if begging the universe to grant him patience.

"You're too late, Aberforth," Anton spat. "If you're looking for the comforting arms of my sister, de la Cruz beat you to it."

Samuel swallowed hard, ignoring the sudden stab of longing that struck through him. Of course Isaac had turned to Shan; he should have realized that himself. If only he had been a little quicker—perhaps met Isaac at the same time, upon the doorstep, then maybe—

But no. He had come here, to the LeClaires', with blood on his hands. Every time he closed his eyes, every time he so much as blinked, he saw the girl again. The way she had struggled, the blood pouring from her neck as she tried in vain to stop the flow. He hadn't held the blade, but he had done nothing to stop it, and Samuel knew that it would haunt him for all his days.

It didn't matter that she had been a traitor, not when her brother was dying. Not when Aeravin could have saved him but chose not to.

And even coming here—even thinking that he could turn to Shan, or to Isaac—was the worst kind of selfishness. They were both better than him and he didn't want to drag them down into his darkness.

No, this was his burden to bear.

But that was not something he could think about now, not with Anton glaring up at him in anger, defying him to speak.

"I see she is popular tonight" was what he managed, pushing past the tension that had crept up and tightened his throat, and Anton's face twisted into an ugly grimace. "What of you, Anton? Are you all right?"

"I am fine," Anton replied, though that was a lie if he had ever heard one. "But I'm sorry that I cannot say the same for you. You'll have to find someone else's shoulder to cry on. Shan's is occupied."

Samuel tried to temper his expression—though he was glad they had each other, he was still so, so lonely—but he must not have been very successful, for Anton sighed, rubbing at his temples. "I'm going to regret this, but have you ever been to a gambling hell, Aberforth?"

"Uh, no?"

"Consider this an education then," Anton said, stepping up beside him. "Give it a couple of hours and you'll forget whatever ails you." He led him across the street, calling for a hack.

"This isn't necessary," Samuel began, but fell quiet when Anton shot him a look so harsh that he was reminded, uncomfortably, of Shan.

"Something is," Anton said, "and this is the best I've got. You coming or not?"

Samuel considered saying no, turning away and continuing down the street, passing right on by the LeClaire townhouse and heading towards his own home, to his cold and lonely bed to stew in the darkness that plagued him.

It certainly wouldn't do. He already felt like he was drowning.

He looked up at Anton with a false smile on his face, saying, "I'd be a very poor student if I left my teacher, wouldn't I?"

Anton beamed, suddenly looking so much more alive. "To the Fox Den," he said to the driver, then slung himself into the carriage. He held out his hand, pulling Samuel in after him. "To adventure."

Samuel grinned, for real this time, and let Anton LeClaire sweep him away into the night.

———————

The Fox Den was so much more than Samuel anticipated—not simply a gambling hell, but an experience that cultivated a sense of danger and delight. The gambling hell was built into the basement of a hotel, one of the few in Dameral, and they had entered through a staircase cut into the ground itself. Anton smiled at him as they arrived at the thick wooden door and rapped a distinct pattern against it.

A panel in the door opened, revealing the harsh face of a doorman who glared at Samuel with suspicion, but when Anton vouched for him let them pass. He opened the door, ushering them into a shockingly small room. There was a bar along one wall, stocking everything. But it was the counter along the other wall that had Anton's attention—the one that turned money into small wooden chips used for gambling and back again.

"It's not the most exclusive club, but still," Anton said, leading him to the money changers. "One does not simply join the Fox Den. You either need an invitation or a referral."

"If it's so exclusive, how did you get in?"

Anton bared a laugh and dropped a handful of coins in front of the teller. She swiftly swiped them away, replacing them with a stack of differently colored chips. "I may be Unblooded, Aberforth, but my coin spends as well as any other."

Samuel nodded, glancing over at the conversion chart. It was an easy enough transaction, and he pulled the money from his coin purse. He placed it on the counter, and the teller shot him a coy smile as she made the trade. "Welcome, Lord Aberforth," she purred. "May luck be on your side."

He grabbed the stack of coins, but she caught his wrist, placing a velvet bag in his hand. It was embroidered with a fox's face, the creature looking strangely fey and wild. "On the house," the teller said. "For every new patron."

Samuel nodded, slipping the chips into his pouch. Anton already has his tucked away, slipped back into his pocket where he wouldn't lose them. Samuel held onto his, feeling the weight of it in his hand. It was a small sum to many Blood Workers, but what he held in his hand in this moment would have fed him for months in his old life. Strange to think that such a small thing was the ruin of so many people. It was, in a way, harder to even think of it as money in this form. They were just chips—bits of colored wood—signifying something far more valuable than themselves.

"What's your poison?" Anton asked, turning away from the teller. He walked to the edge of a small balcony, staring down into the pit where the games were run. Samuel followed wordlessly, taking in the sights. There was roulette and hazard, vingt-et-un and piquet. All around the room were dozens of people, men and women, laughing and betting and flinging their coins against the tables like they meant nothing.

And they probably didn't—they probably had so much more where that came from.

That bitter old hate rose in him, and he clenched his bag of coins hard enough that it hurt. But all he said was "I am not overly familiar with gambling."

Anton nodded at him, neither surprised nor impressed. "Let's start simple. Vingt-et-un is easy enough."

"I know the principles. Don't go over twenty-one."

"Good." Anton led him down the stairs, giving him a quick run-down of the rest of the rules as he went.

Here it was easy to slip into the crowd, just another one of the dozens who came to drink and gamble the night away. If he got a few looks of recognition, well, they were quickly pulled back to their games of chance, too busy losing money to ponder the appearance of the Lost Aberforth.

It was freeing, and Samuel hated how much he enjoyed it.

Anton found them seats at an open table and they settled in to play. The dealer winked at Anton, smiling like he was an old friend, and Samuel supposed he might be. A reputation like his didn't come out of nowhere.

"Go easy on my friend, Sarah," Anton said. "It's his first time."

The girl—Sarah—smiled at him, though the effect was chilled by the fact that her lips were painted the color of blood. She was a pretty girl, clearly Unblooded, given that she worked here, but there was something about her that seemed almost ethereal. "I'll be gentle," she promised, laying down the cards, and Samuel smiled.

Until he lost his first hand.

The night went quickly after that, Samuel learning the game—winning some, losing more. He had a feeling that Anton was folding more often than he normally would to give him a chance, but he found he didn't mind. He was fun to play with, and Samuel thought he would really enjoy these card games if they were played for fun and not for money.

But that was not the case, and with each successive hand Samuel grew more bitter. It didn't matter that the money he was losing was, relative to his accounts, negligible. Nor did it matter that he was one of the cheapest gamblers.

It was the principle of the thing.

Here both Blood Workers and Unblooded came together, money slipping carelessly through their fingers, money that could be better spent throughout Dameral, helping those who needed it.

Perhaps he slapped his cards down too hard, perhaps his frown was too severe. But Anton swept up his chips and gestured for Samuel to do the same. "Thanks, darling," he said to the dealer, flashing her a wink.

She gave him a smile and a wave, then turned to Samuel. "Come back any time, my lord." She fanned her cards in front of her, too over the top to be taken seriously, and Samuel had to laugh.

Anton gestured towards a door, nearly hidden away against the design of the wallpaper. If it hadn't been pointed out to him, Samuel wasn't sure he'd have ever noticed it. But Anton was already there, and Samuel had no choice but to follow or be left alone in a gambling hell full of strangers.

He hurried after him.

Anton had already passed through the door, which hid a staircase. It wound up and up, curling around itself as they rose above where the gambling floor had been. "Where are we going?"

"To the High-Rollers' Lounge," Anton said, over his shoulder. "You looked like you could use a break, and I could always use another drink."

"Oh." It made sense now that he thought about it, that the Fox Den would have one of these, but he didn't think that Anton would be one of the members. For one, he was Unblooded, and for another, given the rumors about the LeClaire fortune, it didn't seem wise for them to spend their money so frivolously.

"I can feel your judgement, you know," Anton said, as they emerged into what looked to be the lushest parlor he had ever seen. Into a wide room, filled with low couches and chairs in deep colors. The glow of witch light shimmered down from above, casting the room in low light.

It was much less crowded than the gaming floor downstairs, small groups of people gathered around tables as they spoke in quiet voices. It was still so rich that Samuel felt like he was a bit of an impostor for being there at all, but some of the tension still ebbed away.

"What do you want to drink?" Anton asked, already shifting towards the bar.

"Tea, if they have it."

Anton, to his credit, didn't argue. "They do. Sit where you like, I'll be right back."

Samuel chose a collection of chairs away from any other groups of people—and also by an open window. He crashed into the chair, turning towards the soft breeze that came in off the sea, the early summer breeze feeling cool on his skin. He was considering if it would be too rude to tear off his cravat when Anton came back, shrugging off his jacket and tossing it onto his chair.

Well, if Anton was stripping his jacket, then surely he could loosen his cravat.

"So, do you want to talk about it?"

Samuel froze. "Talk about what?"

"Whatever is on your mind, Aberforth," Anton said, though he paused as a waitress brought them their drinks. A fresh pot of tea for Samuel, and a glass of dark amber for Anton, served quickly, and she was gone. Anton didn't even reach for his drink; he just rested his elbows on his knees as he stared at Samuel. "I'm not that much of a fool to see that something is bothering you, and it doesn't seem like the tables are helping."

"Am I that easy to read?" Samuel quipped, and Anton chuckled in spite of himself. "Also, just Samuel, please."

"Fine, fine," Anton shrugged. "I suppose we are friends now, aren't we? You came to my house, depressed and dejected, and I took you out gambling. What greater display of masculine bonding is there?" His tone dripped with sarcasm, but his eyes were kind. "I'm just sorry it didn't work out like I had hoped."

Samuel stared at him in surprise—given their past encounters, he was surprised to see this sort of kindness from Anton. Not that he had ever been cruel, or crueler than anyone else who had been born to a Blood Worker family, but he had clearly been pursuing his own agenda. Tonight, he just seemed tired, caught up in his own cares and worries, and yet here he was, trying to cheer Samuel up.

He appreciated it more than he thought he would.

"It's still strange to me," Samuel said. "Spending—wasting—money. I know it's ridiculous, that I have more than enough of it now. But old habits are hard to break."

Anton nodded, sympathetic. "It's ridiculous, isn't it? Tossing so much money for the chance—the thrill—of winning more." Samuel looked at him in surprise, and Anton smiled wryly. "What?"

"I just thought you would enjoy the game more," Samuel muttered. "I mean, you have a—"

"Reputation," Anton said in a low voice. "Yes. People see me as a dissolute gambler, as no threat, and they don't mind their words as much around me." He gestured at his face. "And my beauty doesn't hurt things either. We all have our parts to play."

Samuel just stared at him, taking in the carefully constructed persona that made up Sir Antonin LeClaire the Second. The tailored clothes, well-made and fashionable. The carefully cut and styled hair. He had designed himself to be a rake, frivolous and dissolute, and Samuel had fallen for it.

He remembered Shan's words, back when she had first found him and started transforming him into Lord Aberforth. How he needed to come up with a version of himself that wasn't entirely true, a mask he could wear before the other nobles of Aeravin.

It looked like he wasn't the only one who had gotten that advice.

"Are you happy with it?" Samuel asked.

Anton's brows drew together in thought, and Samuel wondered if anyone had ever bothered to ask him that. Happiness didn't seem to be the lot of the LeClaires, after all, but duty and power.

"I am good at it," Anton said, his voice surprisingly bitter. "And it's not like I have a lot of options, anyway. I'm not the eldest, so I have no seat in the House of Lords. Not that they'd allow an Unblooded in there anyway."

"You know much about the House, then?"

"A bit," Anton hedged. "I was fascinated by politics when I was young, but that was before I learned it wasn't my place." His hand clenched at his side, reflexively, as if he recalled an old pain. "But that was a long time ago."

"Well, perhaps you can help me out," Samuel said, an idea

sparking. "They already have me sitting in on meetings, but I'll be damned if I can figure any of it out."

Anton shook his head. "I appreciate the offer, but it would be better if we didn't. Trust me on that, Samuel." Before he could ask what that meant, Anton stood and grabbed his jacket. "Anyway, I do have a reputation to keep."

Samuel just looked away, knowing a rebuff when he saw one. "I understand."

"Care to rejoin me downstairs? I think it's time for roulette."

Samuel shook his head. "I need to head home."

"Ah, I tried. Just speak to Mary-Ann at the front, and she'll call a hack for you." He turned to walk away but stopped at the last second. "Oh, and Samuel? You're not that bad."

He laughed, because it was so patently untrue. The King had seen to that. "Thanks, you too."

Anton only shrugged. "We'll see how long you think that."

Chapter Thirty-One

Shan

S han and her brother had avoided each other. It wasn't the accidental passing of two ships in the night, busy people with busy schedules and no time to meet. It was the calculated, deliberate work of two people who knew each other—and their schedules—well enough to ensure there were no chance encounters. The only communication they had was the nightly arrival of his notes upon her desk, write-ups on all that he had seen and heard, delivered after she had gone to bed.

She was used to being ignored, to receiving the cold-shoulder. Blood and steel, in her debut year she had received the cut direct a few times. But she had never imagined that it would come from *Anton*. They had always relied on each other, two halves of a whole, the way twins were supposed to be.

When had that changed?

She stood at the door to her brother's room, her fist raised to knock, but the resolve fading fast. Despite the fact that she had cleared her schedule, had rearranged things so that she could barge in on him while he was getting ready for another night out upon the town. It shouldn't be so hard. They could still talk, mend whatever was going wrong between them, and return to the way things had been before. She just had to be open with him.

Shan dropped her fist and walked away.

It was a little early to begin her rounds, but she couldn't spend another night cooped up in this damn house, surrounded by silence and judgement, her shoulders tense as she sorted through folders of information and ledgers of financial records, constantly switching back and forth between the spymaster and Lady LeClaire.

She could have gone to one of the many parties in Dameral, seeing the boost to her reputation over recent months. But that would just be another kind of stress—a world of lies and false masks and games.

Tonight she needed something simpler. She needed to be the Sparrow.

By the time her transformation was complete, night was starting to fall. She slipped out of the house through the servants' door and crept through the alleys, leaving the fine district she had grown up in and trading it for something raw and real.

Pulling her hood up over her face, she moved through the streets and let everything fall away until she was simply a body in motion, heading by rote memory to the appointed place. At last she arrived in the dark alleyway and slipped into the shadows, preparing to wait. She grabbed a slim case from her pocket, and a moment later had a cigarette at her lips, the burnt match crushed under her heel.

It was a vice she didn't normally indulge in, even with the Blood Healing she had access to. It was a vile habit, addictive and nasty and far too smelly, but she had picked it up from Isaac when they had spent late nights at the Academy, reading texts and preparing for exams. Then it was a source of camaraderie and comfort, and lately she needed that. To ground herself and calm the nerves she couldn't quite shake.

Besides, it only added to her disguise. Here she was just another soul taking a smoke under the night stars.

She took a long, harsh drag on the cigarette, the pale stick of paper and tobacco turning to ash in her fingers. The only light in the alley was the burning tip, a spark of red between her lips.

Then a flash of shadows in the corner of her eye and Bart dropped down from the roof, landing beside her in a fluttering of cloaks. "I didn't expect to see you tonight, Sparrow."

She hid her smile behind a long drag on her cigarette. "I was feeling restless."

He nodded, understanding, but there was humor in his voice as he said, "So you thought you could swipe my bird out from under me?"

"Hey," she elbowed him lightly, "she likes me."

As if to prove her point, the sound of light footsteps barreled towards them. Their informant ran right up to her, her eyes shining with an excitement that made Shan preen. It still shocked her that she earned such loyalty, that her birds seemed genuinely happy to see her. This bird was a small thing, no more than twelve, dark of skin and decidedly plain—which fortunately was helpful in her line of work. She slid right under most people's attention.

"Sparrow! I haven't seen you in so long."

Turning towards the girl, Shan dropped the cigarette, leaving it to burn out on the cold cobblestones. "Hello, Naomi."

"And Hawk?" the girl asked, breathless and eyes wide. She peered around Shan, as if Bart were just a figment of her imagination. "Both of you? Must be serious."

Blood and steel, she was clever. Checking to ensure they were alone, Shan pulled the young girl closer to the wall and dropped her voice to a whisper. "I'm helping Hawk tonight," she said by way of explanation, and to pull her attention back from him. Bart always charmed the young ones with sleight of hand, pulling coins from behind their ears. "So, do you have anything for us?"

Naomi then remembered her place, squaring her shoulders and lifting her chin like she was giving a report to a queen. "I have news for you."

"Please, continue," Shan said, giving her the ceremony she wanted.

"It's about the murders," Naomi said, dropping her voice low. "I've been telling Hawk that people are growing more nervous—they've stopped going around after dark anymore, and if they have to, they go in groups."

"What about you?" Shan interrupted. "Are you being safe?"

"My brother is working the corner," she said. "He's a pickpocket. I distract, he steals. We've not split up lately."

Shan didn't know if she should be worried or amused. Bart was fond of this girl—she was quick and clever, and she had a knack for hearing things she shouldn't. But these were dangerous times. The killer had yet to take someone so young, but Shan didn't want to be careless, and the blade tucked into Naomi's belt was little more than a sharpened piece of scrap metal. Slipping one of the small daggers from a sheath up her sleeve, she pressed it into the girl's hand, ignoring the gasp of surprise from Bart. "Keep this on you, just in case."

Naomi's eyes went as wide as saucers. "Wow."

"You know how to use it?"

"Stab them and run?"

Shan laughed. "Basically. You'll be fine." She passed her a coin, more than Naomi would normally make in a month, and added, "Get yourself a proper sheath for it. I don't want you accidentally cutting yourself."

The girl slipped the coin away into one of her hidden pockets, but she kept the dagger clenched in her fist. "Yes, ma'am."

"Anyway, I interrupted you," Shan said, courteously. "You were saying?"

"Right." She drew her shoulders up again. "I found something out." She leaned in, dropping her voice. "They just found another body, not even an hour ago."

Shan grabbed the girl's arm. "Where?"

Shan had Bart see the girl back to her brother, ordering them home for the night and bribed them with another piece of shiny gold. It was more than she was used to spending in a night, but she didn't want to risk it, even if Bart was watching her with surprise in his eyes. The girl was a good bird, she had a bright future ahead of her, and she shouldn't waste resources.

It had nothing to do with her being so young. Shan was *not* going soft.

Besides, she still had a body to see.

＋

Dameral was dark and quiet. The crowds that had been present and thriving at dusk had already dispersed, and Shan never felt so exposed as she did then. But the empty streets at least allowed her to make good time as she hurried down to the waterfront, to the place her bird had said the body had been found.

She quickly glanced up at the moon, tracking its movement across the night sky. It had only been a couple of hours—maybe they hadn't moved it yet. Maybe they hadn't touched anything. Maybe she could actually find *something*.

Shan threw off her hood as she approached the perimeter, the spray off the sea kissing her skin. Several members of the Guard were already in position to keep civilians away, blocking off the area where the edges of Dameral clashed against the ocean.

Not that anyone was attempting to get closer. The sector was completely shut down—everyone hidden behind locked doors, as if that was enough to protect them against a determined enough Blood Worker. But Shan wasn't going to shatter their illusions of comfort. Even she wasn't that cruel.

Slinking around the perimeter, she searched for a familiar face to grant her access, when she was stunned to see a shock of familiar golden hair. Samuel stood at the edge of the pier, hands in the pockets of his coat, staring out across the water. The breeze caught his hair—loose and unbound—whipping it back and forth in a way that shouldn't have been so striking.

She hadn't seen him in days, not since before Isaac had come to her. He had refused her messages, and Isaac's as well, and they had both decided to give him what he seemed to want—time.

But time had run out and, and damn it all, she wanted to comfort him, to let him know that she was still on his side, but she couldn't bring that up now. Not when they had a corpse to examine.

Stepping across the perimeter, she passed by the Guards, holding her head high and acting as if she belonged. No one ran to stop her, though she did earn a few strange looks. As she came up beside Samuel, he turned his head and tried to offer a smile.

It came out closer to a grimace.

"I understand," she said, quietly. "The circumstances being what they are."

Samuel nodded, then took a step back to take in her outfit. "Been a while since I've seen that." His smile was more natural this time.

A small flare of warmth rose through her. Very few people had seen her as both sides of her herself, the Lady and the Sparrow, and fewer yet seemed comfortable with both of them, expecting one or the other to beg a mask. But that wasn't the truth—the truth was far more complicated than that. She was both in equal measure, moving between the noble and the spy with a fluidity that couldn't quite be pinned down.

"How did you come to be here?" Shan asked, and Samuel gestured down to the shallow beaches below them to where Alessi stood, directing her Guards with a quick and efficient hand.

"A note. Didn't you get one, too?"

"Possibly," Shan admitted. "But I wasn't home. I do have other sources of information."

"Ah, right. Foolish of me to assume that you didn't find your way here on your own." Holding his arm out to her, the perfect gentleman, he added, "Let's not waste time. Alessi's holding everything for us."

Samuel grabbed a lantern of witch light and led Shan down a short flight of stairs, leaving behind the warehouses and the docks, heading to where the ground turned to sand. The tide was low, exposing a harsh beach filled with stones and shells, and the moon cast a wan and faint light. Samuel held the witch light, illuminating the ground in a span of a couple of feet in front of them as they walked in silence.

The body was closer to the docks than it was to the sea, looking oddly sad and forlorn. Alessi stood near it, waiting for them as they approached. "It's not the body that I'm concerned about," she said, skipping right past the greetings and straight into business.

At times like this, Shan really appreciated Alessi. There was no need to pretend at propriety and pleasantries now. Shan was thankful that she wasn't wearing one of her dresses as she stepped around the body—a quick glance showed that it was the same kind of death as the previous victims. Desiccated and papery, drained of life and vitality. Only this time, the body had been drained and then thrown onto the beach, salt and sand crusting its dark hair—

Her dark hair. It had likely been a woman. Shan couldn't tell if she had been old or young without seeing the face, but that much had been clear in the shape of the body, the tattered remains of the dress.

Samuel coughed behind her, and she turned to check on him, but he was holding himself together better than she had expected. Then again, this was not his first body—in the past few months he had seen more than his fair share, and that changed a person.

For some reason that made her incredibly sad.

"Here," Alessi said, drawing their attention away from the body as she held up a lantern. "This is what you should be concerned about."

Shan stepped forward, squinting at the dark wall. It took her a second to realize that those weren't smudges on the old, salt-soaked wood, but words scrawled in dark lettering, their edges smudged and dripping.

Five Down. One Left.
Your Secrets Will Out.

"Is that paint?" Samuel asked, reaching out to touch it, but Shan snatched his hand in midair.

"It's blood," she whispered, then turned to Alessi. "Hers?"

Alessi shrugged. "Likely. We've gathered a sample, but we haven't had a chance to test it yet. Or to identify the corpse."

Shan spun back to the victim, her mind whirling with possibility. This message was new—a break in the pattern. And there was a deeper pattern here, something they had been missing.

"There was nothing tying them together," Shan said, mostly to herself. They had just been Unblooded people. Simple people with simple lives.

She had been wrong.

"We must have missed it." Samuel looked towards Alessi. "Can you turn her?"

"I can," she said, though she seemed hesitant. "Why? Do you think you recognize her?"

Samuel just stared down at the corpse. "I ... don't know. Just a feeling."

"Let's do it," Shan said, though she wasn't looking forward to touching it. "In case there is anything we can find—"

"All right, LeClaire." Alessi pulled a couple of handkerchiefs from somewhere in her robes and handed them over. "Here, don't touch the body directly if you can avoid it."

Shan took them gratefully, waiting for Alessi to take her position on the other side of the corpse. Together, they carefully lifted her and flipped her over, laying her back down on the sand.

"Well?" Alessi asked.

She had been young. Under thirty. Shan could see it now, even with her ruined face. But more than that, there was something vaguely familiar about the corpse, a faint recognition that she couldn't quite place underneath all the ruined skin. But it was there, even down to the outfit she wore—a tight, black corset that would have fitted much better on a body filled with life.

Wait.

She leaned forward, studying the corset and skirt, the few faux diamonds that still clung to the fabric. Her blood ran cold—she knew this outfit.

"Hells!" Samuel swore, suddenly and violently, and both Shan and Alessi looked up at him in surprise. He was pale and shaking, the lantern twitching violently in his hand. "I know her. She's a card dealer. Vingt-et-un."

"At the Fox Den," Shan said, and Samuel nodded.

"Her name was Sarah."

Shan closed her eyes, searching her memories of her nights at that place, of the Unblooded workers who came and went. Of a brilliant, bright woman with dark hair and a loud laugh. "Sarah Dean." She turned her gaze onto Samuel, who looked pale and wan in the moonlight. "But how did you know?"

"We need to talk" was all he said. "Alone."

"Yes." She glanced at Alessi. "Check the corpse against the blood on file for Sarah Dean, as well as the ... ink from the message. It should be a match." She was already standing, brushing the sand off her knees.

"Where are you going?" Alessi asked. "They said there will be one more."

"Exactly." Shan looked to Samuel. "There is no time to waste."

"Right." He passed the lamp to Alessi, who took it questioningly, but his attention was entirely on Shan. "Where *are* we going?"

"Somewhere safe." She turned quickly, striding across the sand, knowing that Samuel would be one step behind her.

It wasn't long before she had gotten him away from the crime scene, not all the way fully back towards the noble district, but the streets were quiet enough. Pulling him into an alley, she spun to face him. "What do you know?"

Samuel didn't meet her eyes, staring instead at the cobblestoned street, dragging the toe of his boot along it. "There are a few things I haven't told you."

"Clearly. You gamble, for one."

He winced. "Just the one time. Anton took me."

Shan took a step back. "*Anton* took you?"

"Yes." Samuel still kept his gaze low. "I had—it wasn't important, but I wanted to stop by to see you. But I found Anton instead. He let me know that Isaac was already there, and I was too late. So instead he took me to the Fox Den."

Shan just gaped at him. She had no idea that he had tried to reach her that night—her brother had said nothing of this. But the knowledge that he had wanted her, and had not been able to find her, cut her like a knife.

"Samuel, you could have—"

"No, I really couldn't," he said. "It would have been selfish of me, and I couldn't bring myself to interrupt whatever moment the two of you were having. But that's beside the point."

Though it hurt her in ways she never had imagined being hurt before, she held her tongue. "Right. So, Anton. I didn't realize that you two were that close."

"We're not," Samuel replied, "at least I don't think we are. But this isn't the first time he's come to me." He hurried into the tale, of Anton accosting him at his home, of Anton arranging something behind her back, of wanting Samuel's aid but judging him lacking.

And Shan remained silent through it all, as the pieces started falling into place. Her brother had been growing angrier and more secretive by the year, and she had thought it was merely the ever-growing strain of living under their father. For all the plans she had made, she had just assumed that he would be with her.

But she had never once asked him if he was.

"I am a fool."

"You're not," Samuel said, quickly. "It could be nothing at all."

They both knew it was a lie, but Shan didn't press it. She just allowed herself to lean into him, and he wrapped his arms around her. There was nothing forward about it, nothing demanding—just comfort, freely given.

Shan felt like she was breaking apart.

She stepped away, though the loss of his touch was like a physical ache. "You should go. There are some things I need to do."

"You shouldn't do this alone."

"I have to." She dashed away the tears that threatened. She would not be weak—she *could* not be weak. "I owe it to my brother."

"Okay . . ." He brushed a loose strand of hair away from her face. "Just be careful."

"You, too," she whispered, and then slipped out into the night, leaving him alone in the alleyway. She had to start moving before she broke down completely.

Samuel's fears were justified, but it had to be something else. Her brother might be playing something behind her back, but he wouldn't dare do this.

She had to hold onto that.

Chapter Thirty-Two

Samuel

Samuel stared after Shan as she vanished into the night, wishing more than anything that he could go with her. But she was right about this—whatever was going on between her and her brother was personal, and if she needed time to process it, he could at least grant her that. Forcing his presence on her would only make things worse.

So he shoved his hands deep into his pockets and walked in the other direction, away from the crime scene where Alessi ruled, and away from the district he had just started to feel almost comfortable calling home.

Because, like her, he also needed time—though for an entirely different reason. It was beyond foolish to walk the streets like this, but he consoled himself with the knowledge that the murderer had just killed and that the attacks weren't random.

Whatever was happening, he was safe.

And he hated himself for even thinking that.

His footsteps echoed on the cobblestoned streets as he made his way through Dameral, the lone sound in the empty night. He didn't let himself think about the way, just went where his feet took him, following the route that was imprinted in his soul.

A route he hadn't walked in months.

He walked down the steep side road that wound down the hill of

Dameral, his pace as steady and even as the heartbeat in his chest, following the road down towards the piers. Not the docks where the merchants' ship came and traded, bringing goods in and out of Aeravin—no, he had left that behind with Alessi.

But the little strip of seafront that the Unblooded had been able to hold onto for themselves. A jutting piece of land with a rocky shore and steep inclines, where small-time fishermen eked out a living hauling in daily catches and prayed that their little dinghies wouldn't crash against the rocks.

Towards the little outcropping that had become the closest thing the Unblooded had to a graveyard. If Aeravin could even be said to have a graveyard.

All bodies were burned in the end—Blood Workers and Unblooded, nobles and peasants. For the price of the blood in the body, a family could have their loved ones cremated and the ashes would be returned to them to do with as they wished.

Some kept them—a reminder of the loved one they lost. Most, though, returned them to the earth or to the water.

The outcropping was deserted. Of course it was. Midnight had come and gone, slipping away to the bleak hours when all sensible people were already abed. And even if it weren't so late, no Unblooded was foolish enough to go out alone anymore.

None but Samuel Aberforth.

He climbed the thin, sandy path in his fine shoes, uncaring of the damage the dirt and stones did to the fine leather, savoring the harsh whip of the sea wind against the skin, brine on his tongue and salt in his eyes. It was a precarious climb, but the view at the top was spectacular.

Behind him lay the city of Dameral in all its glory. A city of blood and steel, of finery and tatters. There were buildings that stretched up to the skies, built of brick and marble, that contained the future of Blood Working, and tenement houses of wood and glass, barely standing, where the Unblooded lived.

It was a city of contradictions, of flaws, of pain and beauty and a resilience that Samuel admired. A city that he loved and hated in equal measure.

Before him lay the sea—wild and unstoppable, crashing against the cliffs and chipping away at the stone, smoothing it bit by bit, year by year. The slope down was sharp and slick, stained grey by the ashes of so many Unblooded who had been cast back to the ocean, with nowhere else to go.

Ten years ago, Samuel had first come here to scatter his mother's ashes and to make a promise to himself and to his mother, for everything she had done for him.

He had broken that promise many times over, and for what?

Sinking to his knees, he hung his head, letting the spray of water and salt soak into his clothes, his skin, freezing him to the bone. He deserved it, for everything he had done and become. For all he did and didn't do.

"I'm sorry," he whispered, to no one at all.

For there was no one there to hear him. No one to absolve him of his guilt. He had become everything his mother feared, and there was no going back.

Pushing himself to his feet, he glanced once more towards the ocean—then turned away.

He knew he'd never be back again.

Chapter Thirty-Three

Shan

Shan stared at the invitation from the King in her hand, the weight of the paper comforting despite the words that crossed the card, written in bold, clear strokes. She had been expecting it all night, ever since the last body with its gruesome message had shown up, since the details of that murder scene had leaked immediately, since the rumors had spread throughout Dameral like a wildfire, consuming everyone along the way.

Blood and steel, the reports were in the morning papers.

She should have gone directly to the King. She should have pulled Samuel more firmly into her investigations. She should have hit the streets, searching for more clues to tie these newly dead together and discover the truth behind their shadowy lies.

But instead, she had focused on her brother. She had returned home, scouring through every bit of information she had, looking for something—anything—to absolve him.

And so far she had found nothing.

Now it was time to pay the price for her mistakes. The Eternal King had summoned her and Samuel to a meeting and she was not foolish enough to assume that it would be pleasant.

Leaving the invitation on her desk, Shan retired to her rooms for a bath and a change of clothing. She had spent too much time locked away with her thoughts, avoiding the world around her as she struggled to understand where and how she and Anton had diverged so completely. Instead of focusing on the things she needed to do she had ignored the world around her, nursing her own pain like it was a fine wine.

She was slipping, and it was time to stop that.

Shan dressed soberly, demurely, a change from her normal attempts to impress. It would be useless to attempt to distract the Eternal King with her fineries and fripperies, and she was smart enough to simply take her punishment and carry on.

When she arrived at the palace she found Samuel there already, waiting in the King's study when she was shown in. He was perched on the windowsill, staring out over the ocean as the afternoon light caught his hair, tinting it an even brighter gold than usual. He looked better than she felt, his expression cool and calm, his shoulders free of tension—as if he had let go of a weight he had been carrying.

Good. He shouldn't look guilty before the King. The mistakes were hers, anyway.

Speaking of the King, he had yet to arrive, but someone had brought them a setting of tea and cakes. Her stomach was too riotous for food but she could use the boost that tea gave her. Crossing the room, she poured herself a cup and settled in to wait.

She didn't have to wait for long.

"I was beginning to wonder if you would come to me yourselves," the Eternal King said from the doorway, "but it seems that I had to summon you like the failures you are." His voice was hard as stone, all traces of the reasonable, patient man he had pretended to be for months gone. His expression was cold, his green eyes emotionless and his mouth drawn in a thin, harsh line. It might have taken her ages, but Shan was finally looking at the real King—the power that had held a throne for centuries.

And it terrified her right down to the marrow of her bones.

Shan stood, only to drop into a low curtsy. "Your Majesty." She could hear Samuel rising behind her, no doubt to bow as well, but the King only scoffed. She kept her head low as he closed the door and activated a blood ward to protect them from prying ears. She held her form until he stepped forward, catching her chin and tipping her face up.

"Rise," he commanded, and she did, the tips of his claws surprisingly gentle on her skin. "Both of you."

Shan couldn't look to see what Samuel was doing. She could only focus on the King's touch—on the pure rage and power that rolled off him. This close, she could *feel* the strength of his magic, the vibrancy of his blood—the blood and the lives that he had absorbed over the centuries—as he stared her down. It was like standing too close to a fire, warming and burning at the same time.

He was wrath incarnate, and she couldn't look away.

At last he let go, slipping behind his desk, where he sank into his seat as if it were his throne and they were on trial.

Perhaps they were.

"So, it seems that I have made a grave mistake in trusting you," the King said, looking over them with his steely gaze. "I had hoped that you both would have been clever enough to solve this before it became a true problem." He dragged one claw across the paper on his desk, a copy of yesterday's broadsheet that had leaked the murderer's message, moving it to reveal a pamphlet underneath.

One of the seditious pamphlets.

"The people are in an uproar about this—demanding answers. What good are the Guard if they cannot protect," he paused, picking up the paper with his claws, as if he loathed to touch it, "*even the lowest amongst us.*' Bloody fool considers himself a poet." He tossed it aside with a snarl, digging his other hand into the desk, the metal-tipped claws leaving gouges in the wood. "Now I have a problem on two fronts. Not only do I have this murderer still unaccounted for, wreaking havoc, but a populace that is a hair's breadth away from revolt. So, if you would be so kind, please tell me what, precisely, you have been doing with your time?"

Shan looked to Samuel, catching his eyes, and he just stared back at her with fear. They had tried, hadn't they? Or had they just been fools, getting distracted by all the other pomp and circumstance of Dameral, letting the important things slip through their fingers.

The King watched them for a full minute, the silence stretching tense and unbearable, until he pulled his lips back in a sneer. "Typical. I gave you two the chance to prove yourselves to me and you both have squandered it, not only failing to find the murderer but allowing Dameral to increasingly destabilize in the process."

Shan flinched. "Your Majesty—"

"Don't, LeClaire. Don't think I haven't kept tabs on you. The games you play are simply that, girl. Games. You have so much to learn." He leaned forward, steepling his hands in front of him. "Either you're less skilled than I thought, or you need to find the proper motivation. Listen to me now. This is your final chance—both of you. Either you find the murderer and keep order in Aeravin or face the consequences."

"That's hardly fair!" Samuel snapped, finding his voice at last. "You cannot put that turmoil on us!"

"Oh, I cannot?" The King arched one imperious eyebrow at Samuel. "Do not be so foolish. There may have been unrest, but these murders are giving them something concrete to rally around. And if you cannot deliver the murderer to them then there is no telling what they might do."

Samuel sucked in a harsh breath, preparing another argument, but Shan laid a hand on his arm. He met her gaze, pleading, but she just shook her head once. Oh, how she admired him for it, how she wished that she could join him in his righteous rage, but she knew that would not work. Instead, she remained neutral. Betrayed nothing. Allowed herself to feel nothing.

Instead she focused on what she could control. "You mentioned consequences."

"Oh, there is my girl. So focused on the mission, on the goal. How I have missed you." The King looked far too pleased with himself. "Yes, there will be consequences. But it might be more helpful to think of them as *incentives*. I know what both of you value the most, and if you fail I will take them away from you."

The King turned to Samuel first. "My dear boy. If nothing else, these past few months have proved to be blessing for you alone. You've grown so much in so short a time. You're an exquisite weapon, my child, and if you cannot be a useful ally I will make you a tool to be used. We both know the depths of your talents."

He left Samuel to his terror and turned his gaze on Shan. She wanted to scream, but she didn't even have air to breathe.

"And you, my precious little Sparrow," he purred. Shan startled in her seat, raising her eyes to him in shock. "Oh, I know. I've known all along. You have the capability to be the most vicious, cruel thing. But there is something holding you back and, if I wanted to, I could destroy him." His smile turned sharp. "But I haven't yet, in case I needed a bit of leverage. So, if you value your brother, you had best succeed."

The world came crashing down around her as his words echoed in her ears. Everything she had done—every death, every lie, every bit of pain that she had suffered—had been for Anton. To protect him. To save him. This had never been about power for power's sake.

It was for him.

And even if she had found a bit of joy in it, a version of herself that could fly free, even that was now threatened. The Sparrow was more than just as a mask, more than just a tool. It was the deepest, truest part of her soul.

The King had dragged it into the light, and for the first time in her life she felt stripped bare—naked and exposed and raw.

It was ironic. She had spent her life finding people's weaknesses and exploiting them to her advantage. It was only fair that someone return the favor at last.

Damn it, Bart was right. She had been the fool after all.

"So, my children," the King said. "Am I understood?"

"Yes," Shan said. What other option was there? Either find this murderer—who might very well be her brother—or lose him to the Eternal King.

Fate was a cruel mistress.

"Good." He drummed his fingers on the table. "I am a realist, and I am not entirely without mercy. There are things you should know if you are going to catch this murderer." He stood. "Follow me."

The Eternal King swept away from his desk, stalking towards the bookshelves that lined the far wall. Shan swept aside the confusion that rose in her—she didn't have time for that. Instead, she stood and followed the King, pausing only to rest her hand on Samuel's shoulder. She gave it a brief, desperate squeeze—passing on all the courage and strength that she could in that single heartbeat—then let him go.

It would have to be enough.

Shan refocused her attention on the King, watching as he ran his hand along the spines of the books, until he came to the one he was looking for. He hooked the tip of his claw onto it, glanced over his shoulder at them, then pulled it back.

There was a great groan as the entire bookshelf started to shake. The King took a quick step backwards as the floor itself shifted, the two middle shelves rotating one hundred and eighty degrees, revealing a passage behind it. The way was lit by witch light, illuminating a staircase that twisted down and down and down.

Unable to help herself, Shan stepped forward, looking up at the mechanism which allowed the shelves to spin. She had always wanted something like this, but it had been beyond the means of the LeClaires' wealth.

"Do not dawdle," the King snapped, already stepping through. "You, too, Samuel."

Shan fell into place behind the King as Samuel finally, reluctantly, rose from his chair. She waited with the King for Samuel, and when he joined them in the passageway the King pulled a lever. The bookshelf started moving again, reversing its rotation, until they were trapped on the other side of the wall.

The King simply turned on his heel and started down the stairs, and Shan and Samuel exchanged a brief look. She could see the emotions clearly in his face, free of the masks he had yet to master. Pain, indignation and so much anger it took her breath away.

But this wasn't the time for that. She just brushed her fingers against his as she passed him, following the King down into the depths.

They walked for so long that Shan lost track of where they were, only knowing that they must have gone deep, down below the ground level of the castle. The staircase just kept circling, the same pattern of stones round and round, witch light flickering above their heads. Her thighs ached from the trek, her fine shoes not meant for such a journey, but still she refused to let any of the pain show. She could hear Samuel behind her, his breath coming hard and fast, his anger fading to a fear that she could nearly taste on the air.

She might not be able to pinpoint where, precisely, in the castle they were, but she knew where they were going. The only logical outcome of such a journey.

The Eternal King's dungeons.

Finally, they reached the bottom, the staircase opening into a thin hallway, not quite wide enough for the three of them to stand abreast. A large metal door stood at the end, but there was something more here. A magic ran over her skin like a rush of static, raising all the hairs on her arms.

A ward.

She stumbled forward, one hand outstretched, only to look back at the King. He was watching her with a curious expression, but he simply nodded, granting her permission.

The intensity of his gaze on her was something that she never wanted to feel again—it was as if he was flaying her apart with only his eyes, tearing away every layer of deceit she had so carefully wrapped herself in. Yet she couldn't focus on him; no, there was something more important.

This magic called to her, and gently, tentatively, she ran her fingers across the wards, feeling them hum as they reacted to her presence. It echoed through her, wrapping around her in a familiar embrace, and she could taste the spicy, smoky flavor of his magic on her tongue.

It was Isaac's.

She'd know his magic anywhere, the scent and taste of it imprinted on her soul. Shan closed her eyes, letting the magic wash over her as she parsed through the threads of the spell. It had the strength of a heavy tapestry—each person keyed to it acting as a thread that wove it into the rest, making the overall protection stronger, not weaker.

Blood wards were a tricky business. It was easy enough if all one wanted was to ward for themselves or their families. Like knows like, and Shan could easily allow Anton access to anything she had warded for herself. In fact, she often did. Where things got tricky, though, was wards like this—where it needed to be keyed to a group of people, from different families and different blood. When it was done poorly, the spell broke down, buckling and breaking under the weight of all it had to parse.

Isaac's ward, though, showed none of these signs. It was one of the most complex pieces of magic she had ever seen.

Samuel gasped sharply, and she opened her eyes to find that the door at the end of the hallway had opened. Standing there, looking at them in shock, was the man himself. Isaac was dressed in his formal state robes, splattered and stained with what Shan could only assume was blood. But the true horror was the look on his face—the brief moment of fear, guilt, and shock—that vanished, replaced by a mask as cold as any of her own.

"De la Cruz," the King said, cutting through the silence. He walked through the ward, the magic shimmering and allowing him access. "I do apologize for interrupting your work, but there are some things that I fear I must explain to LeClaire and Aberforth. They have been aiding the investigation into the ... unfortunate deaths. Would you please grant them access?"

Isaac didn't say a word, unwilling to look at her or even Samuel. He just nodded solemnly, and a flash of steel glinted in his hand, a small dagger dangling from his fingers. He sliced his palm open, a thin line of blood welling up, and pressed it to the ward.

Shan shivered as she felt the magic at work, the ward shifting and peeling back to provide them entry. Grabbing Samuel by the arm, she pulled him through quickly, knowing that each second Isaac held the ward open was only a further drain on his power.

The instant they were through, Isaac dropped his hand and the ward snapped back into place.

She had never felt this torn—she wanted to reach for Isaac, to use her claws to tear down this wall he had thrown up between them. She wanted to turn to Samuel, to comfort him and explain away the confusion that he wore so plainly. But the King was watching them, so she did nothing at all. She just followed Isaac through the door and came to a sudden halt as she realized what she was looking at, her brain struggling to keep up with the horrors her eyes beheld.

The stone of the castle had given away to a shining, quartz room—from the floors to the walls, easy to clean and sterilize. She could smell the sharp tang of cleaning agent, the kind they used to destroy stray drops of blood lest they be gathered and used against them. It was a familiar design, like so many of the laboratories across Aeravin, in private homes and in the Academy, in clinics and hospitals, but that's where the similarities ended.

Instead of tables and simple tools, there was row upon row of harsh metal slabs, and on them were strapped people of all ages and types. There was no pattern or reasoning to them that Shan could find, but she would bet everything she had that they were Unblooded. They were stripped to just their underclothes, with needles and tubes pressed into their arms and legs as their blood was slowly, meticulously, drained from them. Under each table were large glass vats of blood, growing more full by the second, and silent Blood Workers moved between them, tending to the people in a sick mockery of a hospital.

It wasn't a dungeon. No, it was something far worse than that. Bile rose hot and sour up the back of her throat as she realized what this was—a blood factory. A place where the Unblooded were unwillingly gathered, drained until there was nothing left but a corpse.

The realization hit Samuel a second later. He pushed past her, and Isaac turned away from them both, his head ducked low in shame as he left them alone with the King.

Samuel came to a stop by the first patient, an emaciated looking man whose age was impossible to determine, his hands flexing over the needle and tube just above the elbow, as if he thought to remove it himself but caught himself at the last moment.

Shan moved quickly, catching Samuel's hands, and he gripped her tightly, so tightly that she feared she might break under the pressure of it. But his eyes—his eyes were burning—a cold fire that she nearly flinched away from.

"What is this place?" he breathed, and Shan just shook her head, helpless.

"My masterpiece," the King said, coming up beside them, glowing with pride. He looked down at the man on the table, who only stared up at them through half-lidded eyes, too drained to have any fight left. The restraints were no longer necessary. If anything, they were just there to hold him up as his died. "The secret that has kept Aeravin strong."

"Why are you showing us this?" Shan asked, surprising herself with the steadiness of her voice. "Our knowing about it would only be a liability."

"Clever girl." The King cast her that appraising look again, and Shan forced herself to not look away. "You are right, it is dangerous to show you. But you were never going to figure out the tie between the murder victims without it."

Shan turned slowly, her vision going blurry around the edges as she watched the silent Blood Workers go about their business. A pair of them were tending to a nearby patient, newly deceased, removing the tubes and wiping down the few spilled drops of blood. They moved with a practiced efficiency, and as they removed the corpse and brought out another bound, gagged prisoner, Shan finally understood. "Suppliers."

The King only nodded, but Samuel looked to her in confusion. "Suppliers of what?"

"People," Shan replied, and Samuel stared at her uncomprehending. She just looked to the King. "How much did you have to pay them to hand over their own?"

The King laughed, low and dark. "It was surprisingly less than you'd think. These are mostly criminals and outcasts, people that the Unblooded won't be missing. If you think about it, they're doing a good service. Less trash on the streets and more blood for us."

"Wait, they sold people?" Samuel said, his voice simmering with the quiet kind of rage that was so dangerous. "The people who have been killed—they were slavers?"

The King wrinkled his nose. "No, not precisely. We're not enslaving these people."

"You're killing them," Samuel said, and the King turned on him, slowly.

"Yes, I am," the King said, levelling a cool stare at Samuel. "But Blood Working demands a price, and it must be paid in blood."

"This is wrong," he snarled, stepping forward.

"Will you never cease disappointing me?" the Eternal King asked, his eyes cold and hard as he looked Samuel over with something akin to frustration. "I've tried to show you that truth—being a King, protecting a nation—is not for the faint of heart. And this is something you'll have to come to terms with. You need to learn that sometimes we must do terrible things—necessary things—for our country."

Samuel started to tremble, and the King scoffed. "If you want to survive here, be more like LeClaire, boy. She is showing true strength." Shan bit the inside of her cheek to keep from screaming, to ignore the terrible implications as they crashed down around her, her entire life restructured and reframed in a matter of moments. Every time they had used blood, from the days in the Academy to the very witch light that lined the streets of the capital, the blood had come from this place. Hells, every time she had requisitioned blood for her home, in her father's name or her own, she had justified the existence of this horror.

But the King just carried on. "We've seen enough. Come, we still have more to discuss."

The walk back to the King's study seemed faster, or perhaps Shan was just in a state of shock. Once they were sequestered back in the study, the King relaxing behind his desk, she focused only on the words.

On the tangled history of the five murder victims, how they had been part of a small but effective ring that had been supplying Aeravin with bodies for generations. How the Blood Taxes had never been enough, only a thin excuse to hide the truth. How a country of Blood Workers needed far more than what a populace would freely, willingly, give. How whoever this murderer was, they had found out the truth behind Aeravin's lies and had destroyed the system from within.

"The murderer has indicated that there will be one more death," the King said, solemnly, "but all the traffickers are accounted for. I believe that the target is Isaac de la Cruz."

"Isaac?" Samuel said, finally breaking his silence of simmering, burning rage. "Why him?"

"Because the role of the Royal Blood Worker is far more than my secretary," the King said, softly. "But few realize it."

"He's the one who does all of this, isn't he?" Shan whispered. It made sense, the change that she had seen in him. The constant circles under his eyes, the pain and guilt that he carried, the fragile way he seemed ready to break. The Isaac she knew would have never accepted this, but once he was made Royal Blood Worker, what could he do about it?

He couldn't deny the Eternal King, not if he valued his life at all.

"Exactly," the King said. "I'll be doing my best to keep him safe. I doubt that this murderer is brazen or capable enough to attack within the palace itself, but there is still a chance that he could fall. Do you understand now why you need to find this murderer quickly? Not just for the country, or for your own selfish sakes, but for the life of the man you both care so much for."

Shan flinched, the first uncontrolled emotion she had shown in front of him, and the King smiled cruelly. "Oh, yes. I am not a fool. I have seen things, heard things. But what the three of you do is not my business, so long as you do not fail in your duties. The summer solstice is coming up, and we have plans in place."

Shan nodded, vaguely remembering that there was a grand celebration scheduled, a new likeness of the King to be unveiled in Dameral's central square.

"The Royal Blood Worker is going to be the one leading that ceremony," the King continued, "and I cannot pull him from it."

"Didn't you just say," Samuel began, but Shan cut him off.

"We don't want the murderer to suspect that we know their plans."

The King studied her. "There is hope for you, LeClaire. Yes. Precisely. So you have a week to find the killer, or you will risk your beloved de la Cruz. I hope I am making myself clear.

"Now get to work."

The words hung heavy between them, somehow all the worse for their truth. Samuel left first, not looking at them or saying a single word, leaving her alone with the King. She wanted to stand, to flee, but her knees were weak and her heart heavy.

"I'm disappointed," the King said, his voice soft and surprisingly tired. "I knew that wrangling Samuel would be difficult, given his foolish ideals. But I expected better from you. You've proven that you have the skill and mind to succeed, and yet . . . It seems that even the brightest of stars can fall to the simplest of weaknesses."

Shan bit her lip, both wanting and not wanting to ask.

But the Eternal King was not so kind as to leave it at that.

"You never should have fallen for them, for either of them," the King whispered, and when she looked up at him he only shook his head. "I had hoped that what Isaac had done to you all those years ago was lesson enough, but apparently not. If you want to succeed in Aeravin you should know better than to rely on anyone. We only betray each other in the end."

His words cut deeper than she had expected—for years she had lived in a strange space of guilt, both hating her father for what he had done to her and desperate to please. But he had never hurt her as much as this. For all that she hated the King and the world he had created, he had seen her potential, her value, and offered to nurture it.

And here he was, offering his own kind of cruel kindness.

"This isn't over yet," she swore. This battle hadn't gone at all as she had hoped, but the war was still far from over.

"Oh, I don't doubt it." The King leaned back, studying her face. "If you fail me in this, you'll still have your life. Your position. As will Samuel. I haven't got this far by wasting potential. But your brother will be dead and perhaps you will finally learn. Your attachments only hold you down."

He glanced past her, and she knew what he was looking at. The portrait of his long dead wife, hanging in a place of honor. She wanted to know what had happened there—what had driven him to denounce attachments when he had once clung to them as strongly as anyone else.

But it didn't matter. Understanding him might be interesting, but it wouldn't get her out of this bind. Only she could do that.

Chapter Thirty-Four

Shan

Shan found Samuel outside the palace, standing amongst the rose bushes, looking utterly and totally alone. She studied him for a moment, remembering the King's warning—that she had brought her failures upon herself, a product of her own attachments and love. And though his threats still hung over her, a weight that she could not shake, as thick and ominous as a storm on a summer's day, she refused to let him dictate her life.

She reached out, taking Samuel's hand in hers, and led him to her carriage. Just having him near soothed some of the tension away, calming the panic in her mind and lifting the darkness over her soul, leaving her free to plot and plan. He had slipped into her life so easily—too easily. It had only been a few months, but he already belonged with her, and that scared her almost as much as the Eternal King's truths and threats.

But she couldn't think of that now.

Instead, she took him home, not hesitating when he invited her in for a pot of tea. He led her into his parlor, though it still felt a little unlived in, sterile and precise and far too formal for Samuel. But a maid brought them tea and refreshments, and they sat in comfortable silence as she turned everything over in her mind.

A murderer's head and peace in the kingdom. That was what she had to deliver to save her brother—and Samuel—from the harm she had put them in. They never would have attracted the King's attention if it wasn't for her. But she had interfered, setting the game into motion.

It was her responsibility to fix it.

Even if it meant turning her brother in for crimes she never thought he could commit. It would destroy what little goodness was left in her, but if Anton was the murderer she'd put him down like the rabid dog he'd become.

Samuel shifted in his seat, his arms wrapped tight around himself, and for a second she wondered if . . . *no*. That plan, the great, grand scheme of hers, was still too far out with too many pieces yet to slide into place. But given the horrors they had just witnessed together, perhaps she could reach Samuel in a way she never could before.

He noticed her watching him, and they sat there for a long moment, Shan's heart pounding as something in the air sparked between them.

"What are we doing, Shan?" he whispered, his voice as soft as a caress, and she fought the urge to lean closer. "I've given up everything that I am, become this farce of a man, and for what? I thought I knew how bad things were, but . . ." He closed his eyes. "Please tell me you didn't know."

"I didn't," she said, fighting back the images of the poor souls strapped to those metal tables, slowly and painfully bleeding to death. "I should have." Samuel cocked his head to the side, his gaze sharp, and for once Shan didn't let herself hide behind her lies. "I never questioned the blood. How whenever we needed it—for our magic, our healing, our training—we could simply requisition it. How even with the Blood Taxes, it shouldn't have been enough."

Their magic, great and powerful as it was, came with a terrible price. And she had ignored it, because she could, because she never had to pay it.

What a fool it made her.

Samuel slid closer, tangling their hands together. "I don't blame you for that. But you promised me that we would change things." That low fire was back in his voice, that passion and rage that had her turning towards him like a flower towards the sun. "I don't see how we can stop this."

Shan took a deep breath, the secrets heavy on her tongue. But they must be said. "There is a way," she admitted, pressing against his side, their tenuous connection the only thing grounding her.

"What way?" His pale hands flexed in his lap, the skin around his nails picked and bitten at. He couldn't stop worrying his bottom lip, turning it red and raw.

This was the chance she had been yearning for, handed to her on a silver platter. And yet she hesitated, not quite able to say it. "I'm surprised you haven't figured it out yet."

"Figured what out?"

"Nature abhors a vacuum," Shan said. "For the longest time I wondered how far my little schemes could go. I knew what I wanted but without a proper structure in place all I would create was chaos. And as much as I'd like to watch Aeravin burn at times, the collateral damage would be too much."

She breathed out slowly, carefully, watching the minute changes as the reality of her plan washed over him. "Then I found you. You were the answer to everything—a hope that I could bring about a smooth transition and create a new Aeravin. One that wasn't led by a man who lost touch with his humanity centuries ago."

"And you think that man is me?" Samuel asked, carefully. He was clearly confused, but he was considering it, and Shan knew that was the first and most difficult step.

Now if she could only get past his morals—or hone them into a blade that she could use.

"I know nothing of politics," Samuel continued, "or bureaucracy, or how to keep a nation running."

"You know what's wrong," Shan said. "You know what the problems are, and you would care for all the citizens, not just the elite." She ran her hand along his arm, feeling him warm under her touch though there were still two layers of clothing between them. "And that's more than we have now."

He shook his head, but he didn't push her away. If anything, he leaned into her touch, craving a closeness she wanted nothing more than to give. Even though it was wrong, so terribly wrong, and she knew that she shouldn't be using this thing between them to pull him to her side, to tie him up in knots until he didn't know up from down. Until he had no choice but to follow her because there was no other option left.

But in all truth she craved this as much as he did, even if it meant it would leave her as entangled as she left him.

"It isn't right," he whispered, his hand coming over hers and removing it from his body. The touch was brief, perfunctory, but it still made her want things she didn't dare name.

"What isn't?" Had she pushed too far, been too brazen? They had only just learned the most gruesome, terrible truth of their nation after all.

"For me to be King," he said. "For anyone to be King, actually."

She wanted to laugh. She wanted to cry. Perhaps she ought to give him a pen and send him off to write pamphlets. "Of course you're a bleeding democrat."

"Is that a problem?" Samuel bit out. "Forgive me for not being greedy enough to fit into your plans."

"It's not about greed." Shan hung her head. "If you were greedy, if you really wanted this, then you'd end up being just as bad as the Eternal King. One monster traded for another."

His brow furrowed, confusion etched across his features, and Shan's heart ached at just how precious he looked. And here she was, hoping to destroy what was left of his innocence.

"I should want the throne," he began, "but I also shouldn't?"

"Yes," Shan said. "You should want it to make Aeravin better, fairer, safer. But not to simply empower yourself."

Samuel huffed. "You almost make me believe it, that I could do good."

"You could," Shan said. "And I'm not asking you to do it tomorrow. As dire as things might seem in the moment, that's not how it would play out. You'd have time to adjust."

He leaned back in his seat, looking at her—really looking at her. "It's strange, Shan. How much you care about me. Your brother. Isaac. But so little about what is *right*."

Shan let his words roll off her, his bleeding heart bare before her cold gaze. "And you think letting the Eternal King continue his reign is the right thing to do? Perhaps we should round up a fresh batch of Unblooded for him to drain, then."

"No, of course not!" He ran his fingers through his hair, tearing at it and leaving it a confused, disheveled mess. She wanted to fix it, to run her hands over it until it was smooth again. "But removing one king to put another on the throne won't fix things, not really. Especially when that new king is me."

"Samuel," Shan said, with more calm than she thought she could manage. "We've been over this. You're a good man."

He shook his head. "Maybe. But there is a darkness in me, a hunger. I don't . . ." his voice broke, and it cut Shan deep. "I'm having a hard enough time resisting it now. And I don't know what I would do if I had that kind of power in my grasp."

She brushed her thumb along the back of his hand, trying to soothe away the tension. "You resist the power you were born with, don't you?"

"I try—"

"You do," she insisted. "It hurts you to use it."

He smiled a bit sadly. "That's not entirely true."

"Oh, no!" Shan widened her eyes dramatically. "Are you telling me that you've made mistakes, that you're human?" He tried to pull back, but she held him fast. "No man is an island, Samuel. Nor should anyone be. You'll have advisers, counsellors, friends to lean on."

"You're forgetting one thing," Samuel interrupted. "I'd need heirs, right? Or are you planning to have me become the next Eternal

King? Watching everyone I love and care for grow old and die around me, taking every last bit of humanity with them."

Shan knew her answer already, but the hunger still rose in her. The King had lived for so long because of Blood Working. He didn't even try to hide it—he made a spectacle out of it—a murder dressed up as a sacrifice, a necessary evil to protect his nation, to give them the one thing that had allowed them to flourish for centuries.

It was so much potential, but the cost was so high.

"I wouldn't make you Eternal," she said. "I don't know if anyone should be made Eternal."

He let out a breath—a sigh, really—and Shan realized that he hadn't been sure what she'd say. How far she'd go. She didn't know if it hurt that he'd expect so little of her, or if she should be proud that he thought her so ruthless.

But there was power and there was monstrosity, and it was a fine line to walk.

"If I am not to be Eternal," Samuel continued, "then I'd need to have heirs."

"And that is a problem?" She smirked, hiding the cut of pain that went through her. If he found her unworthy now, after all that he had learned in the last twenty-four hours, after witnessing the cool and dispassionate face she had worn before the King, she frankly wouldn't blame him. "I'm sure you'll have plenty of young women vying for the role."

He did not look amused. He stood, turning away from her, as if it would somehow make all of this easier. "That's not . . . I mean. It's this thing. This power in me. I inherited it from my father, and my children will inherit it from me."

"Ah." The shape of his fear suddenly made sense, coalescing into the image of sweet little blond children, their every word bringing chaos and tragedy to Dameral. It was bad enough when it was Aberforths, it would be even worse if they were real princes and princesses.

"And what would happen," Samuel continued, looking utterly

stricken, "if somewhere down the line, one of my descendants would be cruel. Harsh. Everything you wouldn't want in a ruler but gifted with a power that makes even Blood Working seem tame."

Shan sucked in a breath, imagining it. A crueler, harder version of Samuel—the power he would have and the damage he would inflict.

"It's better, I think, if this curse dies with me," Samuel said grimly. "I gave up the hope of having a family a long time ago. Hells, even the thought of having … someone is new. I'm sorry, Shan. I was going to tell you—and Isaac—when we had that talk. But …"

"It shouldn't have to be that way," Shan said, crossing to him. She stood too close, she knew it, but the pull between them was like a magnet. "You should have a chance at a family, if that's what you want. Besides, Isaac and I haven't given up yet."

For a second, she thought she had reached him, but then Samuel's expression turned dark, a harsh frown on his face as he studied her. "No. Please tell me this isn't what I think it is."

"Samuel?"

He wrested himself away from her, wiping his hands on his vest, as if he could remove the stain of her from his skin. "Is this what I've been to you this whole time? A way to the throne?"

"No, of course not!" Shan pursued him. "I would never—"

"You would. Don't lie to me, Shan." Samuel held out his hand, and in that moment she swore she could feel his power—just a hint of it, a taste that slipped out past his lips. But not enough to truly affect her. He held himself much too tightly for that.

It still sent a shiver down her spine.

"I meant it," she said. Taking his hand, she pressed it against her face. "I am a liar, Samuel, and a cheat, and I will do whatever it takes to reach my goals. But I will not—I cannot—do that to you."

Samuel sneered—and at that moment he looked so much like the Eternal King that Shan almost staggered back. "And why not?"

Shan searched for an answer, for one that she could bring herself to say. There were so many parts to it.

She didn't want to hurt him.

He didn't deserve it.

She wanted things with him she never dreamed she could have.

He was a good man, better than any she had ever known.

She could have said any of these things—all of these things—and it would have been the truth.

What she did say was "Because I can't."

When Samuel laughed it was the coldest thing she had ever heard from him. "I suppose that is an answer."

But it wasn't the one he wanted, or needed, and she had known it the moment she put voice to the words, could feel it in the way he closed off. "Please," she whispered, barely knowing what she was asking for. "Please believe me."

He hesitated. "I want to. But I don't know if I can. If I can trust anything in this damned city anymore."

Shan felt her heart crack. He was turning away from her—not because of the deepest, darkest parts of her soul, but because she couldn't say the words he needed to hear. Not to herself, not out loud. So she did the only thing she could do. She hoisted herself up on her tiptoes and pressed a kiss to his lips. It was different from the last one they had shared—that had been violent, harsh and full of promise.

This was soft, desperate and full of all the things she never learned how to say.

Samuel melted into her touch, his hands cupping her face. He returned her kiss with a hunger, a fervor, that had her trembling against him. She twisted her hands in his jacket, pulling him close as the kiss turned heated—teeth and tongue and so much passion that Shan felt as if she were about to burst into flames, a phoenix reborn from the ashes.

Blood and steel, she *wanted*.

"Shan," he gasped, against her lips, pushing her hair back from her face so that he could touch as much skin as possible. "I—"

"I know," she said, interrupting him, not wanting to hear it. Not able to hear it. She already felt as if she was teetering at the edge of an abyss from which she would never claw her way out of, and she was afraid of even the tiniest of pushes. Instead, she pressed her face into his neck, whispering words against him. "I found you with the intention of making you king, yes, but I never wanted to be your queen. I never meant for this to happen."

He drew in a deep breath, and she could feel the erratic beat of his heart against her. "I believe you, Shan. But we're here now." He wrapped his arms around her, not pulling her in for another kiss, not pushing her away, just holding her.

It was this—these little things—that he seemed to understand, that he so easily offered her. He wasn't demanding, he wasn't pushing. Though she could never bring herself to ask for this—she was raised to take, not to beg—he understood her perfectly.

He was a perfect partner in every conceivable way, except that if she were to have her way, she could never be with him. She was not meant to be a queen—she was far more powerful in the shadows.

Raising her hand to his lips, he pressed a gentle kiss to the back of it, and it felt like forgiveness.

It felt like a beginning.

Her smile was a fragile, brittle thing.

"Samuel," she said, "I am entirely at your mercy. I am planning treason. Will you help me?" She waited, breathless, as he stared down at her, as he contemplated.

As he held her entire life's work in his hands.

"All right, Shan." He straightened his shoulders, steadied himself. At that moment he almost looked regal. "I'm not saying I agree to all of this. But you're right. We cannot simply do nothing. Just promise me something."

"What's that?"

"That whatever you're planning in that brilliant, clever mind of yours, you include me."

Shan sighed in relief. "All right. But I ask something in return." He arched a brow, and she barreled straight on, not giving herself a chance to stop and reconsider. Reckless, for one brief, shining moment. "If you decide to take the throne, you'll do it because you want it. Not because of me. Not because of us."

Because if he took the throne, she would lose him forever.

Something changed in his eyes then. A weight lifted from his shoulders, and his eyes grew clear. "I can promise you that, and that I am yours. That much I swear."

She pulled him in for another kiss, feeling the world shift beneath her feet, changing into something wholly new. No longer was she the chess master moving her pawns, making the decisions and gambling their fates, playing all sides and binding allies to her. This was the beginning of something new, something she had never tried before.

And for the first time, she wasn't alone.

Chapter Thirty-Five

Samuel

"Are you sure we should be doing this?" Samuel asked, looking up at the building in front of them. It had taken him a moment to realize what was throwing him off—it wasn't a townhouse, like the Aberforth or LeClaire home. Instead, it was a building full of flats to rent. It was, admittedly, far more secured and updated than where he had grown up, and the neighborhood was solidly in the respectable category, but it wasn't what he had been expecting.

Not for the home of Aeravin's Royal Blood Worker.

"I'm sure," Shan said, lifting her skirts as she climbed the short set of stairs to the door. "We can't . . . I can't just let him wonder."

Samuel understood that much, at least. Isaac had been on his mind all day, that horrified look on his face when he realized that they were there, in the dungeons where he harvested blood for the King. So when Shan told him that she was going to visit Isaac, Samuel knew that he had to accompany her.

He followed her into the tenant house—it was simple, clean, and well-maintained—and up to the second floor, where she knocked soundly on the door. It was clear that she had been here before, that she was comfortable being here, and Samuel swallowed the questions on his tongue.

Now was not the time for that.

The door opened slowly, just a crack at first, before widening to reveal Isaac. He looked even worse than usual—the bags under his eyes as dark as bruises, and his beard was a mess, as if he hadn't been bothering to shave.

"I didn't expect you to come," he said, after a long silence.

"Did you really think we'd abandon you?" Shan asked, and the way Isaac glanced away broke Samuel's heart.

Yes, he had thought that.

"Can we come in?" Samuel asked, softly, and Isaac considered it for a moment.

Instead of responding, he produced a small dagger from his waistband and slashed his thumb open. He pressed the bleeding wound against the air in the space where the door would normally be, and Samuel watched as something shimmered and shattered before him.

Another blood ward—so subtle that he hadn't been able to pick up on it, not without Blood Working himself.

But he entered anyway, a burst of static running over his skin as he passed through the doorway, Shan on his heels. The rooms were small but cozy—the furniture the kind of old that felt more lived in than decrepit, with scuff marks on the corners and faded upholstery. It was a living room and kitchen and dining room all in one—open and bright and clean. Overflowing bookshelves lined the south wall, and there were a couple of doors along the north wall, no doubt leading to the bedroom and washroom. But most striking were the wide windows along the east wall, thrown open and letting in the soft light of the moon and a cool breeze off the sea.

Everything about the rooms suggested that it was not merely a place to live, but a home, and Samuel found himself instinctively relaxing.

"It's not what I expected," Samuel said.

Isaac tensed, stopping where he was putting a kettle on the stove. "I know it's not much. Especially compared to your townhouses. But it's plenty comfortable for one person, and this way I don't have to hire live-in servants."

"I wasn't judging you, Isaac," Samuel said, gently. "Honestly, this seems ideal."

Isaac tilted his head to the side, really studying him. "You mean that, don't you?"

"Of course he does," Shan said with a laugh, grabbing a teapot and mugs off a shelf. "Our Samuel is a simple man, and there is nothing wrong with that."

Samuel couldn't help the shiver that ran down his spine at that, at being called *theirs*, but shoved it aside. "Let us help you, Isaac. You've had a long day."

After a moment's deliberation, Isaac stepped aside, sliding over to the table as he let them take over the tea preparations. Shan bustled about with the tea itself, filling the teapot from a small tin she found, and Samuel scrounged up some sugar and milk from the warded ice box while the kettle boiled.

Eventually, the kettle shrieked, and Samuel grabbed the handle and brought it over to the table, filling the pot and watching the leaves rise and swirl. "There. Everything is better with tea."

Isaac looked up at him, his dark eyes sad. Hells, now that Samuel was looking closer at him, he realized that Isaac was a wreck, falling apart before his very eyes. "I think this might be more than even tea can fix."

Shan reached across the table, taking his hand in hers. "You don't have to explain anything to us. We understand that you're in an impossible position."

"Impossible," Isaac echoed, low and bitter. "You don't know the half of it."

Samuel caught Shan's eye, his brow furrowed, but turned his attention back to Isaac. "Try us then."

Isaac pulled his hand from Shan's, settling them in his lap. "I don't think I can."

"Can't?" Samuel asked, "Or won't?"

It earned a small smile from Isaac. "Can't."

"Because you think you'll lose us?" Shan pressed, and Isaac glanced at her. "Because that won't happen."

"You seem so sure," Isaac whispered, "but you have no idea what I've done." He ran a hand over his face. "I never intended for you to find out, not like this."

"How then?" Shan asked.

"It doesn't matter now," Isaac said with a shrug. "You both know. Did he tell you his theory, then? Is that why you're here? To protect me?"

"Yes," Samuel admitted. "And because we care."

"You shouldn't." Isaac pushed away from the table. "And I can take care of myself. I have wards in place, I'm being careful. I'm sure you should be focusing on . . . finding this murderer." He spat the word, and Shan leaned forward.

"Do you not want them found?"

"Yes. No." He ran his hands through his hair, a manic, frantic motion. "It's just . . . what they did. What I've done. It's monstrous. Can we really—"

Samuel stepped forward, seizing Isaac's hand and pulling him to a stop. He rubbed gentle circles against his wrists, trying to soothe him. "They had a choice. You didn't. Besides—whoever is killing them, it isn't justice. It's . . ."

"Murder," Shan said. "Terror. It is just causing trouble in the streets, and it won't solve anything."

Isaac sucked in a harsh breath. "And yet, if they hadn't done . . . this, you never would know the truth." He started to shake. "No one knows the *truth*."

Shan looked away, conflicted. "That is . . . fair. But this isn't the solution. It's what the House of Lords is for. We can change the laws, add in additional protections—"

Isaac laughed, a cruel, cold thing. "You don't really believe that, do you? The House of Lords have no idea this exists, not even the Royal Council knows. It's just between the Eternal King, the Royal Blood Worker and what few necessary staff he deems essential.

"Aeravin is broken."

"I don't believe it," Shan said, hotly. "We can fix it."

Isaac looked at her, sadly, then turned away. "I know we can't."

Shan surged to her feet, but Samuel stepped between them. "Hey. Easy."

For a moment it looked like the argument would continue, but Shan just shook her head. "I know you're hurting, Isaac. You're scared. But I will help you, I swear it. I just need to catch a murderer first." She turned, her skirts swirling around her. "I have work to do."

Samuel started after her, but Isaac's hand found his—his grip tight and desperate. "Please," he whispered. "Stay."

Shan nodded at them. "What I need to do is on my own, anyway." She lurched forward, like she was going to say something, do something, but she just turned and headed out.

Moving back to Isaac, Samuel pressed his hand against his face. "Are you going to be all right?"

Isaac just pressed against him.

"Eventually," Isaac said, so very softly.

Wrapping his arms around Isaac, Samuel held him close, hoping that this would be enough.

It would have to be enough.

Chapter Thirty-Six

Shan

Shan found Samuel exactly where she had left him, with her stacks of notes, telling him to look at anything he wanted. There were official reports, autopsy reports, background information on the victims, detailed breakdowns of magical theory that no doubt went over his head.

It was both overwhelming and disturbing, the life and death of five people reduced to clinical, sterile information. And sitting next to it all was a hastily scribbled note with a simple name—*Sarah Dean*.

She had spent days going over it, determined to find the killer and keep her promises to Isaac, but she had found nothing to help. So, with a fear in her heart that she couldn't quite squash, she had done as Samuel had asked.

She let him in.

She asked for help.

Samuel pushed away from the desk, his handsome features twisted into something dark and grim. He clenched a note in his hand—one that Shan had hoped he wouldn't find. "Anton knew the second victim?"

"Yes," she said. "Jessica James. She imported books for him. Tagalan books."

Samuel dropped the note. "And I know that he knew Sarah Dean. That's at least two of the victims. Multiple ways for him to get into this."

"I know," Shan snapped.

Samuel shut his mouth, then softly ventured, "Shan—"

"No! He is my brother!" She pulled herself tall, as if she could deny the facts by sheer will alone. "My twin. I know him, he would never do this."

Because if he did, she'd lose him either way. Because if he did, she'd have no choice at all.

"All right," Samuel said, holding his hands up in surrender. "All right."

Shan dashed away her tears. "I'm being foolish. It's just … bad luck." Steeling herself, she lifted her chin up high. "And I will prove it tonight."

Samuel reached for her, stepping forward, but stopped himself— an aborted, harsh movement.

Shan pretended not to notice. "We'll prove it," she said.

"Ah, yes," Samuel said. "What exactly is the plan?"

"We're going to the Fox Den, and we'll find out what we can on Sarah. You go in the front, like any normal night—"

"Any normal night I wouldn't be gambling," Samuel interrupted, and Shan shot him an exasperated look.

"*You,*" she said, stressing the word, "will be acting like normal, gambling, having a good time. See if anything is off."

"Wait, *I'm* supposed to do this?"

Shan shrugged. "Well, ideally you'd have Anton's help, but …" She placed her hands on his shoulders, steadying him. If only there was another option. But Isaac was still a wreck, and Bart was too common for this role. "I believe in you, Samuel. You are sweet and charming, and you can handle this. Just act naturally and listen. That's the most important part."

He looked up at her, so trusting, and nodded. "And what will you be doing?"

"I'll be working it from the other side," she stepped back, pulling open her cloak to reveal the outfit underneath.

Samuel's eyes widened as he took it in—the tight corset, the short skirt. The lace and the faux diamonds, the scandalous amount of bare skin visible. His eyes snapped to her face, suddenly taking in the makeup, the curled hair.

She had dressed herself up as a tart in uniform of the ladies of the Fox Den, and Samuel looked as if he were about to faint.

"I— uh— wait—"

Some of the tension faded from her as she smiled fondly at him. "Don't worry, Samuel, I've done this many times before." She dropped the cloak, stepping back. "I know what I am doing."

"That wasn't the issue."

"Oh, I know." She pressed a kiss to his cheek, and enjoying the blush that painted his skin red, more effective than any rouge she had ever used. "But now is not the time for that."

Dazed, Samuel could do nothing but follow, her fingers entwined in his as she pulled him along.

—

When Shan walked into the Fox Den, there was an unusually solemn air amongst the workers. The matron looked at her sharply, sighing in relief, then pointed at a tray of goblets. Doing her best to look slightly confused, she stepped up to the tray.

One of the kitchen workers, a young boy, no more than eighteen or twenty, leaned forward. "Don't worry," he said. "She's been doing that all night, every time a familiar face walks in. Doesn't matter if they're a regular or a part-timer, like you, Sparrow."

Shan flashed him a small smile—Gerome, his name was. "Thanks. Has something happened?"

"One of the dealers never showed up," he said, casting his dark eyes low. "It could be anything, but . . ."

"With the murders," Shan finished for him. That was one thing the papers didn't leak, the name. The Unblooded were already twitchy enough; they didn't need to add more fuel to the fire.

"Yeah, exactly."

"Enough gossiping!" The matron snapped. "We're here to work, not gab."

Shan hoisted the tray of wine upon her shoulder, turning towards the floor. The matron grabbed her elbow, dropping low to whisper in her ear. "My office, end of the night. I'll tell you what you need, Sparrow."

"As you say, matron," she said, inclining her head. Information from the matron wasn't unprecedented, but it was rare. Normally the matron just let her work, allowing the Sparrow to flit in and out. But times were desperate.

Her elbow was released, and she swept out into the Fox Den.

Out there, the atmosphere was completely transformed. All the shades of worry and sorrow were gone as the workers pasted false smiles on the faces—the dealers running their games with confident hands, the servers carrying food and wine between tables. Shan moved through the crowd, taking in the clientele, and noticed something strange.

Usually, the patrons of the Fox Den were Blood Workers—easily nine out of ten being someone she recognized from society—yet there was the occasional Unblooded among them. But tonight there were none. Every single person gambling there was a Blood Worker, and their friends and family who didn't have the gift? They just didn't show up. And worst of all, the Blood Workers didn't seem to miss them.

They continued their gambling and their revelries like nothing was wrong, like people were not being brutally murdered and violated simply for the blood in the veins. They didn't care that people they knew—and presumably cared about—were too afraid to leave their homes.

It sickened her.

She passed by Samuel, surrounded by a crowd of preening

sycophants who were eager to latch onto him, now that he was out in public without a chaperone. There wasn't a LeClaire to ward them away, de la Cruz to charm them, the King to awe them. For the first time, he was truly out in Aeravinian society on his own, and Shan realized that he had done it for her, simply because she asked.

She did not deserve him.

Swooping by his table—roulette—to trade empty cups for full ones, she listened in as he spoke. He was calm and confident, despite the pale cast to his cheeks, and he held up well against the barbs the others threw at him, dancing lightly out of their stings and offering little in return. He was unfailingly polite, and it would only make him a further attraction.

What a novelty this young Aberforth was.

She slipped away, offering a passing smile of comfort, and slid back into her role, none of the other nobles any wiser. Samuel watched her for only a moment as she moved away, then turned back to his entourage.

She allowed herself a breath of relief. He would do well after all—she hadn't been the instrument of his destruction.

The night passed slowly, the work easy but the lies hard, as she waited for the information the matron promised. She smiled and batted her eyelashes at the nobles who didn't recognize her face, hating their casualness, their emptiness.

Eventually, she caught Samuel on the way to the washroom, signaling him to follow her into the storeroom. She tried to ignore the memories that popped into her head of a different man on a different night.

"What have you heard?" Shan said.

"Nothing much," Samuel replied, the easy affability he pretended at all night vanishing. He looked so drained. "As far as rumors, they haven't heard anything that wasn't in the papers. I don't think any-one's even noticed the new dealer. And otherwise—"

"Perfectly normal," Shan spat, and Samuel nodded. Useless, it was all useless. But there was still the matron. Still a bit of hope. She reached out, pressing her hand against his face, and he leaned into the touch. "Thank you for trying, Samuel."

"It's okay," he said. "I wanted to."

They both knew it was a lie, but Shan didn't press it. She just allowed herself to lean into him, and he wrapped his arms around her, soft and comforting. There was nothing forward about it, nothing demanding—just comfort, freely given.

Shan felt as if she was breaking apart.

She stepped back, though she wanted nothing more than for him to keep holding her. "You can go, but there are still some things I need to do."

"Okay," he said, rubbing at his eyes. "We'll talk soon?"

"I'll send you a note about what I find," she promised, and Samuel clenched her hands to his one last time.

"Be careful, Shan."

"You, too," she whispered, and let him slip out first. When she was alone, with only the beat of her heart to keep her company, she whispered, "I really have to stop doing this."

She exited the storeroom only to the find the matron standing there, arms crossed over her chest. "Playing both sides, Sparrow?"

Shan quickly rearranged her expression, hiding away the pain and indecision she felt and replacing it with confidence and a lazy kind of ego. "Both sides have good information."

The matron stared at her for a long moment, but her anger broke. "If it helps you find out who did this to our girl, then how can I judge you?" She turned, heading towards her office, and Shan hurried to follow her.

"You don't think she is alive then?" Shan asked, feigning ignorance though she knew the truth. These people saw her as a beacon of hope, and she needed them to keep seeing her that way. If she came to them with the truth, awful as it was, she didn't know what they would do.

And she couldn't risk that, not now.

The matron shook her head. "It's been five days, Sparrow. No one has seen Sarah. Her home is empty. Her family mystified. We can only assume the worst."

"Tell me everything," Shan said. "Her address, her friends. Who last saw her. Anything that could help."

The matron opened the door to her office. "I have a copy of her file prepared for you to take. It's everything I know. As for who last saw her?" She wrung her hands. "I believe that was me."

Shan leaned forward. "And? Anything unusual?"

"Just that she left after her shift with a dark-haired man." The matron held up a hand. "No, I did not see his face, nor do I know his name."

Shan's breath caught in her throat. "I see."

"That's all I know," she said, "that and what's in the file." The matron looked at her, her blue eyes sharp. "You've got ties to both sides, but I don't care about that. All I care about is keeping my people safe. Do you understand me?"

"I do," Shan said, forcing the words past dry lips.

"Then go out and find this bastard, Sparrow," the matron hissed. "And make him pay."

Shan took the file and held it to her chest. "Thank you for your assistance." She slipped away before the matron could say any more, before she broke down completely.

It was just a coincidence. It meant nothing. There were many dark-haired men in Aeravin. And she would find this bastard and destroy him.

Chapter Thirty-Seven

Samuel

Samuel hesitated at the door to the King's laboratory, his hand hovering inches above the handle. He hadn't seen the King since the day they had been shown where the blood of Aeravin came from. They had been working tirelessly to put together the clues, to find the killer.

To stop it all before Isaac was put at risk in a pointless, ridiculous ceremony.

But they kept coming up empty.

He didn't know if he could continue to do this. He was walking a tightrope, dancing dangerously close to destruction, and if he kept down this path it wouldn't just be his life that was changed. His very soul would be stained beyond all recognition.

The Guard at his side coughed, and Samuel realized that he had been standing there for over a full minute. Squaring his shoulders, he took a deep breath and stepped through the door into the somber, sterile room. The King didn't even glance his way, too busy in a whispered argument with Isaac.

Well, Isaac was arguing. The King just stood there, a glass of amber liquid in his hand as he stared out into the night.

They also weren't alone. There was a third person in the room, a middle-aged man with his hands bound behind his back and his legs chained to a heavy metal chair. *He* looked up, his blue eyes shining with fear, but the gag in his mouth prevented him from saying anything.

Samuel cleared his throat, and both Isaac and the King turned to him. "Ah, you're here," the King said, but Isaac just whispered, "Please."

The King shook his head, a quick but harsh nod. "Enough. Do not forget your place." Isaac stepped back, as suddenly as if he had been slapped, looking completely and utterly defeated. "Now be gone."

Samuel lurched forward, but Isaac was already heading towards the door. He wouldn't meet his eyes, but he did say, gently and softly, "I'm sorry."

For what, Samuel didn't have the foggiest idea, but the dread in his stomach grew stronger. Whatever the King was planning, it must have been something terrible if Isaac had tried to stop it.

And he already knew how terrible the King could be.

Then Isaac was gone, leaving Samuel alone with the King, who tossed back the rest of his drink. "Well, I never thought I'd see the day," he muttered, with no small amount of annoyance as he stared at the space where Isaac had just stood. "But no matter, we have other things to focus on." He gestured to the prisoner, raising his empty glass to him. "Meet Erik. He's going to help with the next step of your training."

Samuel couldn't help the fearful glance he shot Erik, who just stared down at the floor. He didn't even seem afraid or angry. He was just quiet and empty, like a husk devoid of all soul. "I . . . what precisely are we doing?"

"De la Cruz should be thankful for what we're doing tonight. Even he should see that it'll only be to help him." The King smiled, and it was a cruel thing. "It's time we found out the limits of your power."

"Limits?" Samuel echoed, and the King frowned.

"Don't look so timid, Samuel. It's time you let go of this idea that your powers are something unsavory, an unfortunate necessity. This is something you will have to come to terms with if you want a place in my court. If you want to be part of it, you must accept that power—that justice—is not kind."

Samuel turned back towards Erik, remembering how the King had said that when he had killed that poor girl. The traitor. "And tonight we deliver justice?"

"Precisely." The King stepped forward, standing next to Samuel. "This bastard doesn't deserve mercy. He is a treasonous snake and was part of a plan to assassinate me."

Samuel blinked at the man, emaciated and pale, and had a difficult time imagining him as a threat. "I didn't realize there was—"

"It was years ago," the King interrupted. "And I ensured no word of it got out. I cannot have the crown looking weak, after all. But I've been waiting all this time to find the perfect punishment for him. At last he can be of use."

"I see." Samuel tore his eyes away from Erik, who hung his head low. Whatever spark he once had—bright enough to stand up to the Eternal King himself—had long ago burned away, leaving this broken and empty man. It seemed almost too cruel to contemplate, but Samuel was learning that the King specialized in that. In finding the exact right way to draw out the most pain possible.

It would have been awe-inspiring if it wasn't so horrible.

"What will you have me do?" Samuel asked at last, and the King relaxed for the first time that night.

Samuel had given up the fight, and the King knew it.

"We test just how much your gift can affect the body, not simply the mind and the will." He poured another glass of the amber liquid and brought it over to Samuel. "Here, this will help you relax, son."

Samuel stared down at it, hiding the flinch as he stared at the whisky. He hated being called that. *Son*. Like the King could ever be a father to him. Like he'd ever known what a father was like.

It was all bullshit.

"I don't need to be drunk," Samuel said, at last.

"Are you so sure?" The King tilted his head to the side, his green eyes cold and piercing. "You seem ... uneasy. This will help lower your inhibitions."

"It's not my inhibitions that are the problem," Samuel snapped, with more venom than he intended, but it earned him a smile.

"No, it's your fool heart." He pressed the glass into Samuel's hand. "And while that might be admirable in some people, you cannot allow it to hold you back."

Twisting his wrist, Samuel watched the whisky swirl in the glass. It was actually tempting, and he could already feel his power stirring in his chest, aching to be used. "My heart is the only thing that has kept me from becoming a monster."

"Only fools think of things in terms of men and monsters, and it's time to stop pretending you are less than you are."

"I am just a man," Samuel said.

"Not just any man." The King placed his hands on Samuel's shoulders, leaving him no choice but to look up at him. "You are an Aberforth and a Blood Worker. You are the last of my line. You should be a god amongst men."

But he didn't want that—or at least he had tried his whole life not to. The darkness was a part of him, but still disparate, held back by the strength of his will alone. Every time he was weak, every time he broke—every time he used his power in this mad quest for mastery—it was a bit harder to tuck that power back away. He had started to crave it, the rush that came with using it, the sense of control that he never had before.

And this? This would only make it all the harder.

He took a deep drink of the whisky, the burn giving way to something warm, almost pleasant, in his belly.

"You need to stop thinking of your power as only evil," the King said, his voice soft, not quite a whisper. "I would have hoped you had learned that by now, realized that it can be used to protect, to save yourself and those you care about in times of need."

Samuel could envision it immediately, how the words would flow from his lips, the imagined enemy stopping dead in their tracks. "They have to obey me."

"Not just that." The King stepped back, looking him over. "You're not trained for combat, you never have been. But you have another way to take care of a threat. Permanently."

Unable to contemplate what he might mean—even to dare thinking about it—Samuel took another deep sip of the whisky.

But the King didn't give him that out, choosing to continue, to whisper the words that Samuel feared to hear. "You could order them to stop breathing, for their heart to stop, to drop dead at your feet."

"I thought you said that I am not a monster."

"Is it monstrous to protect others? To protect the ones we love? The ones we have a duty to serve?" the King asked. "Isn't that exactly what we should be doing? Not everyone is a Blood Worker—there are countless Unblooded in Aeravin, in the world. Weak and defenseless. And not a single person like you. So, shouldn't you do everything you can to protect them?"

Samuel turned away, the alcohol turning sour in his stomach.

"Just imagine it, Samuel. We all have enemies." The King's voice was as cold and serious as death. "Not just me and you. Pretty little Shan LeClaire. Foolish Isaac de la Cruz. They both play dangerous games and if they are ever at risk, wouldn't you want to help them? Sometimes you only have a moment—a breath—to act.

"And you don't ever want to waste it."

Samuel blanched, but the King just watched him impassively. Of course. They hadn't found anything on the killer. The Royal Blood Worker still had duties to do—and public appearances to make. Samuel just didn't know if it was hubris or some kind of twisted kindness that motivated the King to dangle such potential in front of him, but either way he knew he had to be prepared.

Perhaps it was the result of living so long, seeing so many born and die. One stopped seeing them as people.

It's what made him such a powerful King, and something less than a man.

Speaking through a suddenly dry throat, Samuel said, "We don't even know if that would work." It was one thing to tell a man to kneel, to force the truth from his lips, to force him to remember something he had thought forgotten. But to force him to actively work against his own survival instincts? To end his life—the thing that most clung to so strongly?

Samuel acknowledged that he had a great and terrible power, but he wasn't so arrogant to assume he could do this.

"That is what Erik is here for," the King said, turning back to their guest. He had listened the whole time in enforced silence, but somewhere along the line he had started trembling, violently shaking in his seat. "I picked him specifically for you. I realize your morals still bother you, but this man is a traitor and a murderer, and I am not so cruel as to force you to kill an innocent." He stalked behind Erik's chair, wrapping one hand around the man's throat.

"He killed not just the Guards but servants as he made his way to me. A girl, only sixteen, left dead on the floor in a pool of her own blood. My valet, a man who had served me for more than two decades, who left behind a wife and two young children. He tore families apart in his insane quest to kill me, and for what?" Tearing off the man's gag, he looked at Samuel. "Ask him."

Tossing back the rest of the drink, Samuel stepped closer to Erik, close enough to smell the fear and sweat that rolled off him. "Is what he said true?" Samuel asked, letting the power flow through him and hang heavy on the air.

"Yes," Erik gasped, his voice hoarse, harsh, like he hadn't used it in years. And perhaps he hadn't, locked away in the King's dungeons. "I killed six servants on my way to the King."

Samuel let out a harsh breath. "Did they have to die?"

"No." Erik flinched. "They didn't."

"So why did you do it?"

"Because they were complicit," Erik snarled. "Because it didn't matter. All that mattered was getting to the King. Any cost was acceptable."

The King wrapped the gag around Erik's throat, pulling it back until he started to choke. "It was a foolish plan, ill-thought-out. Erik and his compatriots had no idea what to do once I was gone—they just wanted me dead and did not care who got in the way."

"What happened to the others?"

"They died in the attempt," the King said, relaxing his hold. Erik sputtered for air; it seemed that death would not come to him so soon. "Our friend here was the only one unlucky enough to survive. But now he can join his allies. All you have to do is say the word."

Samuel looked Erik in the eyes. "Do you regret? Their deaths?"

The answer was immediate. Erik didn't even try to fight it. "No."

The darkness stirred in his veins, and a single word fell from his lips.

"*Die.*"

Chapter Thirty-Eight

Shan

Shan swept through the streets of Dameral, her slate-colored cloak fluttering behind her as she trailed after her brother, just another body in the crowd. She hated that she had sunk to this, but she knew she couldn't plead ignorance, not anymore. The solstice was the next day, and she had yet to find proof to exonerate her only lead. If anything, the proof only further damned him.

So Shan did the only thing she could: she followed her own brother.

She kept one eye on the back of his head as he moved with purpose, heading towards his destination. But this time, when he left home, he didn't take the carriage or a hack to one of his favorite gambling hells, theatres, or taverns.

No, he was going on foot, leaving no trace of where he was heading, almost as if he didn't want to be found. He had also discarded his normal trappings, leaving behind his noble outfits for something far more plain, far more simple. Whatever he was planning, it was something he needed a disguise for.

Shan clenched her hand at her side, digging her nails into her palm, using the sharp bite of pain to dispel the paranoia that ran through her, that hadn't left her for hours. She couldn't ignore the fact that her brother had been acting strange lately—distant and different—but to even contemplate this of him felt like the worst kind of betrayal. He had always been the better of them, the reason she had accepted the darkness within.

When had he followed her down? When had he changed, and what had she been doing that she missed it? Her brother might have become a murderer, and she had refused to see the signs. It had been easier to pretend but now the blindfold was gone, and each step she took felt like a knife in her heart.

But she never lost sight of him.

He led her on a circuitous path through Dameral, descending from the lush noble sector where they made their home into the bustling warmth of the middle-class district. As they slipped between sectors, Shan found it more difficult to remain inconspicuous as the crowds grew thinner. The Unblooded, even those with the relative safety of money, were still retiring to their homes early, unwilling to risk even the slightest chance of being caught by this murderer.

Those who had to venture the streets did so in groups, moving as quickly as possible, their heads ducked low and their eyes on the streets before them. The Blood Workers around them, though, with their daggers and their claws, acted as if nothing had changed. The dissonance was disorienting.

Finally, Anton slipped down a small side street, and Shan hurried after him. By the time she had rounded the corner, he had already vanished, but there was the brief flash of a door closing.

There. That must be it.

Glancing round, she found that that street was completely empty—it was still the middle-class district, but he had led them away from the main streets and the shops. No, this was far more residential, where the shops catered to locals, not the broad spectrum of society. And at this hour, this twilight hour when fear ruled Dameral, there was not a soul to be found.

Shan slipped down the street, pressing her ear up against the door and listening for something—anything. She could make out the faint sound of voices, but nothing distinct, and even that was fading as they made their way deeper inside.

She could use her Blood Working, if she wanted—enhance her senses and maybe pick up on what they were saying. But she'd still be standing there, out in the open, completely vulnerable to whoever happened to pass by. No, that would never work. And these buildings were pressed so tightly against each other, with no spaces between, no gaps in which she could press herself.

Her brother had done a good job when he had picked this place. He might not have the ability to protect it with wards and traps like she did, but given his limitations it was a fine setup indeed.

Laying her hand against the doorknob, she made her choice. There wasn't enough time to waste with a slow and careful reconnaissance—and he was her brother, still.

She had safety in that.

Biting down on her tongue, she let her mouth fill with blood and strength infused her body. It was always a rush when she did this—though it wasn't something she often needed—to push her body to the limit, to find the strength she shouldn't have.

Pulling her arm back, she slammed her fist into the door right underneath the knob, the wood fracturing and splintering under the force of her blow. Shoving her fist through the newly made hole, she unlocked the door from the inside and let herself in.

Only to find Anton standing there, flanked by two people she vaguely recognized, filling the narrow hallway with their breadth. Her brother had looked ready to fight her intrusion—a short sword in his hand—but he lowered it instantly. The anger, though, was still there. She knew that look in his eyes—the cold flint of steel in his gaze—but she had never seen it directed at her.

"Shan. I should have expected this eventually." He was furious, and in that moment she could almost believe that he was a murderer.

How could she have missed that this was simmering beneath the surface for all this time?

She slipped the door closed behind her. "I was concerned about you, dear brother," she replied, but she focused her attention on his comrades.

One was a young woman their age, with dark skin and even darker hair that she wore in tight braids pressed to her scalp and bound at the nape of her neck. The other was a bit older, a tall, towering figure, though he was cramped awkwardly in this space that was too small for him. His pale complexion shimmered in the witch light, but his expression was shadowed by the fall of brown hair across his face.

These strangers were too well dressed to be just any Unblooded— the cut and make of their clothes, though in the style of the middle class, were just a bit too fine. But they wore no claws or daggers, and it took Shan a moment to understand why.

They were like her brother, born to Blood Working families but without an ounce of power—a source of shame and bewilderment to most. This was a part of her brother that she had never been able to understand. Blood had always called to her, filling her with power and singing beneath her skin. As terrible as Blood Working could be, it was as much a part of her as anything, and despite the color of her skin and the shame of her father it had granted her just a modicum of acceptance.

Her brother had never had that. None of these people ever had that. And perhaps, just perhaps, it was enough for them to turn against the system.

All it would cost was their souls.

Anton looked back at them, waving them off. "Go on without me, I'll catch up in a minute."

The woman leaned into him. "Don't do anything we'll regret, LeClaire."

His smile was forced. "Do you really think I'm that much of a fool?"

She shook her head. "For your family? Yes." She grabbed the other man by the hand, pulling him along. "We've got work to do." The grim giant shot Shan one last warning look, but he followed the woman out.

Shan tilted her head to the side, listening as they went, their footsteps fading as they took some stairs down, heading lower into the ground.

Interesting.

"Stop that," Anton snapped, too familiar with her antics for her to get away with such things. "We need to talk. This way."

Shan didn't fight him. They had been avoiding each other long enough and it was time to face the truth. She followed him into a parlor, realizing what this place was. It had been a home, once, but they had converted it to their needs. She wanted to peer into each room, to see what she could find, but Anton did not give her that chance.

He ushered her into the parlor and slammed the door behind him. "I need a drink" was all he said, crossing to a liquor cabinet that was stocked with half-empty bottles.

Shan settled into a chair. She didn't have the energy to be mad or anxious anymore. The right thing to do would have been to confront him outright, but she still hesitated. There was so much unspoken between them, and if this was to be her last night with her brother, she wanted to dally a little bit.

He reappeared in front of her, holding out a glass of whisky. She took it, and for a second the anger dimmed as she caught a glimpse of her brother again.

Terrified, lonely, hurt—but hers.

It only made everything more difficult.

He knocked the drink back, downing it with a practiced vigor, and slammed the glass down on the table. Shan watched him curiously. There was something rougher about him, something harder that she didn't fully recognize.

"So," he said, crossing his arms across his chest. "Do you want to tell me what this is about?"

She didn't respond, just stared into the glass of whisky he had brought.

"Dammit, Shan." He crossed over to the window, clasping his

hands behind his back. Shan sucked in a harsh breath. Anton might never look like their father, neither of them would—but that pose, those mannerisms? That was Lord Antonin LeClaire, back from the grave.

"You were the one following me, then?" he asked, still looking away, hiding his face.

"Yes," Shan said, "I was."

He cursed, low and soft, but there wasn't anger in it. Just pain. "Why?"

Shan wrapped her arms around herself, her facade finally cracking. She prided herself on being impervious, on being so strong that she never showed a hint of weakness, but . . . he was her brother, and this pain was real. "I—" her breath caught in her throat, the words refusing to come. "Can't."

"Can't?" Anton said, at last turning. His eyes were dark and empty. "Or won't? Does this have anything to do with the fact that you've locked me out of your study? That you haven't truly spoken to me since before you murdered our father? I thought we didn't lie to each other, Shan."

"I haven't been lying," she said, though the words felt hollow.

"No, I suppose you haven't." He rubbed his hand across the shorn side of his head, messing his meticulous hairstyle. "But you haven't been truthful either."

Shan didn't deny it—it was true. She had only stayed faithful to their long-time vow by a technicality, though she had broken it many times over in spirit.

"So, let me begin," Anton said, surprising her. He stepped forward, taking her hands in his. She wasn't wearing her claws—it didn't fit her simple disguise—and it felt strange to be holding her brother's hand like this again. They hadn't done this since they were children, clinging together against the darkness that was their own family. "I have not been entirely truthful either. Tonight, you met Alaric Rothe and Maia Aedlar."

"Ah." The names clicked into place as Shan drew upon the great family trees of Aeravin. Maia was a bastard daughter, the child of a long-time mistress, but her father had a kindly heart—he raised her in his household, with his name and his wealth. She could never inherit, especially as she had shown no skill at Blood Working, but it was better than the streets.

Alaric was a bit of a radical, though—he should have been the heir. He had no siblings and was the last of a long line but gifted with no magic. After the death of his mother, his cousins immediately started fighting each other for control of the estates, but Alaric held his ground, fighting them tooth and nail, refusing to be denied his birthright.

Or any more of it than he had already lost. The Rothe seat in the House of Lords had sat empty for nearly a decade. Lineage or not, an Unblooded couldn't fill that spot.

It all made too much sense. "Are they your birds?"

Anton rolled his eyes. "They are my friends, Shan. Not that you would know what that is like." He stopped her before she could counter him. "And I don't count. I'm family."

She bit her lip. "There is Samuel."

"Oh, Shan," Anton said, with a cruel little laugh that reminded her a bit too much of their father. Of herself. "Don't believe your own lies. You're using him just as much as you use anyone else. He's no different than Isaac."

He might as well have slapped her across the face. It wasn't true—at least not in the way that he thought it was. Samuel wasn't that different from Isaac, but Isaac wasn't some simple tool to be used either.

Her heart aching many times over, she sighed and reached for her drink. "Alaric and Maia, then. They're your friends."

"Yes," Anton said carefully. "And my . . . allies."

"Allies in what?" she asked, needing to hear it. Needing to know if he'd tell her the truth, even now, or if everything between them was lost forever.

Anton looked away. "It's complicated."

She clenched her hand around her glass, trying to hide the trembling that started. This was the moment—the one that she had been fearing. When she forced the words past her lips, it barely sounded like her voice at all. "Try me."

"It would be easier to show you." He stood, offering her his hand.

And, foolishly, she took it.

—•—

Anton led her down into the basement, following the steps that Alaric and Maia had taken earlier. This place was more than a meeting spot—she had quickly figured that out—it was a headquarters and a safe house and, as they entered into the basement, a printing press.

An illegal, unsanctioned, hidden printing press.

Shan stared at the process, Maia and Alaric working in silent coordination as they took the type and set it against the paper, creating a stream for production. They did the work themselves, despite their noble upbringings. Alaric had his sleeves rolled up past his elbows, ink splattered on his shirt, and Maia worked the type, setting rows of letters in order.

She crossed over to the far wall, where bundles of pamphlets and slim booklets were stacked, ready for distribution. Grabbing the first one she could, she ran her fingers on the freshly dried, slightly offset title.

A DECLARATION ON THE RIGHTS OF THE UNBLOODED

BY THE FRIEND OF THE UNBLOODED

So this was it. This was the big secret that he had been working on behind her back. It wasn't murder, it wasn't illegal Blood Working. It was these damn radical texts that ranged from speculative to outright seditious.

Anton was whispering behind her, and she hardly paid attention to him as he told Alaric and Maia to leave. She just stared at the amount of damning material spread before her and wondered what she was supposed to do with all of this.

It was only the closing of the door behind them that moved her to action.

Crushing the pamphlet in her hand, she spun on him. "It's been you all along. You're *The Friend*."

Anton inclined his head, and she cursed. "Not just me, but, yes. I've been one of the writers and organizers."

"Don't you realize what you've done? What you're all doing?"

"You're brilliant, Shan," Anton began, and she braced herself for the *but* that was coming. "But your plans ..."

"Will change Aeravin," Shan said. "You know this."

"Actually, I don't," Anton snapped. "What you fail to realize is that you're a Blood Worker, and that Aberforth you intend to replace the King with will be a Blood Worker, too. And, yes, he's—" Anton had had the grace to look pained "—he's a good man, but changing one man won't fix anything. There is still the House of Lords, there are still systems and institutions that will keep the Unblooded in their place."

Shan stepped back. She had expected many things, such terrible things, but the idea that he had lost faith in what she was doing was the most painful option of all. "Everything will change."

"Nothing will change," Anton said, sadly. "They won't let it. They won't even allow Alaric to hold his seat in the House of Lords."

Shan wanted to argue, but he was right. The House of Lords would never let someone like Alaric amongst them. Not unless they were forced to.

"It will be revolution, then?" she asked.

"Is it so different than what you are doing?"

"In my plan," Shan said, quietly, "there would be no innocent deaths."

"There are already innocents dying." Anton stepped over to a desk, pulling out paper after paper, laying them in a pile before her. "People are starving, people are being worked until they die, people cannot afford midwives or doctors or healers, though we have the ability to care for them. And," he started making a different pile, "that's not even getting to the crime."

Slamming a bundle of papers down, he hissed, "This is a partial list of Unblooded who have vanished in the past year, Shan. One year. And there were no investigations done, no bodies found. This many people don't just disappear. It should be a crisis, but our government does nothing for them."

He looked up at her and Shan realized that this wasn't some idle fancy, some fit of righteous passion, that had taken over her brother. No, this was a long-thought-out, carefully crafted plan. A revolution that had grown out of the problems that simmered under Aeravin's facade.

Problems that even she—the Sparrow, with her dreams of making the country a better place for the Unblooded—had not seen. Had not bothered to look for.

Because she hadn't truly cared about the Unblooded, not really. She had just cared about her brother.

And he had outdone her in every way, even without magic.

"They will kill you," she said. "They will kill all of you."

Anton didn't argue. "I had hoped that it wouldn't come to that, honestly, but I know that it will come to violence eventually. I've seen your bill."

"I'm trying to save people!" she screamed, and he just smiled sadly.

"I know you are. But you never stopped to ask how they wanted to be saved, or if they were willing to risk fighting for the hope of a better chance."

She turned away, trembling, and Anton wrapped his arms around her. "I have to do this, you understand."

"I do," Shan said, because she was the same. "But know that I will keep fighting to protect you, as much as I can."

"I know you will." He let go. "Now it's best you leave. We have to move our operations."

"I wouldn't—"

"I know," Anton said. "But we need to be safe nonetheless. The fact that you know that I am involved—that Alaric and Maia are involved—is bad enough."

Shan cupped her brother's cheek. "When did you grow up so much?"

"Right in front of your face," Anton said. "You just weren't looking. Now go."

Nodding, she made her way towards the stairs, still clutching the ruined pamphlet in her hand. Anton watched her go, and all the words she wanted to say died on her tongue.

What a fool she had been, thinking he was involved in the murders. What a fool she had been for not seeing what her brother had been capable of.

Perhaps if she hadn't been so blind, they could have worked together.

But now it was too late.

Chapter Thirty-Nine

Samuel

The morning of the summer solstice dawned warm and hazy, and Samuel wished he didn't have to attend this event, wished he didn't know what he could do, simply with the power of his voice.

Hells, he didn't understand why it was still happening at all. Isaac's safety aside, it was still a terrible idea. Sure, the Eternal King had spent a lot of time and money renovating the central square of Dameral, but with everything that had happened in the past few months—the murders and demonstrations and the growing unrest in the country—continuing with it just felt ill-advised at best and a snub at the worst.

Though most of the park was already there to see—with its fountains and benches and endless weaves of rose bushes—the central dais was still hidden behind high cloth barriers that covered it from top to bottom, waiting for the Royal Blood Worker to unveil it. And he was in danger.

Because they hadn't found the murderer. Because—both thankfully and regrettably—it wasn't Anton.

That meant that they had no leads, save the chance that Isaac would be a victim. And so he was here. Praying that he wouldn't need to step in and command something heinous. Again.

The man's death lingered with him. Samuel kept seeing it—when he tried to sleep, when he allowed himself to stop for even a moment. The way he had gone rigid, how he had stopped breathing, choking on nothing as his heart gave out. He had at least died quickly, but Samuel would never forget it. Would never let himself forget it.

He was at last the monster he had feared becoming.

A monster hoping that today would somehow end in peace.

But the same couldn't be said of the others, the Unblooded who had turned out to watch in disgust and frustration. He could sense it in the crowd around him, simmering with an undercurrent of rage that frankly revitalized him. The crowd was divided into sections—most of the nobles watched from above, sitting on the balconies of restaurants and cafés and clubs, but Samuel had turned down the invitation that Shan had offered him. She would be watching from above, but he would be here, feet on the cobblestones and shoulder to shoulder with those he wanted to save. There was something about being with the people he had grown up with that was just so grounding, despite the changes the last few months had wrought.

No amount of finery or money or magic would ever take that away.

Besides, if he was to save Isaac, he couldn't do it from so far away.

But he was still here not simply as Samuel, a man, but as Lord Aberforth. Dressed to the nines in his fine suit, in his cravat and tails, with his hair neatly pulled back into a queue and the soft hint of cologne wafting off him. He tried to ignore the stab of pain that came whenever he caught a sneer from the corner of his eyes, or when someone leaned pointedly away from him.

He wanted to scream, to yell that he was one of them, that this farce wasn't who he really was. But he knew that wasn't true, not anymore, so he just kept moving forward through the crowds, not having to fight his way to the front where the Guards kept watch. The Unblooded parted for him, giving him ample space—not out of respect or deference, but because they did not want to be near him.

He wished he could have accepted Shan's invitation after all.

It was too late for that, though, so he just wrapped his bare fingers around the cool metal fence in front of him. At least he didn't have claws. He might dress like one of them, might have their blood and their money, but he still had this. They hadn't made a Blood Worker out of him.

The crowd quieted, but it wasn't the respectful, reverential silence that he expected. No, there was a fragility to this, a tension that was ready to break. Samuel looked up to find that Isaac had appeared, and suddenly it felt like no time had passed at all. It could almost be the spring equinox again, when he had been caught in the crowd before the Eternal King's annual sacrifice, and if he closed his eyes none of this would have happened.

But he couldn't close his eyes. There was no sacrifice to be killed, no Eternal King to scorn. There was just a man—Isaac—who looked just this side of broken, trapped in a position that Samuel couldn't even imagine.

Four months ago, Samuel wouldn't have cared about the lines around his eyes, about the tension he carried in his shoulders. But four months ago, he didn't care about him, and watching him now, his heart broke.

Knowing what he knew now, about what the King expected of him, what the King made him do, Samuel wondered how he functioned at all.

Isaac crossed in front of the hidden gardens, taking his place front and center as members of the Guard took theirs, standing by large, decorated ropes as they awaited their cues. When Isaac gave the signal, they'd yank on the ropes and the curtains would fall, revealing the new park that the Eternal King had commissioned.

Any other year, it would have been a lovely ceremony. But not a single person wanted to be here, not the Royal Blood Worker who hosted it in place of a King who never could be bothered, or a people who were tired of dying.

"My friends," Isaac said, not with a smile or cheer, but with a solemnity that rooted Samuel where he stood. "My fellow citizens. Thank you for coming out this morning, especially in such dark times. I know that we have been living under a veil of fear, some of us more than others, but I believe that is why we need this more than ever." He took a deep breath, letting the moment sink in. "For even in this, there are still moments of hope to be found, and we cannot lose them all to darkness."

"Easy for you to say!" a voice cried out, somewhere to the back and right of Samuel.

"You're not the one dying!" another called out, this time just to the left.

It was enough—the final drops that overpowered the dam and released the flood. All around Samuel more and more voices cried out, their words growing confused and muddled as they blended together.

The specifics didn't matter, though. Their intent was clear. Their anger was palpable, and it was being held back by only the thinnest of threads.

A couple of Guards stepped forward, flexing their claws, but Isaac threw up a hand. "No, they are right, after all. We don't know what it has been like to be you. To be Unblooded in a time like this. You have been scared and ignored and mistreated, and we—the Blood Workers, the nobles, those who have sworn to lead and protect you— have done nothing about it." The crowd quieted suddenly, confusion spreading as Isaac stared at them with something like pain in his eyes. "We have abused you in ways that you have never known, but it is time for that to change."

He snapped his fingers, once, and the Guard hesitated only a moment before pulling their ropes. The thick curtains around the dais fluttered, and like a shimmering curtain of blood they flowed to the ground. But where there was to be a statue of their king—Eternal and proud and strong—there was something else. A scene of horror.

A metal table where the statue should have been.

A dead man strapped to it, brutalized and mutilated.

A glass vat of blood underneath, the last drips of blood filling from the tubes in his arms and legs.

It was the exact image of a victim of the Blood Factory, and all of Aeravin stared on in shock.

Samuel's heart came to a stop. They had been wrong. They had been so terribly wrong.

"The Blood Taxes you pay are a lie," Isaac said, his voice carrying over the sudden silence. "The Blood Workers demand far more than you give for their magics, and it has been my duty to ensure that needs are met. The Royal Blood Worker sees that the coffers of blood are filled, and the murders that have plagued this city were those who saw that we were supplied with the people—the poor, the unwanted, the criminal. And Lord Kevan Dunn has been kind enough to model what we do with them."

He turned to face the people. "And for my part in this, I know I can never be forgiven."

The silence shattered, the crowd suddenly surging forward. The combined force of them knocked Samuel off his feet, sending him crashing into the fence, which then tumbled to the hard cobblestones below. He caught himself awkwardly, skinning his hands on the rough surface, but a quick check showed though his hands were roughed up, there was no blood.

He almost laughed at the ridiculousness of it. Even in a moment like this, old habits died hard.

Staggering to his feet, he immediately looked for Isaac. But he was already fleeing, his blood-red robes fluttering behind him as he ran, covered by the indistinct figure of a Guard.

So he had an accomplice, then.

Samuel tried to follow, but they were moving too fast, disappearing into the chaos. Something like relief fluttered through him—something he knew he shouldn't feel—but he didn't have time to focus on that now.

Instead, he moved with the flow of the crowd, keeping an eye out for the Guards. They had thrown themselves against the press of the Unblooded, trying to hold them back at points where the fence had fallen through, holding the line until their reinforcements arrived.

Good: if they were focused on the Unblooded that meant that Isaac had a chance.

What was he thinking? Isaac wasn't a damsel to be rescued. If this demonstration made anything clear, he was the very one they were looking for. The murderer they had to bring before the King if they had any hope of surviving. The one that they needed to capture if they wanted to keep peace in Aeravin.

But peace was already lost, and it was *Isaac*. His Isaac. The kind, proud, broken man who had only ever tried to help him. Who wanted to protect him from the horrors of the Blood Workers, all while being forced to commit the worst of them in the shadows.

In that moment Samuel hated like he had never hated in his entire life, the rage and darkness in him twisting into something new, something ugly, something *true*. While chaos raged around him—a cacophony of shouts and screams and cries, the press of bodies knocking against each other, the scrabble of madness unleashed— Samuel found a place of pure calm.

"Out of my way," he called, his voice low and threaded with power. The crowd immediately parted around him, allowing him to pass straight through to the dais.

Despite the riots around him, spreading through the square and the gardens, this place was left untouched. Perhaps the Unblooded were too afraid to approach it, the gruesome and raw display of Blood Working. But Samuel wasn't afraid, not anymore, and he stepped closer to Dunn, reaching out to check for a pulse.

There was none. Of course not. Isaac was smart enough to ensure that. *One to go*—and Isaac would not fail in that. Whatever his plan had been, he had achieved it.

And then left them to deal with the aftermath.

"My lord!" Samuel didn't turn to a Guard who had run up beside him, who stared down at the tableau before them for an uncomfortable long moment before speaking. "We need to get you out of here."

Turning away from the Guard, Samuel looked out over the riots. More Guards were starting to appear, coming in from the side streets and pressing in from the other side, pincering the Unblooded between two fronts. So far, Samuel hadn't felt the brush of Blood Working, but it was only a matter of time. The magic would come, the Guards would take them in, and arrests would be made.

Unless someone did something about it.

He glanced up towards the balconies, where the nobles were supposed to be, but they were already gone. Emptied. They had fled at the first sign of trouble, leaving the people to riot and the Guards to handle it. What cowards.

So be it, then.

Ignoring the look of disbelief on the Guard's face, Samuel shoved Dunn's legs aside, wincing at the clammy feel of his skin. Hauling himself up on the metal table, though careful to not touch Dunn's corpse, Samuel stood tall over the crowd, throwing his shoulders back as he played at strength.

Summoning his power—just a breath of it—he shouted one word. "Enough!"

His voice carried over the square, his power flowing over the crowd, sweeping over them as everyone turned to him. Samuel forced back the urge to flee, terror creeping up the back of his neck as he realized the precarious position he was in, but as he caught the Guards shaking off the moment of stillness he had bought, he knew that he had to do something.

"Please," he said, words coming fast and unfiltered. "I know that this is a shock, that this injustice cannot stand. But rioting is not the answer. There are those of us who will see this corrected. Do not throw your lives away."

For a moment silence reigned, and he thought that just maybe it worked. But then he felt something cold and wet collide with his cheek, sending his head snapping to the side. Raising his hand, he pressed it to the mess dripping down his face.

It was rotten fruit.

"Fuck you, *Aberforth*," a voice hissed from the crowd.

Samuel used the back of his hand to wipe away as much of it as he could, trying to avoid grimacing. Trying to fight the spike of anger that rose in his chest, tempting and insidious. "Please," he began again. "Give me a chance. I am one of you—"

"You are *not* one of us!"

Another fruit was lobbed at him, this one striking him hard in the chest, sending him staggering a couple of steps back.

"Traitor!"

"Blood Whore!"

"Coward!"

More insults and projectiles came his way, and Samuel crossed his arms in front of his face as the Guard helped him off the table. The crowd had erupted again, even more incensed than before, but Samuel didn't have time to dwell on that. He reached for the body—wanting to do something, anything, to keep Dunn from being overrun—but a cadre of Guards had appeared around him, forming a protective triangle as they pushed their way through the rioting crowd, shoving people to the ground and stomping over them as they ferried Samuel to safety.

There was the great heaving sound of the table being overturned, followed by the harsh sound of glass shattering. Screams filled the air, and as he tried to turn around one last time the Guard on his left just shoved him forward and out of the square, away from the violence that he had been unable to stop.

Quiet and a little bit broken, Samuel stopped fighting. The people were right—he wasn't one of them, not anymore.

No, he was Lord Aberforth, protected by his own personal group of Guards as he was guided to a carriage that he did not recognize. The same Guard who had found him pushed him into the carriage, gave it a quick once over, and then shouted something to the driver.

And he was off, carried swiftly to safety.

Samuel slumped in the seat and cried.

Chapter Forty

Shan

Shan paced back and forth, her hands clasped behind her back as she tried to process the discoveries of the morning. She had watched the unveiling from above, one eye on the crowd and the other on Isaac, all the better to keep an eye out for threats. Foolish, in the end. Isaac was never in any danger at all.

After his revelation, after the shock wave hit, Lady Belrose had gathered the remaining members of the Council and all the Lords and Ladies she could summon, calling them to an emergency session at the Parliament House. The riots that had started in the square were only growing, and the government needed to step up and do something.

Belrose had brought Shan along in her own carriage, muttering something about needing her for the next step, but Shan barely paid attention to it.

Her mind—her heart—was elsewhere.

She had been placed, ironically enough, in Lord Dunn's office to wait for the session to begin. Sequestered away to wait as the other Lords and Ladies trickled in, a slow process as they evaded the riots and demonstrations that were breaking out across the city, a fire that had started and was growing out of control.

The door suddenly opened, and she turned, about to ask if they were ready to begin, but it was only Samuel, weary and strangely covered in rotten food. He was ushered in by a distressed footman, who simply bowed and then slammed the door on them.

"Oh, Samuel," she said, stepping forward and holding out her hands. "What happened to you?" She knew that he had been in the crowds below, but she hadn't once feared for his safety. She trusted him enough for that.

But this mess? This she didn't understand.

He took her hands gratefully, claws and all, his shoulders hunching in on themselves as he whispered, "We've made a terrible mistake. Looked in the wrong place." He closed his eyes, as if by avoiding saying it they could avoid the truth. But they had both been avoiding the truth for too long. "It was Isaac."

"I know," she said, squeezing his hand, though pain lanced through her like ice, leaving her numb. Suddenly, everything fit together. The way the murderer had known who to target, the advanced Blood Working that had been used in the murders. The fact that Kevan Dunn, noted for his anti-democratic stances and his commitment to keep the Unblooded in their place, was the final nail in the coffin.

It could only have been Isaac, and he had just as much reason to hate Aeravin as she did.

"You never found what you were looking for," she murmured, her heart shattering like glass, never to be fully repaired. "But this?"

"Was he caught?" Samuel asked, and Shan shook her head.

"The moment the riots started it was chaos. I saw him running with the help of one of the Guard, but, no, he got away." She didn't mention the relief she felt when she saw him flee. "And then we were all fleeing."

"It was terrible," Samuel said, pressing the heels of his hands into his eyes. "I tried to stop them, Shan, I tried to make them listen, but I couldn't—"

"Ah." She grabbed his hands again, pulling them away from his face, as she suddenly understood. "It was good of you to try. But this has been building for far too long—longer than these past four months. Longer than you've been a part of it." She swallowed hard, finally accepting what she had refused to see. "It was bound to happen sooner or later."

Samuel clenched his fists at his side. "What do we do?"

"We keep moving," Shan said, simply. "And we try to make sure there is as little blood shed as possible."

"But . . . the King." Samuel trembled, looking pale and frightened. "We've failed him."

"No." Shan brushed the hair back from his face. "Things have changed, yes, but the final battle is yet to come. We can still swing this."

He took her hand, and she clasped it tight. Oh, how she wanted to break. She couldn't. Samuel was on the verge of falling apart, and she needed to be strong for him. For both of them. This was a disaster, still, she could save it.

They had to act fast.

"I know you're afraid, but we don't have time for that now," she said, cupping his cheek. "I know you feel guilty and foolish for not seeing this. You cannot carry that weight. I missed it, too, and the burden lies on my shoulders as well. For now, we must be strong and we'll deal with the aftermath later."

Samuel nodded. "Okay."

"All right then, you can't go into the House of Lords like that." She stood, pulling him to his feet. "Get out of those dirty clothes and I'll find you something clean to wear."

"How—"

"I'll handle the particulars," she said, stepping towards the door.

"I— all right." He turned to her, his green eyes shining with unshed tears. "Thank you, Shan."

"For what?"

"For doing what you always do," Samuel replied. "Keeping it together."

She almost laughed at that—it was absurd. She wasn't holding it together; she was just falling apart slower. "I'll be right back, Samuel."

—†—

By the time she had gotten him a fresh set of clothes—not as good a fit as his tailored suits, but close enough—and changed, Belrose had reappeared at Dunn's office. She didn't say anything about the sudden appearance of Samuel, just looked at Shan and said, "It's time."

Shan only nodded, following the Councillor out of the office, Samuel questioningly on her heels. They made their way to the Council Chamber in silence, but Belrose stopped at the threshold. "Take your usual seat, LeClaire, but pay close attention. Today's session will be special in many ways, and we have both of you to thank for that."

With that, she swept off, her skirts swishing softly as she made her way down the stairs. Samuel caught her gaze with an arched eyebrow, but she had no answers for him. Whatever the Councillor was planning was beyond her, but she appreciated the warning.

Most of the sitting members of the House had made it, Shan noticed with relief. Not all, of course: it was rare to have a full turnout even at the best of times. But there was enough to pass any motions that were brought forth, and she knew that was precisely what the Royal Council had been counting on.

The nobles who had come were muttering amongst themselves—whispers and accusations and snippets of discussions that Shan knew she should be paying attention to. Isaac's revelation would shake up the entire Court of Aeravin, and she should use this opportunity to get ahead of it. To find out who—like her—was appalled. And who found it to be a necessary evil.

But her heart was heavy, and Shan couldn't bear it. Not now. So she focused on the Royal Council, pushing aside the whispers.

Lady Belrose stood on the central dais, slowly turning to take in all the members as quiet settled over the chamber. Shan couldn't help but be taken in by her strength, her presence, as she commanded the room with the grace of a queen.

"Thank you," she began, soft and solemn, "for coming on such short notice. I know that not all of you were present for the debacle this morning, but I'm sure you know the details." She stopped to take a deep breath. "One of our own was murdered this morning by the Royal Blood Worker, and one of Aeravin's most important state secrets was revealed."

Mutters broke out, only to be immediately hushed as she raised her hand. "That issue, though important, is not the most pressing matter. Riots have broken out across Dameral as the Unblooded learn the truth about how we fill our coffers. Civil unease has become civil unrest, and if we do not move to fix it, there might not be a country left for us to save.

"For this, I turn to a proposal that was submitted to us by one of our newest members—"

The door to the Council Chamber flung open, startling Belrose out of her speech. She flung her hand over her chest as the entire assembly turned to see who dared to interrupt the session, only to find the Eternal King staring down at them all.

Shan sucked in a harsh breath. *He wasn't supposed to be here.* He was their king, yes, but the House of Lords was theirs—theirs to run, theirs to use. A way to propose bills and laws and temper the power of the King. It was sacred, and he was not supposed to interfere.

And in all the history of Aeravin, Shan had never heard of him doing so.

But he was here now, his expression as unmovable as if it were carved from stone. Though the weight of every member's gaze was on him, he walked down the stairs as if he belonged, his steps echoing on the marble as he approached Lady Belrose.

With nothing else to do, Lady Belrose dropped into a formal curtsy, her head bowed low in supplication. "Your Majesty."

He only sneered at her. "Rise."

When she did, he thrust a thin package of papers at her, and she took it wordlessly.

"I have declared a state of emergency," the King said, his voice soft but still echoing in the chamber. "And with that come several new laws."

Gasps rose across the chamber—the King did not propose new laws. That was the entire purpose of the House of Lords. Certainly he had a hand in things, working with his Royal Councillors to prepare motions. But something as brazen as this?

It was unprecedented.

"These are quite ... thorough," Belrose said, flipping through the packet.

The King didn't even look at her. "But they are necessary. Lady Belrose, if you would be so kind?"

Her mouth drew into a hard line, but she nodded. "First amongst these, a curfew is to be enacted for all Unblooded Citizens of Aeravin," she began, and Shan leaned forward in her seat, her claws digging into her skin as the list grew worse and worse.

As the Unblooded were banned from gathering in groups of four or more.

As the writing and distribution of literature deemed seditious was made a crime.

As the Guard were given the right to search the properties of the Unblooded under the mere suspicion of a crime.

As the quarterly Blood Taxes rose from a single pint of blood to two.

As the few rights and protections of the Unblooded were stripped away to nothing at all.

At last, Belrose came to a stop, lowering the pages. Her voice was harsh and rasping. "I suppose we should begin the vote."

"You misunderstand," the King said, turning on her. "This is not for a vote. This is a courtesy. These are the new laws of Aeravin, and I trust that you all will help enforce them."

"But that's not—" Belrose's protest died on her lips as the King turned to her. "I see. Anything else?"

"Yes." He turned his back on Belrose, as if she meant nothing. "Aeravin is in chaos, but this state of emergency is temporary. Until it has been lifted, though, I am suspending the House of Lords."

The questioning murmurs turned to shouts, but the Eternal King just stood there, turning his claws against himself as he trailed it down his own arm, cutting through the fabric of his sleeve to reveal the scarred skin beneath. He didn't need to say a word, the sheer force of his magic rising, building, the same power she had felt before slowly spreading through the chamber.

Silence fell as his aura grew stronger, to the point where Shan feared that she would choke on it.

"As I said, this is only temporary," the Eternal King said, tapping the blunt tip of his claw against the vein in his wrist. "There is important work to be done containing the problem, and after it has been contained you can revisit these laws. Am I understood?"

No one responded, not until Lady Belrose stepped forward. "As you will, Your Majesty."

"Good." He lowered his arms. "Now, there is work to be done. For those of you with estates and vassals, see to it that the new laws are spread and enforced, even outside of Dameral. For those of you idle nobles—"

Shan swore his eyes found hers.

"—I am sure you can find other ways to be useful." The King tilted his chin up. "The Unblooded think they can force change upon us? They are wrong."

He swept past Belrose, ascending the stairs and disappearing through the doors.

The assembly sat there, motionless, until Belrose snapped, "You heard him!" Turning away, she sank into her seat, staring down at the list of laws the King had forced upon her.

Shan stood, slow and wobbly, and it didn't take long for Samuel to reach her side.

"Can he do that?" he whispered.

"He's the Eternal King," Shan replied. "There isn't much we can do to stop him." He had all the power, and in the end she had no choice but to play into his hands.

Even if it shattered her heart.

"We need to find Isaac."

Chapter Forty-One

Samuel

After the Eternal King's announcement at the Council of Lords, Shan had spirited Samuel away to the LeClaire townhouse, keeping him sequestered in her study.

Part of him resented that she kept him so close, as if she didn't trust him not to do anything foolish if he was left unsupervised. But he had to admit that it was smart of her—if he'd been left alone, he might have tried to take to the streets, to mitigate what damage he could.

She knew him too well.

So she held him fast, keeping him safe as terror swept through the streets. The Guards were out there in full force, breaking up riots and filling the jail cells, using Blood Working where simple force was not enough. Despite the calm—the peace—he felt in Shan's study, Samuel knew that the rest of the city was embroiled in a battle he couldn't even imagine.

And worst of all? He didn't even want to know the details. He was happy in his ignorance, focusing on the one thing they could control. He stood above her, watching as she took all the information they had—and didn't have—and laid them along the floor, searching for hints and patterns they had missed. Everything they had on Isaac's life, reducing it to nothing more than scraps of paper.

"Are we sure we should be doing this?" Samuel asked, finally voicing the question that had been hanging unspoken between them for hours.

Shan stopped what she was doing, the pen in her hand going limp as she stared ahead. "Because it's Isaac or because you agree with him?"

"I don't know." Samuel pressed his thumbs into his temples, trying to ease the dull headache that had been building all day. "Both? He wants the same thing that we do, doesn't he?"

"We don't know what he wants, precisely," Shan said, carefully.

She always spoke so carefully. Normally, Samuel admired that about her, but in this moment, it drove him mad. How could she be so calm through all this when here he was, seconds away from falling apart?

And for someone who had spent his whole life carefully keeping all of his emotions and dreams on the shortest leash possible, Samuel wasn't sure how he was supposed to be handling all of this. He hadn't allowed himself so much for so long, but now that he had a taste, he didn't want to let it go.

"He wants the Eternal King gone," Samuel whispered, even though they were safe in her study. He would never feel fully safe speaking treason.

"Yes, but . . ."

"But what, Shan?"

"But people are dying!" Shan snapped the pen in her hand in half, her expression twisted into something ugly, something fearful, and Samuel sank to his knees beside her. "He started a *riot*, and now . . ." Turning her face to the window, she sighed at the darkened night sky. "Now it's curfew."

He had been wrong. She wasn't calm—she was furious. The same kind of fury that he had felt that morning, that all-consuming peace that was far more dangerous that any fire could ever be.

They were more alike than he realized.

He wrapped his arms around her waist, tucking her against him.

She didn't fight him, leaning into his embrace, and he could feel the minute tremors that ran through her. "Then he has to die?"

"He has to be brought in," Shan murmured, so softly against him. "It's the only way we can temper the Eternal King's wrath. If we cannot stop that, then ..."

"Dammit." He reached up, wiping his eyes with one hand, and Shan just sighed.

"I know. But we bring him in, alive, and then we will see what we can do."

It wasn't much—it wasn't a promise, it wasn't the future he had started to hope for. But it was a chance.

And he'd take it over nothing.

Hells, Samuel hated himself for even hoping. He wasn't a child to believe in such foolish things—in life, there were no truly happy endings.

She pulled out of his arms, and he let her go. He would always let her go when she needed it—she was too strong and free to be caged. "It's late, Samuel. We should get some rest. Tomorrow we pick up the pieces."

"What is the plan?"

"We wait for calm. I check with my birds—they are everywhere. He can't hide forever."

Samuel licked his lips. "And me?"

"For now? Prepare yourself." She looked at him, with such kindness in her dark eyes that it felt like a knife. "You'll have to be the one to bring him in, Samuel. If he won't listen to reason, then you'll have to force him."

"I see." Her hand came to rest on his arm, comforting, and he didn't fight it. Not her touch or the pain that lanced through him. It made sense, he understood that. If Isaac was going to live, it would be the only way.

"I'm sorry," Shan said, "to ask this of you."

"Don't be." Samuel knew that eventually he'd have to embrace the monster within. Better to do it for Isaac than for the Eternal

King. Better to bring him in alive than to murder him with a word. "I'll be fine."

It was a lie, and he knew that Shan knew it was a lie, but she didn't press him. She just brushed her lips against his, a ghost of a kiss.

"We'll get through this," she promised. "One way or another."

—

Samuel didn't recognize his city. The riots were over, the Unblooded driven back to their homes—or worse—and Guards patrolled the streets, riding horses down the cobblestoned streets, holding lanterns of witch light high as they kept curfew. They nodded as they passed him, taking in his clothes, his hair, the Blood Worker's dagger that Shan had strapped around his waist—marking him as one of their own in a glance—before continuing on.

Fear hung heavy in the air, driving even the bravest of Blood Workers into their homes, leaving the streets empty and cold. Come morning, most of Dameral's elite would flee the city, taking unplanned vacations to their country homes and estates. Those who didn't have the option would likely lock themselves in their houses, not leaving at all. In one day, everything had changed, and no one knew where the pieces would fall.

It gave his city a new shape and texture, so different from the bustle and life he was used to. Aeravin was a city of flaws, and a city of blood, a city of tragedy, but it had still been so *alive*. Now he felt exposed and alone, a stranger in the only home he had ever known.

It was past midnight by the time he arrived back at his home—though it still felt wrong to call it that, even after all these months. He let himself in the servants' entrance, not wanting to disturb his staff, who should all be abed by this point.

Except for dear old Jacobs, who he found fast asleep in a chair in the foyer, where he must have been waiting for him. Samuel woke him gently, thanking him for his diligence, and sent him up to bed, insisting he did not need a valet that night.

It took surprisingly little convincing, and Samuel let out a sigh of relief, climbing the wide staircase to his bedchamber. He wanted to shed his skin, to tear away all these pieces of him that didn't feel like they belonged, and then crawl into his bed and sleep for a year.

But when he opened the door to his rooms he found them occupied. It was dark, and the figure had his back to the window, the moonlight spilling over his shoulders and hiding his face in the shadows. Yet Samuel would recognize that exhausted slouch anywhere, the hand holding the burning cigarette, the shape of the silhouette.

"Isaac," he whispered, the name almost like a prayer on his lips.

Isaac moved, flicking the cigarette out the window. The meager light caught his face, drawing Samuel's attention to the scraggly almost-beard, the even worse circles under his eyes, the sheer exhaustion that was writ into his skin. Hells, the man was falling apart before his very eyes.

And Samuel should have seen it coming.

Stepping into the room, he closed the door behind him. "I'm surprised to find you here."

Isaac smiled—but it was a false thing. "What? Never had a fugitive in your bed before?"

"No, don't," Samuel said. He crossed to him, his steps loud on the floor, but he had to touch him, catch him, prove that Isaac wasn't some figment of his imagination. A ghost here to haunt him. "Please don't hide. Not now."

Samuel's hand found its way to Isaac's cheek, and he leaned into the touch like he was starved. "I didn't know what you would do," Isaac said, "when you found me here."

"Honestly? I don't know what I am going to do either," Samuel whispered, and Isaac just leaned his forehead against his. "I know what I should do, what's expected of me. But now that you're here . . ."

Isaac twisted, fisting his hands in Samuel's jacket, yanking him forward so he could crash his mouth against his. Samuel let him take command of the kiss, let Isaac shove him hard against the wall, his back cracking against the wood as Isaac ran his tongue along the seam of his lips, coaxing him open.

Samuel gasped as Isaac dropped a hand to his waist, nails digging into his skin as he pulled him flush against him, taking and plundering, and *hells*, biting. Isaac's teeth sank hard on his lower lip, and Samuel groaned as the blood welled and spilled, Isaac sucking lightly on the wound.

Clasping his hands around Isaac's shoulders, Samuel could feel the flex of the muscles under his hands, could hear the flutter of Isaac's heart in his chest, could taste the desperation on his lips. Something like magic was thrumming between them—blood spilt and mingled in a way that pulled the tension beyond them as taut as a wire, and Samuel felt like he was about to burn right out of his skin.

"Isaac," Samuel said, his voice weak and shaky. "Isaac, we ... I ..."

Isaac pressed a gentle kiss to his bloody lip, more soothing than inflaming, and stepped back. "You're right. We should talk."

Wiping his mouth with the back of his hand, Samuel cleared away the blood and the spit. He hated himself for stopping ... whatever this was, but he knew if he hadn't done it then, he never would have. "Why are you here?"

"Why?" Isaac blinked. "Why else? For you."

"For me?"

The air in the room suddenly cooled as Isaac took a step back, his brow furrowed as he tried to understand. "Yes. I thought—given your reaction—that you would want to join me?"

Samuel closed his eyes, unable to look at him. "Isaac—"

"I thought you'd understand!" Isaac said, the words pouring from him madly, raw and unchecked. "You've seen it. The King—everything he is, he's shown you!"

"I do understand," Samuel said. "But."

"But what?" Isaac shouted. "But fucking what?"

"The riots. The consequences." Isaac stilled, turning so cold that he might as well have been made of ice. "The martial law the

King has enacted. Yes, you've exposed the horrors of Aeravin—but now what?"

"Now," Isaac said, "we take him down."

"How?" Samuel begged, and Isaac just eyed him with disgust, his lips curving into a sneer.

"Join me and I will show you." He held out a hand, but Samuel didn't take it. "Revolution does not come easy. I thought that you of all people would have the courage to see that."

Samuel stared at the hand still offered to him. "But what about the price? Shan has her—"

Isaac laughed, unhinged and breathless. "Fuck Shan. Fuck Shan and her schemes and her plans. Aeravin doesn't need a Sparrow—it needs to be burned to the ground. Cleansed. And I will prove that to you."

Before Samuel could even do anything, before he could breathe or think or speak, Isaac was surging forward, dragging his mouth against Samuel's wounded lips, halting his words with teeth and tongue.

Blood filled his mouth, and despite himself, Samuel groaned with pleasure.

And then he couldn't move. He tried to push himself off the wall, to scream, to beg, to do anything at all, but it was like his body refused to respond, the very blood in his veins holding him still.

Hells, was this what his powers were like? Was this what he was planning to do to Isaac, only turned on him first by the power of blood and stupidity?

He had been a fool to ever hope at all.

Isaac stepped back, blood trickling down his chin. "I'm so sorry, but you will understand."

His vision started to fade around the edges, the room spinning as the very beat of his heart dimmed and slowed. Samuel fought it for as long as he could, but Isaac was relentless.

At last, Isaac turned away and Samuel knew no more.

Chapter Forty-Two

Shan

Anton was waiting for her in the parlor, lounging on a couch with Bart curled up against him. Shan took in their expectant looks—Anton's curiosity, Bart's worry—and she pushed right past them, heading straight for the liquor cabinet. "Well, we might as well get it over with, then."

"Oh, so you're finally going to explain what's going on?" Anton drawled. "How kind of you." His smile was sharp enough to cut. "It seems that I was right about de la Cruz."

Shan didn't respond. She just slammed her hands down on the table, the echoing crash cutting through the room as an awkward silence descended.

Bart got to his feet. "I can't deal with this. You two—you talk, and when you figure things out, let me know."

"Bart ..." Anton reached for him, but the young man just pulled away.

"No," he said firmly. "This is on both of you, and I refuse to be caught in the middle." To soften the blow, he pressed a kiss to Anton's forehead. "I'll be nearby, going through some correspondence."

Anton watched him leave with a frown, and Shan hid her smile behind her hand. As the Sparrow, she shouldn't tolerate him giving commands, but she had to admire the way he stood up for himself.

Because he was right—this wasn't his problem. Everything between her and her brother was of their own making.

Sighing, Anton joined Shan at the liquor cabinet. "Honestly, I never thought that de la Cruz had it in him, standing up to the Eternal Bastard like that, but he has made quite a mess of things."

Pouring a glass of whisky—Anton's whisky—she turned around and sipped slowly, the burning liquid heavy on her tongue. "I thought you'd be happy. These new laws will give your ... society much to print about."

He scoffed. "Perhaps. But the threat of imprisonment will not help circulation."

She hardly dared to breathe for hope. "Does this mean you'll stop?"

"Of course not. There is always the hope that making it a crime makes it more enticing." He downed his whisky, then turned to pour himself another. "Also, you all have just proved how necessary our work is."

She didn't bother correcting him—how it wasn't them, not all of them. This wasn't the will of the nobles, but the will of one man exercised over all. Because, in the end, it didn't really matter. In the end, he was the one who was most at risk.

Instead, she whispered, "I think you should take a trip, Anton. You and Bart."

He blinked at her. "What are you going on about now?"

"When we were young, you used to beg Mother to tell you stories of her home." She sank on the settee, the glass suddenly heavy in her hand. "You would sit at her feet as she'd tell you tale after tale. You remember that, don't you?"

Anton squatted in front of her so that they were at eye level. "I do."

She drank again. "Do you ever wonder what happened to her?"

"All the damned time."

"I tried not to think of her," Shan said quietly. "Trained myself to forget her. To cut out every bit of her and let her die."

"I know." Anton hung his head, surely to hide the pain that was still raw and real, even after all these years. "I was there."

"But *you* didn't," Shan said. "You clung to her memory, even after she abandoned us."

"Shan," Anton said, quietly. Gently. Like she was a fragile thing about to break. "You know it's not that simple."

"I know that now." Shan drained her glass. "It was different then."

"You were a child," Anton said, "and father was there, whispering poison in your ear."

"She was still my mother," Shan spat. "And I let myself be fooled." Anton's hand found hers, squeezing tightly, and she had to blink away tears. "I just let him fill me with so much hate."

"Shan . . . it's not that I mind this conversation, but why now?"

She pulled away, creating a deliberate amount of distance between them. "Have you considered trying to find her? We have the funds. We can get you on a ship tomorrow. You can find her, bring her back to us."

Anton stood. "I would love that one day. But I am not a fool. This timing is suspicious."

Shan followed him, filling his glass and pushing it into his hand. "Can't I just want to make you happy?"

"You can," Anton admitted. "Sometimes I think you want it too much. Sometimes I think you want it so badly you don't care about what would actually make me happy."

Shan exhaled slowly. "Sometimes I wish you didn't know me so well."

"And sometimes I wish you knew me better." He raised his glass in a mocking toast. "But I am your twin, and if you think I don't see the way you're trying to manipulate me, then you'd be dead wrong."

She wanted to lie—no, not just wanted, ached to. It was her first instinct, the words gathering on the tip of her tongue as she prepared to cover up her weaknesses. But it wouldn't do her any good. Not with Anton.

"Fine," she ground out. "I wanted to protect you, but it seems you won't have it."

Anton rolled his eyes. "Do you really expect so little of me? I cannot abandon Aeravin now. Not when it needs me."

Turning away, Shan wrapped her arms around herself, digging her nails into her own skin as she forced the truth from her lips. "It's not that."

"If it's about the new laws, do not fret. I will not let myself be caught."

"Of course," she said, tightening her grip. "But that is not it either. Remember how the King tasked us to find this murderer? Well, you can see how well that went. Samuel and I have wasted too much time, and the King has given us an ultimatum. There will be consequences for our failure."

"And that worries you?" Anton laughed. "He may be the King, but you've never let yourself be threatened before."

"He didn't threaten me!" Shan looked up at him, fighting the sudden tears in her eyes. Tears of anger, tears of frustration. Telling him hurt more than she expected. Telling him made it *real*. "He threatened you."

"He what?" Anton froze, all the cocky humor and brazen attitude slipping away, like water running down stone. "Why?"

"Why do you think?" She buried her face in her hands, fighting back the great sobs that shook her entire frame though she didn't utter a single sound. It was a silent sorrow that threatened to tear her apart, but through it all Anton remained by her side.

When at last it was over—minutes, hours, days later—she lifted her head, feeling spent and dry. "It's all about leverage," she explained. "Father taught me that. It's why every secret, every bit of information, was important. You never knew when it would be useful. And the King ... he reminded me that I am not immune from this myself."

Anton didn't look away. "And you're saying that I am your weakness?"

Shan hung her head. "You're one of them. You're my brother. Everything I do is for you. For us."

"And that's why you want me to leave. Not because of the laws, or my work. It's so he can't get to me." He pulled at his hair. "There you go again, making decisions for me."

"I am protecting you!"

Anton stepped away from her, and she felt his absence like a physical wound. "You're protecting yourself . . . and diminishing me. Just because I'm not a Blood Worker doesn't mean that I don't have a few tricks up my sleeve."

She glared. "I am the head of this family."

"Even so, it's not your choice to make. I am my own person, capable of making my own choices and taking my own risks. And it's time you accepted that." He shrugged, as if it was that simple, but his mouth was drawn into a hard line and his hands were clenched at his sides.

"Anton, I was just—"

"I am not a child anymore," he said, softly, and the calmness hurt more than any amount of rage or anger could. "And I know you're just trying to take care of me in the best way you know how. But I can't—" He choked on the words, and Shan knew that everything between them had finally broken—completely, totally, irrevocably. "I can't keep living like this. We're going to spend the next few days focusing on Isaac, and you're going to bring him in. But then I am moving out."

She just closed her eyes, letting the pain wash through her. "I see."

"I'm not going to interfere with your plans," he said, softly. "I know you think it's best. And I trust that you won't interfere with mine."

Shan didn't say anything—she didn't have to. For all the ambition and darkness she held in her heart, she knew that the one person in the world she would never be able to turn against was her brother.

And, thankfully, he felt the same.

When he left her, Shan just stared down at her hands, wondering when everything had started to fall apart.

The door to the parlor slammed open, and Shan woke with a start. The faintest bit of morning light was starting to stream through the windows, and she realized that somewhere in her pain and her loneliness she must have drifted off to sleep.

Rubbing sleep from her eyes, she turned to find Bart there, panic on his face. "There is something you need to hear. Immediately."

—•—

"You can't go alone," Anton said, catching her outside her bedroom. She had changed remarkably fast, but her brother was just as quick. "You don't even know where they took him."

"I can track him," Shan said, shoving past. Her ears hadn't stopped ringing since Bart had told her the message—Samuel had been taken, kidnapped. Her bird in the Aberforth house had discovered it that morning when she had gone to start the fire in the Lord's chambers. A sign of a struggle. Blood on the floor.

It could only have been Isaac. The King wouldn't have resorted to kidnapping, and who else would want him? Only the man who played both their hearts.

She was the biggest fool of all, letting Samuel leave in the first place, exposed and unguarded, but she'd deal with that later. She needed to save him, first.

Anton followed. "How?"

"I have some of his blood." She still had a vial left from what she had drained from him ages ago—the last she had saved from the tests she had run. It had to be enough.

Anton arched an eyebrow, but he didn't argue the point, instead switching tactics. "You don't know what you're walking into. It could be dangerous."

"Which is exactly why you need to stay here," Shan said. "Because I can't be looking out for you, too." She saw him wince but pressed on. "If I don't make it back, you'll need to go to the King. Tell him everything—your blood or his, as long as Samuel or I live—"

"We can find you," Anton said. "But why don't you go to him now?"

"Because I don't trust him with Samuel!" She stopped, the truth that she had been avoiding hitting her hard. "I don't trust him to save Samuel."

Anton stared at her for a long moment. "He means that much to you?"

Shan didn't bother lying. "He does."

"Then go." She turned to him in shock, but he just nodded—encouraging.

She didn't say goodbye—she didn't make any promises she couldn't keep. She just pressed a kiss to his cheek and turned on her heel, her feet light and silent as she ran to her laboratory to grab the vial of blood. She didn't even stop to reset the ward afterwards, she just continued on her way.

Dragging a claw against the back of her hand, she quickly lapped at the fresh blood. As it passed her lips, everything around her stilled and sharpened, her magic reaching out to find bridges to build and bind. But she didn't want that now, so she focused her power inwards, making herself quicker and stronger. Not superhuman, but peak human. She might be slight, but she was determined, and she had years of Blood Working and training on her side.

Throwing open the trapdoor to the rooftop, she pulled herself up onto the cold tiles. The sky was an endless void above her, just starting to turn light. For a moment the panic she felt vanished, her focus crystallized into this one, vibrant thing. This freeing moment, here on the rooftops, thrumming with the power of the magic in her veins.

Grabbing the vial, she thumbed off the top and pressed it to her lips. She let Samuel's blood flow into her, filling her with power and life. And best of all, just the faintest sense of where he was. The thinnest of threads, but still.

It was enough.

The vial slipped from her fingers, and she let it fall to the roof, where it clattered and rolled off the edge. She heard it break on the cobblestones below, shattering into hundreds of pieces.

"I'm coming," she swore.

She turned west, away from the sea, and burst into motion.

Chapter Forty-Three

Samuel

Samuel woke slowly to the sound of a bitter argument, the voices rising and falling as they went back and forth. He attempted to lift his hand to his eyes, to rub the sleep from them, only to feel it snap against a slab of cold metal, pinned by leather restraints.

Isaac.

He tried to sit up, to scream for help, but he was bound and gagged, strapped to a metal table like an offering to a dark god. Panic seized him, and he thrashed against the bindings, tugging at the leather. But they were too tight, and he collapsed back against the table, gasping into the gag.

"You're awake," Isaac said, moving into his line of sight. Beyond him, Samuel could make out that he was in some kind of laboratory, implements of Blood Working scattered around them. But unlike Shan's laboratory, or the Eternal King's, this room was dark. Cramped. Dank.

"I'm sorry," Isaac continued. "We couldn't let you . . ." he gestured vaguely towards the gag, and Samuel narrowed his eyes at him. Of course. They couldn't risk him using his power, marching them straight to the King and forcing them to confess—exactly like they had planned to.

Though—we?

He pushed himself up as much as he could and was just able to spot a familiar figure hanging back against the wall. Cold, ice eyes. A shorn head. The dark robes of the Guard.

"Ah." Isaac glanced over his shoulder. "Yes. I didn't do this all by myself. You know Alessi, don't you?"

She stepped forward, her face expressionless as she studied him like he was some kind of specimen. Samuel lurched away. It made too much sense—they had seen a Guard helping him flee the central square, and Alessi had been the one finding all the bodies, leading the investigation. She was perfectly positioned to deflect attention away from the real culprits.

It was brilliant.

"Listen," Isaac said, drawing Samuel's attention back to himself. "It doesn't have to be this way. You can still join us."

"You're wasting your time," Alessi said. "You're not going to convince him."

Samuel wanted to strangle her.

"We're not killing him," Isaac said, running a thumb along the back of Samuel's hand, as if to comfort him.

Samuel flinched away as best he could, and Isaac stepped back.

"Stop being weak, de la Cruz," Alessi hissed. She lifted a wicked looking dagger, long with jagged edges, and placed it over Samuel's throat. "I can do it if you're too squeamish. I'll even make it quick."

"No!" Isaac grabbed her wrist, pulling her away from Samuel and shielding him with his body. "You will not do that."

"He's not going to join us!" Alessi wrenched away, jamming her blade back into its sheath. "And you cannot let him go—you've jeopardized everything for this Aberforth." She spat his name like it was a curse.

"Let me take care of it," Isaac said, his voice soft and heavy with a dark promise that Samuel didn't want to see fulfilled. Even if his other option was facing Alessi. "When he sees what we can offer he'll reconsider."

Alessi studied him for a long moment. "You really think it will work?"

"I know it will," Isaac said. "Let me prove it."

"You'd better be right." She stalked away, leaning against the wall to watch. "Do it."

Isaac turned around, closing the distance between them. Samuel raised his head, trying to say his name, to reach him somehow, but it was only a slurred mess of sounds that carried no power or significance. Frowning, Isaac dragged the claw-tip on his thumb against Samuel's throat, the skin splitting and hot blood leaking out.

Dipping his head, Isaac sank his teeth against the soft skin of Samuel's throat, and he sucked hard enough to bruise. Samuel tilted his head back, his eyes fluttering closed, as both fear and pleasure coursed through him.

He would always be weak for Isaac, and it would be his greatest downfall.

Isaac pressed his lips to Samuel's cheek—a promise, and then whispered, "I swore to help you, and I will. But this will hurt."

A little blood glinted at the corner of his mouth, and his tongue peeked out, lapping it up. Then it began.

Fire.

It was fire.

Samuel's whole body arched against the table as the heat raged through him. Somehow, Isaac was burning him alive, and he couldn't even scream—couldn't even breathe. Sweat broke out across his skin as his blood literally boiled in his veins, burning and healing and burning and healing.

Isaac took his hand, his fingers unnaturally cool against him, and he broke the skin at Samuel's wrist. Lowering his head, he sucked the hot blood into his mouth, taking and taking and taking. Samuel watched, helpless, tears leaking from his eyes. He could feel his energy, his very life, slipping away with each pull of Isaac's mouth, only to feed back into him in the form of fire.

He could see the effects of it in his hands, the way his very veins were darkening as the blood continued to burn, standing out in stark contrast to his pale skin. He could feel it working in him, as something deep within, as delicate and ephemeral as lace, was destroyed—burned away until nothing but ashes was left. The tattered remains of the power he had carried within him for so long.

Somehow, some way, he felt the brush of Shan's mind against his—a faint and tenuous bridge. Her fear and panic seeped into him, but all he could hear was the roar of blood in his ears.

He wanted it to stop. He wanted to pass out. He wanted to die.

But Isaac's grip kept him painfully, awfully conscious, until at last Isaac stepped away, snapping the bridge of power between them like it was nothing at all.

And Samuel collapsed back on the table as the last rush of Blood Healing flowed through him, leaving him whole but spent, broken by the sudden lack of pain, but consumed by the sudden aching emptiness of loss.

No one moved—neither Isaac nor Alessi did a thing. They just stood in silence. Watching. Waiting.

"Ungag him," Alessi commanded.

Isaac swallowed hard, then did as he was told.

The mask fell from his face, and Samuel gulped down deep breaths of air. Isaac vanished, reappearing seconds later with a glass of water—it was warm, but it was clear and clean, and it felt blissful against his parched mouth.

"It's okay, Samuel," Isaac whispered as he carefully tipped more water past his lips. "Do it."

He knew what Isaac was asking for, and he reached for that power deep within him, digging through the ashes and dust. "Let me go," he commanded.

But, as he feared, it was gone. All that remained was an empty cavern in his chest where he should have found the power he had spent his entire life trying to master and control. That lived within him, creeping out and tainting his words, desperate to be used. The thing that had shaped his entire life. It simply wasn't there.

He was empty.

"No," he snarled. Not now. Not like this. Not when he actually needed it. Everything he was—everything he had, everything he fought for—was gone. "I said, *let me go*."

Alessi crowed. "You actually did it! It's gone!" She clapped a hand to Isaac's shoulder. "If you can destroy the Aberforth Gift now, can you imagine what you could do with a few more blood bags? What other secrets of Blood Working we can unlock?"

Isaac turned away, wiping at the blood on his lips, but Samuel spat, "What is she talking about?"

It didn't have the power of a command. He wasn't forced to speak. But Isaac closed his eyes and let the truth fall anyway. "The murders weren't just about the trafficking. I mean, they were, but we couldn't let such an opportunity go to waste. There are things you still don't know about the Eternal King, Samuel. He's too powerful to be taken down by conventional methods. We needed more power to match his centuries of knowledge, all the power he has consumed year after year. So, yes, we killed to stop the trafficking, to make a point to the King. But we also used those deaths to ensure that we can actually take him down."

Samuel couldn't bear looking at Isaac—not after that. "So you are a monster after all."

"But I kept my promise!" Isaac whirled back on Samuel, grasping his hand. "I took this curse from you—the King would never have let you do it. He would have turned you into a weapon, forced you to do unspeakable things. But now it is gone! The Aberforth Gift is ended!"

Still staring straight up, Samuel whispered, "So instead you do unspeakable things yourself, feeding on the blood of others like they are nothing more than a tool, and then wonder why I am not pleased to hear it?"

"They were murderers," Isaac snapped, a raw desperation in his eyes that Samuel could hardly bear to see. "Murderers and slavers! Do you know how many Unblooded they sent to their deaths for just a bit of money? If it gave me the power to help you, isn't that worth the price?"

"That doesn't matter." Samuel pulled at his restraints, a snarl on his lips. "That does not justify it! This kind of Blood Working is still an atrocity!"

Alessi laughed, the sound harsh and cutting to his ears. "I told you he wouldn't change his mind." Her dagger was in her hand, and that cruel smile was back on her face. "I guess we'll have to kill him after all."

Isaac whirled on her, but before he could say anything, the walls shook. A boom echoed through the room as the wards started to flicker violently against the door, sparks flying off it in a blinding, brilliant spray.

Chapter Forty-Four

Shan

Shan was furious. She didn't know what was happening to Samuel, but she felt the pain and terror that echoed down the bridge, its strength and potency terrifying. The thread that tied them together had grown stronger and brighter with each step she took, to the point where it nearly overwhelmed her. Though she had run across the rooftops of Dameral as fast as her magically enhanced body could, she feared she was too late.

She stumbled down the stairs, rushing to the basement door in the shadows between the buildings, the bowels of an old boarding house, forgotten and empty of life. Another casualty of Aeravin, left to rot in silence.

Still, the echoes of whatever had been done to Samuel slid across her nerves, leaving her shaky and unbalanced, and she almost ran into the ward that blocked her from him, a shimmering, barely visible mist in front of a ramshackle door. She recognized the ward immediately, tasting the magic in the air—the smoky, spicy scent that was quintessentially Isaac. And Samuel was just past it—she could feel it in her bones.

They both were, but first she needed to get through this ward.

She didn't have time to do it safely or carefully, not with Samuel still hurting. Biting her lip hard enough to draw blood, Shan plunged both of her hands into the ward, a scream tearing from her throat as it seared her. She was strong enough that it wasn't able to outright reject her, though it tried, so she reached forward to wrap her hands around the carefully constructed threads of power and *pulled*. They fought her, but she poured every ounce of strength that she had into it, tangling her fingers in the weave, and shredded it like lace.

Cracks started to shatter around her, the wards flashing brighter and brighter as she dragged her hands from edge to edge, rending its bind and sending the ward shattering to the ground like a pane of glass.

The resulting explosion of magic ricocheted back and forth, turning the simple wooden door to ash and shaking the very ground. Shan slumped to one knee from the force of it, her hands left as raw, flayed pieces of bloody meat.

Just beyond she saw Isaac and Alessi staring at her like she was some kind of god, their jaws hanging open as they stood in front of a ruined, broken Samuel, who was strapped to a table. She spared him a quick look, taking in the darkened veins that stood out, blackened and burned, against his pale skin.

Swaying, she pushed herself to her feet, pressing a ruined hand to her lips. The pain was beyond comprehension, but she needed the blood. She needed the strength. She licked the blood from her wounds as she forced the skin to start healing over, Isaac flinching from the very sight of it.

"How did you find us?" Alessi hissed, twin daggers in her hands. They were brutal and jagged—designed to tear and hurt.

Shan pulled back her lips in a snarl. "So, you're part of this, then?"

"Surprise," Alessi said, moving forward with a deadly speed. She closed the distance between them in a heartbeat and Shan barely managed to duck. Her hands were still healing over, her claws ruined and shattered shells.

Alessi pressed forward, giving her no quarter as she swung her daggers, Shan desperately dodging and ducking in the tight space.

Shan fell to one knee, then swept out with a spinning kick as she tried to knock Alessi off her feet, desperate to buy time for her hands to heal enough to hold a weapon.

Jumping back, Alessi hopped over her kick, and Shan surged to her feet, abandoning all pretense of finesse. She drove her shoulder into Alessi's side, sending her sprawling onto the floor and sliding hard into the metal table where Samuel was still bound. Alessi groaned but quickly scrambled to her feet, holding her knives out in a defensive position.

"Why?" Shan said. "Alessi—I don't understand. I thought we were—"

Alessi threw one of her daggers—it flew awkwardly, but it still sliced along Shan's arm. She didn't even flinch, though she felt the sticky drip of blood welling and spilling down her arm.

"As if you could even understand," Alessi spat. "With your grand schemes and slow plans, with your finery and your lords and your damned King."

"So that's it, then," Shan said, finally able to wrap her fingers around the hilt of a dagger. "You weren't satisfied."

Alessi laughed, lunging forward. Shan whipped her dagger up, parrying the blow with the distinctive ring of steel on steel. "Satisfied? People were suffering while you partied!"

Shan gasped for breath, the effect of using so much Blood Working so fast left her empty and woozy. Her grip on her dagger was weak, the handle slipping in her own blood, and Alessi was fresh and strong, approaching her with a near maniacal gleam in her eyes. This time, when their blades met, Alessi bore down with all her strength, sending Shan skidding backwards as her boots slid on the floor.

"You think you're powerful with your ancient bloodline and your money," Alessi growled, as Shan started to buckle. "And what do you do with it? Drink and gamble and flirt while so many suffer."

Shan twisted, spinning under Alessi's arm to drag her blade across her ribs. Blood blossomed, and Shan felt a rush of relief. Bouncing back towards the wall, she ran her tongue across her dagger, lapping up her enemy's blood. The bridge snapped to life between them, and Shan threw all of her will against her.

Alessi stilled, her chest heaving as she struggled to raise her arm.

"And what did you do?" Shan said. "But cause death and destruction?"

Alessi howled, frustrated, as she tried to move, but it was time to end this. Shan ran forward, pressing her dagger to Alessi's throat, slicing through the flesh down to the bone, when—

"Enough!" Isaac shouted, loud enough to draw Shan's attention away from Alessi.

But it was too late. The deed was done, Shan's dagger hanging from her throat like a twisted pendant. Isaac just watched as Alessi's body crumpled to the ground, his expression darkening to something frightening.

It was only then that Shan noticed the shattered glass on the floor, lying in pools of wet, dark blood. Isaac had circled around them as she had fought Alessi, setting this trap, placing his back to a second door, and she realized what he was going to do. Blood dripped from his hands, and she lurched forward.

"Let it go, Shan," he said, as a rush of fire swept across the floor, "or let Samuel burn."

Shan staggered back, the burning heat of witch fire roaring to life around her—a perversion of the mechanics behind witch light, an explosion born when a Blood Worker unlocked all the power within blood in one fell swoop. Hells, just how strong was he? It burned brighter and longer and hotter than anything Shan had ever known, fueled by Isaac's magic and rage.

But it was a distraction and she knew it. Isaac had left her with a choice—go after him and leave Samuel to burn alive or save Samuel and risk him escaping. She knew what the correct choice was—her duty demanded that she let Samuel burn if it meant protecting the future and stability of Aeravin. The right choice was clear—and she chose the other path without hesitation.

Dropping her daggers, she dashed towards Samuel, her stiff and ruined fingers prying at the buckles that held him down.

"He's getting away," Samuel wheezed, his voice a pale and broken husk of what it should be.

"I'm not letting you go," she said, tugging at the restraint on his hand. The fire was burning hotter, climbing up the walls, spreading so, so fast. "I've got you."

"Your hands," he gasped, and Shan flinched from the shock in his voice.

"They'll heal." She freed his hand, and he made quick work of the rest of his restraints. The flames continued to roar, the heat pressing in on them, as the entire back of the laboratory turned into a wall of flame.

"Come on," Samuel said, standing on unsteady feet. He was trying to pull her towards the door she had come through, where the fire had yet to spread.

But she couldn't tear her eyes from the fire, from the shimmering opening that Isaac had disappeared through.

Samuel followed her gaze and cursed. "Leave him."

But she was already moving forward. She had let her heart lead her, and though she had saved Samuel, Isaac had still got away.

And if Isaac got away, Anton would die.

She could still catch him.

Chapter Forty-Five

Samuel

"Shan!" Samuel called, but she didn't listen. She just moved closer to the fire that burned so bright, so potent and wild that it felt nearly alive. "Don't!"

She gave him one quick look, her form shimmering in the heat of the fire. "Get out of here, Samuel," she said, then dove into the flames. She didn't even scream, but he could feel the flames recoiling from her, bending away as she strode through the fire, as if they couldn't bear to touch her skin.

Wait.

He could *feel* the flames—not just their heat, but their power, their essence. Something new and terrible sang in his veins, and the realization hit him hard. His power was gone, that choking, cloying ability that had stifled his Blood Working since he was a child was no longer there. Isaac had seen to that.

But there was something just as terrifying in its place.

Grabbing a jagged blade from the ground—Alessi's, discarded when she had flung it at Shan—Samuel sliced his hand open and sent blood flying everywhere. "Here goes nothing."

He pressed the wound against his lips, and his world flooded with power.

Everything was suddenly clear and sharp, the world coming to a near standstill around him, slowing to match the steady beat of his heart, thrumming in his veins. Suddenly, he knew what to do, the magic guiding him in a way that was all instinct.

Slamming his fist into the ground, he called the witch fire to his hands, pooling it into a single, blinding ball of fire that threatened to sear him alive, but he held it fast—the world shaking as the fire died around him. It swarmed in his hands, sinking into his skin, absorbed by his blood, and he felt unstoppable.

He crossed the ruined, burnt remains of the room, moving faster than he ever had. The distance disappeared beneath his feet, and he burst through the door and up the stairs, emerging into the streets of Dameral, into the bright light of the morning. He followed after Shan—still able to feel her, to follow the trail of her agony, but quickly surged past her, leaving her behind.

Because just beyond, he could feel Isaac. The power within him pulsed, recognizing the source that had set it aflame, and it drew Samuel to him like a magnet. Like recognized like, and nothing could stop him.

He caught up with Isaac easily, seizing him around the throat, lifting him up off the ground. Isaac gasped, his eyes bulging as he tore at Samuel's hand.

Some part of Samuel recoiled at this, but another part of him— that dark part of him that he thought was lost—relished this. Relished seeing Isaac so helpless, so desperate, and knowing that with a simple squeeze he could end every problem that faced them.

Distantly, he heard Shan calling to him, begging him to let Isaac go, warning him about something.

He couldn't concentrate on her words—he was consumed by the power that he held within him, in his blood, burning and alive. The fire broke through his skin, swirling around his arms, seeking to be used. He was a living, breathing god, and he felt like he was full of light, like he had tapped into the essence of life itself.

Shan shoved herself in front of him, her still healing hands on his face. He tossed Isaac aside, not caring that he threw the man against the hard brick wall of a building, his head snapping against the stone.

Isaac fell to the ground and did not move again.

Samuel turned to Shan, catching her fingers in his mouth, sucking the blood off them. The magic happened immediately, binding them together with a bridge that left them tied in a way that felt far too intimate. Far too right.

You have to let it go, he heard, her voice a gentle whisper in his mind. They were so tightly wound together they might have been sharing the same body—her thoughts were his thoughts; her pain was his pain. *It will destroy you, eat you from the inside out.*

He shook his head—he controlled the power, not the other way around. He released a rush of it, letting it wash over her. Her screams were loud as her flesh regrew all at once, knitting back together in a wave that left her reeling. Her touch on his cheek was once again soft, her burns gone, the shine of her hair restored.

Running his fingers through it, he murmured soft words of praise. She was beautiful, so damned beautiful, and she was his now. He had the power to protect her, to break the world and leave it at her feet, and he'd do it without even being asked.

Come back to me. She threw her thoughts at him, her feelings, everything that she was. It overwhelmed him, sent him staggering, but she clung to him. *Don't become him.*

Become who?

She pressed herself against him, tucking her face into the crook of his neck so that their hearts beat against each other. "The King," she whispered, the physical sound of her voice drawing him in, so soft against him. "Don't become addicted to the power. You're better than that, Samuel."

Shuddering against her, he buried his face in her hair. She was right, wasn't she? This power felt so right in his hands, but it wasn't him.

This was not him.

He didn't know if he could let it go, but she wouldn't have asked him if it wasn't important.

"What do I do, Shan?"

Her relief hit like a wave, rushing over his too hot skin like the cool balm of water on a summer's day. "Ground it, Samuel. Give it back to the earth."

"The fire—"

"Make it burn through," she whispered. "Make it burn through the blood and the power and then it will die."

Nodding, he sank to his knees, pressing his hands against the cobblestones. He focused on the power that flowed through him, trying to parse out what was his and what was the fire—fueled by the blood of others and Isaac's delusions. Shan stood behind him, running her fingers through his hair and murmuring words of comfort.

He let it out.

The fire rushed from his hands in a shining sheet of power, sweeping across the ground. It burned so bright and beautiful, swirling and shimmering and dancing. But as certain as the dawn it passed, and he slumped backwards into Shan's arms, empty and boneless.

"I've got you," she whispered. "I've got you."

The last thing he saw was her face, tears in her eyes and the early morning sun a halo against her hair. Her fingers brushed his skin, her lips forming words he didn't quite catch, and then he knew no more.

Chapter Forty-Six

Samuel

Samuel didn't know what time it was. Hells, he didn't know what *day* it was. All he knew was that the sun was shining brightly in his eyes and his entire body hurt. It was an ache deep in his bones, unlike anything he had ever known, and he groaned.

"Get Shan," someone said sharply—Anton?—and then he felt the bed sink under the sudden weight. Anton leaned over him, blocking the brightness of the sun and coming into focus. "Hey, Samuel."

"When is it?" he asked, the question mostly nonsensical, but Anton nodded all the same.

"You've been out for a week," Anton said. "And it's mid-afternoon. You've just missed lunch."

Samuel licked his lips, realizing that his mouth was terribly dry. A week? Pushing himself up on his elbows, he nearly collapsed under his own weakness, but Anton caught him, rearranging the pillows with one hand so that he could settle into a sitting position.

"What happened?" he rasped out, and Anton looked away.

"We should probably let Shan answer that," he said, moving away to fetch some water. "You gave us all quite a scare. But she'll be here shortly; we've been taking shifts looking after you."

He pressed the glass to Samuel's lips, and he gratefully sipped at the cool liquid. Anton held the glass firmly, only giving him tiny sips, and Samuel chased every drop. "Easy now," Anton chided. "You've been on a diet of just broth. Don't rush yourself."

"I didn't realize you were a nurse," Samuel muttered, and Anton laughed.

"I have many hidden depths, you know," he said, placing the glass to the side. "But, no, we just hired one. And his instructions were very strict. Oh, there she is."

Samuel glanced up to see Shan standing in the doorway, relief on her face as she took him in. He felt so terribly exposed, lying in bed with nothing more than a nightshirt while she stood there in one of her lovely day dresses, her hair neatly pulled back in a braid, fresh-faced and gorgeous.

He ran his hand across his jaw, wincing at the feel of a scruffy beard against his fingers. Hells, he must look a mess.

But Shan didn't say anything, only crossed the room, shoving her brother aside so that she could take his place on the bed. "You're awake."

"I am," he said, dumbly, as she ran her hand over his face, turning him this way and that, as if afraid that he was some kind of illusion. "I hear it's been a few days."

"You had us worried," she admitted, sitting back and placing her hands demurely in her lap. The door softly closed behind her, and he looked up to see that Anton had left them alone. Behind a closed door with no chaperone. Well, he supposed that he had been an invalid in her guest room for nearly a week, and propriety was long gone between them anyway.

"What happened, Shan?"

"What do you remember?" she countered, looking up at him with a question in her eyes.

He leaned his head back against the pillows. It was all a blur. Isaac. The betrayal. Pain like nothing he had never known.

Fire.

Power.

Shan.

An overwhelming sense of emotion that felt too raw to be real.

"It's . . . not all clear," he admitted, flexing his hands to study the new scars that ran across his skin. A gift from Isaac, burned into his very flesh. "But I'm different now, I know that."

"You're a Blood Worker," Shan said, quietly. "You're just what you were always supposed to be, if the power in your blood hadn't been stifling it."

He shuddered, the memory rising in him. His power had always been addicting, but what he had done, what he had accessed, was beyond everything he ever dreamed of. It had been a madness. "What did I—" he choked on the words. "Did I kill him?"

"Isaac lives," Shan said gently, squeezing his hand. "The King has him imprisoned, for now."

He let out a breath he hadn't realized he was holding. "I was so scared." Shan was looking at him with something like awe, and he wanted to hide from it. "Please don't look at me like that."

"You drew the power into yourself, Samuel," she said. "The blood that Isaac had spilled, the blood he used to light the flames. You called it into yourself, harnessed it to your will. Twisted his magic away from him. Blood and steel, you're so strong."

"Shan," he whispered, but she just moved closer.

"Most people don't realize how easy Blood Working really is. It's as natural as breathing, and once you taste the power it turns into something instinctual. But it nearly destroyed you." She brushed her hand against his cheek, barely a touch. "I've never seen anyone take to Blood Working like you did, but, even so, you weren't ready. You weren't trained. It nearly ate you alive."

"You saved me," he whispered, remembering. It had been her connection, that bridge between them, that had pulled him back to his humanity.

"Maybe we should just accept that we saved each other?" Shan smiled at him, and he swore he could *feel* a lingering echo of her relief.

But that was madness. The bridge had clearly shattered when he released the fire.

"Yes, we did." He leaned into her touch. "I'm sorry."

"About what?"

"About everything."

"No," she said. "We were both fooled by Isaac. By Alessi. They wanted to take down the King, and I cannot fault them for that even if I cannot abide their methods." She stared at the wall, her eyes unfocused and sad. "Damn it all, Isaac. I should have reached out to him sooner. Perhaps if I had—"

"It's not your fault," Samuel said, though he wasn't sure he believed it. Secrets and lies and schemes had brought them to this point, and they played a dangerous game.

"We could have been allies," she said. "We *should* have been allies. But now we're enemies."

"He still lives, Shan," he said, though he remembered the way Isaac had explained his power. His methods.

"Yes," Shan whispered, "but he is in the grasp of the King. And even if he wasn't, I don't know if we could trust him."

He inclined his head. "We still have each other, at least."

She looked at him in surprise. "You mean that, don't you?"

"Well. I am trapped in your bed, aren't I?" Her lips quirked into an amused smile, and he groaned. "Not like that, Shan."

"Of course not," she said, slyly. "I'd never take advantage of an ill man."

"Thank goodness you have some morals after all," he grumbled, and she threw back her head and laughed. "What now?"

"The King hasn't been back here since the day of . . . well, everything. But don't worry, he is pleased with us." Shan ran her thumb across the scars on the back of his hand. "He tried to heal you, but there wasn't anything he could do. You just needed time. I suppose I should send him a message. He'll probably want to see us."

"Can I get a bath and a shave first?"

Shan studied him. "I don't know, the beard makes you look more mature."

"It itches," he replied.

"Do as you like," she said with a grin. "Besides, you kind of smell."

"You wound me, dear lady," Samuel said, placing his hand over his heart, and she rolled her eyes at him.

"Focus on getting your strength back and let me worry about the future." She stood, smoothing her skirts. "I'll call for a bath to be drawn, and I'll see if the cook can make you some soup." She held up a finger as he started to protest. "Easy food first, Samuel."

Frowning, he crossed his arms over his chest. "Fine."

Leaning forward, she pressed her lips to his forehead, gentle and kind. He pushed himself up on his elbows, trying to chase her, but she grabbed him by the shoulders, holding him fast.

"Samuel, wait," she said, as he tried to ignore the way she affected him so. "You're still recovering, darling." Brushing the hair from his face, she added, "We have all the time in the world."

"You're right," he admitted, though he did not want to. They had already wasted so much time, but now that his power was gone, he could at least have this.

Isaac was lost to them, perhaps forever, but he could still have her.

"Hey, Shan," he called, catching her with her hand on the door-knob. "Thanks."

She glanced back, her brow furrowed. "You don't have to thank me, Samuel. I take care of my own."

With that, she was gone, leaving him with a feeling of warmth that had nothing to do with the sun on his face.

Chapter Forty-Seven

Shan

It had been three weeks since that disastrous day, two weeks since Samuel had awoken, and the King had planned an exceptional celebration—a gala that would honor them for the work they had done.

Shan didn't think they had done much to be honored for—the killer had achieved his goals, and she had lost half of her heart for it—but the King would not be dissuaded. He had given them the date and told them when to arrive. He would handle the rest.

While the King had spent two weeks planning a ball that would put the rest of Dameral to shame, Shan had spent that time with Samuel, helping him regain his strength, teaching him the basics of Blood Working, scheming and plotting. They both knew that the King was going to do *something* at this ball, but none of her birds could find out what. Not that her birds were having much success of late, with the new laws that held Aeravin in a stranglehold.

So the time ticked away, and all they could do was prepare for the worst.

But the night of the ball finally arrived, and they showed up at the palace hours early, as promised. Servants ushered them apart, taking them to different dressing rooms, where the outfits the King had commissioned for them waited.

Laurens herself presented it to Shan, and Shan clasped her old friend's hands. When Laurens leaned in for a kiss on the cheek, she whispered, "Trouble is coming, Sparrow."

Shan leaned back, wishing she could do more, but she was trapped by the role the King had demanded of her. She could only squeeze Lauren's hand as she was helped into the dress, knowing that her country hung on the brink of destruction. But what could she do?

At least the dress was beautiful, unlike anything that she had ever seen—a rich silk gown the color of blood itself. It hugged her torso, bands of silk wrapping over her breasts and flowing into a loop around her neck, leaving wide swathes of skin exposed. The skirt flared out at her waist, layers of silk in various lengths that fell to the floor.

The servants styled her hair carefully, pinning it back so that it flowed like a waterfall down her back, twisting in dark curls that hung like shadows. Her eyes were lined with kohl—sharp and harsh—and her lips painted a deep red. She was beautiful and deadly, and she smiled at her reflection in the mirror. It was bolder than she would have chosen for herself, but she loved every bit of it.

"It's time," one of the serving girls muttered, and Shan followed her towards the sounds of the ball. She wasn't ushered down the stairs, right in the heart of the party like she had anticipated, but moved to a small interior balcony. "Please wait here," the serving girl instructed, then disappeared with a curtsy.

Not knowing what else to do, Shan stepped to the ledge, looking out over the ballroom beneath her. All the nobles of Aeravin had been gathered, called back from the country with an invitation that could not be ignored. But though the Eternal King had not thrown a ball on his own in centuries, all those years of inactivity hadn't dulled his skills as host. If anything, they just made him all the more intense about it. There was food and music and the tinkling of conversation—every detail precise and perfect.

Shan ached to be down there—to slip into the heart of the party, flitting from conversation to dance to conversation, drawing out useful bits of information as she captivated those around her.

But she had to wait, the time slipping past her as more guests arrived. She wrapped her hands around the banister, her ceremonial claws—dull and decorated with rubies to suggest blood without actually drawing it—tapped an incessant beat.

"Shan?"

She spun around at the sound of her name, turning to see Samuel step from the shadows into the light. Her breath caught as her eyes roved hungrily over him—she couldn't help it. If the King had been bold with her style, it was nothing compared to what he had chosen for Samuel.

He looked positively indecent, and Shan couldn't tear her gaze away.

His trousers were tight, form-fitting black breeches tucked away into leather boots. He wore no jacket, just shirtsleeves and a waistcoat, delicately embroidered red roses on a black background—the King's own royal design. Scandalously, he wore no cravat, the neck of his shirt open to bare his throat and part of his chest. His sleeves were also tucked up past his elbows, leaving his forearms bare to the touch.

His scars—still as deep and dark as the day he had received them—were proudly on display for all to see. They crossed over his hands, ran up his arms and disappeared into his sleeves. They crawled up his neck, drawing her eyes to every bob of his throat, and Shan was consumed with the ridiculous urge to put her mouth on them.

"You look lovely," he said, stepping closer. She forced her eyes to his, only to find her own hunger mirrored in his gaze.

"You look like a scandal," she muttered, and he laughed.

Turning his hands over, he rolled his wrists and studied the movements of his scars. "It will leave quite an impression, won't it?"

"It will cause a riot," she muttered, turning back to the banister. She couldn't bear to look at him—it was too much.

"I doubt that," Samuel said, coming to her side. "Your dress, though . . ."

She felt his gaze drop to the expanse of flesh between her breasts, laid bare for everyone to see. She could feel him against her, his blood burning hot in his veins, his power no longer dulled by his curse.

She swore that she could still feel him sometimes, an echo of the powerful connection that they had shared. Lust and longing and fear rolled off him in waves, and she wanted to press against him until all the hesitancy disappeared. But she didn't.

He was still getting used to living without the fear of his gift, as if he was afraid it was just a hoax. If he needed time, she could give him that.

Blood and steel, look at what rushing into things had earned her last time.

"There you are." The King appeared behind them, and Shan glanced over her shoulder, disappointed to see that his outfit was entirely normal. Well, it was expensive and expertly tailored—but there was nothing about it that would draw attention.

It seemed that he wanted them to be the stars of tonight's ball and made it so that all eyes would be on them.

The King beckoned them forward, directing them to stand in the center of the balcony, where he walked around them, taking in their appearances from every angle. "Good. One last thing." He snapped his fingers, and a serving girl rushed towards Samuel, carrying a box in her hands.

Samuel looked up at him, brow furrowed.

They must have pleased the King very much indeed.

The girl lifted the lid, revealing a set of claws. They weren't the decorative kind that Shan wore tonight—they were sharp and dangerous, and Samuel looked at them in fear.

"You're a Blood Worker now," the King said softly. "You've earned them." He lifted them from the box. "Hold out your hands, son."

Shan saw the flicker of something run across Samuel's expression, too quick to catalogue, but he did as he was told. The King slipped the claws over his fingertips, then secured the chain over the hand and around the wrist. Samuel held them up, flexing his hand in the light as the King arranged the other one, his green eyes narrowed in discomfort.

"Now we're ready," the King said, shooing the serving girl away. "Remain in the shadows until I say."

Shan looked at Samuel, raising her shoulder in a delicate shrug. He held out his arm, and she gratefully accepted it, falling into place behind the Eternal King as he led them off the balcony, round to a set of wide stairs that opened down into the ballroom. He held up his hand, and she held Samuel back, waiting to see what the King was doing.

The music came to a stop as the King approached the top of the stairs, and every head in the room turned to him. "My loyal subjects," he said, his voice carrying across the room. "I thank you for attending. It has been far too long since I opened my home, and I apologize for that neglect."

The people applauded, but he held up his hands, demanding silence that he was immediately granted. "But tonight is not all fun. A month ago, a rash of murders that plagued Dameral came to an end and riots erupted across the city. A state of emergency was declared and new laws were brought into being. But we have finally found peace again, stability again, and we are here to celebrate those who are responsible for returning that to us. Please welcome my last living family member, Samuel Aberforth, recently returned to us, and Lady Shan LeClaire."

He crooked his fingers behind his back, and Shan pulled Samuel forward. The crowd started whispering immediately, and this time, the King did nothing to stop them. Whether it was their presence or their appearances, Shan did not know—but she held her head high, a soft smile plastered on her face. She would not show them weakness.

"They both suffered greatly in their quest to bring in the murderer, and Lord Aberforth will forever bear the scars of it on his skin. But without them, we never would have unrooted a conspiracy in the heart of our world and Isaac de la Cruz would not have been brought to justice. For his crimes, he will be punished in a manner befitting treason, serving as an example for those who dare defy the crown. There is still work to be done, my subjects, laws to be refined and broken systems to be restored.

"But that is not the point of tonight. Tonight, we celebrate our heroes. For their work, they shall both be rewarded."

Samuel clenched his hand against her arm, his new claws threatening to break her skin, but Shan didn't flinch.

"For his part, Lord Aberforth will be appointed to my council, taking the position recently vacated by Lord Dunn."

The crowd cheered, and Samuel let out a low breath, his hand relaxing. It wasn't so bad—Shan's mind was already racing with how they could use this to their advantage.

"And for Lady Shan LeClaire, well, we have another vacancy to fill, don't we?"

Shan looked to the Eternal King, her heart pounding in her chest as she hoped that he wasn't about to say what she thought he was.

"I admit," the King said, placing a hand over his heart, "that I carry some of the blame for what happened. I appointed de la Cruz to a position far above his station, hoping that raw skill would outweigh his legacy. But blood will tell, won't it? Shan is the heir of the LeClaires, a bloodline that has been with us since the founding of Aeravin. She was born to our world, moving through it with a grace and elegance that cannot be taught."

Her knees buckled under her dress, but Samuel slipped his arm around her back, holding her upright when she wanted nothing more than to faint.

"She was the top of her class at the Academy, and she has proved her loyalty a hundred times over. So please let me present to you, Lady Shan LeClaire, Royal Blood Worker."

The crowd erupted, and Shan did the only thing she could.

She curtsied to all of Dameral, accepting the new chains that bound her.

Epilogue

Isaac

Isaac was used to the sound of his Guards' heartbeats.

After months of imprisonment, he had gotten used to the individual rhythms of the Guards that rotated in front of his cell. He did not know their names, their passions, their wants or their dreams, but he knew the steady beat of the woman who watched over his cell at night and the slight arrhythmia of the man who watched over him now. The gentle pitter-patter that had worsened, slightly, over the past weeks, a dangerous clock that ticked away in his chest, hardly noticeable. One that Isaac could have warned him about, if he cared to.

But he didn't care.

What use was caring at this point?

Everything that he worked so hard for, all the atrocities that he had committed in the Eternal King's name, and all the atrocities he had done to try to atone for it, all of it had been ruined by one simple mistake.

Trusting the wrong man with his heart.

He heard the new heartbeat before he heard the footsteps, before he felt the first of protective wards, wards of the King's own making, shudder and split. It wasn't the King—he would have sensed that, the overwhelming power of his presence almost enough to choke him. Logic sparked in the back of his mind—there was only one person who could even cross that line without the aid of one of the Guard's tools—but he already knew. He would recognize that heartbeat anywhere.

His own downfall, come to visit him at last.

He sat up straighter in his chains, pulling against the manacles that held his hands apart, pressed against the edge of the chair he had been chained to for his disobedience. He dug his teeth into the bit that had been fitted into his mouth, the muzzle that held him fast, wishing he could steal even a mouthful of his own blood.

When he had first been imprisoned, he had tried just that. The beating the Guard had given him hadn't even been the worst of it; no, that had been what happened after. When the King had come down to speak to him personally, the one time he had been graced with his royal presence since this imprisonment began. When he was told that if he wouldn't behave like the man he was supposed to be, he would be treated like the rabid dog he was.

He didn't think he could sink any lower, but he had been wrong.

So very wrong.

Samuel rounded the corner, looking even more handsome than Isaac remembered him. Isaac couldn't help but compare them—he knew what he looked like, how thin and emaciated he had become. He knew that his hair had grown long, an unimpressive shag of curls, and his beard was patchy and rough from the careless way an uninterested valet handled him on those blessed days when he was freed long enough to bathe and receive his treatments under the careful eye of an entire squad of Guards.

He was a ruin of what he was once, but Samuel was perfect, his skin glowing with health and vitality, his hair tied back at the nape of his neck, hanging over his shoulder in a luscious fall of sunshine. His suit was impeccable, though he wore a higher collar than fashion called for, and pristine white gloves on his hands.

So the scars Isaac left hadn't faded, then. He did feel somewhat bad about that.

But still, there was something different about Samuel. Something colder. They hadn't seen each other since that ill-fated morning, but that sweet and awkward man he had fallen for was gone, and in his place stood the very thing Samuel had feared the most. A Blood Worker.

An heir the Eternal King could be proud of.

"Lord Aberforth," the Guard said, snapping to attention before dropping into a bow.

Samuel barely even looked at him, his eyes only on Isaac, cool and assessing. He held out his hand. "Keys, please. Then leave us." The Guard hesitated, then Samuel turned his head. So cold. So regal. "Now."

"As you say." The Guard stepped forward, pulling the keys looped on his belt and handing them over before turning sharply on his heel. There was something strange about the way he acquiesced so easily, but no—

That couldn't be.

He didn't have long to contemplate it, for the second the Guard was gone Samuel was slipping the key into the lock, opening the door to the cell and stepping through. He hesitated for a moment in front of Isaac, hands flexing in the air, then he reached forward, soft fingers working the muzzle free.

Isaac gagged as it came loose, his mouth so damned dry, but Samuel was already moving to the pitcher of water in the corner, pouring a glass and returning to hold it to his lips. He was so much gentler than the Guards usually were; who cared not if more water ended up splashed against his shirt than down his throat.

Samuel let him drink slowly, carefully, brushing the tangle of Isaac's hair away from his face. "They're not treating you well."

"No shit," he wheezed, his voice harsh and drained, even to his own ears. "But you must have expected that."

Samuel glanced down at the empty glass in his hands, fiddling with it idly, as a flush of shame flickering across his cheeks. Suddenly, Isaac understood the change in him. "Ah, I see Shan has been training you well, Lord Aberforth. I'm sure the King is pleased with your progress."

"Isaac, please. I need to ... I came to ..." He glanced over his shoulder, towards where the Guard had been standing.

"If you're worried about being overheard," Isaac offered, "you needn't be. He's back past the ward."

Samuel turned back, brow furrowed. "How can you be sure?"

How indeed?

That was a question that had been plaguing him for nearly a year, since he first began this mad plan with Alessi. The more bodies he drained, the more blood he consumed, the more something shifted inside of him. It wasn't only his Blood Working that had been enhanced, it had been all of him.

His senses were sharper, more acute than any human's should be. It wasn't just the heartbeat that he could hear, he could see the minute lines by Samuel's eyes, so faint that no one would even know they were there. He could taste the tang of the sweat on the back of Samuel's neck, smell the lingering traces of blood from where he had pricked his finger to pass through the King's ward.

His throat clenched, aching in a way that mere water could not sate, no matter how much he drank. Running his tongue against his teeth, he pressed his own flesh against the tips of his canines, nearly sharp enough to pierce.

"I'm sure," Isaac assured him, at last. "Trust me, if you can find it in yourself to do that."

What remained of the mask Samuel wore shattered. "I don't know ... that's why ..." He cut himself off, glancing up towards the ceiling as he blinked away tears. "I have two questions."

Swallowing hard, Isaac could only nod.

"Do you regret how you did it?"

"How I did it?" He shook his head, holding back a mad laugh. "I do not regret killing them. If that is what you have come here to ask, then you can leave right now."

"No, that's not what I meant." Samuel stepped closer, his gloved hand catching Isaac's chin and tipping his face up. He wasn't close enough to kiss, not with the chains that still bound Isaac, but he was close enough to share breath. "I meant this."

Oh, that's what this was. "What I felt for you was true," he confessed, too exhausted for artifice. "That you should never doubt. I only wish I could have—"

He halted. He didn't know what he wished. Alone in his cell, with no one to talk to but the ghosts he had made, he had tried to figure out a different way he could have done things. But there wasn't a different way, not truly. There was only one mistake.

"I wish I could have trusted you sooner."

Samuel nodded, rested his forehead against Isaac's. The words he spoke were barely a whisper, and Isaac had to strain to hear them. "And would you still take down the King, if you could?"

Isaac didn't even have to think about it. "I would."

Soft lips brushed his skin, then Samuel was pulling back, slipping the muzzle back into place. Isaac didn't resist, accepting the bit with something like reverence. He had already resigned himself to his fate—the gruesome death that awaited him. If he lived, it would only be by the grace of the one he had hurt the most.

And if he didn't, if they left him to face the consequences of his own actions, who would blame Samuel and Shan for casting him aside?

"Wait just a little longer, my dear Isaac," Samuel said, stepping back towards the door with one last, longing look. A twist of the wrist, and the door was locked again, a single sigh, and he was gone from sight.

Isaac closed his eyes, listening as Samuel's heartbeat grew fainter and fainter.

The story continues in ...

LORD OF RUIN

Keep reading for a sneak peek!

Acknowledgments

First and foremost, I want to thank my incomparable agent, Jennifer Azantian. Thank you for plucking this bloody mess of a book out of the slush and whipping it into shape, for advocating for me and my stories every step of the way, and always being there for all of my overly complicated, rambling questions. You have been a lifeline.

To my editor, Nadia Saward. Your enthusiasm for Shan, Samuel, and Isaac was palpable from day one. You have been the champion that this story needed, and I am so grateful to work with you. To my US editor, Priyanka Krishnan, thank you so much for welcoming me into the Orbit community. To Tiana Coven, for stepping in and guiding me the rest of the way. To the entire Orbit Team, including Aimee Kitson, Nazia Khatun, Anna Jackson, Zakirah Alam, Blanche Craig, Serena Savini, Jess Dryburgh, Lauren Panepinto, Stephanie Hess, Alex Lencicki, Natassja Haught, Kayleigh Webb, Ellen Wright, Bryn McDonald, Rachel Goldstein, Angela Man and Tim Holman. And a special shout out to Felix Abel Klaer for the beautiful art and to Ella Garrett for creating a stunning cover out of it. Shan has never looked so good!

To my Guillotine Court—Alyssa Coleman, Ashley Northup, Brittney Arena, Jennifer Gruenke, Jessica James, Kalyn Josephson, Rae Castor, Sam Farkas, Tracy Badua! I am truly blessed to have found you all, and it is no exaggeration to say that I would not be here without you. Thank you for helping me through all the iterations of this story, and for becoming some of the dearest friends I have ever known. May our Court rise and flourish!

To all the friends I have made along the way—Rae Loverde, Ashley Shuttleworth, Sarah Hashem, Elian K. Wells, Alechia Dow, Guthrie Adams, Laura Samotin, Andrea Hannah and the entire Unearthed Crew. Writing is a lonely business, and publishing is a difficult industry to navigate, and I would have been so lost without you all.

To the wonderful indie and hybrid writers who have welcomed me into their community—Ladz, Rien Gray, Kellan Graves, rafael nicolás, C.J. Twining and Rien Nadie, DC Guevara, Elle Porter, Moira Carn, and Morgan Dante. I am honored to call you friends.

To the family that welcomed me—Barbara and Alex. To the cousins I gained—Marie, Johnny, and Brittany. Thank you so much for embracing me, flaws and all. I would not be here with the support you so unwaveringly gave.

To Eric, my love. You have been the strongest support, helping me through every rough patch, through all of my health issues, believing even when I lost all hope. Thank you for not letting me give up on myself.

To my cat, Zuko. I know you can't read, but I love you, little bean.

extras

orbit

meet the author

K. M. Enright

K. M. ENRIGHT is a Filipino American writer of romantic fantasy for teens and adults. When not writing, he can be found playing too many video games, cooking, or listening to Broadway musicals. He currently lives in New Jersey with his spouse and their black cat, Zuko.

Find out more about K. M. Enright and other Orbit authors by registering for the free monthly newsletter at orbitbooks.net.

if you enjoyed
MISTRESS OF LIES

look out for

LORD OF RUIN

The Age of Blood:
Book Two

by

K. M. Enright

Look out for Book Two of the Age of Blood.

Chapter One

The grandfather clock chimed one, startling Shan out of her light doze. It was much later than she had intended to work; she had planned to stay only an hour after dinner to finish up the latest inventory, but she'd lost herself as she dug into the ledgers that were her main responsibility. The ever-dwindling supply of blood for the Kingdom of Aeravin, diminishing a bit more each day as they ran through what remained.

She cursed Isaac de la Cruz under her breath; the Blood Factory was abhorrent, but so was every other option. He had achieved his goal, he had seen the horrors ended under the threat of civil unrest, but here she was, left to pick up the pieces of his mess.

It was her greatest duty as Royal Blood Worker, and still, months after her appointment, she had found no reasonable solution.

She gently closed her notebook, setting it aside with the ledger for the next day's efforts. It looked so small on the grand desk, a mahogany monstrosity etched with hand-carved details of roses and thorns. It matched the rest of the furniture she had inherited with the office—large, oversized pieces that made her feel small, from the chair that dwarfed her to the shelves that covered the walls to the wide bay window that overlooked the capital and the grand sea beyond. Some nights, she wished she could fly out that window and never look back, but every time she so much as dared to dream, she remembered the shackles that held her fast and the work she had yet to do.

There was nothing she could accomplish now, not with ache in her back and the way her eyes threatened to drift closed once more. She needed rest, her soft bed, and the comfort of Samuel's arms if she had any hope of solving the great issues left at her doorstep.

428

Pushing herself up, she carefully brushed the stray locks of hair from her face, taking a moment to refresh her appearance. Despite the hour, there would still be people flitting about the Academy—students cramming for exams, instructors frantically preparing the next lesson, and nearly invisible servants gliding between them, ensuring that everything ran smoothly. As soon as she stepped out of her office, the sole bit of privacy she had would vanish as the performance began again.

Appearances had always been important, as a LeClaire, as a child with foreign blood. As the Royal Blood Worker following de la Cruz, they had become *everything*, the entire court of Aeravin watching her every movement, waiting to see if she would make the same mistakes he had, if the quality of her blood would be as poor as his.

Yet another mess he had added to her plate, another bitterness left where there had once been the hope for something more. It was uncharitable of her, she knew that, but it was better to be angry at all he had done than to mourn everything she had lost.

That was the lie she kept telling herself, anyway.

Prepared to face the night, she exited her office and stepped out into the grand hall that made up the top floor. The witch light had been dimmed for the night, casting a warm glow over the couches and low tables throughout the space, places for the enlightened of Aeravin to mingle as they discussed the newest bits of theory and magic. Empty, thankfully, except the door to the Eternal King's Archives. The sole door was cracked open, light spilling out across the marble floor.

And Shan's heart sank into her stomach as she realized who was there. There was only one person who could access it on their own, whose blood would allow them to pass through the ward and into the room beyond.

It seemed that the Eternal King had stirred from his own offices again, as he had many times in the past few months, poring over the knowledge he had spent a millennium collecting as he tried to understand what had been done to Samuel. It was a great puzzle in his eyes, nothing more; a bit of intellectual inquiry that he wanted to solve. Whatever pain Samuel went through did not matter.

Still, she squared her shoulders as she stepped through the ward, the buzz of her own magic sizzling against her skin—no doubt the King knew she lingered, and it would be better for her to go to him. She had learned that lesson the hard way.

The room was large but windowless, bookshelves lining the walls and reaching almost all the way up to the ceiling. A long ladder was braced against the shelves, attached to a railing that allowed one to roll it to the proper stack, climbing through the very ranks of history itself. Each shelf was carefully preserved against the ravages of time by being encased in specially made glass, protecting the collection of journals and books dating back all the way to the founding of Aeravin itself.

Journals full of knowledge that Shan, in her time before serving the King, had not even been able to imagine. There were too many of them to get through in her meager lifetime, not unless she devoted herself solely to this endeavor, but there was a part of her that ached to try.

The Eternal King stood in the middle of the room, the brightness from the witch light casting shadows across his face, as inexorable as ever—a man who never changed or aged. There was a sternness to him that she knew waited just beyond the surface, a promise of unyielding will and cruelty, but she had learned to walk around the edges of it, managing his moods just as she managed everything else.

Still dressed in his court finery, the Eternal King stood with his hands pressed into the wood of the table, a slight frown marring his otherwise flawless features. Before him was one of his old journals, bound in leather and filled with his own thoughts written in his own hand, a journal that he protected even from his own skin with the special gloves he wore to flip through the pages.

"Good evening," the King said, without looking up from his work. "How goes your work?"

Shan still had to fight the urge to lie; the words already hung on the edge of her lips, but she swallowed them down. "Things are not going as well as I would have liked, even with the rationing we've established. We are burning through blood faster than our initial projections called for, even with the increased Blood Taxes."

There were some areas that they had been able to cut back in, fat that they had been able to trim from the endless requisitions that came to the Royal Blood Worker's office. Under Isaac, it had been brushed off to aides and secretaries. But in these new conditions, she had to account for every single drop of blood in their coffers, and there was only so much rationing that the nobles would allow.

The entire balance of their nation hung on a tightrope, and with each step, Shan feared that she would fall into the abyss.

The King only hummed, turning the page in his journal with a careful hand. "I am sure that you will come up with something. I know you are too clever to let something as minor as this defeat you."

Fear thrummed a heady beat in her veins. Shan still didn't know how she withstood it, the level look the Eternal King sent her way, eyes as hard as emeralds, peeling away all her schemes and lies to get to the heart of her. His faith was a burning potential, almost too much to bear, but she could not flinch away.

"I will," she swore, though she did not yet know the particulars of how she would appease him. She just knew she had no other option, lest she end up like all the others who had crashed and burned. Like her father.

Like Isaac.

The King only smiled, gesturing her forward with a gloved hand. "What do you think of this?"

He stepped aside, allowing her to take his place at the research table, but lingered close enough that she could still feel the warmth of his body, the nearly overwhelming taste of his magic on the air. He had stopped masking around her, when it was just the two of them, no longer even bothering to play at being merely human. Perhaps it was meant as an intimidation tactic, a reminder of just how far above her he was. Perhaps it was a kind of trust, the only way he could show it.

But it did not matter why. In truth, all it did was make her hungry. What would such power feel like, in her hands? Who would dare challenge her? Would it let her, for the first time in her life, know what it was like to be free?

The journal before them was one she had seen before, one of the first he had shown her after her ascension to Royal Blood Worker. In those early weeks, they had spent so many nights in this very room, poring over theories and details as they struggled to understand exactly how the Aberforth Gift had been decoupled from Samuel. It had been entirely fruitless, but here was the Eternal King once more, searching for answers they could not find.

She bit her lip, trying to find what exactly he wanted her to see. It was always like this with him—he never just gave the answers, she had to find them first. And when she succeeded, his praise felt like a buoy for her faltering soul, the only thing keeping her afloat when she felt like she was drowning.

Leaning over the notebook, she scanned the lines, used to the untidy scrawl of the King's handwriting, a slight flaw in his otherwise perfect persona. The journals were not neat or well organized, a sprawling stream of consciousness as the King's mind jumped from one perch to another, interspersed with sketches and notes and the odd equation. It was difficult work, parsing out the information from the chaff, but part of Shan relished it.

Perry worries about the cost, the blood. What we are trying is such an elemental rewriting of his Blood Working, and to do it will require more power than the typical Unblooded will provide, but access to blood is not an issue for me.

Shan blinked slowly, the thought hovering just out of reach, as ephemeral and difficult to catch as mist. She read it again, slower, muttering the words under her breath, as—

"Ah."

"You see it, then," the King said, less a question and more an affirmation. She had passed the test, and the weight of fear slipped from her shoulders.

"I do," Shan said, tilting her face so she could meet his expectant gaze. "Dunn." That was the piece they hadn't dug into; they hadn't known if his death was part of Isaac's experiments or merely a statement that he felt necessary to make.

"De la Cruz is not the first to use Unblooded in this manner," the King said. He stepped between her and the table, carefully gathering up his journal as he went to return it to its normal resting place halfway up the wall, where it was shelved chronologically with all his other notes. "Even if he used all the Unblooded that he murdered to enhance his own ability, it shouldn't have been possible to do what he's done. But Dunn..."

The King slid back down the ladder with a sigh. "Kevan was powerful, and compounding that power into his own body? Perhaps that might be enough."

Shan swallowed hard, ignoring the way she hungered for this knowledge. This bit of magic that no one besides their King was allowed to practice, the very way he had extended his life and his power across generations. "Have you ever done it with a Blood Worker?"

"No," the King admitted, turning back to watch her. He wasn't upset with the question, with the discussion. Sometimes, she wondered if he actually enjoyed it. "I have never needed to, and the consequences of such actions... Well, the price isn't always worth the power."

"The price?" Shan echoed, wondering which of the endless journals could tell her what such a cost might be. If he would show it to her, or if he expected her to find it on her own.

"Mm-hmm," the King replied as he pulled the ladder to another stack and climbed up it. "It was something I discovered early in my reign, something that I strove to keep hidden. To think that de la Cruz stumbled upon it entirely by accident."

Shan donned a pair of gloves, stepping to his side to receive the tome he handed down. This was a thicker one, an older one, the very binding that held it together starting to fray and fail. "Your Majesty, may I ask a question?"

He glanced down at her, imperious as ever, but he nodded.

"Why did you not show this to me until now?"

"Ah, that is a good question, Shan." His smile was as cold and sharp as the claws she normally wore on her hands. "Because this knowledge is dangerous, and I did not want to share it with you unless it was necessary."

It was almost crueler in its simplicity than it would have been if he had meant to be unkind. The fact that, despite elevating her to be his right hand, he still did not trust her. Not fully.

She could spend the rest of her life proving herself to him, and it still wouldn't be enough.

"So I followed other paths," the King continued as he climbed back down, "all the way down to the bitter end. But now there is only one thing to do, only one option left. Truths that I hoped had faded entirely to myth, monsters that I hoped the world had forgotten."

Shan dragged her thumb across the spine of the journal, her curiosity piqued. Myths and monsters, false tales of what countless fools had thought of Blood Workers. Perhaps there was some truth to them after all. "Are you saying that vamp—"

"Read it," he repeated, cutting her off before she could even finish the word. "Read that, then tomorrow night we'll see to Isaac."

Shan clenched her hands around the journal as she bit back a sigh. Another night without sleep, then. It was foolish to resent it—she had never wanted the position of Royal Blood Worker, but now that she had it, it was more power, more knowledge, more access than she ever could have dreamed of.

She had been foolish to think that any of her previous schemes or ploys were power. That she, as bright as she was, as capable as she strove to be, could ever hope to bring about real change. Her little network, her little games, that wasn't power.

This was power—standing next to the Eternal King, his knowledge gifted freely, his experience guiding her to places she had never dared to reach for.

And now that she had it, she would never let it go.

"As you say, Your Majesty." She clutched the tome to her chest as she bowed before her King, ready to serve.

if you enjoyed
MISTRESS OF LIES

look out for

LONG LIVE EVIL

by

Sarah Rees Brennan

This adult epic fantasy debut from Sarah Rees Brennan puts the reader in the villain's shoes for an adventure that is both "brilliant" (Holly Black) and "supremely satisfying" (Leigh Bardugo). Expect a rogues' gallery of villains including an axe-wielding maid, a shining knight with dark moods, a homicidal bodyguard, and a playboy spymaster with a golden heart and a filthy reputation.

As her whole life collapses, Rae still has books. Dying, she seizes a second chance at living: a magical bargain that lets her enter the world of her favorite fantasy series.

She wakes in a castle on the edge of a hellish chasm, home to the Once and Forever Emperor—her favorite fictional character. He's impossibly alluring, as only fiction can be. However, in this fantasy world, she discovers that she's not the heroine but the villainess in the Emperor's tale.

Time to assemble a rogues' gallery of villains and hatch an evil plot....

CHAPTER ONE

The Villainess Faces Death

Ours is a land of terrible miracles. Here the dead live and lies come true. Beware. Here every fantasy is possible.

Time of Iron, ANONYMOUS

The Emperor broke into the throne room. In one hand he held his sword. In the other, the head of his enemy. He swung the head jauntily, fingers twisted in blood-drenched, tangled hair.

A scarlet trail on the hammered-gold tiles marked the Emperor's passage. His boots left deep crimson footprints. Even the ice-blue lining inside his black cloak dripped with red. No part of him was left unstained.

He wore the crowned death mask, empty of the jewel that should adorn his brow, and a breastplate of bronze with falling stars wrought in iron. The red-gleaming metal fingers of his gauntlets tapered into shining claws.

When he lifted the mask, fury and pain had carved his face into new lines. After his time in the sunless place he was pale as winter light, radiance turned so cold it burned. He was a statue with a splash of blood staining his cheek, like a red flower on stone. She barely recognized him.

He was the Once and Forever Emperor, the Corrupt and Divine, the Lost and Found Prince, Master of the Dread Ravine,

Commander of the Living and the Dead. None could stop his victory march.

She couldn't bear to watch him smile, or the shambling dead behind him. Her gaze was drawn by the hungry gleam of his blade. She wished it had stayed broken.

The hilt of the re-forged Sword of Eyam was a coiled snake. On the blade an inscription glittered and flowed as if written on water. The only word visible beneath a slick coat of blood was *Longing*.

The girl with silver hands trembled, alone in the heart of the palace. The Emperor approached the throne and said—

"You're not *listening*!"

"That's a weird thing for the Emperor to say," Rae remarked.

Her little sister Alice sat on the end of Rae's hospital bed, clutching the white-painted steel footrest as if she'd mistaken it for a life raft. Alice was giving a dramatic reading from their favourite book series, and Rae wasn't taking it seriously.

Life was too short to take things seriously, if you asked Rae. Alice's rosebud mouth was twisted in judgement. Rosebuds shouldn't get judgemental.

When Rae was four, her mom promised her a beautiful baby sister.

Alice came to her in springtime. The apple blossoms in their yard were snowy white and tinged with pink, dawn clouds in front of Rae's window all day. Their parents carried baby Alice over the threshold, wrapped in pink wool and white lace that made her seem another curled blossom. Under Rae's eager gaze, they drew back a fold of blanket with the reverence of a groom unveiling his bride, and showed the baby's newborn face.

She wasn't beautiful. She looked like an angry walnut.

"Hey funnyface," Rae told Alice throughout their childhood. "Don't cry. You're ugly, but I won't let anybody tease you."

Life turned out ironic so often, fate must have a sense of humour.

As Alice grew, the bones in her face clicked into the perfect position, even her skeleton shaped more harmoniously than anybody else's. She was beautiful. People said Rae was pretty too.

Rae wasn't pretty any more. Even before, Rae knew pretty wasn't the same.

Beauty was like a big umbrella, both useful and awkward to handle. Three years ago, the sisters had gone to a convention for fans of Alice's favourite books.

Time of Iron was a saga of lost gods and old sins, passion and horror, hope and death. Everyone agreed it wasn't about the romance, but discussed the love triangle incessantly. The books had everything: battles of swords and wits, despair and dances, the hero rising from humble origins to ultimate power, and the peerless beauty who everybody wanted but only he could have. The heroine overcame her rivals, through being pure of heart, to become queen of the land. The hero clawed his way up from the depths to become emperor of everything. The heroine was rewarded for being beautiful and virtuous, the hero for being a good-looking bastard.

Alice attended the convention as the villainess known as the Beauty Dipped In Blood. Rae didn't understand why Alice wanted to dress up as the heroine's evil stepsister.

"*I'm* not the one who gets confused between costumes and truth." Softening the words, Alice had leaned her newly darkened head against Rae's shoulder. "The truth is, she looks like you. I can pretend to be brave when I look like you."

At the time Rae hadn't read the books, but she wore her cheerleading uniform so they'd both be in costume. A line formed asking Rae to take their picture with Alice. The guy at the end of the line stared, but another guy carrying the First Duke's double-bitted axe told jokes and made Alice laugh. It was nice to see her shy sister laughing.

When Rae held up the last guy's phone, his hand strayed to Alice's ass. Alice was thirteen.

"Hands off!" Rae snapped.

The guy oiled, "Oooh, sorry, m'lady. My hand slipped."

"It's fine." Alice smiled, worried about his feelings even though he hadn't worried about hers. "Everybody say 'cheese!'"

Alice was the nice sister. Rae considered the guy's smirk and his phone.

"Everybody say 'Fish for it, creep!'"

Rae tossed her ponytail, and tossed the phone into a trash can overflowing with half-eaten hot dogs. Being nice was nice. Being nasty got shit done.

The guy squawked, abandoning underage ass for electronics.

Rae winked. "Oooh, sorry, milord. My hand slipped."

"What are you dressed as, a bitch cheerleader?"

She slung an arm around her sister's shoulders. "*Head* bitch cheerleader."

The guy sneered. "Bet you haven't even read the books."

Sadly, he was correct. Sadly for him, Rae was a huge liar, and her sister was obsessed with these books. Rae shot back with one of the Emperor's lines. "'Beg for mercy. It amuses me.'"

She strode away, declining to be quizzed further. Usually she remembered every tale Alice told her, but Rae was already worried about how much she was forgetting from classes, conversations, and even stories.

That was the last time Rae could protect her sister. The next week she went to see the doctor about her persistent cough, and the weight and memory loss. She began a battery of tests that ended in biopsy, diagnosis and treatments spanning three years. Part of Rae stayed in that final moment when she could be young, and cruel, and believe her story would end well. Forever seventeen. The rest of her had skipped all the steps from child to old woman, feeling ever so much more than twenty.

Rae was past the time of hoping for magic, but Alice fulfilled every requirement for a heroine. Alice was sixteen, beautiful with-out knowing it, and cared more about her favourite book series than anything else.

Sitting on Rae's hospital bed, Alice pushed her glasses up her nose and scowled. "You claim you want a refresher on the story, but you get surprised by key events!"

"I know every song from the musical."

Alice scoffed. Her sister was a purist. Rae believed if you were lucky your favourite story got told in a dozen different ways, so you could choose your favourite flavour. None of the musical's stars were hot enough, but nobody could ever be as hot as characters in your imagination. Book characters were dangerously attractive in the safest way. You didn't even know what they looked like, but you knew you liked it.

"Then tell me the Beauty Dipped In Blood's name." When Rae hesitated, Alice accused: "It's as if you haven't even read this book!"

That was Rae's guilty secret.

This was her favourite series, and she *hadn't* really read the first book.

Rae and her sister used to have book sleepovers, cuddled together reading a much-anticipated book through the night or telling each other tales. Alice would tell Rae the stories of all the books she was reading. Rae would tell Alice how the stories should have gone. Back then, Rae hadn't believed Alice when she said *Time of Iron* was life-changing. Alice was a literary romantic, falling in love with the potential of every story she met. Rae had always been more cynical.

Reading a book was like meeting someone for the first time. You don't know if you will love them or hate them enough to learn every detail, or skim the surface never to know their depths.

When Rae was diagnosed, Alice finally had a captive audience. During Rae's first chemo session, Alice opened *Time of Iron* and started to read aloud what appeared to be a typical fantasy adventure about the damsel in distress getting the guy in a crown. Rae, certain she knew where this was going, listened to the fun parts with blood and gore, but otherwise zoned out. Who cared about saving the damsel? She was astonished by the end, when the Emperor rose to claim his throne.

"Wait, who's this guy?" Rae had demanded. "I love him."

Alice stared in disbelief. "He's the hero."

Rae devoured the next two books. The sequels were wild. After his queen was murdered, the Emperor visited ruin upon the world, then ruled over a bleak landscape of bones. The books were grim and also dark. The series title might as well be *Holy Shit, Basically Everybody Dies.*

Under the eerie skies of Eyam, monsters roamed, some in human form. Rae loved monsters and monstrous deeds. She hated books which were like dismal manuals instructing you of the only moral way to behave. Hope without tragedy was hollow. In the strange, fascinating world of these books, with its glorious horror of a hero, pain meant something.

By the time she finished the sequels, reading began to make Rae feel sick, adrift on a sea of words. Even listening to the books led her mind into the fog. She did want to find out the actual events of the first book, so she tricked Alice into reading it aloud as a 'refresher'. If any voice could hold Rae's attention, it would be that best-beloved voice.

Except they were now at the end, and Rae had still managed to miss a lot from the first book in the *Time of Iron* series. She feared her super-fan sister was catching on.

Time to play it cool. Rae said, "How dare you question me?"

"You constantly forget characters' names!"

"The characters all have titles as well as names, which I find greedy. There's the Golden Cobra, the Beauty Dipped In Blood, the Iron Maid, the Last Hope—"

Alice gave a scream. For a minute, Rae thought she'd seen a mouse.

"The Last Hope is the best character in the book!"

Rae lifted her hands in surrender. "If you say so."

The Last Hope was the losing side of the love triangle, the good guy. If you asked Alice, the flawless guy. Alice's favourite wasted his time longing for the heroine from afar, too busy brooding to use his awesome supernatural abilities.

The parade of guys professing love for the heroine was a blur that bored Rae. Anybody could say they loved you. When the time came to prove it, most failed.

Alice sniffed. "The Last Hope deserved Lia. The Emperor is a psychopath."

The idea of deserving someone was wrong-headed. You couldn't win women on points. Alice must be thinking of video games.

Rae overlooked this to defend her man. "Have you considered the Emperor has great cheekbones? Sorry to the side of good. Evil's just sexier."

Rae wanted characters to have tormented backstories, she just wished they wouldn't be annoying about it. The Emperor was Rae's favourite character of all time because he never brooded over his dark past. He used his unholy powers and enormous sword to slaughter his enemies, then moved on.

Alice made a face. "The thing with the iron shoes was creepy! If a creep is the true love, what does that teach girls?"

What thing with the iron shoes? Rae decided it wasn't important. "Stories should be exciting. I don't need to be preached at, I can do literary analysis."

Rae was supposed to be valedictorian and get a scholarship. Instead Rae's and Alice's college funds were gone. Rae was twenty and never going to college.

They didn't talk about that.

"If the Emperor were real, he would be horrifying."

"Lucky he's not real," Rae snapped back. "Everyone who thinks books will make women date assholes underestimate us. If stories hypnotize people, why isn't everybody terrified movies will turn boys into drag-racing assassins? I don't want to fix the guy, I want to watch the murder show."

She refused to have another argument about the Emperor being problematic. Clearly, the Emperor was problematic. When you murdered half the people you met, you had a problem. Stories lived on problems. There was a reason *Star Wars* wasn't *Star Peace*.

After Lia was killed, the Emperor put her corpse on a throne and made her enemies kiss her dead feet. Then he ripped their hearts out. 'Now you know how it feels,' he murmured, his face the last thing their fading vision ever saw. Villainous characters had epic highs, epic lows, and epic loves. The Emperor loved like an apocalypse.

In real life, people let you go. That was why people longed for the love from stories, love that felt more real than real love.

Alice's sigh could have blown a farmhouse away to a magical land. "It's about troubling patterns in media, not a specific story. Specifically, you're basic. *Everyone* likes the Emperor best."

That was ridiculous. Many appreciated the Last Hope's chiselled misery, the Golden Cobra's decadent antics, and the Iron Maid's cutting sarcasm. Few liked the heroine best. Who could be as good as the perfect woman, and who wanted to be?

Fewer still liked the wicked stepsister. The only thing worse than a woman being too innocent was a woman being too guilty.

"*Nobody* likes the Beauty Dipped In Blood best," Rae pointed out. "I don't need to remember her name. That incompetent schemer dies in the first book."

"Her name is Lady Rahela Domitia."

"Wow." Rae smirked. "Might as well call a character Evilla McKinky. No wonder the Emperor liked her."

"Not the Emperor," corrected Alice.

Right, the king didn't become emperor until later. Rae nodded wisely.

Alice continued, "Rahela was the king's favourite until our heroine came to court. The king was dazzled by Lia, so Lia's stepsister went mad with jealousy. Rahela and her maid conspired to get Lia executed! Any of this ringing a bell?"

"So many bells. It's like a cathedral in my brain."

Her sister's voice grew clearer in Rae's memory. Rae always appreciated a big death scene.

The chapter started with Lady Rahela, wearing a signature snow-white dress edged with blood-red, realizing she had been imprisoned in her chamber. The next day the king had Rahela executed before the entire court. Everybody enjoyed seeing the bitch sister get hers.

Rahela's maid was offered mercy by Lia, who was always saying 'I know there's good in them,' as the people in question cackled and ate the heads off kittens. The heartbroken former servant became an axe murderer known as the remorseless Iron Maid.

All great villains almost got redeemed, but instead plunged deeper into evil. You kept thinking, *they might turn back! It's not too late!* The best villains' death scenes made you cry.

Alice offered, "Want to read more? We need to be prepared for the next book!"

The next book would be the last. Everyone expected an unhappy ending. Rae was dreading one.

Hope without tragedy was hollow. So was tragedy without hope. Rae had always told her sister this was a story about both. Darkness wouldn't last for a grim eternity. People wouldn't keep getting worse until they died. She'd believed the Emperor could resurrect his queen and snatch victory from the jaws of defeat, but her faith was fading. Fiction should be an escape, but she suspected nobody was getting out of this story alive.

"I'm not ready for an ending." Rae feigned a dramatic swoon. "Leave me with the Emperor in the throne room."

Alice turned toward hospital windows that went opaque as mirrors when night drew in. Rae was startled to see a tell-tale gleam in Alice's eyes, reflecting the shimmer of the glass. This wasn't worth crying over. None of it was real.

Alice's voice was low. "Don't act as if what matters to me is a joke."

Rae should be able to transform into who she'd once been, for her sister. She should be smart and strong with sympathy to spare. She used to be overflowing. Now she was empty.

Her voice went sharp as guilt. "I have other things to worry about!"

"You're right, Rae. Even when you get everything wrong, you believe you're right."

"It's just a story."

"Yeah," Alice snapped. "It's just imagined out of nothing, into something thousands love. It just makes me feel understood when nobody in my life understands me. It's *just* a story."

Rae's eyes narrowed. "Has it never crossed your mind why I might not want to reach the end of these books about everybody dying?"

Alice launched to her feet like a furious rocket, spitting sparks as she rose. "You don't even realize why the scene when the Flower of Life and Death blooms is my favourite!"

Rae was speechless, with no idea what happened in that scene.

In this hospital, doors had metal loops set in the white doors. You could grab onto the loops if you were feeling unsteady, and ease the door open. The door swung behind Alice with a force that made the squat water glass beside Rae's narrow bed shake.

Her sister leaving was no surprise. Rae had already driven everyone else away.

Rae turned her head on the pillow and stared out of the silver-blank window, pressing her lips tight together. Then she heaved herself out of bed like an old woman emerging from a bath. She tottered towards the door on legs skinny as sticks that tried to slide out from under her and skitter across the floor. Sometimes Rae felt it wasn't her legs betraying her, but a world that no longer wanted her tipping her over the edge.

When Rae opened the door, Alice was standing right outside. She fell into Rae's arms.

"Hey, ugly," Rae whispered. "I'm sorry."

"*I'm* sorry," sobbed Alice. "I shouldn't make a fuss over a dumb story."

"It's our favourite story."

Rae was the organized sister. She'd colour-coded their schedule at the convention to optimize their experience. She'd helped Alice make her costume. The story was something they did together.

The story wasn't real, but love made it matter.

Alice pressed her face into Rae's shoulder. Rae felt the heat of

Alice's cheeks and the tears sliding from under her glasses, leaving wet spots on Rae's hospital gown.

"Remember how you used to tell me stories?" Alice whispered.

Rae used to do a lot of things.

For now, she could hold her sister. It was strange to be skinnier than reed-thin Alice. Rae was withering away to nothing. Alice had grown more real than Rae would ever be again.

She pressed a kiss to her sister's ruffled hair. "I'll tell you a story tomorrow."

"Really?"

"Trust me. This will be the greatest story you ever heard." She gave her sister an encouraging push.

Alice hesitated. "Mom will come by if she manages to close the deal."

Their mother was in real estate. She worked long past visiting hours. They both knew she wasn't coming. Rae did the cheesy pose from their mother's posters and delivered the slogan. "'Live in your fantasy home!'"

Alice was almost gone when Rae called, "Funnyface?"

Her sister turned, trembling with dark beseeching eyes. A fawn lost in the hospital.

Rae said, "I love you."

Alice smiled a heartbreakingly beautiful smile. Rae staggered back to bed, and lay on her face. She hadn't wanted Alice to see how exhausted she was from simply raising her voice.

She reached for *Time of Iron* beside her bed. The first grab failed. Rae gritted her teeth and grasped the book, then found her fingers shaking too badly to open it. Rae hid her face in the pillow. She didn't have the energy to cry long before she passed out, still holding the closed book.

When she woke a strange woman sat by her bedside, Rae's book in her hands. The woman wasn't wearing a white coat or a nurse's uniform, but black leggings and an oversized white T-shirt. Box braids were twined into a bun atop her head, and her gaze on Rae was coolly assessing.

Blurred with sleep, Rae mumbled, "Did you get the wrong room?"

The woman answered, "I hope not. Listen carefully, Rachel Parilla. There is much you don't know. Let's talk chemotherapy."

Shock dragged Rae into wakefulness. There was a lever on the side of her bed that propped it up on a slant. Rae pushed the lever so her mattress jerked upward and she could glare from a better angle.

"What is it you think I don't know?"

Rae gestured to her head with one chicken-wing arm. She got sweaty in her sleep and knew the sheen of moisture on her bald scalp gleamed in the fluorescent lights.

The woman leaned back as if the hospital chair was comfortable. She traced *Time of Iron*'s cover with a fingertip, her golden nail polish a glittering contrast to her deep brown skin and the glossy book jacket.

"The tumours in your lymph nodes have grown more aggressive. Your prognosis was always grim, but hope remained. Soon the doctors will tell you hope is gone."

Rae's head spun, leaving her sick and out of breath. She wanted to sink to the floor, but she was already lying down.

The woman continued, relentless: "The insurance isn't enough. Your mother will re-mortgage. She will lose her job. Your family loses their house. They lose everything, and their sacrifice means nothing. You die anyway."

Rae's breath was a storm shaking the wreck of her body. She scrabbled for any emotion that wasn't panic and clutched at anger. She grabbed her water glass and threw it at the woman's head. The glass smashed onto the floor into a thousand tiny sharp diamonds.

"Do you get a sick thrill from torturing cancer patients? Get out!"

The woman remained composed. "Here's the last thing you don't know. Will you save yourself, Rae? Would you go to Eyam?"

Had this lady escaped from the psychiatric ward? Rae hadn't even known there was a psychiatric ward. She stabbed the button to summon the nurses.

"Great suggestion. I'll buy a plane ticket to a country that doesn't exist."

"Who says Eyam isn't real?"

"Me," said Rae. "Bookstores who put *Time of Iron* on shelves marked *fiction*."

She stabbed the button repeatedly. Come save your patient, nurses!

"Consider this. You say 'I love you' to someone you don't know. Is that a lie?"

Rae regarded the woman warily. "Yes."

The woman's eyes were still in a way that suggested depth, much happening below the tranquil surface.

"Later you learn the heart of the person you lied to. You say the same words, and 'I love you' is a great truth. Is truth stone, or is it water? If enough people walk through a world in their imaginations, a path forms. What's reality, except something that really affects us? If enough people believe in something, doesn't it become real?"

"No," said Rae flatly. "Reality doesn't require faith. I'm real, all on my own."

The woman smiled. "Maybe somebody believes in you."

Wow, someone was getting the good drugs.

"It's a story."

"Everything is a story. What is evil? What is love? People decide upon them, each taking a jagged shard of belief and piecing the shards together. Enough blood and tears can buy a life. Enough faith can make something true. People invent truth the same way they do everything else: together."

Once Rae led her cheerleading team. Once her family worked as a team, helping each other, until Rae couldn't help anyone any longer. Once upon a time was a long time ago.

"What gives a story meaning?" the woman pursued. "What gives your life meaning?"

Nothing. That was the insulting truth of death. The worst thing that had ever happened to Rae didn't really matter. Her desperate struggle made no difference. The world was moving on without her. These days Rae was all alone with death.

That was the true reason she loved the Emperor. Finding a favourite character was discovering a soul made of words that spoke to your own. He never held back and he never gave up. He was her rage unleashed. She didn't love the Emperor despite his sins, she loved him for his sins.

At least one of them could fight.

In Greek plays, catharsis was achieved when the audience saw treachery, twisted love, and disaster. They purged through impossible tragedy until their hearts were clean. In a story, you were allowed to be wracked by feelings too terrible for reality to hold. If Rae showed how furious she felt, she would lose the few people she had left. She was powerless, but the Emperor shook the stars from the sky. Rae shook with him, in the confines of her narrow hospital bed. He was company for her there.

Rae refused to be a hopeful fool. "I can't go to Eyam. Nobody can."

A real country would have a map, she wanted to argue, then remembered the map of Eyam that took up the best part of Alice's bedroom wall. Rae had seen the jagged peaks and pencil-thin swoops of the Cliffs Cold as Loneliness, the sprawl of the Valerius family's great estate, and the palace's intricate secret passages, grand throne room and greenhouse.

Rae had never been to Eyam. She'd never been to Peru either. She still believed in Peru.

The woman gestured. "I can give you an open door."

"That door leads to a hospital hallway."

"Does the door lead, or do you? Walk out of this room and find yourself in Eyam, in the body of the person most suited to you. A body the previous occupant is no longer using. In Eyam, the Flower of Life and Death blooms once a year. You get one chance. Discover how to get into the imperial greenhouse and steal the flower when it blooms. Once you have the flower, a new door will open. Until then, your body sleeps waiting for you. If you get the flower, you wake up, cured. If you don't get the flower, you don't wake up."

"Why are you doing this?" Rae demanded.

There was a serious note in the woman's voice. "For love."

"How many people have taken you up on your offer?"

"Too many." The woman sounded a little sad.

"How many woke up cured?"

"Maybe you'll be the first."

The button to summon the nurses was obviously broken. Rae could stick her head out into the passage and yell for help, or stay here getting ranted at.

Rae chose action.

She swung her legs over the side of the bed, setting her feet on the floor. Moving through the world when sick took focus. Every step was a decision Rae made while weighing her odds. It was like being on top of the cheerleading pyramid. A wrong move meant a bad fall.

The woman's voice rang at her back. "When the story takes and twists you, will you beg for mercy?"

Desire flew through Rae sharp and bright as a burning arrow. What if the offer was real? Her lips curved at the wild sweet notion. Imagine a door could open as a book does, right into a story. Imagine a big adventure instead of hospital walls closing in and life narrowing down to nothing. Being not an escape artist but an art escapist, running away to imaginary lands.

Behind a bathroom door while Rae threw up bile and blood, she'd heard a teacherly voice tell her mother, *Time to let her go.* Rae couldn't let herself go. She was all she had.

Once she believed her future would be an epic. She hadn't known she would only get a prologue.

She no longer had a ponytail, but she tossed her head and fired a wink over her shoulder. "By the time I'm done with it, the story will beg *me* for mercy."

Rae grabbed the loop of the door handle. She pushed the door open with all her remaining strength.

Light broke like sparkling glass in her eyes, followed by rushing darkness. Rae looked over her shoulder in alarm. Colour drained from the world behind her, leaving her hospital room black and white as ink on a page.

Rae took her waking slow. These days she fainted whenever she stood up too fast. She usually regained consciousness eyeballing linoleum.

Now Rae found herself drowning in the broken pieces of a world. Fragments blue as the earth seen from space, with cracks running through the blue as if someone had shattered the world then fitted the pieces back together.

She scrambled up to stare at the ground. Blue mosaics depicted a shimmering pool the richly draped bed beside her seemed to float upon.

As Rae gazed incredulously down into the deep blue, rubies winked scarlet eyes up at her. Blood-red jewels, adorning softly rounded hands. Rae's hands were claws, the hands of an old woman with paper-thin skin stretched over bones. These were the hands of a young woman.

These weren't Rae's hands.

This wasn't Rae's body. She had been accustomed to suffering so long that pain wasn't something that happened to her, but was part of her. Now the pain was gone. She spread her fingers before her face, the easy turn of her wrist a wonder. A heavy bracelet in the shape of a snake slid down her arm, red light striking the metal coils like bloodstained revelation.

Someone might kidnap her, but they couldn't change her body.

She lowered ruby-ringed hands to her sides, and for the first time noticed her clothes. Her skirts poured over the floor, white as snow, the edges dyed deep crimson. As though the immaculate white had been dipped in blood. This was the dress Alice had worn to a convention, the costume she believed made her brave.

Rae bolted from the bedroom into the tiny hall beyond. Walls and floor were white marble, gently shining as if Rae was caught inside a pearl. When she tried the door, it was locked. Through the single stained-glass window she saw a sun sinking into smoky clouds and a moon already reigning over obscured night. The moon was cracked like a mirror that cut reflections in two, broken like the window of a house in which you were not safe.

She knew this sky. She knew this scene. She knew this *costume*.

A laugh forced its way from the pit of Rae's stomach, coming out as a cackle. Her beautiful hands clenched for a fight.

She was in the land of Eyam, in the Palace on the Edge.

She was Lady Rahela, the Beauty Dipped In Blood. She was the heroine's evil stepsister. And she was due to be executed tomorrow.

orbit

Follow us:

📘 **/orbitbooksUS**

𝕏 **/orbitbooks**

▶ **/orbitbooks**

Join our mailing list
to receive alerts on our
latest releases and deals.

orbitbooks.net

Enter our monthly
giveaway for the chance
to win some epic prizes.

orbitloot.com